Touch Me

JAX BURROWS

BOOKS

Vinci Books

vinci-books.com

Published by Vinci Books Ltd in 2026

1

A CIP catalogue record for this book is available from the British Library.
Paperback ISBN: 9781036708115
The EU GPSR authorised representative is Logos Europe, 9 rue Nicolas
Poussion, 17000 La Rochelle, France contact@logoseurope.eu

By Jax Burrows

Chapter One

'Della! Get your arse in here now.'

Sapphire Bell-Johnson was in bad mood, and everyone in her immediate vicinity was in danger of the fallout. She cringed a little at her manners. Della had been her loyal PA for many years, and Sapphire valued their relationship. She depended on her for so many things and was grateful to her for many more. And, as her mother had drummed into her, good manners cost nothing.

'Now, please. If you don't mind. Thank you.' *There, that should do it.*

Sapphire knew Della could hear her. Both doors to their adjoining offices were open, and Sapphire could hear Della's nails clicking on her computer keyboard. Yes, she had definitely heard her shout. Everyone in the executive suite would have heard her. Hell, her voice had probably resounded all over the top floor of Sapphire Enterprises.

She liked shouting, it made her feel good. Her parents had never allowed her to make much noise growing up.

They hadn't let her do anything fun, for that matter. She was making up for it now though.

Sapphire had just opened her mouth to let fly another command when Della strolled into the office as if she had all the time in the world.

'Did we get out of bed on the wrong side this morning?' Della asked.

Sapphire lounged back in her cream leather chair and looked her up and down. She was dressed conservatively, by Sapphire's standards, in a smart, tailored navy shift dress. Her blonde hair was cut in a sleek bob, with gold highlights. Pleasingly, she was wearing stilettoes designed by House of Sapphire. The more advertising her products got, the better.

'Can't answer for you, sweetie, but I certainly did. It was my own bed, sadly.'

'Hot date not up to expectations?'

She had hoped to end up in bed with the man who had wined and dined her for some no-strings sexy-time, but instead she'd ended up on her own with cocoa and Netflix.

'He was charming, talked excessively about himself all evening and bored the knickers off me if you must know.'

'Oh dear.'

'Why are all the good-looking men so self-obsessed? They all think they're God's gift.' Sapphire knew why she was feeling so irritable. She was sexually frustrated and horny as hell. She'd always had a high sex drive and if she didn't get down and dirty with some gorgeous hunk on a regular basis, she couldn't function, and she had to function at a high level to be the owner, CEO, and Chairwoman of Sapphire Enterprises.

'He was obviously trying too hard to impress you. You know how intimidating you are to some men,' said Della.

'Well, he failed. Miserably,' said Sapphire. Only she was

the one left feeling miserable and crabby. 'How about that coffee?'

Della leaned over the desk and collected the documents from Sapphire's out-tray. Her PA was wearing their latest fragrance, Sparkle by Sapphire, and she felt a glow of satisfaction as she inhaled the scent. It was gorgeous. Light, but evocative, with undertones of spice. It was proving popular with women of all ages.

'Don't forget you've got a meeting with James Lewis at eight.'

'Oh God! I'd forgotten all about him. Another boring man.'

'How do you know? You haven't met him yet. Give him a chance. He's here to take the pressure off you. You've been spending too many nights burning the midnight oil. You're working too hard.'

'I've heard a rumour that he never smiles, is distant and wears dark colours.'

'That doesn't make him boring,' said Della, 'perhaps he's just shy.'

'Well it hardly makes him the life and soul of the party either.'

'You shouldn't listen to gossip.' Della strolled off to make her boss's coffee.

Sapphire personally interviewed all the staff that worked for her at an executive level. She'd handpicked her team of secretaries and admin staff but, when the co-CEO employed to assist her in running the business had been interviewed, she had been in hospital. She had, however, managed to run her eye over the CV's and agreed that James Lewis stood out from the pack in every respect. He had excellent experience and qualifications and had once owned his own company. He looked okay in his photo, if a bit serious. She didn't know whether she could work with someone with no sense of humour.

She would have to charm him out of that protective shell of his and get him to crack a smile. Otherwise, she'd be looking for another co-CEO.

James Lewis straightened his tie and ran his palms over his hair before knocking lightly on Sapphire's office door. Her secretary had told him to go straight in as Sapphire was expecting him, but he decided to play safe and wait for an invitation.

He wasn't sure what he would find on the other side of the door. The lady had a reputation for being a hard task mistress, pedantic to the point of obsession, and shouted a lot. Such women could be tiresome; he'd worked with too many of them.

Sapphire's company needed him. From what he'd seen of the finances and future projection of Sapphire Enterprises, it was being run inefficiently and required some order brought to proceedings. That's what James did. He brought order out of chaos. And once things were running to his satisfaction, he would move on.

Since losing his company, he spent his working hours helping other CEO's to achieve glory. He didn't resent it... much. One day he would own his own company again but until that happy time, he had to be content with helping others. James knew that with his qualifications and experience he could pick and choose where he worked which made him feel slightly better about having to settle, temporarily, for a co-CEO's post.

After hours spent studying the businesses he was interested in, he stumbled on the Sapphire Enterprises website and knew he'd struck gold. He could have chosen a more lucrative organisation, of course; there were plenty of jobs in London for someone as qualified as he, but he had been swayed by something unassociated with profit and loss. The clincher had been the photo of Sapphire Bell-Johnson on the company's home page. She was beautiful, in a way that caused his heart to race and his trousers to tighten. With long red-gold hair that fell to her shoulders in a tangle of curls and the most expressive green eyes he had ever seen, he'd felt like a teenager again, masturbating to pictures of beautiful women. He'd always loved redheads, and this redhead was stunning.

'Come!' The loud shouted command from inside the office confused him for a second. He admonished himself to get his act together and opened the door cautiously.

Sapphire was at her desk, staring hard at her computer, and James took advantage of the fact that she wasn't looking at him to study her.

Her hair was loose and excessively curly as it tumbled over her shoulders. She wore a sleeveless dress in bright rainbow colours, and her bare shoulders were tanned and unblemished. The neckline was low, and her breasts pushed at the material, so it stretched tight over her chest. Her nipples stood out prominently and he wondered if she was wearing a bra. He decided, after intense scrutiny, that she wasn't.

James took a deep inward breath and coughed slightly.

'James.' Sapphire looked up as if she had only just realised he was there, 'are you okay?'

'Yes fine. Thank you.' He straightened his tie again.

'Well, don't just stand there, come in, I don't bite. Well,

not until we get to know each other better, anyway.' She laughed, and James did too.

He strode in, then stopped in front of her desk.

'Listen to this and tell me what you think. I'm preparing a statement for an interview a local radio station has asked me to give concerning women at the peak of their careers.' She glanced at him for a second over the top of bright blue glasses, before her gaze returned to her computer screen. 'That's me, by the way. I'm one of the women at the top.'

He smiled and nodded. *She may think she's at the top, but she won't be for long unless she does something about the contracts Sapphire Enterprises is losing.*

"My goal is to make Forbes Annual List of Billionaires by the time I'm forty. At present the youngest woman to achieve this up to the present is forty-six. Only ten percent of the list is female—inspiring women, all of them. I intend to be a role model to the next generation of business-women, especially to those who have been told all their lives, that they can't do something. I want to show them that they can and help them smash through the glass ceiling and let in more light to shine on all the talented young female entrepreneurs, not just in the UK, but the world over."

She leaned back in her chair and removed her glasses, her gaze penetrating, and her expression enquiring. 'So—what do you think?' She was waiting for his response, but James wasn't sure what she wanted him to say. If she expected a round of applause, she'd be waiting a long time.

'Were you one of the women who were told they couldn't do something?' he asked quietly.

'I was talking generally. It applies to a lot of women, being told they're not as good as the men.'

'So—you have ten years to achieve your goal. It's a big

ask.' He knew she was thirty from the extensive research he'd done on her and her company.

'Would you have said that to a man?'

'Yes. Although if ninety-percent of the people on the Forbes's list are men, the odds are obviously in their favour.'

She stared at him for a long time, but he refused to drop his gaze. Then she smiled. 'Let's sit down. Make ourselves more comfortable.' She brushed her hair back from her face with her fingers and stood up to lead him to an L-shaped sofa in the corner of her spacious office.

James sat on one side, expecting Sapphire to sit on the other, but she squashed up next to him, invading his personal space. Their knees almost touched, and he wondered if he should move away, but the sight of her dress riding up her thighs and the thought of the delights hidden underneath the soft material, pinned him to the spot. Did she wear stockings? Or hold-ups? His preference would be for the second, with a lacy band at the top and a few inches of bare flesh above them. And if she wasn't wearing any panties...

'Tell me about yourself, James.' She leaned forward, and her cleavage was on full display. He wanted to shut his eyes, so he wasn't tempted to stare at the luscious mounds that were so tantalisingly close, but, by an extreme force of his will, he held eye contact with her.

'You have my CV, Sapphire. Everything you need to know is in there.'

'I've read your CV, and it's very impressive. You used to have your own company. What happened?'

He knew this question would come up, maybe not quite so soon, but he had been prepared for it. He decide to proceed on a need-to-know basis. She could check if she was really that interested. He leaned back on the couch and stared at a painting on the wall opposite Sapphire's desk. It was an oil painting of London at night.

'Well, let's just say that I was a fool for trusting the wrong people. But we live and learn; I'll never make that mistake again.'

'Are you planning on running your own company again one day?' She was moving nearer to him and James knew now that she was deliberately provoking him. He didn't know why, but he could feel the beginnings of an erection and if she didn't stop soon, his body would take over, regardless of what his mind decided to do.

'Of course. That was always my goal. I won't let anything stand in my way.'

'Good for you,' she said softly. Then she leaned towards him, so their faces were almost touching. 'What do you think of this perfume? It's our latest product. It's called Sparkle by Sapphire.' She tilted her head, inviting him to inhale the scent of her neck. She lifted her hair out of the way, and he wondered what she'd do if, Dracula-like, he sank his teeth into her.

He breathed in obediently, then sat back, his arm casually draped across the back of the couch. 'It's lovely. Really very nice.' He knew nothing about perfume but the whole incident was so bizarre, and his cock was so hard now, that he realised he was beyond caring what she thought any more.

'The reason I ask is that, if you are going to be part of Sapphire Enterprises, you need to familiarise yourself with our products.'

'Of course.' He pulled slightly at his collar which was threatening to strangle him. She must have noticed his condition. Should he say something? Apologise?

Sapphire grasped his knee, then slowly moved her hand

upwards until she was almost touching his groin. She squeezed slightly and said in a breathy voice, 'I hope you don't mind me mentioning it, James, but you appear to be in a bit of distress.'

It was too much. He put his head back and laughed out loud. He couldn't help it. Her outrageous behaviour was inexcusable, but it was strangely exciting, and he felt his inhibitions falling away.

Her demeanour changed suddenly at his response. She removed her hand and moved away from him slightly. But her smile was genuine now and her eyes bright with laughter.

'Is this a test Sapphire? Do you always sexually torture newcomers to see if they're able to cope with your weird sense of humour? Does my raging hard-on mean I've passed or failed?'

She had the grace to look a bit sheepish. But not sorry. 'It means you've passed, of course. And yes, I apologise, I was testing you. I heard that you were too serious for your own good, so I was teasing you to see how you'd react. Forgive me?'

'On one condition—that you let me take you to dinner tonight so we can talk properly.'

'Okay, but I have a condition of my own.'

'Oh?'

Sapphire looked more like the entrepreneurial business-woman she claimed to be than the sexy call girl of a moment ago. James started to relax.

'We wrap up the business meeting now so that we can enjoy the meal tonight without any distracting talk of figures and spreadsheets.'

'Have you forgotten, James? We have a meeting with

Hector, the head of accounts in about...' Sapphire looked up at the clock on the opposite wall, 'five minutes.'

James frowned. 'This is the first I've heard of it.' James was meticulous in diarising his meetings and appointments and knew he hadn't been told about this one.

'Really? May I suggest you check your emails more often?'

Before James could reply there was a knock on the door and a middle aged man opened it cautiously and looked in.

'Hector, come in and take a seat. Have you met James Lewis, my co-CEO?'

'No, Hector Winthrop, pleased to meet you.'

'James Lewis.'

They shook hands and then sat on the sofa, while Sapphire settled herself at her desk.

'Good. So, James, what did you think of the figures I gave you?'

Sapphire was all business now, and James realised he would have to have his wits about him in future.

'I think the company is in trouble. You're losing too many contracts to sustain the level of growth you are aiming for. The industry is hyper-competitive right now and you need to do more than just produce the goods at the present rate. I'm afraid it's just not enough.'

'What do you suggest?' Sapphire was frowning, clearly not liking what she was hearing.

'My recommendation would be to diversify. You need to expand into other areas.'

'Fashion is my life, it's what I'm good at.'

'You don't need to be an expert to run a business. You hire the experts to do the technical stuff for you. My advice would be to invest in a company that's going places and be part of the growth of that industry.

'Hector? What are your thoughts?'

Hector cleared his throat and leaned forward slightly. 'I agree, Sapphire. I have the figures for the last three months and there is a definite decrease in sales. I don't think we've quite recovered from the loss of last year, I'm afraid.'

'What loss is this?' James asked.

Hector looked at Sapphire who sighed deeply. 'I made the same mistake you did, James—I trusted the wrong people, or in this case person. I invested money in his company which subsequently went bankrupt.'

'How much did you lose?' James was starting to wonder what he had taken on.

'Too much,' Sapphire said abruptly. Obviously, a sore point with the lady.

'But we have managed to recoup some of the loss, mainly as a result of Sapphire working around the clock and making herself ill.' Hector smiled at Sapphire who frowned.

'This is my company, Hector and therefore my responsibility. I'm not letting it sink without a fight.'

'I understand, my dear, but you have to look after yourself. You're no good to anyone if you're ill.' Hector smiled and James remembered that Sapphire was in hospital when he had his interview for the job.

'Let's move on. What about James's idea of investing in another company. I have to admit, the idea makes me nervous having been bitten once, but if you, Hector, think it's a good idea, then I'm on board.'

'I think it's worth a shot. James, I'm sure, will pick a winner this time.'

They both looked at James expectantly. 'Would you like me to look into the areas that are ripe for expansion and report back to you?'

She sighed, and then smiled. 'Yes, James, that would be helpful.'

Hector looked at his watch. 'I have another meeting soon, so, if there's nothing else?' He stood up and held out his hand to James.

'Good to have you on board.'

'Thank you, Hector, good to be here.'

The accountant left and James, still standing, looked to Sapphire for direction. She stood up and strolled around her desk, so she was standing in front of him.

'So… tonight. We'll have dinner in the restaurant of a hotel we often use when we invite guests to London to attend our shows. The Grand Rossini. The food is superb. About seven?'

'Would you like me to pick you up?'

'No, I'll meet you there.'

She put her hand out and James took it. He lifted it to his lips in a gesture he knew was old-fashioned and could impress or annoy a modern kick-ass woman like Sapphire. He was curious to see which one it was. Her skin was cool, her fingers slender and her nails perfectly manicured.

She said nothing, but stared at him with bright emerald green eyes, assessing him. Finding him wanting? He decided to push things a little further.

'Just for the record, I find you devastatingly attractive. Oh, and it's been quite a while since I had sex. I just thought you should know.'

She watched him for a few seconds. Then she started to smile. A slow lifting of the corners of her mouth that moved upwards to cause the skin around her eyes to crinkle. Then she laughed; a low and sexy sound that reverberated through his body, tightening his balls and causing sweat to break out under his arms.

He smiled back and wondered how he was going to work with Sapphire Bell-Johnson without wanting to lift her skirt around her waist, push her over the desk and take her like a caveman until she screamed.

'Thank you for your honesty, James. I do believe it's going to be interesting working with you after all.'

Chapter Two

Sapphire was late.

Deliberately.

She nodded to Cyril, the Concierge, as she entered the hotel, then made her way to the restaurant. A waiter opened the door for her and greeted her by name. James was sitting alone at a table for two, tucked discreetly in a corner, but in a space that commanded a view of most of the restaurant. It was her regular table, one she used when she fully expected the evening to end in a sexually satisfying way. And this night was no different.

She'd been delighted with how James had responded to her teasing. He was attractive, albeit a trifle conventional, but had stood up admirably to her tormenting. She smiled at the thought of something else that had stood up. The bulge in his trousers had been reassuringly large and Sapphire was looking forward to seeing him naked.

His declaration of attraction had pleased her, but he could have been using the situation to his advantage. He'd had an effect on her though, as she'd found it difficult to concentrate the rest of the day, imagining him naked and helpless on her four-poster bed, begging her to end his suffering.

'James—sorry to keep you, am I very late?'

He stood up and held her chair out for her. 'You're half an hour late, Sapphire, as I'm sure you know. I've ordered some champagne.'

'Champagne? What are we celebrating?' Sapphire glanced at the bottle nestling snuggly in its bucket of ice. Dom Pérignon. Impressive.

'A new era in the history of Sapphire Enterprises.'

'Oh splendid. I like that. Thank you, James.'

'You're most welcome.'

James was wearing another dark suit, but she approved of this one. It fitted beautifully across his broad shoulders and the pale blue shirt intensified the blue of his eyes. It was more casual than the suit he had worn at work, but Sapphire knew it was designer, almost definitely Italian. And the silver tie he wore was silk. She had to hand it to him, the man knew how to dress.

She examined the menu, although she knew exactly what she was going to have. Sapphire loved her food and had been anticipating this meal for hours.

'I've ordered for us too. I hope you don't mind. I didn't know how much longer you were going to be.'

She felt a rush of anger. How dare he order for her? She was perfectly capable of ordering for herself. But not wanting to cause a scene when the evening had barely started, she forced a smile.

'What are we having?'

'Oysters, followed by rib-eye steak, then for dessert, caramelized white chocolate and almond cake with passion-fruit ice cream. I hope that's to your liking.'

She tried to keep a straight face as she said, 'Perfectly. You've done well.' It was exactly what she would have chosen. Clever boy.

James didn't seem phased by her patronising attitude but poured them both a glass of champagne. They raised their glasses and clinked them together.

'Cheers.'

'Here's to us—and Sapphire Enterprises, of course.' She sipped the champagne, the cold sharpness of the bubbles fizzing on her tongue.

'You're wearing the same perfume.'

'Yes, I wear it all the time.'

'It's beautiful, truly. It suits you. What makes a good perfume in your opinion?'

'You really want to know? We did say we wouldn't talk business.'

'I really want to know.' He leaned forward and inhaled deeply.

'Exactly what you're doing now. Perfume should never be applied so heavily that it repels. It should be subtle and draw you closer so that you want to breathe it in. Then it becomes part of you, embedded in the brain, and you imagine that you smell it everywhere.'

'Interesting.' He leaned back in his chair and sipped his champagne.

The waiter brought the oysters and immediately Sapphire's stomach growled. She'd had back to back meetings and had missed lunch. The effect that had on her body wasn't good, but it couldn't be helped.

The smell of the sea wafted up and she put her face to the plate and inhaled the aroma. 'Beautiful,' she said. She picked up an oyster and sipped from the shell. Then she tipped the oyster into her mouth and started chewing, her eyes closed, murmuring appreciation.

James had poured tabasco sauce on his and swallowed it whole. He was watching her with a frown on his face.

'You should chew it, James,' said Sapphire sternly, 'It brings out the sweetness and umami.'

'I've never heard that before. You're obviously a foodie.'

'One of life's greatest pleasures, good food—that and good sex.'

She took another oyster and relished it. Soon, her plate was empty.

'What about relationships? Even a busy lady like yourself has to make time for love.'

'Love, James? Or sex?' She wiped her mouth daintily with her napkin and sipped from her champagne. 'I have one-night stands to satisfy my sexual needs. Occasionally friends with benefits but have no intention of tying myself down to any man.'

'Why?' The question was direct, but honest. It deserved an honest answer.

'Simple. I've yet to meet a man who can accept that I am in control—of every area of my life. Men want a woman to be compliant, to look good on their arm, to obey their every command. But what they don't want is one who is more intelligent, capable, and rich.'

'But surely you meet successful businessmen every day. Men who are your equals.'

She thought about the men she came across and grimaced. 'They're either married, gay or arseholes. No, I'm happy as I am, thank you very much.'

'Not all men are arseholes, Sapphire. I'm not.'

Just then she spotted someone entering the restaurant. Her good mood evaporated at the sight of him as he strutted in with a gorgeous woman on his arm. A model. Sapphire recognized her from the catwalk. Beautiful, but vacuous. Much more his type. Sapphire had trusted him, and he had betrayed her in the worst possible way. She vowed to never trust another man. Especially in business.

'Earth to Sapphire.' James waved his hand in front of her face. 'Am I boring you?'

'No—sorry. I just saw someone I know. What were you saying, James? Something about men being arseholes?'

He glared at her but didn't speak. With perfect timing, the waiter arrived and cleared away the empty plates while James poured them both another glass of champagne. She watched him, wondering if he was or he wasn't. An arsehole. The jury was still out.

'Okay. We've talked about me. What about you? Why aren't you married?'

'I nearly was once. Biggest mistake I almost made. She was having an affair with my business partner. I ended up walking away from my fiancée and my business.'

'I'm sorry. That must have been tough.' James couldn't meet her eye and he was tugging at his collar. It must have been a blow to discover he'd been taken for a fool like that. 'But you've obviously moved on.'

'I have moved on. As I said to you before, I intend to own another business one day, but for now I'm enjoying the challenge of working with CEO's to help them build up their own. People like you.' He looked up and smiled.

'And marriage?'

'Never going down that road again, especially if there's an altar at the end of it.'

'A toast.' She lifted her glass of champagne, 'To singledom.' James clinked his glass against hers and they drank deeply.

The waiter brought the steaks with chunky chips and green salad and they both set to. The oysters had whetted her appetite and Sapphire ate without speaking. She was aware of James doing the same and she realised, with pleasure, that they were in tune on several levels. That thought led, naturally, to her wondering if they would be compatible in bed. Her guess would be yes. He'd found her attractive and her teasing had elicited a satisfying response. She wanted to take things further and see if she was right.

By the time their dessert was served, Sapphire had mentally stripped James and was doing unmentionable things to his body. These wicked thoughts spread heat from her middle down to the area between her legs. She was wet and hungry for satisfaction of another kind.

As soon as the waiter placed the passionfruit ice-cream and white chocolate dome hiding the spicy almond cake, in front of her, her mouth started watering. It was her favourite dessert and she would go without a lot of her favourite foods so she could indulge occasionally.

James watched her with an amused lift of his dark eyebrows. He made no attempt to pick up his spoon but sat back and studied her every move.

Not prepared to wait for him to start, she pulled the bowl nearer to her, dug her spoon into the ice-cream and lifted a generous helping up to her mouth. The sharp, distinct taste of the passionfruit in contrast to the sweet creaminess of the white chocolate made her groan aloud. It was cold and smooth and Sapphire wanted more.

'This is heaven,' she muttered, as the second spoonful quickly followed the first.

'It sounds it,' said James, amusement sparkling in his eyes.

'Why aren't you eating?' she demanded, 'Your ice-cream's melting.'

'I'm having too much fun watching you. I love the sight of a woman receiving such simple pleasure. And…' he leaned forward across the table and she caught the woodsy scent of his aftershave, 'I like to eat my ice-cream when it's nearly melted. When all that soft creaminess flows across the tongue. It tastes so much better like that.'

Sapphire's skin started to burn at his words. Her crotch was wet and sticky, and her dress suddenly felt restricting. Damn the man, he was trying to gain the upper hand. Payback for her teasing earlier on? Well, it wouldn't work. She was in charge and James Lewis needed to learn that.

She finished her dessert, pushed the bowl away, then reached across the table and pulled his bowl towards her. The expression on his face nearly made her laugh out loud. He looked like a little boy who'd just had his sweets confiscated.

'If you want another dessert, I'll call the waiter,' he said frowning.

'No need,' she replied. She took a scoop of the ice-cream and held the spoon out to James. 'Open,' she commanded.

He looked at her in surprise, but to his credit, he obeyed. She fed him carefully, marveling at how straight his teeth were and the motion of his Adam's apple when he swallowed.

She could feel the wetness between her legs increasing, especially when a dribble of ice-cream started to run down his chin. She put the spoon back in the bowl and caught the dribble with her thumb before it fell onto the silk tie. She held her thumb to his lips. 'Lick,' she said as she tried not to laugh.

He obeyed, and the heat from his mouth on her ice-cream covered thumb, nearly made her come then and there. He licked from the bottom of her thumb to the tip, slowly and lasciviously, as if he was savouring it, then he took her thumb in his mouth and sucked on it.

Sapphire shivered and tried not to squeeze her legs together. If she did, she would orgasm on the spot. She took a deep breath in and bit her bottom lip to stop herself moaning. Reluctantly she pulled her thumb out of his mouth.

She sighed, leaned back in her chair, and wiped her thumb on her napkin. Then she took her phone out of her handbag and started pressing buttons.

'Sapphire, you have the attention span of a gnat. I hope that's not work.'

She looked up and was satisfied to see that Mr "I'm the one in control" was looking most put out.

Sapphire smiled sweetly. 'Oh, no James, it isn't work. Tonight is purely for pleasure as we agreed. Actually, it's the concierge, he's a personal friend of mine.'

'The concierge?' James looked bewildered.

Her phone pinged to alert her to a text. 'Ah—that's his reply—I've just booked us a room.'

'A room?' James stared at her. He realised he was repeating everything she said, making him sound like an imbecile, but he was astounded at the speed Sapphire moved.

'Yes, James, a room. You know—a room here in the hotel. We're in a hotel, in case you hadn't noticed.'

Sapphire was staring at her phone almost as if she had forgotten he was there. He took the opportunity to study her. He'd wanted her from the second she'd walked into the hotel's restaurant. The food had been delicious, and was cooked to perfection, but he couldn't even remember what they had eaten.

She was dressed entirely in red. Blood red. Scarlet. He didn't know what the fashion industry called the colour she was wearing, he only knew the effect it was having on his libido. Whoever said redheads should never wear scarlet were wrong. So wrong. Her hair was arranged in an elaborate up-do that looked as if it had changed its mind halfway through. Tendrils and curls hung down, having escaped their prison and were now dancing around her face and swirling over her shoulders.

Her dress was simple. Sleeveless, extremely low cut and indecently short. She wore a simple gold necklace and red stilettoes. Her fingernails were the same colour as her dress. Heavy, blood-red lipstick that made her lips stand out on a face almost devoid of any other make-up except black eyeliner. So sexy he was going out of his mind.

She looked up and put the phone carefully on the table. 'It's as much a shrewd business decision as anything else.'

She looked at him with raised eyebrows as if her logic was so obvious she shouldn't need to explain it to him. He shook his head helplessly.

'You want me.' She waited.

'Correct.' His voice was croaky, and he coughed to clear his throat.

'And I want you.'

'Good to know.'

'But we have to work together. So—the sooner we get this,' she waved her hand between them to indicate, he imagined, that "this" referred to the raging sexual tension that was threatening his equilibrium and his very sanity, 'out of the way, laid to rest, put to bed, whatever cliché you'd like to use, the sooner we can get down to the important task of running Sapphire Enterprises together and making me an extremely rich woman.'

She grinned as if it was simple. But James knew it wasn't. Being a businessman had taught him not to take anything for granted. You had to be on your guard at all times.

'And you think that we can get this,' he waved his hand in a parody of her movement, 'out of the way in one night?'

'I don't see why not. It usually works for me. One-nighters and friends-with-benefits remember.'

'Is it possible we could be the second?'

'Not if we intend to stay working together, James, no. I'm afraid if that is what you want, I'll have to look for another co-CEO, and that would be a shame. Don't you think?'

'You drive a hard bargain, Ms Bell-Johnson.'

'I'm a businesswoman.'

'You are indeed.' *And you are going to get so fucked tonight, lady, that you won't be able to sit down for a week.* He smiled sweetly at her. 'Well then, let's get to this room.'

He stood up and held her chair while she stood up.

'Thank you, James. You're such a gentleman.'

'I try my best.'

He walked beside her as they made their way to the lifts.

'Goodnight Cyril,' said Sapphire as they passed the concierge.

'Goodnight, Ms Bell-Johnson, Sir.' Cyril replied.

'Goodnight, Cyril,' echoed James.

James wondered how many men Sapphire had taken to bed in this hotel. How many had been led by the nose, or the cock, to the glory of a king-size bed with Egyptian cotton sheets and a well-stocked bar? And how many of those men had lasted more than one night?

The thought that they could assuage the uncontrollable lust they felt for each other in twenty-four hours was either coldly calculating or unbelievably naïve. He had until daybreak to prove to her that he was different from all the other men she had fucked. He would make her need him. Rely on him. In bed and in the boardroom.

If she believed herself to be in control, Sapphire Bell-Johnson was in for a rude shock.

Chapter Three

James took control from the moment he shut the door. He shrugged off his jacket and threw it on the bed. Then he loosened the tie that was threatening to choke him.

Sapphire had turned to him, still holding her clutch bag, preparing to speak. To ask him to pour her a drink perhaps or tell him which side of the bed she favoured, or something else. He really didn't care. The time for anything but sex was over.

He grabbed her clutch bag and threw it on the bed on top of his jacket, then cupped her face and kissed her. Her mouth opened in response and he plundered her, his tongue seeking hers and his hands in her hair. Her lipstick tasted of cherries and her signature perfume wafted over him. He let the kiss go on, not preparing to release her until he was ready. He held her head, so she couldn't move and, gratifyingly, she reached up and caressed the back of his neck with one hand, while reaching down and stroking his hard-on through his trousers with the other.

It was only when she cupped his balls and squeezed that

he ended the kiss. He was so close and desperate to be inside her, that he wondered if he should forget about finesse and take her then and there. But he wanted to make it good for her tonight, so he needed to control his urges a little bit longer. He was in control of this act and she would follow his lead, not the other way around.

He stepped away from her slightly and took the hem of her dress, pulling it upwards, over her hips, to bunch it around her waist. Then he looked down and gulped. He heard her soft laughter as he examined her beautiful naked body. She hadn't been wearing any panties. The whole time she had been sitting across the table from him, taunting him, she had been naked underneath her dress. Now he was up close to her, he realised she hadn't been wearing a bra either. Her nipples pushed against the thin fabric of her dress like cherries on an iced bun.

'It saves time, James,' she murmured in his ear, 'and as any good businesswoman will tell you, time is money.'

'You shave,' he said as he scrutinized her hairless pudenda. He was disappointed, imagining his face buried in a glorious fire of red bush. He loved women's pubic hair, the fierier the better. He felt deprived.

'You sound cross, James. Don't you approve?'

Not wanting to come across as prudish or old-fashioned, he touched her smooth hairless labia and felt his cock harden at her silky, smooth skin, hot against his fingers.

'You're gorgeous—of course I approve,' he whispered as he slipped one finger between her wet folds and stroked her. 'Open your legs.'

She did so and then gasped as he carefully inserted his forefinger into her vagina, testing her. She was tight, and her muscles contracted automatically around him. He replaced one finger with two and she grabbed hold of his shoulders to steady herself as he used his thumb to make teasing circular movements around her clitoris, avoiding touching the sensitive nerve endings until he felt she was ready.

'Oh, god, yes...' she cried, her fingernails digging into his flesh through his shirt.

He removed his fingers and she gasped again, this time with indignation.

'Take your dress off and lie on the bed,' he instructed, fully expecting her to refuse to obey orders, but she was obviously having too much fun to argue. She pulled the dress off in one swift movement and threw it aside. When she bent down to remove her shoes, he stopped her. 'No, leave them on.'

She looked at him with a raised eyebrow but lay back on the bed anyway.

'Take the pins out of your hair.' She did as he asked, and he watched in fascination as the rest of her thick locks, released from their prison, cascaded over her shoulders in curls and twists of red-gold waves. 'Shake your head,' he commanded, and she did.

He stood and watched her. She was lying width ways across the bed, completely naked except for red stilettoes, her hair in a tangle, her lipstick smudged and her eyes sparking green fire as she waited for him to speak. Her breasts were full with dark pink nipples and her legs were open, inviting him to come and play. He had never seen anything as sexy as Sapphire in that moment and his throat was dry and his cock as hard as steel.

He dropped to his knees at the side of the bed and put his face between her legs. He licked her, delighting in her taste and the shudder that went through her. She was wet and swollen, ready for him, but she would have to wait a while longer yet.

He could hear her chuckle as she grabbed his hair and tugged. He nibbled her labia with his lips and sucked her, keeping away from her clit until he was ready to let her come.

'Yes, James, that's it,' she encouraged him. But he didn't need any encouragement. He was being carried away on waves of uncontrollable lust. He grabbed her by the hips and pulled her so she was right at the edge of the bed, then he pushed her legs open as wide as he could. She was with him every step of the way and bent her knees so that she opened further to him.

'Yes, yes,' she cried. Her arousal was building fast and her eyes were closed as her head thrashed from side to side on the bed.

This time he used his fingers again, three of them in her vagina and his thumb teasing her clit.

'Oh,' she cried, 'I'm nearly there!'

He pulled out of her and stroked her inner thighs instead. 'Not yet,' he murmured.

'Don't tease me, James,' she said, lifting her head to glare at him.

He kissed her between her legs and caressed her lower abdomen, then reached up and put a finger into her belly button, tickling gently. She writhed on the bed and he held her down easily as she bucked and thrust up. Liking the reaction, he moved up the bed so he could use his tongue instead. She wriggled and squirmed, grabbing onto his hair.

'I want to come,' she said, and he laughed.

'I know you do. And you will. Patience Sapphire.'

'You're a bastard—do you know that?' She put her legs

on his shoulders and tried to pull his head down to continue his administrations.

'Am I?' He laughed and stroked her legs from her knees to the top of her thighs. When he got to her labia he gently opened her up and put his face between her legs again. She was so hot and wet he didn't think she'd hold out much longer. *Well, let's see.*

He resumed his leisurely kissing, nibbling, and licking, with the occasional caress. She was squirming around on the bed now and he was finding it almost impossible to hold her still. Sapphire was a lot stronger than she looked but she wasn't going to get her release until he said so.

'James…' she panted.

'Tell me what you want.' He stopped and held her legs open, blowing gently on her heated skin. She jumped, and he laughed.

'You know what I want.' Her voice was desperate now and he knew he could get her to beg if he wanted. And he did.

'Ask me nicely.'

'I want you to make me come, please.'

'Are you begging me?'

'Yes!'

'Then say it.' He didn't know what had come over him; he wasn't normally cruel with women. He was a gentleman. Kind. But he wanted to control Sapphire. To see the need and yearning in her eyes. And to know that he was the only one to give her what she wanted.

'I'm begging you to make me come – now!'

Then suddenly he didn't want to tease her anymore. He put his mouth to her again, but this time his licks were purposeful and controlled and in exactly the right place to send her over the edge. She screamed and tried to close her legs. He held on to her as wave after wave of her orgasm moved through her, nearly pushing her body off the bed.

She squeezed her legs tighter, trapping his head in the process. It took all his strength to keep her legs open and hold her down on the bed.

As her orgasm started to wane, she shouted, 'More! Don't stop!" so he kept licking, caressing, rubbing and tickling her until her screams must have been heard all over their floor of the hotel.

James had heard that some women could have multiple orgasms, but he had never met one who could. Sapphire didn't seem to be able to stop.

'Oh God!' she screamed. "Yes…no… keep going. Harder, faster… Oh…!'

His mouth was getting sore from all the sucking and licking he was doing, but Sapphire was insatiable. She was out of control, flaying around on the bed, but he kept going, giving her orgasm after orgasm, until they started to decrease in strength, and she began to calm down.

She lay on the bed like a rag doll that had been partying all night. Her legs were open, one shoe was half off, and her labia were wet and red. He wondered if he had made her sore. He would offer to rub cream into her skin, to help alleviate the pain. He grinned at the thought and scrambled up the bed to lie beside her. Her chest was still heaving slightly as she panted, and her mouth was open, her lipstick smeared across one cheek.

Lifting a lock of her hair, he curled it around his finger, then leaned over and kissed her demurely on the forehead.

'How was that for you?' he asked.

'Oh, James,' she gasped, 'that was… well, the only way I can describe it is—fucking amazing!'

'Really? So, your other lovers don't give you as many as

that then?' He was fishing for compliments—shamelessly—but he didn't care.

'No. One or two maybe—never that many.'

'So—how many did you have in the end?'

She chuckled and lay on her side facing him. 'I don't know, I lost count.'

She kissed him, and he felt the lust that had been kept on simmer while he pleasured her start to reach boiling point.

She ran her hands lightly over his chest and then her fingers caressed his cock which was so hard it was becoming painful. He was still fully dressed, and he had been sweating. He wanted to get naked.

'Okay. Now it's your turn.'

***

Sapphire was still aroused. Even after her multiple orgasms, she knew that it would simply take a short rest and then she'd be ready to go again. It was one of the many ways that women were superior to men who, poor dears, always took so long to recover.

James looked as if he was going to burst, so she pulled off his tie and slowly unbuttoned his shirt, running her hands through the dark, curly chest hair that arrowed down to his trousers. She took her time undoing his belt and lowering his zip. She could tell even before she pulled his trousers down to his ankles, that James was big. His cock strained against his zip and when she freed him, he sighed with relief.

'Better?' she asked solicitously.

'You bet,' he replied.

'Let's get you naked, then,' she said with a smile, kissing

his stomach and sticking her tongue in his belly button as he had done with her. It was a sensitive area on some people, and she was glad to see that it was on James. His body jerked as if she had given him an electric shock. Lovely. She continued to tongue him, wondering how long she could tease him before moving on to the organ he was desperate for her to touch.

'I want to make love to you.' His voice was croaky and held a hint of desperation.

'I know you do,' she replied, 'and you will. Patience, James.' He groaned in pain as she repeated his words back to him.

'You're going to punish me, aren't you?'

'Whatever for?' she asked sweetly as she pulled his shoes and socks off and then his trousers and briefs. She folded them neatly and put them on a chair. She stuffed his socks in the shoes and put them side by side underneath. James watched her every move but didn't make any attempt to get up. He lay, as she had done, completely naked, his cock so hard that it glistened with precum.

'For making you wait for your orgasm.'

'But that's part of the pleasure.' She stood at the side of the bed, looking down at him. 'Would you like a drink?'

'What?' His eyes were as dark as caves.

'I think I'm going to have a Scotch. You?'

'Yes. Thank you. No ice.' He was still lying sideways across the bed; his cock must be throbbing, but James was as polite as ever.

She fixed the drinks and put lots of ice in hers. Then she clambered onto the bed and gave James his glass.

'Thanks. Cheers.' He knocked it back in one and handed the glass to her. She couldn't help grinning at the puzzled look on his face. He put his head back and closed his eyes. 'I don't know what you've got planned for me, Sapphire, but I would be grateful if we could get back to the sex now. Please.'

'Of course, James. Straight away. She got off the bed and put his empty glass on the table. Then she strolled back to the bed sipping her drink. 'What I want you to do is put your arms above your head and keep them there. It's a pity I don't have my handcuffs with me, but we'll have to make do.'

'Handcuffs? What are you going to do to me?' He sounded really worried now and she stifled a laugh.

'Don't worry, you'll enjoy it. I always do.'

'So—does that mean I can do it to you afterwards? Whatever *it* is?'

'Steady, cowboy—one step at a time.'

'Okay.' He put his hands over his head obediently and watched her with an excited, but scared look in his eyes. 'Now what?'

She sat cross-legged on the bed beside him and drank the rest of her Scotch. She shook the glass slightly and the ice tinkled against the sides. She stared at James to see if he had guessed and his eyebrows shot up to his scalp as realization dawned.

'Oh, no...'

'Oh, yes, James. You need cooling down. In order to prolong your orgasm as long as possible, we need to take drastic measures and decrease your body temperature. Ice is the best way—don't you think?' She knew it would have the opposite effect and drive him insane.

Sapphire took an ice cube in her mouth and put her lips to James's right nipple, gently rubbing the ice over the nub.

'Oh fuck!' he cried.

She continued rubbing gently, then moved to his other nipple.

When the ice cube melted, she selected another and trailed it over his stomach with her fingers, using her tongue to retrace the path. The differences in the temperatures were driving him crazy and he writhed on the bed, crying out for her to stop.

'Don't you like it?' she asked innocently.

'Yes, but…'

'I know—you want to come.' She smiled as he looked at her in anguish. 'Very well.'

She put an ice-cube in her mouth and then shuffled down the bed and took his cock in her mouth. He groaned and covered his face with his hands.

'That's … Oh my God!'

The ice melted rapidly from the heat of her mouth and James's body. She felt his cock hit the back of her throat, so she relaxed and took him in further. Alternately massaging his balls and stroking his inner thighs, she worked on him expertly so that, in a matter of seconds—or that was how it seemed to Sapphire—James orgasmed with a loud cry and she swallowed his semen before lifting her head to see what state her co-CEO had been left in.

He was lying in exactly the same position he started, but his eyes were closed, and he was groaning.

'Oh God,' he said quietly.

Worried that if she lay beside him, he might want to cuddle her or indulge in other displays of affection, she got off the bed and padded over to the mini-bar.

'How about another drink? While we both catch our breath for round two?'

James lifted his head, looked up at her and gave her the

sexiest grin she'd seen on him yet, then said, 'Great idea, but definitely no ice this time.'

Chapter Four

James was back in charge for round two.

'I have an idea. It's called the "hot seat", he told Sapphire, whose face lit up at the suggestion.

'Tell me more,' she drawled.

'I'll show you.' He sat on the edge of the bed, sheathing himself with one of the condoms that he had, conveniently, stashed in the inside pocket of his jacket before leaving his house for the evening.

Sapphire's eyes were shining as she walked towards him slowly. He turned her to face away from him and she maneuvered herself onto his lap then he buried himself inside her.

He held her tightly as he thrust up into her and buried his face in her hair. He loved her hair; it was the most glorious colour and so soft he wanted to wrap it around himself. He fondled her breasts, tweaking her nipples, and she reached between her legs and played with his balls.

James quickly reached the point of no return, encouraged by the endless climaxes Sapphire was enjoying. He came again and was overjoyed when Sapphire showed no sign of slowing down. She obviously loved sex and seemed very experienced. He didn't want to disappoint her. He loved listening to the guttural animal noises she made when she climaxed. And he loved how she completely let go and gave in to the pleasure. He felt so involved. He wasn't just doing something to her, as he had felt with previous lovers, he was right there with her, almost feeling what she did.

'I am going to have a long soak in a bubble bath,' Sapphire stretched like a cat, 'How about you order us some coffee? Or tea if you prefer?'

'Which would *you* prefer?'

'Tea.'

'Me too.' Coffee would keep him awake. Not that there was any chance of either of them getting much sleep that night. He was going to make sure of it.

He phoned down to room service and asked them to bring some fruit and a selection of cheeses with the tea, and to just leave it on the coffee table in the lounge if they knocked and no one answered. He didn't want them to be disturbed if they were engaged in more sex. They could eat later if they were otherwise occupied. He didn't imagine their sexual appetites would decrease any time soon. His certainly wouldn't; he could have sex with Sapphire all night.

Just as he put the phone down, the sound of his mobile went off. He moved swiftly to where his trousers lay, neatly folded over the back of the chair, to retrieve it from one of the pockets, but it wasn't his phone that was ringing.

The sound was coming from Sapphire's clutch bag. They had the same ring tone. The bag was open, and James could see the phone. He hesitated, wondering whether to ignore it, but then picked it up to look at the number. He wasn't going to answer it, obviously, but he wanted to be able to tell Sapphire who had called. It might have been urgent.

It wasn't. It was a London number, but one he recognized as a cold caller. He picked up the clutch to return the phone and noticed something in the bag. Something he recognised immediately. He'd seen one like it many times. An object that looked a lot like a fountain pen but wasn't.

After sitting on the edge of the bed, deep in thought at the implications of what he'd discovered, he got up, replaced the clutch bag where he had found it and, without knocking, went into the bathroom.

Sapphire was lying in the large, luxurious bath, which sat at an angle to the front of the floor-to-ceiling windows that afforded the best view that London had to offer, the city stretching out to the horizon.

They were on the tenth floor of the hotel, with no danger of being overlooked, and there were no blinds on the windows. He could see Tower Bridge, the lights of small boats on the Thames and the windows in nearby office blocks lit up like a mosaic.

It wasn't the view from the window that fascinated and enthralled him. It was the sight of Sapphire in the soapy water. She had tied her hair up and laid her head back on the rim of the bath. Her long legs were stretched out and a foot placed on each side of the bath tub. Her feet, with scarlet toenails, glistened and small collections of soap bubbles hung from her legs, reminding James of dandelion seeds that he and his sisters had played with when the girls had been tiny.

Sapphire's hands were under a layer of bubbles that floated like a raft on the top. She must have used half the bottle as the bubbles were thick, white and creamy and the most evocative aroma of flowers, spices and exotic fruit wafted up from the water. The bathroom was steamy, reminiscent of a sauna, but the window was clear. Perhaps they used special glass to keep it that way.

A groan from the bath alerted James to where Sapphire's hands were. 'Are you playing with yourself?' he asked incredulously. She couldn't be, not after all the sex they'd just had. Could she?

'Do you want to do it for me?' Her sleepy voice woke up his dozing erogenous zones and his cock hardened instantly.

He walked over to the bath and helped her to lift her head and shoulders up, and he climbed in behind her.

Sapphire leaned back, her head on his shoulder, her buttocks pressing into his groin. She bent her knees and dangled her legs over the sides of the bath, so she was exposed for him. She was wet from the soapy water, and sticky from her arousal. He took his time, stroking her with the tips of his fingers. She squirmed and pushed her buttocks harder into his groin. His erection pushed back, and she wriggled, setting up delightful sensations that vibrated all through his body.

He took her hand and guided her fingers back to the place where they had been. 'Show me how you like it. I want to see every little movement.'

She turned her head slightly and he saw the sweat on her top lip. 'It was pretty good before.'

'Yes, but it can be better. There's always room for improvement.'

'Spoken like a man with ambition. I like it.'

She showed him. He held her hands loosely while she masturbated. She used both her hands, her palms and fingers. She varied the pace, sometimes with a touch like a spider's web, sometimes rubbing as if she was trying to polish herself. James was riveted.

She orgasmed and tried to squeeze her legs together, so James kept her legs apart by placing his feet inside hers and forcing her legs open. She cried out and struggled, so he pushed her hands away from her vagina and stroked and fondled her, circling her clit until she orgasmed again—and again.

She was splashing and thrashing around, and water spilled over the side of the bath and soaked the floor. The whole bathroom, floor, and walls, was tiled in a beautiful black and ivory marble pattern.

James was grinning as Sapphire came multiple times.

Once she was still and her panting and thrashing had come to an end, he put his arms around her and held her tightly. If they had been having a normal relationship this would be the perfect time to tell her how much he loved her. All of her. Her beauty, sexiness, funkiness, spark, and her ability to have multiple orgasms that tore through her body like a tsunami. They would have talked, quietly and intimately before falling asleep in each other's arms.

But he didn't love her, and she certainly didn't love him. They liked each other and, perhaps they would work well together, but this was sex. Nothing more and nothing less. Pure physical release. And it was good. But there were two things worrying him. The item he'd found in her clutch bag and the fact that when daylight came, the thing he had with Sapphire would be over.

'Oh, my giddy aunt!' Sapphire moaned, 'I need a rest.'

'Good idea,' said James climbing out the bath and grabbing a huge bath towel to rub himself down with. 'The food should be here by now and we don't want the tea to get cold.'

'Okay.' She sighed and, when he was dry, he left her to it and wandered back to the bedroom. This time, to avoid temptation and because he wanted to talk to her, he slipped on the robe provided by the hotel. Then he sat in their separate living area, eating grapes, and waiting for Sapphire to join him.

She strolled in, looking relaxed and replete in a matching robe, her hair brushed and flowing around her shoulders, gold lights mixing with the red. She wore no makeup at all, not even her signature eyeliner which she usually applied quite heavily, James thought. She looked gorgeous, utterly kissable and totally fuckable.

'I'll pour, shall I?' He watched as she poured the Earl Grey into delicate china cups, then added milk but no sugar. He picked his cup and saucer off the table.

'Thank you. Have you taken your insulin today?' He kept his voice quiet and matter-of-fact, but she jumped as if he had hit her and then put her cup and saucer back on the table, slowly and carefully.

'What did you say?' Her voice was low and threatening and he felt a frisson of something cold pass across his skin.

'I found your insulin pen in your clutch bag. I'm just checking that you've taken your insulin. In the excitement of tonight and all the sex, you could easily—'

'You went in my bag?' Her voice was loud now, and he cringed. 'How dare you? What were you looking for?'

'I wasn't looking for anything—your phone rang and I—'

'You answered my phone?'

'No, I didn't need to, it was a cold caller, but I found—'

'Well you had no right. No right at all.' She stood up and marched around the room. He stayed where he was and watched her. 'How dare you go through my things? I don't think I need to remind you that, technically, I am your boss and I do not take kindly to my employees snooping through my personal belongings.' Her voice grew louder until she was almost shouting.

He said nothing but smiled to himself. She wasn't looking at him, fortunately, but the thought of her indignation after all the things he'd just been doing to her body struck him as amusing.

Her reaction was way over the top. Some people liked to keep their private lives private and never spoke about their medical conditions to anyone, but Sapphire looked almost afraid that he had discovered she had diabetes.

'Sapphire, come and sit down and talk to me.' He kept his voice calm and controlled.

'I don't want to discuss it. It's absolutely none of your business, and I'd appreciate it if you'd never mention it again.' She was shaking now, whether from rage, cold, or fear, James wasn't sure.

'What are you afraid of, Sapphire?'

'I'm not afraid of anything—or anybody. I just begrudge people knowing things about me.'

'You're a social media darling—all your personal details are there for anyone to read. Why is it such a big deal that you've got diabetes?'

'Will you stop saying that!' She was yelling now, and all the good vibes and ambience of the evening they'd spent together disappeared fast. James wanted it back. He intended to fuck her again, hard, more than once. But the way things were now, she wouldn't let him near her.

'How old were you when you were diagnosed?'

'None of your business,' she snapped. She sat down, her arms crossed, and her legs crossed, one foot bouncing up and down to the rhythm of her rapid breathing. It was the most stressed he'd seen her. And the most defensive. Interesting.

He poured himself more tea. Sapphire hadn't touched hers. Then he put some cheese, figs and grapes on a plate with a couple of crackers and sat back in the chair, his legs stretched out, utterly relaxed. He watched her from the corner of his eye.

'Lulu was diagnosed when she was eight. It was a shock for the poor little girl, but she took it stoically. The way she took everything.'

As he knew she would, Sapphire asked, 'Who's Lulu?'

'My baby sister. She's twenty-five now. She's an infant support teacher. Loves the little ones.' He smiled at the thought of his little sister. She had been a cutie when she was small. 'My other sister is twenty-eight. She's a tougher version of the Lewis women, a lawyer—Phoebe.'

'How utterly fascinating,' said Sapphire sarcastically.

James hid a smile by stuffing his face with edam cheese on a sesame seed cracker. Sapphire may be feigning boredom, but her body was starting to lose its rigid control. She was deflating somewhat, like a party balloon that knew the party was over.

'You're an only child, aren't you?'

She turned her head away. 'I suppose you read that on social media?'

He laughed. 'Yes, I did, as a matter of fact.' He ate in silence for a while. Sapphire looked as if she wanted to cry and he wondered why she was so upset. Diabetes was easily treatable these days. He'd get to the bottom of it eventually. He'd make her talk if he had to sit there all night.

It was ruined. All of it. And she'd been having such a good time. James was attentive, sexy and seemed to want to please her. She'd had the best orgasms she'd ever had at his hands, and mouth—and then there was his cock. Boy, did he have a lovely cock. He was big, but not huge. She had a small pelvis. She'd couldn't cope with a man if he was huge.

There was no point trying to hide it now. He knew. She'd have to make the best of it. If only she'd been prepared, she wouldn't have lost it and she could have played a role. Pretended that she was fine with it, that it was no biggy. Just another challenge that she, as a business-woman and entrepreneur in the modern world took in her stride. Instead, she'd thrown a tantrum like a child.

'I was eight, too, when I was diagnosed.' He looked up, and his dazzling blue eyes were full of interest. Not pity, she was glad to see.

'And how did you feel about it?'

Angry. Sick. 'Well, I wasn't happy, but you just have to get on with things, don't you?'

He looked unconvinced. 'So why were you so upset just now?'

She sighed. 'Okay, I'll level with you. Women at the top still have to put up with a lot from men. We have to work harder than they do to get to the same place. And my rivals will use anything they can to bring me down. And women have plenty of things that men can use against them, believe me.'

James was watching her, drinking in every word. His look was hard to read. Interest, but not sympathy. She would have loved to know what he was thinking at that moment.

'Such as?' he asked finally.

'Menstruation, pregnancy, motherhood, menopause, and just being a wife to some selfish, chauvinistic—'

'You sound bitter.'

'I'm not bitter, James,' she said angrily, 'just realistic. To add a chronic condition like diabetes to the list just adds fuel to the fire.'

'So who, in your immediate support team, knows about it?'

'Only Della.'

'Is that wise? Surely you need people to be aware in case you're unwell at work. You could have a hypo, or DKA...'

'Della knows exactly what to do in case I have a hypo or diabetic ketoacidosis so please don't worry on my account.' She wanted to steer the conversation away from illness, but James seemed to want to know everything. Perhaps, if she told him the bare minimum, he would be satisfied, and then they could get back to the sex.

'What if she's on holiday or at lunch?'

'Oh James, for God's sake, you sound just like my parents!' *Shit!* She hadn't meant to say that.

He raised his eyebrows. She knew she'd have to tell him the truth now.

'Did they wrap you up in cotton wool? Treat you as if you were a fragile flower with a serious illness?'

'Exactly that.' He was more perceptive than she'd given him credit for. 'They wouldn't let me play out, go to other kids' houses, have sleep-overs. They were terrified something would, "happen to me".' She put the last phrase in air quotes and put on a silly voice, and then felt a stab of guilt at being disloyal. But her childhood could have been so different...

'That's tough. Luckily my parents were the opposite. They refused to treat Lulu differently to Phoebe and myself.

Even though she's the baby, they made her get out there and live her life. She was scared sometimes, poor kid, but she just put her brave face on and went out there and did it. Lulu's had more than her share of problems and coped admirably with all of them.'

'I wish my parents had been like that. You sound proud of your little sister.'

'I am. She's very special. And not just because of the diabetes.'

'She's lucky to have you.'

'That spell you had in hospital—when the interviews were going on—was that because of your diabetes?'

'Yes, but I don't wish to discuss it.'

'Maybe you *need* to discuss it.'

'You don't know me James. If you did, you'd realise that I never talk about it.'

'There's a first time for everything, and I'm a good listener.'

'It wouldn't change anything.'

'I disagree,' said James. 'We all need to be able to offload now and again. It'll make you feel better. In fact—how about this for an idea? Let's get naked again and get into that bed and you can tell me all about it. Get it off that gorgeous chest of yours, then we can make love again. How about it?'

'Okay.' The two things that resonated with Sapphire about that suggestion was the thought of cuddling up to James was suddenly appealing and the fact that he had said "make love" not "have sex". Things were changing, and she wasn't sure how she felt about it. They only had one night, maybe an innocent cuddle wouldn't hurt. Didn't mean they were engaged.

When they were lying together, James on his back with

Sapphire next to him on her side, one leg thrown over his legs, his arm around her and her head on his chest, his hand gently playing with her hair, in the muggy cocoon-like darkness, Sapphire poured her heart out to him.

She told him how claustrophobic her childhood had been. Her parents wouldn't let her have a bike, or a skateboard. She hadn't been allowed a kitten, even though, at the age of ten, she had set her heart on one. Germs, apparently, according to her mother. Not worth the risk. Everything was not worth the risk when she was a child. She had sometimes wondered if life itself was not worth the risk.

James had listened quietly, stroking her hair and occasionally kissing her on the forehead. He was a solid, comforting presence. Non-judgmental and supportive. She'd never had that before.

When she finished talking, she took his cock in her hand, to find him hard as a rock.

They made love then without moving their positions much. Sapphire just rolled the condom on James, then they lay facing each other and she guided him into her. It was slow, leisurely. There was more kissing, fondling and hugging.

Was this the last time they would make love? Sapphire had made the rule that they only had one night to get it out of their systems. Had James done that? She certainly hadn't. She'd never had a lover like him, and she wanted more.

They fell asleep in each other's arms as the first light of the new day crept up over the horizon and bathed London in its milky glow.

Chapter Five

'Is she in yet?' James asked as he peered around the door of Della's office.

'Not yet. She's on her way though, she just texted.' Della smiled.

James liked Della, she was calm, sensible, and rational. The perfect foil for the woman she worked for, who was the complete opposite. The memory of the night he had spent with Sapphire still melted his bones and ignited his erogenous zones. A week had gone by since then and nothing had been mentioned about a repeat performance. Sapphire had stipulated one night to get it out of their systems, and it seemed she was sticking to it.

James understood what Hector had meant when he said Sapphire was working around the clock and in danger of making herself ill. She was always in the office when he arrived—except today—and was the last one to leave in the evening. James, wanting to prove his worth to her, had kept the same hours, but their paths rarely crossed as Sapphire was often in meetings that he wasn't part of, and he was out and about, looking at prospective businesses to invest in.

'You need a secretary, James,' said Della as she folded a letter and put it in an envelope, 'judging by the amount of paper littering your desk.'

'Do I?' He hadn't thought of it, but as co-CEO, with all the administration that went with the role, he needed someone to assist him. 'Can't I share you?'

'I don't think Sapphire likes sharing. Shall I see who's available in the secretarial pool?'

'Yes, thanks. That would be good.' He came into her office and sat down in an upright chair in the corner. 'Do you mind if I wait?'

'Of course not.' Her gaze fell on the object he had placed on the floor at his feet. 'What have you got there?'

'A present for Sapphire.'

'It looks like a—' Della was peering at it and frowning. A tiny noise made her laugh and put her hand to her mouth. 'It's a cat!'

'Kitten to be exact. She's ten weeks old and her name is Sparkle.'

'Oh my God, she's so cute! I love tortoiseshells.' Della rushed around her desk and bent down to see her better. 'Can I take her out?'

'Of course.'

He opened the door to the cat carrier and scooped up the tiny body. She was meowing, her open mouth pink with sharp little teeth. He handed her to Della, who cuddled her and cooed to her.

'Where did you get her and why, if you don't mind me asking, do you think Sapphire needs a cat?'

'My sister's cat had kittens, and she's been trying to find

homes for them all. Sparkle is the last one. Everyone needs a cat, don't they?'

He looked at Della, deliberately keeping his expression blank, before breaking into a huge grin. 'Actually, she told me her parents wouldn't let her have one when she was a kid and so I thought—'

'You thought what, James?' said Sapphire from the doorway.

He stood up as she sashayed into the room.

'What have we here?'

'A present. For you.'

'A kitten? I've had many presents from men—flowers, perfume, chocolate. Even a pair of silk stockings once—but I don't recall ever being given a kitten.'

'I like to be different,' said James.

'You sure know how to spoil a girl,' she murmured.

'Look, Sapphire, she's got a little collar with gems around it. They're not real, are they, James?' Della asked.

'They're real imitations,' he said, still grinning.

Even though Sapphire was eyeing the cat warily, he could see she was itching to cuddle her.

'She's had all her vaccinations and been wormed and flea'd. So, she's good to go. Why don't you hold her and get to know her?'

Sapphire sighed as if she really didn't have time for all this nonsense. Della put the cat in her arms, and the little thing snuggled up into Sapphire's neck and started purring like a miniature engine.

'Ah, she likes you,' said Della.

'Excellent.' James was feeling rather pleased with himself. He'd helped Lulu home the last kitten and found something for Sapphire to shower her love on. For it was obvious to him that, no matter how much she protested about being in control of her life, she needed a hug on a regular basis. He suspected she wasn't as tough as she liked to think she was.

'James, I have very important meetings in my office, I can't have a cat getting under everyone's feet.'

'Don't worry, she can stay with me,' Della said, 'We'll need to get a bed and food bowl—oh, and some toys.'

'That's all taken care of.' James stepped out of the office for a second and returned with a large carrier bag he had left outside the door and pulled out a small cat bed, food, two bowls in pink and a selection of toys including what looked suspiciously like a dead rodent dangling from a stick. Lulu had assured him it was the kitten's favourite toy.

'Fine. But what will happen to her at night?'

'She can go home with you,' Della said.

'Then bring her back in the morning. At least until she gets bigger and can stay on her own.' James was enjoying himself. Teasing Sapphire was becoming one of his favourite pastimes, especially when he knew she was just thinking up excuses to annoy him.

'I have work to do.' Sapphire handed the kitten to Della and flounced out of the office.

James winked at Della and followed her.

Sapphire sat behind her desk and tried not to stare at James. Their night of hot sex hadn't dampened her ardour one bit. In fact, it had achieved the opposite effect. She was desperate to get him back into her bed. It was, however, going to be an incredibly busy week and she needed to focus on work.

'Do you have the statistics ready for the directors' meeting?'

'Of course.' James sat on the couch they had used at their first meeting, his papers in neat piles on the coffee table in front of him. 'All ready, just as you asked.'

'And what about the information you were going to gather about companies that we could, potentially, invest in?'

'Yes, I was on it first thing this morning. I've emailed all the notes I've made, with my recommendations, and the spreadsheet containing the risks involved and the profits we are likely to receive going forward, to all the directors and shareholders. And you, of course.'

'Thanks.'

'You're welcome. You look very sexy in that trouser suit by the way. I haven't seen you in trousers. They look good on you.'

'It's because of the meeting.'

'Really? The directors like you to wear trousers?' James looked totally bewildered and Sapphire smiled in an evil fashion. She didn't know whether to tell him the truth, but she needed to pay him back for presenting her with the kitten as if she was ten years old.

'No, James, they have no say in what I wear. Nor does anyone else. It's because I get bored in meetings. My mind tends to drift—to sex. And then I feel the need to orgasm. Well—the trousers help with the process.'

'No,' he said, shaking his head, 'you've lost me.'

She pushed her chair away from her desk, so he could see what she was doing. His gaze was riveted on her legs as she crossed them.

'If I sit like this, and squeeze—and if I'm visualizing

what I would like to do to a lover and get turned on—then I can come.'

James stared at her open-mouthed. 'You're shittin' me!'

She laughed. 'No, I'm not. Some women can have orgasms by squeezing their legs together, and trousers, especially those made of a certain fabric that you can feel against your clitoris, aid the process. Especially if the seam is in exactly the right place. These trousers are particularly good. In fact, I'd say they are definitely my favourite. Nice colour too, don't you think?'

'Are you winding me up?'

'No, it's the truth. Google it if you don't believe me.'

'You actually orgasm in the middle of a meeting, in a room full of people, and nobody notices? I don't believe you.'

'Well, of course, I have to be discrete about it. I can't shout out or swear or anything. Once I did have to pretend to have a coughing fit…'

James did something that made Sapphire want to strip his clothes off and mount him right then and there as he sprawled on the couch. He put his head back, closed his eyes and laughed until he cried. Real tears were streaming out of his eyes and down his cheeks. His whole body was shaking uncontrollably, and as he started to get up, he fell back down again helplessly. The thought of James helpless ignited her engines and she wanted to swerve the meeting and take him back to the hotel room for an orgy for two.

There was something so exquisitely sexy about the sight of a man in the throes of uncontrollable laughter. It turned her on more than anything else. Sadly, it wasn't a sight she saw very often.

She couldn't watch for much longer or she'd be incapable of doing any work at all.

'James,' she said loudly and sternly, 'pull yourself together. We've got work to do.'

'Sorry…' he struggled to sit up and wiped his face with his hands. But his body was still shaking, so she got up and went into the bathroom to give him time to recover.

As Sapphire stared at herself in the mirror, she smiled. She looked good. She knew she did. The sex she and James had enjoyed had given her a boost. She felt happy, confident, in control. She waited a full ten minutes and returned to her office.

James wasn't laughing any more, but he couldn't look at her, so she sat down and put her glasses on, peering at him over the top of them.

He looked at her. His lips twitched, and his eyes were shining. "While we are on the subject of sex, there's something I want to say.'

'Oh?' She waited.

'Yes. I've given this a lot of thought and I believe I've been short-changed.'

'In what way?'

'Well —our arrangement was that we have a night of sex to get it out of our systems. Correct?'

'Yes, I believe that *is* what we agreed.'

'But you—as you ably demonstrated and have described in such interesting detail—are in the habit of having multiple orgasms. While I can only have one at a time.'

'That's because you are a man and therefore inferior in that department.' Sapphire made a conscious effort to keep her face straight. She enjoyed this kind of silly banter with James. He was such a serious man in the office, but she suspected he had depths and layers she intended to peel away as easily as she had peeled off his clothing.

'While I concede that to be true, I can't help feeling I should be compensated in some way for the deficit.'

'What do you have in mind?'

'Another night together.'

James looked at her steadily. Properly looked. His blue eyes seemed to stare down into her soul, searching for something. He was telling her he didn't want them to stop having sex. She didn't either. Her heart leapt for joy. Or for lust. Yes, lust, obviously.

'Well—I suppose we could extend the terms of the agreement. Just for one more night.'

'Excellent.' He grinned and, leaning towards her, he whispered, 'Always a pleasure doing business with you. I look forward to another long and satisfying night.' She couldn't help herself—she grinned back.

'Right. I need to go. The directors' meeting starts in half an hour, so I'll see you there, okay?'

'Fine.'

'Oh, and don't forget the fashion show tomorrow, will you?'

'Fashion show? Is it tomorrow?' James looked surprised and Sapphire realised that she hadn't mentioned it before.

'Yes, it is, and I really think you should be there. I'm showing my autumn collection and a lot of very important people will be attending. You need to meet them.'

'Okay, no problem. Where is it?'

Sapphire mentioned a warehouse conversion in Soho. 'I think this time it would be nice if we went together. We need to be there for about six. Is that okay?'

'Perfect. Right in the centre of London in rush hour traffic. Couldn't be better.'

'We could get a driver if you prefer?'

'No. I'll sort it. Leave it with me.'

James had never spent an important meeting in such a state of heightened sexual arousal. After Sapphire's admission, he couldn't take his eyes off her. He hadn't believed her, thinking it was another of her teases, so he'd Googled it to find she was telling the truth. From then on, the thought of being able to concentrate on boring facts and figures went straight out of the window. Even though his future, and the future of Sapphire Enterprises, depended on getting those facts and figures right.

He tried to listen as the directors gave their views, the toing and froing of arguments and the repetition as each one was thrashed out over and over again.

Sapphire looked calm, for her, and seemed to be listening intently. Every now and then she interjected with a comment or a question. There was a time, during a particularly dull patch, that her eyes seemed to glaze over slightly, and she coughed and looked down.

Was she doing it? Had she come?

He couldn't look at her, but he couldn't concentrate either.

As the meeting ended and everyone filed out, he grabbed her arm and said in a loud voice, 'Can I have a quick word, Sapphire?'

They both nodded at people and shook hands with others, then Sapphire lead him to the executive bathroom and locked the door behind her. They were on each other almost before they had heard the click of the lock. They tore at each other's clothes, trousers falling around ankles, swiftly followed by underwear.

James nearly dropped the condom in his haste and Sapphire had to help him to put it on.

'Did you?' he rasped, 'in the meeting?'

She kissed him, her mouth a hot cavern. 'Yes, but only once.'

He picked her up and sat her on the space next to the sink. He pushed her legs open and placed two fingers in her vagina. She was wet and open. She cried out and he kissed her again.

'What were you thinking about when you did it?'

'You James. I was thinking of all the things I want to do to you.'

He groaned and thrust into her. She grabbed him around the neck and pushed her body as close to him as she could. She seemed to be trying to take him in deeper, so he picked her up and she wrapped her legs around his waist. He carried her to the wall, so she had her back against it and one leg on the ground, the other wrapped around his body. He thrust harder and faster and they climaxed together.

When their breathing started to return to normal, he put his forehead against hers and whispered, 'Sapphire—what are you doing to me?'

Chapter Six

Sapphire couldn't sleep. She rarely could the night before a show. It was humid, and she had the windows open to try and move the still, heavy air.

It was after midnight and she lay on her couch in her spacious living-room with Sparkle curled up on her stomach, staring out at the London skyline, lit up as if it was still day. She didn't know about New York being the city that never sleeps, London didn't seem to do a great deal of it either. Whatever time she looked out of her windows at the view—evening, midnight or early morning—there were lights on everywhere. People were awake; in offices, apartments, on the streets. The sirens of the emergency service vehicles formed a constant background music to a Londoner's life.

She loved it. It was vibrant, exciting and made her feel alive.

She loved her apartment too, in the Elephant and Castle area of the city. Bequeathed to her by her first employer,

Monty Ferrante, the designer who had taken her on as an apprentice when she won a design competition at nineteen and he had fallen in love with her work. He'd fallen a little bit in love with her, too, and their working relationship had spilled over into a sexual one.

He was a lot older than her and died of a heart attack at the age of forty-nine. He left her his apartment and enough money to start her own business. He'd taught her about sex, opened the door to her future as a designer and showed her that life was for living.

Life in the fast lane. Short and sweet. Her parents wouldn't approve, but she was in control of her life and no one could tell her what to do with it. Sapphire was determined not to let the diabetes stop her from achieving her goals.

Another thing that Monty had taught her was not to trust anybody, especially when it came to money and sex. Advice that she wished she'd taken to heart.

Seeing Roland again in the restaurant had unsettled her. She had, once, imagined herself in love with him and when he asked her to invest in his company, promising her a return on investment of several hundred percent, she had believed him and taken money out of Sapphire Enterprises. Hector had been against the whole thing. Sapphire bitterly regretted not listening to him. Roland's business went bankrupt and the money was lost.

She stroked Sparkle's tiny head and thought about James. He was a different kettle of fish to Monty and Roland. Completely different. James was thoughtful, considerate and could be intensely serious. But he also had a fun side, when he fell into uncontrollable laughter... Sapphire smiled at the memory.

He was fit, sexy, had muscles in all the right places and quite a tidy six pack. He must work out or run—or both. And then there was his cock... delectable!

Sapphire sighed. Thinking about sex was not the way to fall asleep, unless she wanted a session with one of her vibrators first. There was quite a collection in her bedroom, vibrators having come a long way since the first rabbit she bought. They were so sophisticated these days, she even had one that simulated oral sex. No matter how technically proficient it was, it wasn't the same as the real thing and the memory of James's mouth between her legs caused a rush of heat to envelop her. She groaned.

It was no good, she would have to take a sleeping pill. She stood up, kissed Sparkle on the top of her head and padded into the bathroom. She swallowed a pill with water, then carried cat and glass into the bedroom.

'Okay, sweetie, let's go to bed. It's going to be a long day tomorrow.'

As Sapphire got into bed, she reminded herself to eat properly the following day. She would take some food with her in order to keep her blood sugar level even and to avoid people getting on her case. It was nice that people cared and were watching her constantly but would be even better if they didn't have to.

———————

Sapphire overslept and woke up feeling sick and groggy. There was no time to prepare her food, so she would have to send Della out for snacks. Sparkle wouldn't go in her carrier and Sapphire spent a frustrating twenty minutes chasing her around the apartment, which left her irritable and tetchy.

When she arrived in the office, she discovered that Della was off sick with a heavy cold. She had sent her a text, but Sapphire hadn't checked her phone. But, like the good PA she was, Della had arranged for a girl from the secretarial pool to fill in for the day. She was a potential candidate for the role of James's temporary secretary.

Sapphire disliked her on sight.

James was in Sapphire's office when Angie arrived. She ignored Sapphire, who was at her desk holding Sparkle, and went straight up to James to shake hands.

'Della says I'm going to be working for you. Isn't it exciting? May I call you James?'

She fawned over him and fluttered her eyelashes. James said nothing but shook Angie's hand.

'You'll be working for me today and there's lots to do, so you'll need to keep your wits about you.' Sapphire was feeling stressed already and the arrival of Angie with her over-the-top enthusiasm was guaranteed to get on her last nerve.

'Oh, a cat! How sweet...' Angie greeted Sparkle by leaning over Sapphire's desk and kissing the cat on her head. Sparkle rubbed her head against the secretary's face. *Traitor!*

'I meant to ask you what I should wear tonight,' James said, 'I was wondering what the dress code was.'

Sapphire sat back in her seat and looked him up and down. As usual, he looked smart in a dark blue pin-striped suit, blue shirt and black tie.

'I wouldn't have thought it mattered,' said Angie, 'You look to me like the kind of man who would always look smart.'

Sapphire gave Angie a look that most perceptive secretaries would have read as the sign to disappear and leave the bosses to talk. Angie was obviously not very perceptive as she looked as if she wanted to be part of the conversation.

James was sitting on the couch and Angie was hovering around him like a fly around spilt sugar.

'Do you know anything about the fashion industry, Angie?' Sapphire asked sweetly.

'A little,' the girl said nervously.

'Well, I know a lot. And it matters a great deal what we wear to these shows. The fashion on display isn't only on the catwalk. The place will be full of the industry's finest and they will all be watching each other. Watching for any fashion *faux pas*. And then there's the press, who will, obviously be doing the same. We all dress to impress.'

'Oh,' said Angie.

'Shit,' said James.

'What you wear depends directly on the image you are trying to project. It has to be fashionable, more glamorous than you usually wear, and incorporate your style statement.'

'My what?' James was looking baffled, but Sapphire hadn't finished tormenting him yet.

'Your style statement is the essence of who you are. As someone in the industry once said, "You, fully expressed." It isn't a label, of course, as fashions change and so can your style. You won't be the same now as you were at twenty and, again, you will have a different style statement at fifty.'

'Can't I just wear a suit?' asked James looking a bit pale.

'Well, of course, you can James, if you think that's who you are.'

'Casual?'

'Smart casual.'

He grinned, and Sapphire felt the familiar warmth

spread down to her lower abdomen settling in wet waves of desire between her legs. He looked completely different when he smiled. So fuckable she wanted to strip him and show Angie how real adults had sex.

'Would you like a coffee, Sapphire?' her secretary for the day asked.

'That would be delightful, Angie, thank you.'

'Right—I'll go and sort my wardrobe out. Pick you up at five Sapphire?' James got up and strolled to the door.

'Thanks. See you later.'

When James had gone, Sapphire looked in her drawer for pain killers. Her head was banging. Why did she take that sleeping pill? Stupid idea. She swallowed two with some water and debated sending Angie out for food. She didn't want anyone to know about her diabetes, though, and would probably have to fend off too many questions. She needed to buy glucose tablets as she'd run out. It would be too difficult to explain.

So, she got stuck into the mountain of work she needed to get through before the show and tried to ignore the fact that she was sweating too much, and her stomach was growling with hunger.

Angie came back with the coffee, chatting away as if they were old friends.

'Oh, I love working here. The fashion industry is so fascinating, isn't it? I wish I was coming to the show. So glamourous. All those models and designers…'

'Angie? Would you be a darling and pop out to the patisserie on the corner? Get me a croissant, would you?'

'Of course, Sapphire. Is there anything else you want?'

'No, that's all, thank you.'

At least that would give her blood sugar level a boost

until she could find the time to eat a salad for lunch. Sapphire gave a sigh of relief when Angie had left. She was feeling a bit disorientated and had a sudden desire to cry. Not good. Not good at all.

The phone rang on the dot of five. It was the concierge telling her that her visitor had arrived.

She loved these apartments, she felt like a celebrity having someone vet her visitors for her. There was a gym for her to use too, but she never used it. Never had the time or the inclination.

When she arrived in reception, she thanked Victor and left the building to look for James. She found him outside on the pavement, leaning on a motorbike, dressed completely in black leather. He held a motorcycle helmet in his hands.

'Is this your style statement?' she asked, gazing at him with a mixture of horror and excitement.

'No, it's my standard protective gear when I ride my bike.'

'Your bike?!'

'Yes. How else do you think we're going to get through the traffic jams at this time of the day?'

'I never thought... I didn't know you rode a bike.'

'I imagine there's a lot about me you don't know.'

'Yes, I imagine there is.' She was feeling weak again suddenly. She'd worked through lunch and the only food item she managed to find was a tuna and mayo sandwich, which she ate at about three o'clock. Unfortunately, because she hated tuna and mayo and because her nerves were kicking in like demented mules, she had thrown up in the toilet half an hour later. All she'd managed to keep down since was water. She'd raced home with Sparkle and just had the time for a shower and a glucose tablet. She hoped it was going to be enough.

'Is something wrong?' James was watching her, and she didn't want him to know she wasn't feeling well. She wouldn't put it past him to march her back upstairs and put her to bed. Not for a bout of hot sex either, unfortunately.

'No, James, everything's wonderful. What make of bike is it?'

He looked at her with narrowed eyes. 'As you can see by the badge on the side, it's a Harley-Davidson.'

'Oh yes, of course. I didn't see that.' She was finding it hard to focus and hoped that she wouldn't have to watch the show through blurred vision.

'Are you alright, Sapphire, you look a bit vague.' He was watching her intently and she knew she couldn't fool him for much longer.

'Truth is, my blood sugar is a trifle low—you don't have a mint or something, do you?'

'Of course.' He unzipped his jacket and felt around in the inner pocket. 'I always carry some with me. Here.' He handed her an extra-strong mint and she nearly bit his hand off in her haste to consume it.

'Thanks. I'll be fine now.'

'Good. You will tell me, won't you, if you're not feeling okay?' He looked concerned and suddenly she was grateful he was going to be with her at the show.

'Of course. Right—shall we go?'

'After you've put these on.' He handed her a leather jacket and trousers to match, similar to the ones he wore. 'The trousers might be a bit short. They're Lulu's and she's not as tall as you. And don't forget the helmet.'

As Sapphire struggled to pull the trousers on, grateful

that she was wearing a dress short enough to tuck into them, she wondered at James taking his beloved diabetic sister out on a beast like the one sitting a few feet away from her. The bike was big, electric blue and scary as hell.

'Have you ever ridden on the back of a bike before?'

She was tempted to say yes, as what modern woman about town hadn't? Well, she hadn't for one.

'Actually, no.' She tried to keep her voice cool as if it wasn't a big deal.

'Ready for an adventure?' he asked, a grin firmly in place.

'Of course. Bring it on!' She wished she felt as brave as her words sounded. In her mind's eye, all she could see was the body of a young man lying in the road, with a paramedic in a green uniform leaning over him, and a smashed-up bike a hundred yards or more further down the road. She'd been in a taxi, on the way to a dinner/dance and the scene flashed by in seconds, but the image had stayed with her for years. She often wondered if he'd survived.

'Right then, let's go.'

James was in his element. Riding his bike at any time made him happy, even in London in the middle of rush hour traffic, the warm air of early summer mixing with the smell of diesel and dust. And to have Sapphire pressed up against his back, her hands around his waist, the distinctive feel and smell of leather mixed with her perfume, was the height of erotic pleasure.

She had looked stunning when she came out of her apartment building, wearing a short animal-print dress that was off the shoulder, and just about covering her breasts from the nipples downwards. Bare legs with knee-length boots in soft brown leather. Her hair was loose, and copper lipstick and eye shadow, made her green eyes more luminous than usual. She had looked like a jungle cat—sleek, sexy and slightly dangerous.

He would have liked to have ridden off with her, out of London and into the countryside to find a secluded, intimate pub that offered bed and breakfast. They could have made love all night, away from the city, the stress, and the thought that their time together was finite.

He had asked her for another night, and she agreed readily. Almost eagerly. Which gave him hope their liaison might be stretched out to more days and, more importantly, nights. Possibly even weeks if he played his cards right. He never had such satisfying sex in his life.

All too soon they were there, and he was directed to a carpark at the back, where he could leave his beloved bike in safety. He cut the engine, turning slightly to see how Sapphire was doing.

'Are you okay?' She looked shocking. Her face was pale, and she had bags under her eyes. She was trembling slightly and trying to smile, but he could tell it was an effort.

'I'm fine,' she snapped.

'No, you're not fine. Here,' he reached into his inside pocket again, 'have a couple of mints.'

She took them without thanking him, then clambered unsteadily from the bike and started walking away. He followed, after generously tipping the carpark attendant to keep an eye on his bike. She had disappeared inside the building without waiting for him by the time he reached the door.

Sapphire was exhibiting some worrying symptoms of hypoglycaemia. She was irritable, sweating, shaky, and letting him feed her mints which may fend off an attack for a short while but wasn't a long-term solution. She was a proud woman and hated asking for help. He knew, having seen the disease in his sister, how easy it is to miss meals, not realise how much time has passed since eating, and slip into a hypo without even realizing it was happening. He would have to keep an eye on her.

'Come on, we need to store the leathers before anyone sees us.' She was standing in front of a door that, by the noise coming from the other side of it, was the changing room for the models. He couldn't believe such a loud cacophony of sound could emanate from such a small area.

'In here?' he asked suspiciously.

'Yes, James, in here,' she snapped. 'There are wardrobes we can store them in. Hurry now, I've got work to do. The models are already getting changed and I need to make sure all the outfits are perfect.'

'Right.' He shrugged off his jacket and removed his trousers in the corridor and handed them to her with the helmet. He didn't fancy getting in the way of the models getting changed. The little he could see through the door that Sapphire had opened would strike terror into the heart of any red-blooded male. The straight ones anyway. There were gorgeous, skinny young women in stages of undress everywhere he looked.

If he spent the whole evening with a hard-on because of the sights that were spread out before him in that room, Sapphire would never forgive him. And he needed to get her a sugary drink and fast.

'I'll be back soon,' he shouted as she disappeared into the melee.

After wandering about for twenty minutes or so, he eventually tracked down a vending machine selling soft drinks and he bought a fizzy orange. That should hold her for a while at least, until he could get her to eat some proper food.

He hurried back to the changing room and stuck his head around the door. A young girl stopped him from coming in any further.

'You can't come in here, sir, it's for models and designers only.'

'Right. Then, would you be an angel and make sure Sapphire Bell-Johnson gets this drink. It's very important.' He smiled his most winning smile, hoping she understood the urgency of his request.

'Yes, of course,' she said as she took it and scuttled off, looking harassed.

He went to find their seats, then sat, gazing around at the fashion world in all its splendour. It was a sight to behold, but his thoughts were still on Sapphire and her impending hypo. He phoned her mobile and got the voicemail.

'Sapphire, it's James. I've sent a girl to find you with a fizzy orange. Drink it please. It's important. Okay. Hope it's all going well backstage. See you soon.'

He could do no more. Sapphire would be distracted with her designs and models, but hopefully she had enough sense to know that her health was more important than all of that. Lulu always had. But his little sister and his new lover were like chalk and cheese. Lulu was sensible and thoughtful, considering the pros and cons of every decision she made. Sapphire was wild and impetuous, throwing herself into situations with no thought whatsoever. She was also the sexiest woman he had ever met. The mere thought of her made him think of endless hot nights spent on satin sheets drinking champagne and eating oysters. She was exotic, domineering and magnificent.

Tonight, she was also vulnerable and unwell. He wanted to look after her, ride to her rescue like a knight in shining armour would do.

And then, when she was back to her normal feisty self, fuck her senseless.

Chapter Seven

It was hell backstage. It always was the few hours before a show, with models having tantrums, things going missing, clothes not fitting as they should, and the thought of everything that was riding on the evening being a success. Usually Sapphire had her wits about her, adrenaline flowing, excitement surging, and she was proud and happy to be exhibiting her new work.

Tonight, she was scared. Her deepest fear—that she just wasn't good enough—was never far from the surface when she had to appear in public. Not just any public. The FROW, as the front row of a fashion show was known, would be filled with important people. Fashion magazine and newspaper editors, celebrities, social media darlings, the odd minor actor or two and even a few reality TV stars—all people she needed if House of Sapphire was going to thrive and if Sapphire Enterprises was going to pick itself up out of the doldrums and if she was going to start her ascent to the top ten richest businesswomen on the coveted Forbes' list.

Sapphire felt sick. Physically and mentally. Physically because she hadn't eaten enough, and she knew she was in serious danger of falling into a hypoglycaemic state if she wasn't careful. Mentally because she cursed her stupidity for letting herself get into this position on one of the most important days in her calendar. She also cursed the diabetes for controlling her life. She wanted to be the one in control. Of her working life, personal life and sex life and her body. But sometimes, control slipped away from her and she felt herself falling with no safety net to save her.

It was too late to do anything about it now. The show was about to start. Thank goodness for James and his can of fizzy orange. She would thank him properly later, when this circus was over.

As she arranged a costume on a rather bad-tempered model, she mused on the fact that, for the first time since she became a designer—due to this damned diabetes—she wasn't looking forward to a show.

Sapphire collapsed into the seat next to James and gave a huge sigh.

'Ready to rock and roll?' he asked.

'As ready as I'll ever be. My chief stylist will take over now and make sure the models are catwalk perfect. Thanks for the drink by the way, you're a life saver.'

'You look a bit better, more colour in your cheeks.'

She smiled at him, taking in his "style statement" of black jeans and a white silk shirt, worn loose over the jeans with the sleeves rolled up to his elbows. Dark chest hair peeked out where he had left the top button undone, and the only jewellery he wore was a gold Rolex watch. He looked sensational in an understated way and Sapphire wondered if he knew more about fashion than he was letting on.

'You look good. Well done.'

'Actually,' he said with a shy smile, 'I have a confession. I rang Phoebe and asked her what to wear as I didn't have the faintest idea and wasn't going to risk embarrassing you.'

'Phoebe is your other sister?'

'Yes, Lulu is almost as clueless as I am about fashion. Phoebe is a lawyer and knows how to look good.'

'I'm going to have to give you some lessons then, seeing as you'll be an important cog in the wheel of Sapphire Enterprises.'

'Lessons from you would be a thrill.'

Sapphire wondered if James would be up for a spot of role play later, then decided that thinking about sex would be a bad idea until the show was over. Her brain was still a bit fuzzy and she needed to stay alert.

'Have you never wanted to be a model, Sapphire?' James asked. 'You're beautiful enough.'

The sudden compliment sent heat to her already flushed cheeks. Did he really think she was beautiful? 'Not with this rack,' she said cupping her breasts and thrusting them upwards to emphasise their size. 'Models have tiny tits. Haven't you noticed?'

'Uh, no, can't say I have.'

James was staring at her breasts, so she pulled the material of her dress down so her nipples were hinted at, but not on display. There were too many people around waving mobile phones; she wanted her designs to appear on Instagram and Twitter, not her tits.

'Well,' said James dreamily, his gaze still firmly fixed on

her chest, 'I would be honoured to be seen with all three of you.'

Sapphire chuckled and straightened in her seat as the first model appeared and began her walk. She had taken a risk with this one. Her signature look was bright, vivid colours and plenty of bling, but this time she had decided to try a completely different approach.

The model was black and beautiful in a "don't touch me" kind of way. She wore a black sheath dress with three-quarter sleeves that was so short it could almost be worn as a T-shirt, and her long legs were bare. Her fingernails were like talons and painted silver. Her eyeshadow and lipstick were the same shade of silver that shimmered in the light. A long, thick silver chain reached her bellybutton and she sported skintight, thigh-high silver boots with platform soles.

The feature that held everyone's attention, however, was the model's hair extensions. Her scalp was a helmet of thin silver plaits that extended all the way to her bum. Sapphire knew how many hours the girl had endured at the hair-dressers, getting them put in, but from Sapphire's point of view, it was worth every second. The effect was mesmerizing.

The risk seemed to be paying off. The audience murmured and there were a few "oohs" and "aahs" from the row behind them.

She glanced at James to see his reaction. He was staring open-mouthed at the model and Sapphire grinned. 'Shut your mouth, James, you're catching flies.'

He obeyed while keeping his gaze fixed on the model. She turned at the end of the catwalk, staring resolutely ahead, and flicked her extensions over one shoulder as she walked back. The effect was electric, like steel cables dancing in the breeze. She looked like an exotic robot from the future, emotionless and utterly fascinating.

Sapphire was pleased. Maybe now her critics would stop accusing her of churning out the same old stuff. Not that the clothes she was famous for weren't still popular. They sold extremely well on the high street. But she knew it was time for a change.

Her next model was wearing a hat almost as large as a sombrero and then three models walked together, with similar designs in Sapphire's signature colours—lime green, sunshine yellow and candy-floss pink.

The applause was enthusiastic, and James joined in.

'Are you enjoying the show?' she asked him.

'Immensely,' he answered. 'You know how to choose your models, I'll give you that.' He appeared to be paying far too much attention to one young woman who sashayed down the catwalk, her head perfectly still, her expression blank, but her body working "the walk" for all she was worth.

'Her?' Sapphire gave her a brief glance then looked away. 'She's not one of our best. Her arse is too big for a start—like two puppies in a pillowcase.'

James looked down, so she couldn't see his expression. His shoulders were shaking, and she knew he was desperately trying not to laugh. Gotcha!

She suppressed a smile, feeling that familiar surge of heat that started somewhere deep inside and spread outwards, becoming visible in the pink tinge that she knew was settling in her cheeks. The part of her that was affected the most wasn't visible, but she could feel the dampness start and wondered if it was time to invest in disposable knickers. If she spent any more time in the company of James Lewis, she may need them.

He had a reputation for being too serious, but she seemed to have the knack of making him laugh. To see the grin start to crack his face and his eyes dance with mirth. Then his body start to shake. She loved the thought that she could do that to him. To reduce him to helplessness. At that moment, she had him in the palm of her hand. The only thing that topped making him laugh was making him come. The thought of holding James's cock in her hands and what she would like to do to it, made her squirm in her seat. She hoped she wouldn't leave a wet patch when she stood up.

An hour later, Sapphire was feeling very ill indeed. She was sweating, shaking, and finding it difficult to concentrate. She had no idea how much longer she needed to sit still, feigning interest in the models that sashayed past. They were all blurring into one and she couldn't remember which outfits she'd seen already and how many there were left to see. And she was beginning to feel indifferent to the whole thing.

She needed to leave soon and get some sugar in her system before it was too late. The effort of trying to smile and keep up the conversation with James was almost beyond her.

He had asked her twice if she was alright, and she had snapped at him on both occasions. She wouldn't blame him if he got up and walked out. He stayed, watching the models even though it was obvious, by now, he was bored rigid. He was frowning and kept throwing her anxious glances.

If she closed her eyes, she'd be asleep. She pinched herself hard on the thigh in an effort to keep awake.

Then, suddenly, the show was over. The audience stood as one and started clapping. She stood too, on wobbly legs and with a fuzzy head. Her heart was pounding, and she felt sick. She tried to clap, too, then realized with dismay that she was being led to the front. They were clapping her. Why? Oh God. She didn't know what to do.

Sapphire tried to speak, to thank people. But who? The models, of course. And the people who worked tirelessly… somewhere… where? She was slurring her words, her vision was blurred, and she felt herself swaying.

Then, amongst the crowd of people surrounding her, crushing her, talking, asking if she was alright, touching her, she felt herself being swept up by a pair of strong masculine arms.

'I've got you, Sapphire. You're safe. Everything is going to be okay,' a deep male voice whispered.

Then everything went black.

Chapter Eight

'I need to get my bike, it's still in Soho,' said James.

'Oh James, no, you can't leave. You have to be here when she wakes up. She'll be scared and not know where she is.' Lulu's voice was pleading, and James felt bad about mentioning his bike when all his attention should have been on Sapphire. He was concerned for it, that was all.

Lulu was sitting cross-legged at the bottom of his bed, watching over Sapphire, who was lying motionless in the centre of the bed. They had placed her on her side, in case she vomited and choked. Pillows at her back prevented her from rolling over.

'She'll be fine now she's had the glucagon. She just needs to sleep it off. I won't be long.'

'No, James. Please don't go. You should stay until she wakes at least.'

James stifled a sigh. His sister was as stubborn as he was at times, but he knew she was right. He also knew that the car-park attendants would probably have all gone home by now and his beautiful Harley was a sitting target. He wouldn't be able to rest until he got her back safely in the garage, with her cover on her, all safe and sound.

He fidgeted in the chair he had placed at the side of the bed and leaned forward to gaze at Sapphire. She was looking wan and pale, her hair spread out on the pillow like a reddish-gold fan. She was breathing more easily and seemed to be out of danger.

The glucagon injection he had given her had done the trick. He knew how to use it, as he had administered similar ones to Lulu on the few occasions over the years that her low blood sugar caused her to become so drowsy she had almost fallen into an unconscious state. Fortunately, with Lulu being the sensible person that she was, that hadn't happened very often.

Lulu had changed Sapphire into one of his T-shirts, demanding that James leave the room while she did it. It was too big for her and she looked like a child as she lay there, her chest rising and falling rhythmically, and her lips open slightly, making quiet "popping" sounds as she exhaled.

'Stop biting your nails,' James said as he spotted Lulu gnawing on a fingernail and frowning. She dropped her hand quickly and folded her arms as she used to do when she was little and was desperately trying to stop the habit.

'I'm surprised they let you carry her out like you did. Didn't anyone challenge you?'

'Yes, but I told them I was a doctor, and they just let me do it.'

'You lied?' Lulu's eyes were like saucers and he wondered at how his little sister managed to survive in the world so well. She was scrupulously honest and couldn't understand that sometimes lies were necessary.

'There wasn't time to explain and I'm pretty sure

Sapphire has kept her diabetes secret from almost everyone who was there tonight. They were all for calling an ambulance which wasn't necessary. I knew we had the glucagon pack here and I just wanted to administer it as quickly as possible.'

'Good job you keep a spare otherwise she'd have ended up in A&E.'

'She would have hated that. She's better here, with us.'

'I know.'

He stood up and leaned over the bed, stroking Sapphire's face gently. 'Sapphire—you okay?'

She moved her head and opened her eyes slightly, murmured something unintelligible, then closed them again. He moved the pillows, so she could lie flat if she wanted.

'She's conscious now, just deeply asleep. I really think I should go and get the bike. I won't be long, I promise.'

Lulu's long-drawn out exaggerated sigh was a perfect copy of their mother's. Lulu had inherited her looks, but she had also adopted her mannerisms as well as she got older. She raised her eyes to heaven. 'Oh, go on then. You won't rest until you get it back.'

'Right. See you later.'

He practically ran out of the room, grabbing his spare leather jacket—the leathers he and Sapphire had worn to the fashion show were still in the wardrobe in the models' room—then sprinted down the stairs to the front door and out, a litany playing in his head as he ran. *Please be in one piece. Please just let it not be vandalized or stolen or…*

'Taxi!' The black cab screeched to a halt and he leapt into the back and gave the address. 'Hurry, please.'

'Or'right mate, keep your 'air on.'

The driver took him at his word and sped through the

London traffic which, as it was just getting dark, was no mean feat, as there were people everywhere, dressed up for a night out, some looking as if they had been partying for hours, stepping dangerously into the road and shouting at anyone who passed by.

'Bit early to be legless—but that's Soho for you,' said the driver.

'Yes. Interesting place.' James wasn't in the mood for small talk, but the driver was breaking every rule in the Highway Code to get him to his destination, so he forced himself to be polite. They made meaningless chitchat until finally the driver turned down a series of side roads that eventually brought them to a stop.

'Is this it?' asked the driver.

'Yes. Could you just go around the back to the carpark. I need to pick up my bike.'

'No worries, mate.'

As the cab turned into the carpark, James could hardly believe what he was seeing. It was deserted. All except for his Harley Davidson sitting exactly where he had left it. Standing over it, looking nervous but resolute, was the carpark attendant who James had tipped earlier on in the day.

'Thanks,' said James to the cab driver and gave him almost double the fare.

'Oh, nice one! You're a gent.' The cabbie pocketed the money and sped off.

James walked over to his bike and the man standing guard over it. 'I didn't think you'd still be here.'

'Just doing my job, sir. You paid me to look after the bike and I have. No one's been anywhere near it. I heard about the unfortunate collapse of the lady and you saved her life.'

'Well, her life wasn't exactly in danger… not really…'

'No need to be modest, sir, but it was the least I could do, to protect your bike.'

James wondered how long he would have been prepared to stand there and felt a rush of gratitude to the young man.

'Thank you, I'm so grateful. Listen, you don't have the keys to this place, do you? My leathers are still inside.'

'I haven't, but I could ring the caretaker. He doesn't live too far away.'

'That would be very kind and, of course, I'll make it worth your while.'

The man took his phone out of his pocket and made a quick call.

Half an hour later, James was dressed in black leather again, the spares and Lulu's leathers safely secured in the storage box at the back of the bike. He took his time weaving through the London traffic and thought about the peculiar day he'd just had. Then he thought about Sapphire and how she'd nearly fallen into a hypo. She needed help. The lady was obviously not coping well with her diabetes. With his little sister on the case with him, the Lewis's would offer Sapphire their full and unwavering support.

Her throat was dry, her head ached, and she felt sick. Hangover? But she didn't remember drinking recently. Although, she couldn't remember much of anything else either.

Sapphire opened one eye and raised her head off the pillow slightly. There was a pixie sitting cross-legged at the bottom of her bed staring at her. A pixie with short brown hair like a boy's and blue eyes exactly like James's. Dressed in leggings and a baggy sweatshirt. All in green. She had bare feet and she was gnawing on a fingernail.

She closed her eye, then opened both as wide as she could. No, it was no good, the elfin creature was still there.

'Hi, how are you feeling?'

Good question. How was she feeling? And where the hell was she? She tried to sit up. The pixie scrambled up the bed and gently pushed her back down.

'No—stay down until the dizziness goes. You need to get up slowly. Well, that's what happens to me anyway.' The pixie smiled. James's smile when he was being his most charming.

Then the memories started to creep into her fuddled mind. The fashion show, the hypo, two strong masculine arms lifting her up.

'Are you…?'

'Lulu. James's sister. He's gone to get the bike. He loves the thing. Couldn't rest until he got it back safely. I told him he should stay and look after you, but…well, I'm here anyway and I can do it.' She stopped and sighed. 'Sorry, I talk too much. James always tells me I've got no filter. Sorry.'

'No… don't worry…' Talking was difficult. Almost as hard as thinking. But the desire to cry had gone. She just felt overwhelmingly tired, but strangely peaceful.

'Anyway, I need to check your blood sugars now you're awake. They should be done hourly for three or four hours after taking glucagon. I expect you know that.' Lulu leapt off the bed and returned with a blood testing kit. 'You're not pregnant, are you?'

Sapphire shook her head. Pregnant? Why would Lulu think she might be pregnant?

'Although if you were, it's nothing to worry about,' she

continued, 'Glucagon is a pregnancy category B drug, which means it's not expected to harm an unborn baby. Although if you think you might be you should tell your doctor.' Lulu looked at her expectantly.

'I'm not.' Sapphire shook her head as Lulu expertly pricked the side of her middle finger after cleaning it with a perfume and alcohol free wet wipe, then squeezed gently until there was a drop of blood that she applied to the strip that tested the blood glucose.

'Good. Well, it might not be good. You might want to be pregnant. I would. I'd love to have a baby. It must be wonderful.' She stared off into space dreamily and Sapphire wondered what the hell was keeping James. She sucked her finger where it had been pricked and tasted the iron of her blood.

'It's probably good that you're not though, as they don't know for sure if glucagon passes into breast milk or if it could harm a breastfeeding baby. So being pregnant is probably not a good thing for you. But you're not, so it's all good!' Lulu beamed, and Sapphire smiled weakly.

'Great.' What was she supposed to say? She could hardly keep up with Lulu's chatter.

'I should ask you about the medication you're on as some of it could react with the glucagon.' Lulu then proceed to reel off a list of drugs including prescription and over the counter as well as illegal substances. Sapphire didn't do drugs, but she was tempted to tell Lulu that she did just to see what reaction she'd get.

Eventually, taking pity on her, she shook her head.

'Oh—I nearly forgot to mention alcohol.'

'A nice glass of Chardonnay would be good.' Sapphire was starting to feel better and this earnest young girl looked so much like James, she was tempted to tease her.

'Oh no, you mustn't! No alcohol. At all.' Lulu looked distraught and Sapphire felt like a complete bitch for tormenting her.

'Sorry. Just joking. Of course not. I could murder a cup of tea, though.'

Lulu leapt off the bed and said, 'That's exactly what you need now. Your blood sugar is okay so how about a piece of wholemeal toast and peanut butter? I'll have some too to keep you company.'

Without waiting for a reply, Lulu skipped out of the bedroom and Sapphire lay her head back on the pillow, closed her eyes and breathed a sigh of relief.

***

'So, where do you live, Lulu?'

'I live here with James. In Orchard House. I couldn't afford a place of my own when I came to London, so he suggested I cook and clean for him in exchange for board and lodgings. It works well.'

'This is James's bedroom, isn't it?' It was decorated in shades of cream, coffee and nutmeg. The curtains matched the duvet and there was a cream rug next to the bed. Tasteful but a bit boring.

'Yes. Mine is on the top floor. It's an attic room so it's smaller but just right for me.'

'I'd love to see the rest of the house.' Sapphire had a thing about people's homes. They held clues to their characters and Sapphire was curious about James. And also about Lulu. There was obviously a strong bond between brother and sister.

'Okay, I'll show you around when you've finished eating.'

'Right.' Sapphire picked up the toast, generously spread with peanut butter and bit into it gratefully. She was aware that she hadn't eaten properly all day and the hot peanut buttered toast tasted divine.

'Lulu Lewis—that's an interesting name.'

Lulu laughed, a light giggly sound like a child. 'My real name is Louisa. My mum is a big fan of "Little Women", you know, by Louisa May Alcott? She named me after her. Which sister would you be, Sapphire? I think you'd be Amy as she was beautiful and quite sophisticated.'

Sapphire, who had always related to tomboy Jo, smiled and asked, 'And you—who would you be?'

'Probably Beth as she wouldn't say boo to a goose, but I'd prefer to be like Jo.'

'So why are you called Lulu?'

'It's a pet name. James started it and it just stuck. Everyone calls me that now.' She took a bite of her toast, scattering crumbs on the duvet.

'You're very fond of your big brother, aren't you?'

She nodded and put her hand over her mouth, swallowing quickly. 'Oh yes, I adore him. When Dad died…' a shadow passed across her face, '…well, James was just there for us all. Even though his own heart was breaking.'

'Did he get on well with his father?'

'Oh yes, they adored each other. James is just like him; strong, dependable, intelligent. He's our rock.'

Sapphire watched her face. Lots of adoring going on in that family. Or was Lulu painting her a rosy picture deliberately? Lulu appeared to view the world through rose-tinted glasses.

'Louisa Lewis is a cool name. It's a strong name.'

'Whereas Lulu Lewis is just plain silly,' Lulu replied with

a giggle. 'Maybe that was why James called me that. He's always trying to make me laugh.'

'Really?'

'Oh yes. He's a great big brother.' She sighed. 'I just wish...' she trailed off and stared wistfully into space.

'What? What do you wish for, Lulu?'

'I wish he could meet someone worthy of him and settle down. He's not been the same since Ruth broke his heart. I hate her.'

Lulu glanced sideways at Sapphire as if she had said something wrong and was going to be chastised for it. She bit into her toast angrily.

Lulu was sitting at the end of the bed again, cross-legged. Sapphire was sitting up, supported by four pillows at her back. She ate some more of her toast.

'Tell me what happened... with Ruth and James.'

Lulu had finished her toast, so she put her plate on the dressing table and picked up her mug of tea. She was frowning and staring at the carpet.

'They were engaged and James idolised her. No one in the family liked her particularly, but we welcomed her all the same. For James's sake. Mum was happy he was settling down, but I knew she wasn't right.'

'How did you know?' Sapphire put her empty plate on the bedside table and picked up her mug.

'She was selfish. Wanted everything her own way. James bent over backwards to give her the things she asked for, but it was never enough.'

Sapphire forced the picture of a naked James bending over backwards out of her mind and concentrated on Lulu. 'What did she ask for? Material things?'

'Yes, mainly. She loved foreign holidays and jewellery.

That kind of thing.' Lulu seemed reluctant to go into any more detail and Sapphire wondered what was behind it.

'How did it end?'

'It was awful!' Lulu looked as if she was going to cry and Sapphire knew she should change the subject, but the opportunity to learn more about James was one she didn't intend to pass up.

'Go on.' Sapphire leaned forward and forced herself to look sympathetic.

'Well,' said Lulu wiping her eyes with the sleeve of her sweatshirt, 'she started sleeping with James's business partner, Malcolm. The two of them hatched a plan to take over Lewis Leathers and force James out of business. Poor James —it was simply horrible the way they treated him.'

'What did they do exactly?'

'Oh, I don't know the details. I'm not business minded. I'm not sure.' Lulu frowned and shook her head as if it was all too much for her to think about.

'Was she working for them?'

'She was a secretary.'

'Right.' It looked as if she would have to ask James directly. She wanted to know how a business savvy man like James could let himself be tricked. If for no other reason than she could avoid it happening to her.

'Then what happened?' Sapphire settled back on the pillows and sipped her tea.

Lulu sighed. 'James caught them in bed together. Having sex. It was so humiliating for him.'

'What did he do?' Sapphire tried to imagine James losing his temper and throwing this Malcolm out, then turning on Ruth and doing the same to her. The image of an enraged James ranting and raving self-righteously was a bit of a turn-on.

'Do? Nothing. What could he do? He left them to it without saying a word. Later, he found out that Malcolm wanted him out of his own company. It nearly destroyed him.'

Sapphire would have liked to question Lulu further and find out exactly how Malcolm had persuaded James to give up his company, but they heard the front door open and James's footsteps as he ran lightly up the stairs. Further interrogation would have to wait for another time.

Chapter Nine

'You're looking better,' said James as he sat on the edge of the bed, smiling at her.

'Yes, I feel better. I want to thank you, James for helping me. Lulu has told me how you whisked me out of there before anyone called an ambulance. Quick thinking.'

'No problem. Have you eaten anything?'

'Yes. Lulu has been looking after me.'

Lulu blushed as they both turned their attention on her. She was a pretty girl, Sapphire thought, but totally unaware of her charms. She could look quite stunning with the right clothes and make-up.

Just then a cat with similar markings to Sparkle but much bigger, jumped onto the bed and started purring loudly, her paws kneading the duvet.

'Hello darling,' said Lulu stroking her. 'This is Willow.'

'Sparkle's mother?'

'Yes, that's right. She was a stray, but we didn't know at the time that she was pregnant. It was lovely when she had her kittens, wasn't it, James?'

'Inconvenient you mean. She commandeered my sock drawer to give birth in. I had to buy dozens of new ones.'

Willow wandered over to Sapphire who stroked her head gently. Her markings were similar to Sparkle's, but she had more black on her. She was a lovely cat. Her presence reminded Sapphire how long Sparkle had been on her own.

'I should go,' she said.

'Oh, don't go!' said Lulu. 'I was going to cook us all a meal. You haven't eaten properly yet. Toast isn't enough, that was just to keep you going until you could get something decent inside you.'

'I'm grateful for everything you've done, Lulu, but I really need to get back home now. I'll eat something later, I promise.'

'I'll ring for a taxi,' said James, 'I don't fancy driving through traffic at this time.'

'Are you coming with me?' asked Sapphire and James gave her a look that answered her question. She wondered if Lulu had picked up on it, but the girl was fussing the cat and hadn't notice.

———

As they left the house—which was a three storey Victorian terrace with the name of Orchard House on a plaque on the wall—Sapphire asked James where they were. She'd been barely conscious when he'd carried her in and deposited her on his bed and it felt strange not to know what part of London she was in.

'Primrose Hill.'

'Oh…right.' Nice area. She felt a bit deprived that she had missed out on a tour of the house but was anxious to get home. Another time maybe. Lulu stood in the doorway and waved them off.

Neither spoke much when they were in the taxi, crawling through the city streets, but Sapphire was aware of James's hand resting on the seat between them and wondered if he meant it as an invitation. She put her hand next to his, their little fingers touching. James put his hand over hers and she felt the warmth of him stirring her senses. He didn't hold her hand, but just let his hand rest on hers, covering it as if he was protecting it.

Such a small thing, but Sapphire sensed the promise of more to come in his action. He didn't look at her but continued to stare out of the window of the taxi.

She carefully pulled her hand out from under his, then picked up his hand and laid it on her thigh. She was still wearing her animal print dress and had bare legs and she felt the heat from his skin as if it were burning her. Her arousal spiked.

At first, he didn't move, and Sapphire wriggled slightly. Then he slowly walked his fingers upwards until he was grasping the top of her thigh. She opened her legs, checking first that the driver couldn't see what was going on.

She was desperate for him to touch her and felt wet between her legs. 'Touch me,' she murmured almost inaudibly. He slowly ran one finger over her crotch, and she took in a deep breath and tried not to squirm on the seat. He caressed her but not enough to make her come and she felt frustrated and angry with him. He was teasing her, keeping her on the edge on purpose.

He pulled his hand away quickly as the driver stopped outside her block of flats.

'Right,' James said cheerfully, 'There you go. Thanks.'

He paid the driver and Sapphire didn't wait for him to be a gentleman and open the door for her, she scrambled out, desperate to get inside so they could finish what they had started.

As soon as they were inside, and the door shut on the world, Sapphire pounced on James, wrapping herself around him and rubbing against his body. She could feel his erection and her arousal peaked at the steely strength of his hard-on. She kissed him as she hastily unbuttoned his shirt; his hands caressed her breasts through her dress.

After fumbling each other out of their clothes in their haste, they were both naked and panting. Desperate to feel him inside her, Sapphire led James to the couch in her open-plan living area and they fell onto it, kissing and caressing. They should use protection, but as she was on the pill, and she didn't want to break the spell by searching in her bathroom cabinet for a condom, she decided it was worth the risk.

He was obviously feeling the same sense of urgency as he pushed her legs open and entered her almost in one movement.

'Oh God, that feels so good.' Sapphire moaned. She wrapped her legs around his hips and her arms around his neck and clung to him, revelling in his strength, his hard muscles and his all-male musky scent. 'Don't stop,' she commanded as she felt James withdraw.

'I need to wear a—'

'I'm on the pill, it's okay.'

'Are you sure?' James kissed her face; her forehead, her

cheeks, the tip of her nose, his hot breath fanning the flames that grew ever stronger. If he didn't fuck her soon, she was going to burst.

'Positive…' Her voice was low and husky, and she thrust upwards with her hips while tightening her grasp on his neck.

James groaned and entered her again. He pushed in deeper than before and Sapphire tightened her grip even more, her heart hammering in her chest and her mouth dry. They were locked together as one and when James began thrusting, she met his thrusts eagerly and cried out as she felt her orgasm mounting.

'I'm coming…'

'Me too.' James stared down at her, their faces mere inches apart, and she marvelled at the tension in his face and neck, the veins swollen, and his skin flushed and sweaty. Even in the throes of her release, she couldn't help thinking how undignified sexual intercourse was and how, at the point of orgasm, the world could come to an end and they wouldn't be aware of it, or even care too much if they were. It was the ultimate release, a time when a person was at their most vulnerable.

Then there were no more thoughts and Sapphire cried out as orgasm after orgasm surged through her. She couldn't tell when one ended and the next began. Maybe she was just having one tsunami of an orgasm, but no… it definitely felt more like separate waves. Gradually, the sensations abated, and she lay still with her eyes shut.

'What are you thinking about?' She opened her eyes to the sight of James gazing down at her with an uncertain smile on his face. She'd been daydreaming in the aftermath of stupendous sex. She grinned up at him.

'I'm thinking about how bloody good that was and what a great lover you are.'

'Really? Then why were you looking so serious?' Clearly he didn't believe her.

'Because it's a serious subject.'

'You looked distant as if your mind was off wandering somewhere. Anyway,' James said moving away from her and collecting his clothes, 'I know what you need now.'

'More sex. How about we get into bed and have a repeat performance? When you've recovered that is.'

'I've got a better idea.'

'Better than sex?' Sapphire groaned as she sat upright. Her body felt weak as if she'd been suffering from a serious illness and was only just starting to recover.

'You need looking after tonight after that hypo. I'm going to cook you a delicious meal, then you and I need to talk.'

'I like the sound of the first part. What are we having?'

'Pasta. Why don't I run you a hot bath and then you can have a soak before dinner?'

'You're too good to me, James.'

'Nothing is too good for you tonight, m'lady.' James bowed, and Sapphire felt a glow of gratitude that James was there. She wasn't feeling well, despite the glucagon and the sleep. Wretched diabetes, it was in danger of taking over her life.

Despite the late hour, James cooked a substantial spaghetti carbonara and opened a bottle of white wine. He knew from his experiences of looking after Lulu that Sapphire needed some carbohydrate to get her body back to normal. And he'd have to convince her to keep her eye on her blood sugars. He sighed. She clearly was not coping well with her diabetes, but he wasn't the one to lecture her. He only wanted her to be well.

He heard the slap of bare feet on the floor tiles. 'Something smells good.' Sapphire stood directly behind him and put her arms around his waist. The mixed aromas of bath oil, soap and Sapphire's own unique scent nearly caused him to abandon the carbonara and take her to bed as she had suggested. He forced himself not to turn around. He wanted to have a serious conversation, so sex would have to wait.

'Have a seat, it's ready.' Sapphire obediently sat and poured them both a glass of wine. She had piled her hair up on top of her head to have her soak and the damp tendrils crept over her shoulders and stuck to her neck. She was wearing a short satin nightie and it barely covered her bottom.

James put a plate piled high with pasta in front of her and set another one at the other end of the table for himself. 'Parmesan?'

'Ooh, yes please.'

'Black pepper?'

'Just a little.' He turned the pepper grinder expertly and Sapphire smiled. He put the grinder on the worksurface and then sank into his chair with an exaggerated sigh. He watched as Sapphire tucked into the food with little grunts of appreciation. She ate as if she hadn't seen food for days and James was tempted to tell her to slow down. He resisted, however, and picked up his glass of wine, holding it out to her.

'Here's to your successful show, the new contracts that are bound to come flooding in and your good health.'

Sapphire picked up her glass and clinked it against his. 'Cheers. And to your good health too. And thank you again for helping me today. I don't know what I would have done without you.'

James knew she would still be in A&E as most people who were unfamiliar with diabetes would have panicked and phoned an ambulance, but he said nothing.

They ate in silence for a while, James wondering how he was going to broach the subject without upsetting her.

'I like your sister, she's very sweet.'

'And she likes you. I think you made quite an impression on her.'

'Me? I was lying like a corpse in your bed for hours. I must have scared the poor girl senseless.'

'Not at all. Lulu is an expert on diabetes. She wanted to help you.'

'She certainly knows all the medical jargon.'

'It was drummed into her from an early age. Knowledge is power, and it could save her life one day.'

'I'd like to do something to thank her. Do you have any suggestions? Perfume maybe?'

James twirled some spaghetti around his fork and thought about Lulu. He wanted her to help Sapphire with her diabetes without it being obvious. He couldn't think of a time when the two women could be together, in a relaxed atmosphere conducive to Sapphire opening up about her illness. Their personalities and lifestyles were too different..

'I'll have to think about it, although Lulu doesn't wear perfume, it's usually too strong for her.'

'Does she have a boyfriend?'

'No. She doesn't go out much. She likes to stay at home.' James chewed his spaghetti thoughtfully.

'What kind of social life does she have? Does she have

girly nights in watching movies? Or does she prefer wine bars and clubs? She must go out sometimes.'

'Neither. She has friends, of course...' he trailed off. What did Lulu do for fun? He couldn't think of anything. 'She makes things like... patchwork quilts and tapestries... and she reads a lot. She goes home to keep our mother company every week.' That was a bit of a sore point as Lulu was always nagging him to spend more time at home. James was too busy to spare the time. Phoebe was guilty of the same crime and only went home for celebrations like birthdays and Christmas. So it fell to Lulu to spend time with their mother.

'James,' Sapphire leaned forward and waved her fork at him, 'Lulu is never going to find the man of her dreams making patchwork quilts. She needs to get out and have fun. Live a little. You should be encouraging her, not keeping her in the attic like a slave.'

'What!' James nearly choked on his spaghetti. 'Did she tell you that or is it another of your exaggerations?'

'I don't exaggerate—'

'You bloody do!'

'I might embellish a story to give it some spice, but I do not exaggerate.'

'Well, just to set the record straight, Lulu lives with me rent free and does a spot of cleaning now and again in exchange for bed and board. It's a mutually satisfactory arrangement. She's free to go whenever she wants.' James tried to see the funny side of the conversation as he knew that Sapphire was doing her normal teasing just to get him to react. He should have learned by now, but she had inadvertently hit a nerve. For he did feel a bit guilty at the fact he had a better social life than Lulu. Despite the fact he wasn't looking for love, he knew he could phone up any one of a dozen women and ask them out on a date. And most of them would probably say yes. He had never known Lulu bring a man back to the house.

'How old is she?'

'Twenty-five, why?'

'Did you know she wants to be a mother?'

James was astounded. Lulu must have opened up to Sapphire more than he would ever have guessed if she was telling her things like that. 'No, I didn't. Are you sure? She's never mentioned it before.'

'Yes, I'm sure. Women need other women to tell their secrets to. Big brothers are great for some things, but not for secrets.'

'Right.' She was right, of course, but what could he do about it? Lulu needed to find male friends of her own, he couldn't do it for her.

'How about this for an idea? I'll take her shopping to Oxford Street and Bond Street, to buy her some sexy new outfits. Then I'll book her into Pierre's for a new hairstyle and highlights. Then a make-up session. A full make-over.' Sapphire was looking pleased with herself, but James was shocked.

'Oh no, I don't think that would be Lulu's scene at all. She isn't into fashion and make-up, she's a simple soul who likes cooking and crafts. Homemaking type things…' Sapphire wasn't listening to him. She had left the kitchen hurriedly as he was speaking and returned with her mobile a few minutes later.

'What's her number?'

'What?' James watched in fascination as her thumbs moved expertly over the tiny keyboard on the screen of her phone.

'Lulu's mobile number?' She looked up and James knew

he was wasting his time. Sapphire was on a mission and nothing was going to stand in her way. He told her the number and the next minute he heard Sapphire's side of the conversation.

'I just wanted to thank you, Lulu, for everything you did for me today and wondered if you fancied a day out? I can't make it this Saturday I'm afraid, but how about the one after? Just the two of us having a girly day—shopping, lunch and the like.' James frowned as he saw Sapphire's grin. 'You would? That's great. James said you wouldn't be interested, but I had a feeling you might.' James shook his head at her, and her grin broadened. 'Yes, you're right. Men—what do they know?'

James had no choice but to accept defeat. He was still worried. He knew Lulu had a habit of fan-girling celebrities, following them on Twitter and Instagram and trying desperately to think up interesting tweets so that they direct messaged her with a reply. Of course, they never did, and Lulu wasted precious spare time wondering what she could do to get them to notice her. Even though Sapphire wasn't a celebrity, she was a confident and sexy businesswoman who knew important people in the media and fashion world. Lulu could easily have her head turned by Sapphire and James's instinct was to protect his little sister.

'What's wrong James?' Sapphire asked. 'You look disapproving. Don't you want me to spend time with Lulu?'

'Of course. I think it's a kind thing to do. Lulu will enjoy being made a fuss of, but please don't expect her to change her looks. She's fine the way she is.'

'I think we should leave that up to Lulu. Don't you?'

'There's something I think you should know about Lulu—'

But Sapphire wasn't listening. She stood up and held her hand out to him. 'Bed now.'

At the mention of bed, all thoughts of his sister fled. 'How are you feeling?'

Sapphire smiled, and James felt his insides melting a little.

'Horny.'

Chapter Ten

James took Sapphire's hand and let her lead him to her bedroom. The room was spacious with an enormous four poster bed against one wall. It was upholstered in a champagne coloured soft cotton and covered in cushions and pillows of varying sizes and colours. Everything matched perfectly. It was like a photo from an interior design magazine, right down to the view from the floor-to-ceiling windows.

London at night was an exciting place and viewed from the comfort and decadence of such a luxurious apartment, the scene made James's blood pump faster around his body. Sapphire's home was like the set of a modern movie, spacious with high ceilings, and she was perfect as the heroine. A tough go-getter, fighting her way to the top. A beautiful, mysterious and jaw-droppingly sexy woman who wanted him. The thought made him hard and, as he watched her pull off her nightie and throw it casually onto a chair, he grew harder. She stood next to the bed, wearing nothing but a searching look. She was glorious in her nudity, her breasts full and her pink nipples erect. Her head was held high and she never broke eye contact as James licked his lips and let his gaze wander over her body like twin search lights.

He walked towards her and stopped just before they touched. They gazed at each other, not speaking, just looking. Then he slowly unbuttoned his shirt and shrugged it off. It fell on the floor and he kicked it out of the way.

Neither of them spoke. They maintained eye contact as James unzipped his jeans and pushed them down, then stepped out of them and kicked them in the direction of his shirt. His briefs followed. He had an impressive erection, but Sapphire didn't even glance down, she continued to look him in the eye the whole time. James, however, couldn't help himself; he glanced down at her body and breathed deeply at the perfection in front of him. Sapphire was easily the most beautiful woman he'd ever had the pleasure of having sex with. He wanted to stand there forever, breathing in her subtle scent and ravishing her with his gaze. But, more than that, he wanted to take her again and again. To bury himself in her soft heat and feel the connection they had. For he had never felt as close to another human being as he did to Sapphire when they orgasmed together after turning each other on to the point of madness.

James slowly inched forwards until their bodies were touching and took the pins out of her hair, combing it with his fingers until it cascaded over her breasts in red-gold curls. Then he palmed her face and kissed her lips. The touch was light at first, the merest hint of his mouth on hers. Her mouth opened to him and he kissed her deeply and passionately.

Sapphire ran her fingers across the backs of James's hands as he held her head fast, then up his forearms to his shoulders, then down his back to his buttocks. He clenched them tight as the lightness of her touch skimmed over his skin, causing the hairs to stand up. The kiss went on, and he let out a low moan as Sapphire pulled his body into hers, his erection pressing into her.

He tangled his fingers in her hair and scrunched it up in his fists. Sapphire, freed from his grasp, knelt, and took his penis in her mouth.

'Oh God,' he whimpered as she worshipped his cock with her mouth, lips and tongue. He was close to coming and he tried to pull away, but Sapphire held him fast; one hand on his balls and the other at the base of his cock. The lady was in control, so he closed his eyes, his hands still in her hair and let her do whatever she wanted to him. He was adrift in a sea of lust, helpless in her hands, and he gloried in every second of it. For Sapphire was an accomplished lover and it wasn't long before he cried out and ejaculated in her mouth.

His knees gave way and he found himself kneeling on the carpet in front of Sapphire. She was smiling as if she had just won the biggest contract of her career. The lady obviously took her sexual prowess very seriously. And he was the lucky recipient of her skill.

When he had recovered, he stood up and went to the kitchen to open another bottle of wine. He returned with the bottle and two glasses to find Sapphire lying in the centre of the bed, her head propped on her right hand and her phone in her left hand.

'Lulu has sent me a photo of Willow. Isn't that sweet?'

'Delightful.' He poured the wine, then handed Sapphire a glass. 'But I really think we could leave the cute kitten pictures to afterwards, don't you?'

'James, you sound peeved. If I didn't know better, I'd

say you were jealous. Am I not giving you enough attention?'

James sat next to her and sipped his wine. 'It's your turn for the attention and I intend to turn you on so much that you won't remember your own name.'

'Promises, promises,' she purred.

'Don't you think I can do it?'

Sapphire lounged back and placed her glass on the bedside table. 'Put your money where your mouth is mister,' she drawled.

James felt a thrill pass through him. He loved a challenge. Especially one he knew he could win. He placed his glass next to Sapphire's and pulled the pillows away from the top of the bed. He placed them strategically, so they would be under her hips when she lay flat.

'Lie on your stomach,' he commanded, 'and put your arms above your head.'

She did as he asked, and he admired her buttocks, her trim waist and long, slender legs. Instead of looking vulnerable in such a position, Sapphire looked as if she was lying on a beach without a care in the world.

He moved her hair away from her neck and shoulders and gently started to massage her.

'Umm that's nice,' she murmured.

'Do you want some music on?'

'No, I'm good.' There was a background hum of London traffic, very faint, in the distance. There was no other sound and James found it quite relaxing.

Sapphire had turned the overhead lights off and the only illumination was a small table lamp. Shadows danced across the ceiling, and around the canopy of the four-poster bed. Sapphire's body looked pale and ethereal in the half-light.

James sat on the bed and worked diligently on Sapphire's neck and shoulders.

'Where did you learn massage?' asked Sapphire sleepily.

'No talking, you're supposed to be relaxing.' He had learned massage from Ruth who had been a masseur in her spare time. He didn't want to break the mood by mentioning her name.

James kept up his innocent massaging until Sapphire's breathing grew deeper and slower. He knew the exact moment that she was starting to fall asleep. He moved his hands lower and massaged her back, his fingers caressing the side of her breasts with each stroke.

Sapphire groaned and tried to turn onto her back.

'No moving. Stay where you are.'

She sighed but did as she was told. He let his hands move lower down her body until his fingers reached the twin globes of her buttocks. Her breathing was faster now and her body tense. He put one finger between her buttocks, and she gasped. She spread her legs for him as he gently eased her cheeks apart. He put his face between them and licked experimentally.

"Ah…' she cried out, lifting her head off the bed.

'Lie down,' he commanded.

She did but her hands grasped the sheet tightly on either side of her body.

James knew that if Sapphire didn't like what he was doing, she would speak up. She wasn't afraid to ask for what she wanted or tell him what she didn't like. He had heard no such protestations from her, so he continued.

He ran his finger down towards her vulva and was surprised at how wet she was. She groaned even louder and lifted up to give him access. He returned his attention to her anus and stroked his wet finger over her puckered hole rubbing gently to lubricate it.

'Oh God!' Sapphire cried out, squirming under his hands. Satisfied with her response, he gently pushed his finger into her.

'Is that okay?' he asked quietly. Not all women liked their anuses played with although he liked to bet that most men did.

'Yes!' Her voice was harsh and hoarse. She couldn't keep still on the bed and he pushed his finger in further.

'Oh my God!' she cried out.

James kept his finger in her anus and found her clitoris with his other hand. She came almost straight way, her body jack-knifed on the bed. He held her until the waves of her orgasms gently died away.

'Well?' he asked.

'Sapphire Bell-Johnson. I remember my name. But I have to admit, that was good. Ten out of ten.'

'So glad to hear it.'

James wanted to keep going, to arouse her further so she truly forgot her name, but there was something he needed to say first. He couldn't read Sapphire's expression as they lay side by side on top of the duvet, both naked, both still aroused.

'You agreed to us having one more night together.'

'And?'

'So… can I stay the night?'

'Of course.'

'What happens then?'

'Why don't we wait until tomorrow to find out.'

It wasn't the answer he wanted, but it would do for now.

They turned on their sides and faced each other. James stroked Sapphire's hair back from her face and she ran her fingers lightly over his chest and down his stomach to his erection that pushed against her body.

'I want you,' said James.

'I want you, too, inside me,' Sapphire replied.

Then Sapphire rolled onto her back and James rolled with her. She opened her legs and he entered her. They fitted together perfectly, and James wondered at how right it felt to be inside her. They had only made love a few times, but the effortless familiarity of the act took him by surprise. It was almost as if they had been together for years. He gazed down at her face. Her emerald eyes stared back at him in the half-light.

'James?'

'Yes?'

'What are you thinking about? You're staring at me.'

He thrust slowly into her then pulled out a short way, then thrust into her again. Each time he was deep inside her, Sapphire let out a little groan.

'I'm just thinking how much I like this—you and me.'

'Yes, so do I, but this isn't forever, so let's enjoy the now.'

'Agreed.'

He started thrusting then with purpose and Sapphire wrapped her legs around his waist to encourage him to go in deeper. She had her arms around his neck and her hair was a curtain around them. He quickened the pace and she rose up to meet him. It was just sex, he had to keep that in mind. There was no future for them. They were just bodies that happened to be able to give each other pleasure.

His arousal was growing, and he forgot everything else as Sapphire cried out as she came, and he climaxed soon after.

Afterwards, lying on his back, with Sapphire next to him, her leg thrown across his legs and her arm across his chest, he wondered at how comfortable he was with this woman.

She was breathing deeply, fast asleep. It had been quite a day. He needed to sleep, so he could be ready for the following day. He had no idea how Sapphire would react when she saw the papers and magazines, not to mention the social media account of the fashion show. When he was carrying her out the flashbulbs were popping all around them. It would be her collapse that made the headlines, not her designs.

One thing he did know. He would be there for her, to shelter her as much as he could. For all her attitude and feistiness, Sapphire needed him, even though she didn't realise it yet.

Chapter Eleven

Sapphire woke to glorious sunshine and the smell of bacon. The curtains were open, and, next to her, the bed was empty and the sheets cold. James had obviously been up for a while. At least he was still here. She had wondered if he would sneak out of her apartment leaving behind a hastily scribbled message telling her he would see her on Monday, as most of her ex-lovers would have done. She didn't really like the idea of men staying the night, it could be embarrassing the following morning, especially if the sex hadn't lived up to expectation. James had stayed long enough to make her breakfast. And the sex had been superb. She felt surprisingly pleased.

Sapphire stretched luxuriously and yawned.

'Ah, so she lives…' James wandered into the bedroom wearing a full-length apron with a large pocket in the front like a kangaroo's pouch and nothing else. 'I've made breakfast so up you get. You don't want to let it get cold.' He picked up her bathrobe and held it up, so she could slip her arms in the sleeves.

Sapphire sat up and took in the spectacle of James waiting on her hand and foot. She could get used to this but knew that she wouldn't. That was the slippery slope, getting used to having a man around the place. Before you knew what was happening, he had moved in and the woman was waiting on him.

'Any time today would be good, before we burn the sausages.'

She took her time climbing out of bed, then turned around obediently and slipped into the bathrobe. 'What have you cooked? It smells delish.'

'Full English. Bacon, sausages, mushrooms, tomatoes and fried bread. I'm going to make sure you eat properly from now on. No more hypos.'

'What? No hash browns?'

'Didn't have time to make them. Sorry. Maybe next time.'

So, James was planning a next time. She wasn't sure how she felt about that. But the weather outside the window was shaping up to be another gorgeous summer day and she was feeling mellow. A feeling she hadn't enjoyed for a while. Must be all the hot sex.

'Thank you, James, you're very kind.'

'You're more than welcome. Shall we?' He extended his elbow in her direction and she slipped her arm through it. Together they made their way towards the kitchen like an old married couple. Then she chided herself for thinking like that. Their relationship, if you could call it that, had a sell-by date and she mustn't forget it.

The breakfast was delicious, and Sapphire wondered at James's ability to cook. He had Lulu to cook and clean for him, but he had produced a superb meal. The bacon was crisp and the sausages tasty. The fried bread, which she didn't allow herself to indulge in often, was so good she ate two pieces.

'Did you squeeze these oranges yourself?'

'Of course.'

Then she realised that she hadn't had any of this food in her fridge. 'Did you really cook this yourself, or did you buy it from a local café?'

He looked at her with a hurt expression. 'You have cut me to the quick. I had to nip out to the all-nighter on the corner to buy this lot and then slaved over a hot stove to bring you a delicious meal—'

'I hope you didn't wear that to the supermarket.' She indicated the apron and bit into the last piece of fried bread.

'Of course not, I got changed first.'

'Thank heavens for that. I couldn't cope with complaints from the neighbours, this is a respectable area. Is there any coffee?'

'At your command, ma'am.'

James got up and switched on the coffee machine. He busied himself with mugs and took the milk out of the fridge. Sapphire busied herself with staring at his naked back. And long, muscular legs with the buns of steel that were white globes against the sun-kissed skin of the rest of his back view. She idly wondered why, if James had got dressed to go shopping, he then got undressed again and donned nothing but a fancy pinny. He had obviously done it for her benefit. Unless he liked the feeling of being semi-naked. Maybe he was a closet naturalist.

'See anything you like?' James asked without turning around.

'Don't flatter yourself,' said Sapphire as she stood up and collected the dirty plates to put them in the dishwasher.

'Although I have to say, you do have a rather nice body. Do you work out?'

'I run every day. Don't have much time for the gym.'

'I know that feeling. In fact, I have some phone calls I need to make when I've had my coffee, so…'

Sapphire wondered if he would take the hint and leave. She did have work to do, most of which involved making sure she still had a business after the drama of the fashion show.

'I thought we could spend the day together if you weren't doing anything in particular. It's a shame to waste this sunshine.'

'Not the whole day, James, I'm far too busy.'

'Okay. How about some of it then? I'll dash home and get the bike while you're making some calls and then we'll drive out to a nice country pub I know for lunch.'

'It does sound inviting, but—'

'I'll get you back in time for tea, I promise.'

It was a choice between phoning her contacts to try to persuade them that she wasn't ill and at House of Sapphire it was business as usual, or a leisurely Saturday spent in the countryside with her lover of the moment.

'Oh, okay, I suppose I do deserve a day off now and again.' She usually went into the office for a couple of hours most Saturdays, but she doubted she would be able to concentrate much today anyway. She hadn't seen the papers yet and was dreading it. Sapphire wasn't the type of person to put off unpleasant things, especially where her business was concerned. She faced things head on—usually. She knew the papers would be merciless in tearing her apart and the speculations would be rife. There was nothing she could do about it anyway. She wasn't running away exactly, just postponing the inevitable for one day.

'Is that a yes then?' James looked delectable dressed in her apron. She put her arms out and he was there straight away, hugging her tightly.

'Yes, why not. Let's play hooky for one day.' She put her face up for a kiss and James obliged. She ran her hands over his naked back and grabbed hold of his buttocks. He groaned and closed his eyes. She could feel his erection pushing into her. Was this man always hard?

'If you keep doing that, we won't be leaving the apartment.' She let go reluctantly. James stepped back and smiled a shy smile.

'Right. I'll be back in an hour,' he said.

When James had gone, the apartment seemed empty and quiet. Sparkle was nowhere to be seen so she didn't even have her cat for company and moral support. Sapphire sighed and picked up her phone. The first person she rang was her best friend Monica, who expressed concern at her collapse and relief that she was now fighting fit.

Next, she spoke to her chief stylist. The phone rang five times before it was answered, and Sapphire forced a light-hearted tone into her voice.

'Hi, darling! It's me.'

As Sapphire explained that she hadn't eaten enough that day and had merely fainted from low blood sugar, she realised that she was only lying by omission. For that is exactly what had happened. How easy would it be to follow up that statement by saying, laughingly, "this damned diabetes" and making light of it. Questions would follow, of course, but then she wouldn't have to lie anymore.

Something always stopped her from admitting her condition. She suspected James believed she was in denial. Maybe she was. She was scared, that was the truth. Once she told people, she couldn't untell them. They'd be watching her every move, waiting for her to slip up. No, she would never tell anyone else.

An hour later, they were driving through London traffic, dodging Saturday shoppers and cyclists. James insisted they wear the leather protective gear, even though they started sweating as soon as they put it on. Bike riders were vulnerable. Car drivers hated bikes and the easy way they could weave effortlessly through traffic. He knew this because he was a car driver and a bike rider. He could see both sides of the argument. And, of course, everyone on the road hated cyclists. Even pedestrians.

James chuckled to himself at his thoughts. It'll be better when they are outside the centre of London and he can put his foot down on the country roads.

For now, his plan to keep Sapphire away from the papers seemed to be working. He suspected that the journalists would be catty at best and positively vitriolic at worse. They would demand an explanation for Sapphire's collapse and if they didn't get one, they'd make something up. Something far worse than the truth.

Sapphire was holding on to him tightly, with her body pressed against his back. Even through the leather, it was a turn-on. The sun beat down on them exacerbating the aromas that were all around. The smell of hot leather, which he loved, the smell of diesel fumes from the traffic that surrounded them, which he disliked intensely. He wanted to smell Sapphire's perfume and bury his face in her hair.

Once they left London and were on the M40 leading to the Chilterns, they started to make good time. They took the exit off the motorway, and the scenery changed quickly. The roads became quieter and the suburbs were replaced by fields and small villages. The roar of the bike sounded too loud in such a peaceful setting.

James was glad when, finally, they arrived at the Hare and Hounds.

'We're here,' he said.

'So I see,' answered Sapphire. She looked a bit shaken and James wondered if she was thinking of the only other time she had been on his bike. This was completely different. He should never have let her get in that state in the first place. He had learned his lesson. If Sapphire couldn't be trusted to monitor her diabetes, then he would have to do it for her. The day had started off well with that enormous breakfast and now they would have a substantial lunch.

'Right. Lunch.'

'I'm taking these leathers off first. I've sweated off at least half a stone.'

'Good idea.' James took his jacket off and was dismayed to find large patches of armpit sweat on his T-shirt. He pulled off the leather trousers and was glad he'd worn his chinos underneath which were cool but still modern.

Sapphire had taken off her jacket and James watched her as she pulled off the trousers. She had chosen shorts and a sleeveless blouse with a low neck. She wore her hair loose and, after pulling off her helmet, tendrils escaped from their prison and hung down in corkscrew curls. James wanted to reach out and wind one of her curls around his fingers, but he resisted and stuffed the leathers inside the box instead.

James took Sapphire's hand as they left the bike and strolled to the entrance to the pub. It was a lovely old-fashioned establishment with window-boxes bright with petunias, tubs of fuchsias and a bowling green at the back. There were low ceilings with black rafters and a huge stone fireplace in the corner. Two elderly men were playing dominoes, the sun streaming through the window onto their table. A Labrador that looked as old as the men lay at their feet.

'What are you drinking, Sapphire?' asked James.

'Dry white wine, please.'

James ordered and handed a lunch menu to Sapphire. It contained the usual pub grub and James chose scampi and chips and Sapphire decided on a Ploughman's lunch. He was drinking shandy, which wasn't his favourite beverage but was cold and refreshing on such a hot day.

They found a table in another small room off from the main lounge. This room was bright with large windows and high ceilings. It had been built on to the pub at a later date when the landlord realised how lucrative pub food was and advertised the place as child friendly. There was a family of five tucking into their lunch— mother, father and three children, James surmised. He watched the children who seemed to be behaving impeccably. Two girls and a boy of about five who was the youngest. He was having trouble spearing his chips with his fork, so one of the girls leaned over and helped him. He wouldn't mind having kids if they behaved as well as these three were doing. *Now, where had that thought come from?* he wondered. After the Ruth debacle, he had decided against marriage and children. He intended to remain blissfully free and single.

'This is nice,' said Sapphire. 'Is this a favourite pub?'

'Yes. We sometimes celebrate birthdays here. My mother particularly likes it. She says it's genteel without being stuffy.'

'Do you often go out together as a family?'

'Not since Dad died.' He fell silent, thinking of his father. He missed him dreadfully; he had been the lynchpin that held the family together. Since his death, James had tried to step into his shoes and provide his mother and sisters with the support and love his father had given them, but he knew he was doing a poor job of it. He hadn't visited his mother in weeks.

'Sorry. You obviously miss him still.' Sapphire took his hand in hers and they linked fingers.

'I do, but let's not think of sad things. We're playing hooky remember. We've left the real world behind. It's just the two of us today.'

Sapphire smiled up at him and something in the centre of James's being shifted. The look on her face was compassionate and kind. There was no trace of teasing, no superior lift of the eyebrows she usually gave him. With an uncontrollable need to kiss her, he leaned his head down to touch her lips with his, at exactly the same moment the landlord came hustling up with their food.

'On my own today, one of the bar staff is sick. Sorry for the delay.'

'No problem,' said James straightening up and moving things around on the table to make room for the plates. 'Thanks,' he said cheerfully, wondering if the landlord knew what he had interrupted.

'This looks good,' said Sapphire picking up her knife to cut some cheese.

'Would you like some chips?' asked James.

'Just a few, thanks.'

They were silent as they tucked into the food. James was surprisingly hungry and relished the fresh scampi with lemon and crunchy batter. The chips were good too and he pushed a few more onto Sapphire's plate. She ate them without comment.

When they'd finished, they sat back and watched the pub fill up with locals and walkers. James had a sudden desire to be alone with Sapphire. There was a woodland nearby after a shortish walk over easy terrain.

'Let's go,' he whispered as a group of four milled around near them, looking for an empty table.

'Good idea,' she replied.

They left the pub and the noise behind and James grabbed Sapphire's hand as they dodged the traffic to cross to the other side of the road and the start of the path that wound steadily through the countryside towards the woods.

James lifted his face to the sun and breathed deeply. At this exact moment, life was good. He never wanted this feeling to end.

———

Sapphire was glad she had worn her trainers instead of the gladiator sandals she had intended to wear. The path was strewn with pine needles that caught in her laces and crunched underfoot. The trees grew tall and strong and provided a shady path for them to walk down. Sunlight filtered through the foliage and the air was several degrees cooler.

She held James's hand and felt sixteen again. They didn't speak but listened to the sound of the birds, the rustling on the forest floor, the noise their feet made on the well-worn path through the trees. Every now and then, James would squeeze her hand slightly and she returned the gesture. Non-verbal communication was new to Sapphire who was used to men who never stopped talking as if trying to impress her with their knowledge and authority. James didn't need to impress her as he had already succeeded in doing that in the bedroom. He seemed more relaxed today than she had ever seen him.

'Listen…'

'What?' They stopped and James lifted his face up as if he was listening intently. She did the same and waited.

'A woodpecker…do you hear it?'

She listened carefully, frowning. Then she heard that distinctive tapping on the bark of a tree, like a machine gun firing. 'Yes…where is it?' She looked up at the trees, trying to spot it.

'Oh, quite a way from here but it sounds closer because the sound carries.'

'Right.'

'It'll be a green woodpecker, I think. They are the most common in these parts.'

'Are you interested in birds then, James?' Sapphire asked.

'Not really. My dad was a birder and I tried to take an interest for his sake. I learned all the calls and everything. But sitting in a hide staring through binoculars for hours on end just put me to sleep, I'm afraid.'

'Oh dear. The lengths we go to try to please our parents.'

'Yes. People should just be themselves, it's easier in the long run.'

Sapphire tried to picture James as a young boy, desperately trying to please his father. She put her arm around his waist, and he put his arm around hers and they continued down the path like a pair of honeymooners.

They'd walked for about half an hour when they came

to a clearing in the woodland. 'Shall we sit down for a minute? Are you tired Sapphire?'

She wasn't tired and the feeling of being held by James and the nearness of him, was making her feel horny.

'I'm not tired but we could sit for a while and listen to the quiet.'

'Great idea.'

They sat down on a piece of ground that was dry and mossy. It was surprisingly comfortable, and Sapphire lay back with her hands behind her head and stared up at the sky through the foliage. Tiny white clouds drifted lazily across a gap in the tops of the trees and Sapphire stared at them until she felt her eyes closing.

She felt herself falling asleep, until she was awoken by the touch of soft lips on hers. She opened her mouth obediently and James deepened the kiss. Then she felt his fingers gently stroking her face, then moving down to cup one of her breasts through the material of her blouse. His hand moved lower, then crept up under her blouse and squeezed over her bra. He pinched her nipple through the material and played with it. She moaned and waited to see what he would do next.

Pleasingly, he ran his hands up the inside of her thighs and inside her shorts. She opened her legs slightly to give him access and he touched her through her panties which were now damp with her arousal.

'James, I want you. Can we…?'

'Of course. Hardly anybody comes here and, if they do, we'll hear them anyway before they get too close.'

'*I* want to come here. Hurry…'

James chuckled and undressed her quickly. He pulled off his chinos and pants and took a condom from his pocket, quickly sheathing himself.

'I know you said you're on the pill, but I think it's a good idea to have protection.'

'I'm not complaining,' said Sapphire although she loved making love without the condom. It was common sense for him to wear one.

Then she forgot everything as James leaned over her and entered her quickly. She cried out as he thrust into her and he pulled back slightly.

'Am I hurting you?' he asked in concern.

'No, not at all—it just feels so good.'

He relaxed and thrust into her again. After a few seconds, she wrapped her legs around his waist and clung on to him around his neck, relishing the feel of him inside her. As well as the heightening sexual arousal that she loved feeling when engaged in intercourse, she felt something else that was new. The only way she could describe it to herself was safe. She felt completely safe in James's arms, with his body tightly inside hers. It felt right as if this was meant to be. They fitted together perfectly, and she loved the hardness of his totally masculine physique, the strength of him, the flexing of his muscles and the scent of musk that hung in the air mixing with the smell of pine from the trees. They were engaged in an activity so natural in a wonderfully beautiful place that it affected her in a way she couldn't put words to.

She wanted the experience to go on forever, as much as she wanted to climax and feel the soaring sensation of orgasming hard that she always felt with James. He took her to places that no man ever had. It was as if they had become one person and were having an out-of-body experience together.

She cried out when she came, and James followed seconds later. It was all encompassing, totally physical but strangely spiritual as the waves of feeling swept through her. When she opened her eyes, she was amazed to discover that she had tears tracking down her cheeks.

James was still lying over her, his weight supported on his elbows. He wiped her tears away and smiled. She smiled back not feeling in the slightest bit embarrassed. She never cried after sex. Until now.

'That was beautiful,' she said softly.

'You're beautiful,' James whispered.

She closed her eyes then, and James kissed her closed eyelids. Then he lay down beside her and they both fell silent, listening to the birds singing just for them.

Chapter Twelve

James stared in dismay at the fashion pages of the newspapers spread all over the table in Sapphire's office. The headlines jumped out at him mockingly.

"Designer carried out of her own fashion show."

"Who is Sapphire Bell-Johnson's mystery man?"

"Is Ms Bell-Johnson pregnant?"

"Is there a doctor in the house?"

'Have you seen this lot?' James asked Della as she peered down at the papers.

'Yes, I'm afraid I have. Social media is worse. Twitter and Facebook have really gone to town. The good news is that a lot of Sapphire's followers have leapt to her defense. The bad news is that others just think she was drunk.'

'Has anyone mentioned the D word?'

'Diabetes?'

'That's the one.'

'No. She's done a great job of keeping it a secret from the public.'

'We can't let her see this lot. She'll go apeshit.'

James sat down on the leather sofa and put his head in his hands. Della remained standing, flicking through some of the papers to see how bad the damage was.

'Well, one or two of the more serious papers have given a good account of the show itself. One even called Sapphire the designer to watch this autumn. She'll be pleased about that.' Della looked over at James and smiled.

'She should come clean now—admit to the world that her collapse wasn't down to drink, but because of something beyond her control,' said James running his hands through his hair.

Della shook her head. 'No way. That is the last thing she'd do. Sapphire sees her diabetes as the enemy, something she needs to defeat. She thinks other people will see it as a weakness. You don't know her like I do, James. Please don't even suggest it.'

'She can't keep it secret forever.'

'Sapphire thinks she can. But she is going to have to manage it better than this,' Della pointed her finger at the newspapers, 'if she's going to keep it from leaking out to the press.'

'It's not as if diabetes is such a big deal these days. Lulu manages it with no bother.'

'Well, bully for Lulu,' said Sapphire from the doorway. She strolled into the room and threw her handbag on the couch, narrowly missing James's head. He suspected that she could have hit him if she'd wanted to.

'Have you been eavesdropping outside the door?' asked James, standing up quickly in case Sapphire decided to throw something else.

'It's my office. Why would I be lurking outside it? And I don't eavesdrop.'

'So—you didn't hear our conversation then?'

Sapphire narrowed her eyes and stood with her hand on her left hip. She was wearing a lime green suit with a tight pencil skirt and fitted jacket which showed off her red hair to perfection.

'Why, James? What have you been saying about me?'

'Nothing.'

'Della—what have you two been talking about?'

James didn't expect Della to be cowed by Sapphire's attitude. She was the only other person he knew who could stand up to her.

'I'll give you three guesses, but you won't need them. Just take a look at the table,' she said.

Sapphire glanced at the newspapers as if she had only just spotted them, then turned her back on them. 'Well, you know what they say—any publicity is good publicity. Now, I suggest we all get back to work and forget about the gutter press.'

'It wasn't only the gutter press, you're mentioned in nearly all the papers,' James said. Della was shaking her head at him, but he ignored her and ploughed recklessly on. 'Don't you think this would be the perfect time to explain why you collapsed? I'm sure people would be sympathetic. After all, nobody can help having a condition like diabetes… not when it's type one… if you had type two then, perhaps, people could be forgiven for thinking you've brought it on yourself. But then, you're not overweight, so…'

Sapphire sat at her desk, with a fixed smile on her face, but her eyes were flashing a warning. She gave Della a look that her PA understood perfectly.

'Coffee, Sapphire?' Della asked sweetly. 'Would you like one James?'

Before he could answer, Sapphire said, 'James will be

going back to his office in a minute where, I am sure, Angie will be able to make him a coffee. After we've had a quiet word.'

Della turned towards the door with a last lingering look at James. He raised his eyebrows and shrugged in a "What did I say?" kind of gesture. Della raised her eyes to heaven and, shaking her head, strolled out of the office in the direction of the kitchen.

'Now, James,' Sapphire said in a deceptively reasonable tone of voice, 'I'm going to forgive you on this occasion, but in future please do not ever suggest I "come out" about my diabetes—'

'But don't you think—'

'Quiet—don't interrupt!' Sapphire shouted loud enough to make the windows rattle and James stepped back involuntarily. He put his hands up as in surrender.

'Sorry...' he whispered. Sapphire glared at him, her eyes like flint.

'That's better,' she said calmly. 'As I was saying. *My* diabetes is *my* business,' she spoke the words slowly as if she was speaking to an imbecile which is probably how she thought of him in that moment. 'Nobody is going to find out about it. I told Della because I need her as an ally, and I trust her with my life. I told you because you found my insulin pen and, as it turned out, I now know I can trust you with my life as well.'

James nodded vigorously but didn't speak.

'Good. Do you understand the situation now?'

'Well...' he began. Sapphire raised her head and glared at him. Her green eyes were flashing a warning that was as clear as a crystal pool. 'Yes, Sapphire, I understand perfectly.'

'I'm so pleased.' She took a deep breath in and let it out in a long exhale. 'Marvellous. Off you go then.'

James was tempted to bow and then walk backwards to the door bowing all the way as the courtesans did in front of royalty in the days of yore. He knew that would only rile the lady even more than he already had.

He turned around and, as casually as he could, he walked through Sapphire's office door and shut it quietly behind him.

'I told you,' said Della as she opened the door again with Sapphire's coffee in her hand.

'You did,' he replied. 'Next time, I promise I'll listen.'

———————

As predicted by most people in Sapphire's social circle, the dust settled very quickly. She made a few phone calls to the most important people, playing down her collapse and telling the same tale of low blood sugar without mentioning her diabetes, and she rapidly became yesterday's news, and was able to get back to the important business of running her company.

Sapphire, James, and Hector met for their Monday morning finance meeting. Hector gave them the good news that the price of shares was going up.

'I need to mention that there is a buyer who has declined to give his real name. A bit surprising but not altogether unheard of.'

'Do you mean he's been buying shares under a false name?' asked Sapphire.

'Yes. I tried to do a background check, as I do with every shareholder, but got nowhere. This person doesn't want his identity to be discovered.'

Sapphire frowned. 'I don't like the sound of that, Hector, I like to know who our shareholders are. Transparency is important. James—would you be able to do some digging please?'

'Of course. I'll get straight on it.'

'Thank you. Right Let's all get back to work shall we?'

Hector and James left, and Sapphire rapidly became absorbed in her designs for the autumn collection. She wanted to build on her success and design clothes that were up-to-the minute, but affordable by the ordinary people that bought from the high street shops. People like Lulu.

As she worked, she found she was sketching clothes that would look good on James's sister. Perhaps Lulu would agree to model for her. She had an elfin look, almost androgynous, with small breasts, a boyish body and big soulful eyes. She remembered a model from the sixties called Twiggy who looked like that, except the model's legs were long like a racehorse. Lulu was quite short and petite, but with the same "urchin" look.

As Sapphire worked, she found she was looking forward to shopping with Lulu the following Saturday. She would help her to make the most of her best features; her eyes and pretty mouth. She would encourage her to develop her own sense of style with her clothes. It would be fun. Maybe Lulu would inspire her to produce a completely new range for the women who didn't have the fuller figure. Teenagers who were yet to become women and women like Lulu, who would never be buxom with wide hips and big bosoms but have the waif-like figures and appearances that were once so popular.

Sapphire aspired to be a trend-setter. Someone the other designers followed. She would start a trend, with Lulu's help.

She felt quite excited at the thought of reinventing herself and her designs. She would make the Forbes list yet, with hard work, insight and the bravery to step outside her comfort zone.

As Sapphire worked, head bent low over her designs, intense concentration on her face, she didn't notice the time. Periodically, Della bought her coffee and snacks, and a salad for her lunch. She grunted a thanks, not wanting to break the spell her creativity had put her under. It grew dark outside, commuters made their weary way home, lights came on in the surrounding office blocks and armies of cleaners set to with vacuum cleaners, mops and buckets. Still Sapphire worked on, completely in the zone, oblivious to her surroundings, intent only on her designs.

'Are you looking forward to Saturday, Lulu?' James lounged on the couch with a glass of wine while Lulu curled up on one of the armchairs, her feet tucked under her. She was staring at the television and biting her thumbnail. Willow was asleep on the other end of the couch, cuddled up to a cushion.

'Ummm?'

'What are you watching anyway?'

'*Love Island*. It's very good.'

'Is it?' James asked. He hated reality TV and couldn't imagine anything worse than watching people he had no interest in doing things that bored him to tears. But his sister seemed riveted.

'See the blonde girl?'

'The one with the big... voice?'

'Yes her. Well—she fancies *him*,' Lulu pointed at the

screen as a man grinned inanely at the camera, 'but he is secretly seeing another woman. Wait, you'll see her in a minute.'

'Okay,' said James yawning widely.

'There! That one—the one with the blue bikini. Did you see her?'

'Yes. So—what happens now?'

'What do you mean?'

'I mean,' he spoke slowly and wondered why he was bothering to carry on this conversation when he really wanted to talk about Sapphire, 'If two women like the same man, how do they resolve it?'

'They don't usually.'

'Oh. Sounds like a fascinating programme.'

'It is.' James's sarcasm was lost on his sister. He tried again. 'What I was going to say was that you don't need to change your look. You're fine as you are.'

'Thanks.' Lulu was obviously not listening, and he was tempted to grab the remote control and turn the television off, but he bided his time and got his chance when the adverts came on.

'The thing is, Lulu,' he leaned forward and put his elbows on his knees, his hands clasped together, 'Sapphire is a modern designer and some of her clothes are rather... well...out there.' He remembered the model with the grey hair extensions that looked as if she had landed from another planet.

'Out where?' Lulu had turned in the chair to give him her full attention.

'It just means quite unusual—not the kind of stuff you wear to work.'

'Oh, that's okay. I need some casual clothes as well. Most of the clothes I teach in have to be quite hard wearing.

I usually stick to trousers, a white blouse and a cardigan. Sapphire thinks I should make the best of my figure and she's going to show me how to do that. It'll be fun.'

James didn't know what to say. He wanted the two women to be friends so Lulu could give Sapphire guidance on how to monitor her diabetes. He didn't want his little sister to become a project for Sapphire to try out her designs on.

'It will be fun, I'm sure, but what I am trying to say is that you don't need a make-over, you don't need to be transformed into somebody you're not. Just choose clothes that you like, okay?'

Lulu was frowning at him and he leaned back on the couch and stared at the television. There was an advert for dog food and a retriever bounded around a garden, grinning with the joy of being alive.

'James? Don't you want me to go on Saturday? I thought that you'd be pleased about it. You want me to help Sapphire, don't you? You said so.'

'Yes, I do, but I'm just a bit concerned that you'll go along with everything Sapphire says to try to please her rather than doing things because *you* want to do them.'

'Things like what?' Lulu was looking upset and James wished he hadn't started the conversation. He was making a complete dog's dinner of it and even the retriever would have turned his nose up.

'Okay. Let me try and explain. Sapphire wears sexy clothes and lots of make-up… and she wears stilettos,' (even in bed). His thoughts flew to the first night they spent together. 'But you don't, and I don't want you to feel pressured into looking the way Sapphire does, that's all.'

'Sapphire is a beautiful woman and can get any man she wants. She told me that I, too, can attract men if I make the best of myself. I'm not making the best of myself at the moment, I know I'm not.' Lulu spoke carefully and James knew it was because she was trying not to cry. 'She is the only person who has offered to help me in this way, and I am going to do everything she tells me. And if you don't like it, James, well that's just tough.' The last few words were muffled in an inward breath that sounded like a sob.

'No, don't get upset... sweetheart...'

Lulu stood up and hurried to the door. She opened it and left the room without looking at James, closing the door quietly behind her.

Willow, sitting on the couch, next to James, stared at him without blinking.

'Yes, you may well look at me like that,' James said to the cat, 'I'm an idiot. Yes, go on, you can say it, I know it's true.' The cat said nothing, just continued to stare at him.

The door opened and Lulu came back without looking at James. She scooped Willow up in her arms.

'I'm taking my cat. She doesn't judge me.'

'Lulu—I'm sorry. Don't go. I didn't explain myself well. I love the way you look. I'm not comparing you to Sapphire.'

'I think you made yourself very clear. Sapphire is sexy and gorgeous and I'm not. And you don't want me to be.'

'Yes, I do. But you already are... just not in the same way that's all.'

'James—I'm nearly twenty-six and I've never had a proper boyfriend. Sapphire is going to help me. Be happy for me.'

Then she left again.

James stared at the television feeling wretched. The woman in the blue bikini was in a hot tub with two men. She'd taken her bikini top off. He switched the television off.

Maybe he should back off and let Sapphire help Lulu. The two women seemed to have taken to each other. Whether they could stand each other's company for more than an hour or so remained to be seen. Saturday would be the test. Maybe he could arrange to take them both for lunch. After all, he had no plans for the weekend. He had been hoping to spend more quality time with Sapphire. Perhaps he could see her on Sunday.

The thought of Sapphire with her green eyes and her luscious red lips sent a shiver through him. She was getting to be a habit. A luxurious addiction. He was still in control, wasn't he? He could stop seeing her anytime.

He thought of the mystery shareholder. Who is this guy? He needed to find out.

James sighed as he stood up and made his way to his home office. He needed to do some digging and if he couldn't dig far enough into the dirt to come up with the answer, he knew a man who could.

Chapter Thirteen

Lulu had changed her outfit three times before settling on black trousers, flat shoes and a long shirt-style blouse in powder blue with three quarter sleeves.

James looked up from reading the Financial Times and gave her an encouraging smile. 'You look nice.'

'Do I?' She looked as she always did. What she would look like when she returned from shopping with Sapphire, he had no idea. James wished she wasn't so nervous. He needed to reassure her about this wretched make-over.

'Yes, really. Remember what I said though—you're fine as you are. You don't need to change a thing about yourself if you don't want to.'

The doorbell rang and James stood up, throwing the paper onto the couch behind him. 'I'll get it.'

'No, I'll get it,' said Lulu and raced down the hall before him. She got to the front door first and James followed, standing like a spare part in the hallway while the two women greeted each other.

Sapphire was also wearing trousers, but hers were daffodil yellow and skintight. She wore a long white blouse, a bright multicoloured waistcoat and a pale cream glittery scarf draped casually around her neck and over her chest. Her hair was pulled up in a top knot, the usual curly tendrils escaping and hanging over her face. She wore minimal make-up to devastating effect. It was a look that gave the impression of being thrown together, but everything matched perfectly. Her sandals had three-inch heels and her toenails were painted bright yellow.

'Morning, James,' she said.

'And good morning to you, Sapphire.' His voice had lowered an octave and sounded, even to his ears, husky and seductive. He coughed to clear his throat. His baby sister was standing next to him. He needed to act with decorum.

Sapphire smiled in a way that suggested she knew exactly what he was thinking. Which was that he wanted to be alone with her and bury himself in her soft, perfumed body.

'So,' Sapphire said brightly, 'what do you intend to do with yourself today, James? While Lulu and I are indulging in retail therapy?'

'I've got some work to do this morning, then I thought we could all meet for lunch and you can show me what you've bought. My treat, of course.'

Sapphire looked at Lulu. 'This is your day, Louisa Lewis, you choose. Shall we let a man take us out to lunch? Or shall we keep it as a girly day?'

Lulu looked at James for guidance. He nodded slightly.

'Oh no, don't do what James says. This is your choice. Today is the first day of the new you, remember. What do *you* want?'

'Oh, um, well...' Lulu muttered and then turned bright

pink. 'I think yes—don't you?' She turned beseeching eyes to Sapphire.

'Good decision. If a man wants to buy you lunch, it would be rude to refuse. Especially if it's your brother.'

Lulu looked relieved that she'd made the correct choice.

'Okay,' said James. 'Where shall we meet?'

'I'll text you. We haven't decided yet. Now, we need to go, there's a taxi outside waiting to take us to the wonderland that is Oxford Street. See you later, James.'

'Yes, bye…'

Sapphire led Lulu out of the house and down the steps to the front gate. A black cab was waiting on the pavement and he stood on the step and watched them settle themselves into the back. Then the cab took off and he was left alone.

He had given Lulu some cash for clothes as she didn't earn much money as an infant teacher's assistant. She was a sensible girl and would only get useful clothes. He knew from experience, though, how seductive Sapphire could be, and Lulu seemed to have fallen under her spell.

He just hoped she had enough sense to keep the receipts.

By the time the taxi had crawled its laborious way through the Saturday shoppers and stopped outside Harrods, Sapphire wondered if she had made a huge mistake. Lulu had chattered all the way there, her nerves evident in the constant stream of inane questions that emanated from her. She commented on everything as if she had never shopped in London in her life.

'Lulu,' said Sapphire carefully.

'Yes!' she said as she pushed her way out of the back of the taxi and stood on the pavement gazing at the window of Selfridges.

'Take a deep breath and calm down. You need to pace yourself. We have a lot to get through today.'

'Right, I will.' Lulu closed her eyes and put her hand on her stomach before taking a deep breath in.

'And… out…' said Sapphire before taking her elbow and propelling her in the direction of Pierre's Palace. 'Right. Now. We are going to put you completely in the hands of Pierre. He does my hair and is the best in London. Okay?'

'Do I have to have my hair done? Can't we just buy some clothes?'

'No, you are having a complete make-over—hair, nails, make-up, undies, and nightwear. As well as your outer garments, of course.'

'Sapphire,' Lulu whispered, 'I can't afford all that. James has given me some money, but it won't stretch to everything.'

'You are not going to pay for anything today. This is my treat. A thank you for looking after me so well. Now, come on, let's go in.'

Lulu shrunk back behind Sapphire as she greeted Pierre.

'Hello, darling! Here she is, your project for the day. I will leave her in your capable hands and sit quietly in the corner checking my emails.'

'Anything for you *ma chere*', said Pierre who was from the east side of London, but had reinvented himself as a Frenchman when he opened his first salon. 'Don't look so scared, my dear, we'll look after you,' he said guiding Lulu to the backwash.

Sapphire settled herself down to check her emails and look over her favourite social media sites. Someone placed a cup of espresso on the table next to her and she drank it absentmindedly, as she became engrossed in work. She checked her Twitter feed for any juicy gossip, especially if she was the subject, then Instagram to get a look at the designers she followed and what they were up to. She became so involved in commenting and posting that the time flew by.

An hour and a half later, Pierre's "project" was finished.

'What do you think?' he asked as he paraded Lulu in front of her.

'Wonderful! I love the rose gold highlights. And the nails —exquisite. Do you like it, Lulu?'

'Yes…' said Lulu uncertainly.

'What? You do like it, don't you?' Sapphire loved the new look. Lulu's hair was swept back and layered instead of straight and falling in her eyes, and the colour was modern; dark at the roots, with at least three shades of honey, rose gold and amber.

'It's just so different…'

'Well of course, it's supposed to be. What about the make-up?' The make-up artist had given her eyes definition. She had perfectly shaped eyebrows that made her eyes look huge in her face, and her cheekbones were pronounced with just the right amount of blusher. She wore lip liner and now sported blood red lips. The look emphasised her heart-shaped face but also made her look older and more sophisti-cated. 'I think's it's gorgeous, I really do.'

'It is. Thank you, Sapphire. And you Pierre.'

'It was a pleasure.'

'Right. Ready for the clothes?'

'Yes.' Lulu brightened up at the prospect of buying

clothes, so Sapphire phoned a taxi and they left the salon. Lulu attracted a few admiring glances from men passing by and Sapphire smiled. Little Miss Lewis was going to be transformed.

—————

'Oh, I love the feel of these,' said Lulu as she stroked the satin knickers and matching bra set, 'and the colour is heavenly.'

'It's peach,' said Sapphire thinking about the half a dozen matching peach lingerie items hanging in her walk-in wardrobe. And the red, blue, black, navy, champagne… 'What colour do you normally buy?'

'Oh, I'm very boring, I just buy white or natural. You know, the six in a pack for five pounds?'

'Right. And how do those white ones make you feel?'

Lulu frowned. 'They don't make me feel anything, they're just knickers.'

'No, darling, they're not just knickers. They are the secret to a woman feeling good about herself.'

'Are they?' Lulu gazed at her, her new look giving her a sensual innocence that pleased Sapphire. She knew that little Miss Lewis was capable of looking hot and sexy, but now it was Sapphire's job to help her to feel that way as well.

'What I want you to do is try on this dress I have chosen for you, which you will look stunning in. Now, take the dress, shoes and the underwear to the changing room and come back out. I will wait here for you, okay?'

'Okay.' She went off obediently and Sapphire sat down to wait.

A short time later, Lulu emerged from the changing

room and stood, running her hands down the front of the dress nervously. It came to just above the knee, but with the heels, was exactly the right length. A deep midnight blue, it was sleeveless, almost completely backless but with quite a respectable neckline. It accentuated her tiny waist beautifully and was tailored especially for women with small breasts. It surpassed even Sapphire's expectations.

'Wow…you look beautiful, you really do.'

'Really?' Lulu's eyes were shining, and her head was held high.

'Yes, absolutely. Haven't you seen yourself in the mirror?'

'Well, yes, but… I didn't really recognize myself. It was almost as if that person in the mirror was a stranger.'

'That person in the mirror, darling, is the real you. Now tell me, Lulu, how do you feel wearing your new clothes?'

'I feel, well… you know… better.'

'Sexy?'

Lulu blushed, then laughed but this time it wasn't a giggle, more of a woman's laugh. 'Yes, now you come to mention it, I do.'

'More confident?'

Lulu stood straighter and pushed her shoulders back, 'Yes.'

'And the nicks? Do they feel good against your skin?'

'Oh yes.'

'And could you imagine a good-looking man slowly undressing you and caressing you through the satin?'

Lulu put her hand to her mouth and blushed. 'Oh no!'

'Then we need to do something about that, don't we? But first, promise me that you will get rid of all the old knickers and bras?'

'Okay,' Lulu said breathlessly.

'Good. Then my work here is done. Let's phone James and meet him at the restaurant for lunch. All this shopping has given me an appetite.'

Chapter Fourteen

The restaurant that Sapphire had chosen was full to capacity but somehow she had managed to get a good table with waiters buzzing around her like bees around an exotic flower. Make that two exotic flowers, thought James, as he caught sight of his sister smiling up at a young man who was swapping their wine glasses for champagne flutes.

Lulu looked so different he almost didn't recognize her even though she was wearing the same clothes she had left the house in. The top buttons of her blouse were undone, and she had a scarf, similar to the one Sapphire was wearing, draped casually around her neck and tied loosely over her breasts. She was showing far more flesh than normal.

When she caught sight of him weaving his way between the tables towards them, she started waving madly at him. Same old Lulu then. She always greeted people she cared about like an exuberant puppy.

'James—we're over here!' Lulu shouted when he was half-way across the restaurant. He waved discreetly and smiled.

'What are we celebrating?' he asked when he caught sight of the champagne bottle in the ice bucket. He picked it up and studied the label. It was a Veuve Clicquot, not the most expensive one on the market but good enough for a Saturday lunchtime. And it was very dry. Not for Lulu then, she didn't do dry, preferring her drinks to be sweet. And she didn't like alcohol.

'We are celebrating the new Louisa May Lewis. Your sister has been reborn today.' Sapphire looked as if she had already started drinking. Her cheeks were flushed, her hair was loose now and flowed over her shoulders and her eyes were excessively bright.

'Are you drinking, Lulu?' James asked, frowning.

'I'm going to just try a glass of champagne, as Sapphire has kindly bought it for us.'

'But you don't like alcohol,' he said.

'Well, I don't know until I try, do I?'

She had tried beer and didn't like it. She couldn't drink spirits and cocktails made her feel ill. The chance of her suddenly taking a fancy to champagne was remote, but James decided to humour her. Today was a day for surprises and getting out of your comfort zone if Lulu's appearance was anything to go by.

'You haven't even mentioned your sister's new look. What do you think, James?'

James sat down and studied Lulu, trying to think of something complimentary to say. The truth was, he was appalled. The red lipstick didn't suit her and the multi-coloured hair looked silly, at least to his untrained eye. And he couldn't get used to it brushed back in a masculine fashion. He was used to seeing Lulu with little or no make-up and he didn't like what Sapphire had turned her into.

'Well…' he said drawing the word out to give him more time to think, which didn't fool Lulu.

'You don't like it, do you? In fact, you hate it.'

How well his sister knew him, he thought, despite the fact that she wasn't good at reading people's expressions. Body language completely eluded her. Lulu was staring at him and he felt dismay when her eyes filled with tears.

'Sweetheart, it doesn't matter what I think, or what anyone thinks, the only thing that matters is that *you* like it and are happy. Are you happy?' He tried to keep his voice calm and gentle as he had when she was younger and got upset at something. It worked then. It obviously wasn't working now. Especially as Sapphire was glaring at him.

'She was happy, James, until you turned up.'

'I'm sorry, but I told you before, Lulu, that I like you as you've always been. This is so…' he searched desperately for a word that wasn't too insulting. The only words that were spinning around his head were mainly reserved for ladies of the night.

'Different is the word you're looking for, isn't it James?' Sapphire sounded as if she wanted to tip the champagne bucket over his head. Minus the bottle of course, Sapphire would never waste good champagne.

The waiter was hovering near the table and James took advantage of that to say, 'How you two ordered?'

'Yes,' said Lulu quietly.

'Right, then I'll have the lamb chops please.' The waiter nodded and James thanked him as he handed the menu back. 'What have you two chosen?'

'Fish and chips,' Lulu muttered.

'Lovely. Sapphire?' But Sapphire wasn't going to take the hint and get things back on an even keel. She stared at him with angry green eyes and said nothing.

'I think I'll just go to the ladies,' said Lulu. She stood up without looking at either of them then walked away with her head down.

James waited for the fallout as Sapphire clearly had something she wanted to say, and he wasn't going to like it.

'What? Why are you staring at me?'

'You make me so angry sometimes,' she said, grabbing the champagne bottle, pouring it into the flutes and spilling some on the tablecloth.

'Why? What have I done? You're the one who's turned my baby sister into a tart.' He didn't mean to say that, it just slipped out.

'What! How dare you?'

'Well look at her... she never wears red lipstick and her hair...'

'What's wrong with her hair? It's modern and chic. It's lovely.'

James knew he shouldn't be having an argument with Sapphire in the middle of a busy restaurant, especially as Lulu would be back any minute, but he couldn't in all honesty condone what Sapphire had done.

'It doesn't suit her.' He sipped his champagne and tensed in preparation for Sapphire's next volley.

'What is your problem, James?'

'I have no problem.'

'Oh yes, you most certainly do.' Sapphire sat back and watched him with narrowed eyes. 'Explain yourself and be quick before she returns.'

James took a deep breath. 'Okay. Lulu is... well, she's different to other women her age. She isn't worldly and sophisticated like you. I'm afraid that she'll attract the wrong type of men looking the way she does now. They won't understand her. They'll see her looking like that and think… they might take advantage of her, hurt her, maybe even break her heart.'

'And what type of men might they be?' Sapphire asked quietly.

'Men who are only after one thing.'

'You mean men like you.'

James was taken aback. He hadn't meant himself at all, but he'd given Sapphire every reason to think he only wanted her for sex.

'Okay, I admit I was attracted to you at first because of the way you look—'

'And how did I look? Sexy, red lipstick, red dress, high heels…'

No underwear, that was what James remembered about their first date. He started to get hot under the collar just thinking about it. He took a mouthful of champagne.

'Yes, but…'

'And how would you have described that look? Trashy or classy?'

'Classy, of course.'

Sapphire poured them both more champagne. James was amazed to find his glass was already empty. 'Are you sure about that?'

'Of course, I'm sure. You are a devastatingly attractive woman and men will always want you, no matter what you wear or how you look, because whatever you wear, you'll always look good.'

'Even when I'd been sick and lying in your bed looking like a ghost?'

'Yes, even then.' Reminded of that night, James wondered if he dared ask Sapphire if she and Lulu had taken their insulin.

'And are you saying that your sister isn't as attractive as that?'

'Yes, that is what I'm saying. Lulu is pretty and can look good when she tries, but not with all that make-up on and that hairstyle. They just don't suit her.'

'Oh…' At the sound of Lulu's voice, James turned abruptly, knocking his glass off the table.

'Lulu…I didn't know you'd come back.'

'Oh, James, how can you be so hateful!' How much had she had heard?

'Listen, honey, I'm sorry, I didn't mean what I said. You're lovely, you know I think you are…'

The waiter was mopping up the spilled champagne and Lulu was standing with her arms folded, trying not to cry.

'Sit down and let's have a nice lunch together.'

'I'm not hungry, I'm going home. The day's spoiled for me now.'

'Oh, please don't say that Lu. Forgive me. Don't go.'

It was no use, Lulu walked off and Sapphire stood up and glared down at him.

'Thank you for ruining a perfect day,' she said before hurrying after Lulu.

James sat on his own, staring at the wet tablecloth, the ice melting in the bucket and the paper napkin that Lulu had been absentmindedly shredding. What a mess.

'Shall I bring your lamb chops now, sir?' asked the waiter.

'Yes, but could we cancel the ladies' order, I don't think they'll be coming back.'

'I'm afraid the food is already cooked,' said the waiter. Which meant that James would be paying for three meals. He shrugged nonchalantly.

'Fine,' he said. The waiter left.

Good work Lewis, he chided himself. He had managed to upset poor Lulu on her special day, making her think she isn't attractive enough, and he intimated to Sapphire that her look is trashy. It was going to take all his charm and charisma to talk his way out of this one. He almost laughed out loud. What charm and charisma? He'd just proved he had little of either.

It was Lulu's twenty-sixth birthday in a few weeks, and he would make a massive fuss of her then. Make the day extra special and shower her with love and attention. She'd forgive him, after she'd made him sweat a bit. Nothing he didn't deserve.

Sapphire was a different proposition. This was a tricky one. For he *was* attracted to her because of the way she dressed which, let's face it, was nothing if not drop-dead sexy. At first. Now, he would fancy her if she wore a boiler suit. He hadn't been lying about that. But was that all? Was it still just sex or had he started to have other feelings for her? He admired her. And he did feel protective of her, especially with regard to her diabetes. No, it was just sex. Sex with Sapphire Bell-Johnson was like nothing he had ever experienced before. The woman was dynamite in bed.

Which was why he needed to grovel on all fours to get her to forgive him. He didn't want the sex to stop. Not yet anyway. They weren't over. The thought of never making love to that delectable body ever again left him feeling empty.

There was only one thing left for him to do. He called the waiter over and ordered another bottle of champagne. He intended to spend the afternoon getting comfortably hammered.

Sapphire gave the taxi driver her address and sat back on the seat. Lulu sat next to her, sniffling and clutching a wet tissue.

'Listen, sweetie, you need to toughen up a little. I know you were upset about James's foot-in-mouth episode but he's a man and they are indelicate at best and downright stupid at their worst.'

'He said I wasn't attractive,' Lulu said, her lip trembling dangerously again.

'To be fair, that isn't what he said.'

'I heard him,' she muttered.

'He said he thinks you are lovely and don't need the make-up and hairstyle. That isn't the same as saying you're not attractive. And he's right, you are lovely, and with the right make-up and clothes, you can look stunning. The only reason he can't see that yet is because he isn't used to you looking like that. You said yourself it was a different look. He needs time to get used to the new you.'

'Oh.'

'Look—we're here. Come in and I'll make you a coffee.' Sapphire paid the taxi driver and nodded to Victor. They got in the lift together and Lulu smiled. 'That's better.'

'I'd rather have tea if that's okay. I don't really drink coffee.'

Lulu was fascinated by Sapphire's apartment and walked around like a kid at Disneyland while Sapphire made the tea. She put a plate of cheese, biscuits and grapes on a tray, with a slice of ginger cake. After all, neither of them had eaten since breakfast and Sapphire didn't want a repeat of the fashion show.

'It's a lovely place.'

'Thanks. Come and sit down, I want to talk to you about something.'

Sparkle chose that moment to make her appearance.

'Hasn't she grown!' exclaimed Lulu, 'She's got a lovely home with you, Sapphire. I'm so glad.'

'And I'm glad James was kind enough to think of me for her new owner.'

At the mention of James, Lulu looked sad again and Sapphire pushed her to eat some cheese and biscuits.

As she munched, Sapphire showed her a website on her phone. 'This is one that a lot of my friends use, and the men on here are more acceptable than the usual on-line dating site.'

'Oh, I couldn't do anything like that. I'm not brave enough.'

'I thought you wanted to meet someone—a special someone?'

'Oh, I do, but… I don't know…'

'Lulu—now is the time for you to find that courage. You have a new look, and you can't waste it by sitting at home every night. What have you got to lose?'

'I don't think James is going to be happy. He says that the people who have to join dating sites are inadequate somehow. Because they can't meet people naturally.'

Sapphire felt mounting anger at James. He wasn't helping Lulu with remarks like that.

'Okay,' Sapphire said, 'tell me how many dating sites that James has tried.'

'None! He doesn't need to use them. He has never had problems meeting women.'

'Well, if he has never tried them then he doesn't know what he's talking about. I'll help you set up a profile and if you see someone you like, just have lunch with them. Or just phone them for a chat initially. You don't have to meet anyone if you don't want to.'

'Oh, I don't know…'

'How were you planning on meeting men? Do you have friends you can go clubbing with?'

'No. None of my friends like nightclubs.'

'Why don't you register and set up your profile, then think about it. Or go online and read the blogs of women who had tried it. I can give you some names if you like.'

Lulu looked at Sapphire as she cuddled Sparkle. 'Why are you doing so much to help me? It can't be just because I'm James's sister.'

'It's nothing to do with that, actually. I think it's more to do with the diabetes. I don't know many people who have it. I suppose I feel that we have a connection. And I like you, as well, don't forget that.'

'I like you too, Sapphire. Okay—let's do it.'

'Good girl.'

They sat close together and stared at the screen as Sapphire helped Lulu to set up her profile.

'There—done! Now all you need to do is sit back and wait for Prince Charming to waltz into your life!'

'Thank you, Sapphire. Now, can I do something for you?' Lulu looked nervous and Sapphire wondered what was coming next.

'Go on, I'm listening.'

'James is worried that you're not managing your diabetes and he asked me to help you.'

Sapphire's natural reaction was to refuse to talk about it, but Lulu and James were two people who understood and cared. And James *had* rescued her from a sticky situation.

'Okay,' she said cautiously.

'Well, I want to show you how I manage mine, if that's okay with you?'

Sapphire had never been too proud to learn from an expert and Lulu was only trying to help.

'Yes, Lulu, that's fine by me.'

Lulu logged on to a website and handed the phone to Sapphire. 'This is the group I belong to. It's a diabetes support group and they are really helpful. Whatever question you have, they can answer it.'

'How often do you meet?' Sapphire wasn't the type to join support groups, preferring to find her own way out of problems. But Lulu was trying so hard to help her, she could at least ask a couple of questions.

'Monthly. Sometimes there's a guest speaker. The next meeting is about diet and exercise, so I think you should come. You'd find it interesting.'

'Let me get back to you on that,' Sapphire said returning Lulu's phone to her.

'They do other things like fund-raising, increasing awareness and sometimes social events too.'

'Like I say—'

'I think you should come. James has been to one or two meetings to support me but also to learn more about diabetes. Please come to the next one, Sapphire.'

'Oh…okay then.' She could spare one evening for Lulu's sake. The girl was beaming and looked happier than she had all day.

'Great! You'll love it and James will be happy.'

Sapphire suspected that keeping her brother happy was high on Lulu's agenda.

Chapter Fifteen

Sapphire was hard at work the following Monday when James stuck his head around the door of her office.

'Is it safe?' he asked.

Sapphire looked up and smiled. 'Safe, James? Whatever do you mean?'

'I mean you're not going to throw something at me... or attack me for ruining your weekend?'

'You haven't ruined my weekend. It would take more than the misguided preconceptions of a misogynistic alpha-male to ruin anything I do.'

'Ouch...'

'I thoroughly enjoyed spending Saturday with Lulu and had a relaxing Sunday reading the papers then working on designs for my autumn collection.'

'You think of me as an alpha-male then?'

Sapphire sat back in her chair and gave a heavy sigh. 'Trust you to ignore the insults and pick up on the phrase "alpha-male". It wasn't a compliment. Come in and stop hovering in the doorway.'

James came into the room and Sapphire took a minute to admire the sheer masculine presence of the man. He was dressed in a dark suit with a dark tie in almost the same colour. His shirt was pristine white. If he'd been wearing sunglasses, he would have looked like a mafia boss.

'I'm not misogynistic by the way. I love women, not hate them and I don't think I mistreat them. Do I?'

Sapphire thought of how courteous he always was, holding doors open for her and putting her needs first.

'No, you're not, but you are judgmental. Especially when it comes to clothes. Just because you dress conservatively doesn't mean the rest of the world has to follow suit. And this is the fashion industry after all. Big, bright and bold. Larger than life. And Lulu is a young woman who should be out there celebrating her youth and independence.'

'Can we not do this again—please? I have tried to apologise and will do so again if you want, but I am still concerned about Lulu.'

He looked worried, so Sapphire took pity on him. After all, she didn't have siblings and had no idea how strong the bond could be. He adored his family, that much was obvious. Perhaps he was genuinely concerned for his sister, as a father would be for a teenage daughter. But Lulu wasn't a teenager.

'Look, James, I know you are, but Lulu is a grown woman. You have to let her live her own life. Is this because of her diabetes? Would you be so concerned about your other sister?'

James shook his head. 'Phoebe is completely different to Lulu. She's more sophisticated for a start. She's a lawyer, made of sterner stuff. And it's nothing to do with her diabetes either. It's her. She's an innocent when it comes to men.'

'She's a virgin?'

'As far as I know, yes she is.'

'Then it's about time she grew up, don't you think? Are things okay between you?'

'Things are… chilly. They were positively icy on Sunday but this morning she made me a coffee and seemed to want to make up.'

'Well, that's good.' They had moved over to the couch and James took something out of his jacket pocket and handed it to her.

'I need to give you this before I forget. Lulu did them on the computer yesterday.'

Sapphire opened the piece of A4 paper and found an invitation. It was bordered with summer flowers and had text in the centre of the page inviting her to a birthday party. Balloons floated upwards on either side of the text. It was quite an attractive invitation if the birthday-girl had been ten years old. But it was Lulu's twenty-sixth birthday party she'd been invited to.

James winced as she glanced at him with raised eyebrows.

'You're right, Lulu hasn't really grown up yet, I'm afraid.'

'Which is why you're so concerned about her.'

'Right. She was a daddy's girl, cosseted, kept safe from harm… and before you ask, no, it had nothing to do with her diabetes. I think Father would have been the same if she'd not been diagnosed with it. He simply adored her and didn't try to hide it.'

'That must have been hard for you and Phoebe.'

'It was harder on poor Phoebe than me. Father and I

had a good relationship. He played on the two men against three women thing. He always made a fuss of me, but poor Phoebe seemed to be overlooked a lot of the time. I think that was what made her so independent. She's a tough cookie now.'

Sapphire wasn't sure what to say. As an only child she had no real knowledge of the politics of family life. She spent most of her teenage years in her bedroom, drawing and planning her escape.

'So… birthday party then.' She stroked the back of James's hand with one finger. 'Where is she having it? Some high-end hotel? Will there be the chance for us to sneak off for some hot sex?'

He laughed. 'Haven't you read the invite?' She picked it up again and read it properly. She had just skimmed it the first time.

'It's Sunday lunch at Mum's. And there'll just be the family. So, to answer your question, there'll be no hot sex, just a roast dinner, lots of awkward questions and Lulu will take great delight in blowing out the candles on her cake— all twenty-six of them.'

'Then, I may have to plead a prior engagement. Sorry.'

'Sapphire, you will break Lulu's heart if you do. And you don't want that on your conscience, now do you?'

'I'll explain to her. I don't do this kind of event, James, and I don't think it would be a good idea for me to be there at one of your family get-togethers. I'm not family.'

'Sapphire wants you there.'

'Let me think about it. Where are you off to today?'

'I've got a meeting with the CEO of a company that I think you might be interested in. I am going to do a recce and I'll report back to you. Is that okay?'

Sapphire wished that James had mentioned this to her

sooner. She would have gone with him, or maybe instead of him. On the other hand, he was doing all the legwork in checking them out before the real negotiations began. That, she grudgingly decided, was one of the reasons she had employed him in the first place.

'What's the name of the company? Have I heard of them?'

'The company's called Dalton Mackenzie and I have never heard of them. Have you?'

'No, I haven't. Okay, off you go then, but be sure to come straight back afterwards and report to me.'

'Fine,' he said getting up.

Sapphire stood up too. She wondered if she should kiss him but thought better of it. They needed to be ultra-professional in the office. She walked back to her desk and by the time she had settled herself once more in her leather chair, James had gone.

James took a taxi to Dalton Mackenzie and was surprised to find the office was part of a multi-occupied building. It was on the fifth floor at the back of the office block and shared space with a small firm of architects. He had the impression, from the website, and from communicating with a director of the firm during a quite lengthy email correspondence, that this company was on the up, and was already making serious money. It had an impressive portfolio and contracts coming out of their ears. He still hadn't nailed down exactly where their main interests lay which was why he wanted to see them first before taking it any further.

Judging by the size of the premises he had been directed

to, the information he had received was either a gross exaggeration, or they were pouring their money into the product and skimping on appearances. There seemed to be little evidence of a brand or of anything that would attract investors. It was almost as if they didn't want anyone to know they existed at all. Very strange. James was suspicious already.

The waiting area was decidedly sub-standard with a cheap, vinyl-covered two-seater settee and two matching chairs, encircling a glass-topped table. A young woman sat behind the reception desk with a computer and a phone that hadn't rung once since James had entered the premises. There were no staff milling about, no one waiting for the lifts. The place looked deserted.

When he spotted a woman who had wandered in to talk to the receptionist, it all became clear. She had her back to him, but there was a mirror behind the reception desk, and he had a perfect view of the woman's face. She was attractive with a neat bob of chestnut hair. Ruth hadn't changed a bit.

He moved as stealthily as he could away from the area and stood behind a large potted palm tree that occupied too much space in the waiting area. Fortunately, the plant grew tall and wide, with massive leaves that hid James quite adequately. It was off to the side of the waiting area and James didn't think Ruth would see him in the mirror. He was safe until she turned round. He wondered where Malcolm was. Like Bonny and Clyde, where there was one, the other was sure to be nearby.

He examined the dusty palm and wondered what kind of business they were running now. An odd choice of decoration; a plant that most interior designers of cutting-edge office space would recommend their clients avoid. It grew too fast and too much. Obviously Ruth and Malcolm hadn't received that particular memo.

He risked a quick glance at the reception desk. Ruth was still there, chatting to the receptionist. He stayed behind the plant feeling more than a bit stupid.

As he peered through the leaves, keeping an eye on Ruth, his heart started racing and he began to feel slightly sick. He wondered if the person he had been emailing had been Ruth, or even worse, Malcolm. And if so, why had they agreed to meet him today? What game were they playing now?

He suspected that Malcolm was up to his old tricks. He had obviously bought this place and was trading under an assumed name. No wonder he didn't want to draw attention to himself. What was Ruth's role in it? Were they married now? Was she his business partner? He couldn't answer any of those questions, but one thing he did know was that he needed to get out before Ruth or Malcolm spotted him and stay as far away from this company as possible.

'How did it go? Were you impressed?' Sapphire lounged back on the leather couch, sipping a mineral water and looking relaxed and happy. James knew she was pleased with her new designs and had received more than usual interest in her autumn collection. He was happy for her, she deserved to be successful, she certainly worked hard enough for it.

'No, actually, I wasn't.' He flopped down beside her and stretched out his legs. He would tell her as much of the truth as he could without the information that the company was being run by his ex-business partner and his ex-fiancée.

He needed to do some more digging into the mystery share-holder so could easily widen the net and find out what Malcolm the Rat was up to.

'Why?' Sapphire asked curiously.

'Small, pokey office stuck at the back of shared space on the fifth floor. No distinguishing features. No customer service taking into consideration that I was the customer today and would have expected to be escorted to the right floor at the very least.'

'But what about the CEO? Isn't that who you were going to meet?' Sapphire was frowning now, and he needed to play down his disappointment and dismiss the place as not worthy of their consideration.

'Never got that far. I waited… and waited. No one came to ask if I wanted a coffee so I just stood up and walked out.'

'How appalling!' said Sapphire, 'How do they stay in business with that kind of attitude?' James realised he was tugging at his collar and forced himself to stop.

'How indeed.' He was wondering that himself, but suspected it was all a front. But for what? That was the question. 'No idea—and do you know what?' he turned to her with a smile, 'I don't care. They are not a company we need to concern ourselves with. As different from Sapphire Enterprises as you can get. So, onwards and upwards. I'll make sure I get more information about the next prospec-tive investment, don't you worry. I have no intention of wasting any more of my afternoons.'

Sapphire was watching him with heavy eyelids. What was going on behind her expressive green eyes, he didn't know. Perhaps she didn't believe him and had learned to tell when he was lying. The collar tugging was a perfect exam-ple. Lulu had told him that he did it when he was being economical with the truth. Or, maybe, she didn't give a flying fruitcake and she just wanted to rip his clothes off and have her wicked way with him. What a wonderful plan…

He doubted it was the last as they'd agreed an extra night, and that night had been spectacular. James wanted more. He didn't want them to be over. But Sapphire might have had enough and was true to her word of only one more night. If so, he'd have to think of a way to persuade her that it would be a shame to stop now, when they were having so much fun.

'What I don't understand,' she said, clearly not thinking about his wonderful plan and with her mind still firmly on business, 'is the fact that you were impressed by their website and by everything they said when you corresponded by email. It's strange how a company can be so attractive in the virtual world, and so utterly disappointing in reality.'

'Perhaps they've got a strong IT department but are weak in the other areas.'

'The ones that matter.'

'Exactly. Which is why we are not going to touch them with a ten-foot pole.'

Sapphire sipped her mineral water and frowned. 'Maybe we should look into them a bit more. After all, you were keen enough to want to go and meet the CEO. It might be a bad move to discard them altogether. What if they are producing the next big thing and we miss out because they didn't offer you a coffee?'

'It was much more than that. I just got bad vibes from the whole set up. I really don't think we should waste any more time on them. There are many more companies, better ones, ripe for investment. We can't be too hasty. Trust me on this, Sapphire, okay?'

Eventually, and to James's relief, Sapphire agreed.

'What now?' she asked in a husky tone.

'Let's get laid,' he said in a whisper.

'What a wonderful idea,' she murmured, 'Your place or mine?'

'Lulu is home tonight so let's go to yours.'

'What are we waiting for?'

Absolutely nothing, thought James as he escorted Sapphire out of the building and into the muggy London evening air.

Chapter Sixteen

James collected Sapphire early on Sunday morning. It was a glorious summer day, perfect for driving with the top down on the sports car. He had debated taking the Harley but, as he knew he'd be subjected to a lecture by his mother, and possibly one from Phoebe as well, he had decided against it. Today, he would be on his best behaviour so that the day went well for Lulu. The poor kid didn't get a lot of fun in her life and maybe Sapphire was right when she said that she needed to start enjoying being young, free and single.

James parked the car a few hundred yards away from Sapphire's apartment and strolled there, deep in thought. He politely asked Victor to ring and let Sapphire know he'd arrived. He could, of course, just send her a text, but that would be depriving the doorman of a job. The man always looked at him with suspicion which made James wonder, vaguely, what he had done wrong. Perhaps Victor had feelings for Sapphire and was, instinctively, suspicious of any man who showed up to take her away. He wouldn't blame him if he did. Most of the men who found themselves in Sapphire's orbit would want to bed her.

He paced up and down the lobby as he waited for the lady in question to appear.

Then he was gazing into Sapphire's dazzling green eyes, dancing with laughter. 'Hi.'

'Hi.'

James took in her appearance and his breath quickened. She had obviously dressed more conservatively than usual today, in honour of the occasion, and he felt a rush of warmth at her consideration. To his biased opinion, she looked more gorgeous than ever. She wore a dress that came to just above her knees, in a green colour that matched her eyes. She wore shoes with a lower heel than usual, and her hair was loose and flowing. The dress had a tasteful neckline and three-quarter sleeves. On any other woman it would have looked quite nice, but nothing special. On Sapphire, it looked simply stunning.

'You look lovely,' he said.

'Thank you. You look good yourself. Loving the black shirt.'

She took his arm and steered him in the direction of the door. 'Let's go and party! Bye Victor!'

'Goodbye Ms Bell-Johnson.'

Victor studiously ignored James, so he ignored him back. Then, realising how childish that was, he turned his head to shout a muffled goodbye over his shoulder.

As they sped down the M4 motorway towards Surrey, James thought that life couldn't get any better. He was driving a classic car—a 1968 MG Midget MKIII— and receiving admiring looks from other drivers. He was sitting next to the most beautiful woman he'd ever known which elicited more admiring glances. The sun beat down pleasantly and the wind blew their hair back in a way that brought to mind old-style shampoo adverts. He almost laughed out loud with the joy of the moment.

The negative parts of his life would be kept buried deep in his subconscious today. He wouldn't give a thought to Malcolm, Ruth or the mystery investor. Today, no one would have a hypo or faint or argue. The weather was too perfect, and he was in too good a mood.

'What did you get Lulu for her birthday?' asked Sapphire, a strand of red hair blowing across her face as she turned to speak to him.

'I got her gift cards for all her favourite stores—W H Smith, HMV, Hobbycraft, Boots and Argos—'

'Argos?'

'She likes Argos; she's always pouring over the catalogue. She buys stuff for the kitchen and bedrooms sometimes.'

'Gift cards, James—really?'

'What's wrong with gift cards? She can get what she wants then instead of somebody buying her something she may not like.'

'They're so impersonal. It's what you give a work colleague when they leave for pastures new. Not a beloved little sister.'

'I've always given her gift cards, it's what she wants,' he said as if that was the end to it. Sapphire had other ideas.

'And I bet she's effusively grateful and throws her arms around your neck, kisses your cheek and tells you what a wonderful brother you are.'

Sapphire had got it exactly right again. 'She likes gift cards,' he said rather lamely.

'No James, she doesn't like bloody gift cards, but she does adore her big brother. If you gave her half a pound of sausages wrapped up in a pink ribbon she'd love them just as much.'

'Only if they were beef—she's not keen on the pork.'

Sapphire punched him on the arm.

'Ow! That hurt…'

'Oh don't be a baby, it wasn't that hard.'

'It's too late now anyway, she'll have to put up with them.' His good mood was being slowly erased by Sapphire's scorn.

'Then, it's a good job I got her something valuable.'

'You've got her a present?'

'Of course.' Sapphire was stretched out in the passenger seat as far as she could and pulled her dress up to expose as much of her bare legs as possible. She was obviously trying to catch the sun's rays while she had the chance. Her eyes looked closed behind her Ray-Bans. He had an over-whelming desire to run his hand up the inside of her leg, but if he did, they would have to leave the motorway and find a secluded spot which would make them late for lunch. He kept his hands on the wheel and tried to turn his mind away from sex.

'What did you get her?' He was almost afraid of the answer; it was bound to be glamorous and hideously expensive.

'I made up a beauty basket for her with all our products in, including perfume—'

'Oh, she'll love that.' That was okay; not too ostentatious.

'And I selected a special evening gown with matching

shoes and handbag for when she starts getting dates and meets someone with enough about him to take her somewhere special.'

'Right…' Lulu would never wear an evening dress. She'd never go to a venue that called for that sort of attire.

'And I found the perfect drop earrings for the dress that will compliment her new hairstyle. And a necklace to match. Rolled gold.'

'Sapphire! You can't give her all that… it's far too much.'

'Of course I can. It's her birthday. Gift cards indeed!'

James was silent as the sports car ate up the miles and the countryside spread out before them on both sides. He was brooding but he couldn't help it.

'You're too generous Sapphire and Lulu will love everything but, can I just ask one favour?'

'Of course,' said Sapphire sleepily.

'Choose a time to give her the presents when you are alone with her. I don't want the things that the rest of us give her to look sad in comparison.'

'What do you take me for, James? I'm not stupid. I know your mother and sister are not in the same financial position as me, nor do they have access to the fashion world. Anyway, I've already given them to her.'

'When?'

'Yesterday when you were off somewhere doing heaven knows what, I took them round to your house before she left. Then I gave her a lift to the station.'

'Why didn't you tell me you were doing that? I was only having a few drinks with some friends, I could have cancelled.'

'Whatever for? This was between me and Lulu. And she loved everything, thanks for asking.'

James didn't know what to think. They hadn't wanted him there, obviously. Sapphire could have told him about the presents before she gave them to Lulu. They made his gift cards look pathetic.

He glanced down at Sapphire who looked as if she was falling asleep again. She had the ability to look completely at peace in an instant. It took him ages to relax when he was wound up. At the moment he didn't feel as if he would ever relax again. Then he glanced at her once more and couldn't help smiling. For this incredibly irritating, wonderfully sexy and mind-bogglingly fuckable woman was his for the taking. For now anyway.

James wished he could stay on the motorway and keep driving until they reached the horizon. He didn't want this —whatever it was between them—to end. He wanted her every second of every minute he was in her company. He'd never felt that way before about any woman and he intended to make the most of it.

Chapter Seventeen

Once they left the boredom of the motorway and reached the town of Guildford, Sapphire sat up and took notice. She'd been right about the neighbourhood that the Lewis's came from. The houses were detached with tidy gardens filled with regimented flower beds. It was a pleasant, typically middle-class area, exactly what she expected.

James stopped outside a corner house and parked half on the road and half on the pavement. There was a car in the drive already—a silver BMW, parked in the middle of the driveway, almost as if someone had measured the space all the way around to make sure it was exactly in the centre. Sapphire assumed it belonged to Phoebe. She couldn't help thinking that, with a bit of thoughtful maneuvering, she could easily have left enough space for the sports car as well.

'Right,' James said with a strained smile, 'ready for the fun to begin?'

'Of course, I'm looking forward to meeting your family.'

'Tell me that again at the end of the day,' James said and grinned in a positively evil fashion.

What had she let herself in for? Sapphire never met the families of the men she was involved with.. She had never met Monty's or Roland's. And they had never met her parents. It was easier that way. In fact, she was shaking a little inside. She wasn't sure why apart from the simple fact that she hated to be on display. It was a different thing being the centre of attention when it involved work; it was a given that fashion designers were constantly in the public eye. The more media attention they got, the more successful they were. And it was the clothes that were under the microscope, but the scrutiny she anticipated from James's mother and older sister was a different thing altogether.

James rang the doorbell and said, 'I do have a key but only use it for emergencies. Luckily there haven't been any so far.'

'Good,' she replied. Victor had a spare key to all the apartments so that wasn't something she needed to worry about, but James's mother lived alone.

Then the front door burst open and Lulu shrieked, 'They're here!' before throwing herself into Sapphire's arms and hugging her. 'Oh, I'm so glad you've come, and you too, James', she said as she hugged him as well. 'The party can really start now. Come in, come in.'

They were ushered into a spacious hall with photographs adorning the walls of all of the Lewis offspring at various ages. The smell of furniture polish and freesias filled the air. A large vase of summer flowers sat on a small table next to an old-fashioned telephone sitting on a pile of phone books, including the yellow pages. Sapphire didn't think people used them anymore, not now that Google was all the rage. Perhaps James's mum didn't like modern technology.

Lulu, dressed in a summer dress that Sapphire would

have called a "frock" and wearing sandals with ankle socks, skipped ahead of them.

'We're through here—come on,' Lulu said as she stopped outside a door that was firmly closed. It was the front room of the house, a room that some people called the drawing-room. Sapphire remembered her grandmother's house and the drawing-room that was never used except for wakes and visits from the insurance man. The family spent their lives in the kitchen or watching TV in the lounge.

When Sapphire walked through the doorway, after Lulu flung it open for her—no doubt wanting her to make a grand entrance—and took a quick glance around, she decided that things were exactly the same in this family. Mrs Lewis sat in an armchair, wearing a skirt and blouse and lace-up shoes. She looked like a character from an Agatha Christie novel, down to the tightly permed hair and blue eye shadow. Sapphire felt that she had stepped back in time, to the 1950's.

'Hi, I'm Sapphire,' she said walking towards the woman who made no attempt to get up from her chair.

'Yes, I thought you were,' she replied, 'It's very nice to meet you.'

'It's lovely to meet you,' Sapphire offered her right hand to shake and the older woman took it as if she wasn't quite sure what to do with it. Sapphire gripped her hand gently before letting go.

'This is Phoebe,' said Lulu grabbing hold of Sapphire's arm and pulling her around to face her sister. At least Phoebe had the grace to stand up.

Sapphire wasn't sure whether to offer her hand or not, but Phoebe smiled and put her hand out, so Sapphire obliged. Phoebe had a surprisingly strong grip. She was dressed in white trousers with a tailored black top. Sapphire couldn't decide whether it was a jacket or a blouse—it fell somewhere between the two. It was smart and incredibly stylish. Her brown hair was shoulder length and cut in layers that fell gently around her face. Her make-up was subtle, and she wore a hint of perfume. She had the appearance of a successful professional woman who was confident of her own abilities. It took one to know one. The look that she was giving Sapphire wasn't particularly friendly. She was sizing her up as if they were in competition in some way, ridiculous as that thought was. But then, Phoebe was a lawyer, and used to competing.

On an old fashioned sideboard sat six birthday cards, one of which was hers. If each member of Lulu's family had given her a card, then she obviously didn't have many friends. Not ones who gave cards anyway.

'So,' said James rubbing his hands together, 'now that the introductions are over, what would you all like to drink?'

'Sherry for me please,' said his mother, smoothing her skirt and settling herself more comfortably in the armchair. She smiled sweetly at Sapphire.

'I'll have a Scotch, but just one as I'm driving,' said Phoebe.

'Is that a new car?' asked James, 'I don't remember seeing it before.'

'Yes, it is. I see you've still got the Midget.'

'Of course, I wouldn't be without it.'

'And he's still got the bike,' said Lulu.

'Oh, James, you know I don't like you riding that thing, it's so dangerous,' said his mother, her smile quickly turning to a frown.

'It's fine, Mum, honest.'

'What do you think of the Harley?' Phoebe asked turning to Sapphire.

'Umm… well, for London traffic it's practical.' Why had they dragged her into it? She looked at James, but he was pouring Amontillado into a liqueur glass, and didn't appear to be listening.

'You're not one of those Hell's Devil's as well, are you?' said Mrs Lewis peering shortsightedly at Sapphire who was still standing in the middle of the room, having not been invited to sit yet.

James chuckled and gave his mother her drink, then kissed her gently on the cheek. 'Neither of us are Hell's Angels, Mum, don't worry. Sapphire is a famous designer and has just had an outstandingly successful fashion show that I was privileged to be part of.'

'Yes, I know,' said Mrs Lewis, 'I've heard all about it from Lulu. A designer, fancy that.' She took a sip of her sherry cautiously. Sapphire guessed that she didn't sit in this room sipping sherry very often as she looked way out of her comfort zone.

'What's the birthday girl drinking?' asked James and Lulu threw herself into his arms again.

'Oh, I love birthdays! Do we have any champagne? I really enjoyed the one I had the other week.'

Sapphire didn't think that Lulu had even tasted the champagne from the make-over day. They'd left the restaurant before they had managed to eat or drink anything. Which was a shame as it was one of Sapphire's favourite eateries.

'Forget the scotch then, I brought a bottle with me just in case; it's chilling in the fridge. Hang on while I fetch it,' said Phoebe. She hurried to the door.

'Bring the glasses as well…' James shouted after her.

'Champagne?' said Mrs Lewis in amazement, 'We are pushing the boat out today, aren't we? When did you start drinking Lulu? You've never had anything stronger than coffee before now.'

'Since Sapphire and I had a girly day out in London,' said Lulu taking Sapphire's arm and leading her to the couch. 'Have a seat next to me,' she said. 'Sapphire introduced me to a lot of new experiences that day, didn't you?'

'Umm, well, maybe one or two…'

'Did you?'

Mrs Lewis was studying her now, a bit suspiciously, and Sapphire was beginning to feel like a call girl in a convent.

'It's a lovely house, Mrs Lewis,' she said.

'You haven't seen much of it yet, just this room.'

'Well, yes, but—it's a lovely room. Nice colour scheme.' If you were into muddy brown and beige.

'We hardly ever use it. Last time was my husband's funeral. We don't get many visitors. Like to keep ourselves to ourselves.' She sipped her sherry, then put the glass on a table next to the chair and folded her hands over her stomach, as if she would sit out the intrusion into the family's privacy stoically.

'Right,' said Phoebe returning with a bottle of champagne and five glasses on a hostess trolley, 'Who's for champers?' She opened the bottle and Lulu shrieked when the cork flew up to the ceiling, nearly taking out the light bulb. Sapphire noticed the shade was one of the old-fashioned kind with a fringe around the edge.

'I think we can all manage a small glass each, to toast Lulu,' James said. They all watched as Phoebe poured the sparkling champagne into the wine glasses. Obviously not a family that celebrated very much. Or if they did, perhaps they stuck to Prosecco.

'Not for me, thanks, I'll play safe and stick to the Amontillado.' said Mrs Lewis.

'Come on now, Mum, just have a taste.' James swapped the sherry for champagne and she glared at it as if it contained poison.

He handed everyone a glass, Lulu nearly spilling hers as she was jumping up and down with excitement. She took a sip and giggled as the bubbles went up her nose.

When he handed Sapphire her glass he looked into her eyes and said, 'Sapphire—would you do us the honour of proposing a toast to Lulu?'

Sapphire sensing that this was a bigger deal to Lulu than it would be to most women celebrating their twenty-sixth birthday, said, 'It would be a pleasure. Please raise your glasses to a beautiful young woman and wish her every happiness for her birthday. May all your dreams come true, sweetheart.'

"Oh! Thank you, Sapphire.'

Lulu was beaming, James and Phoebe were clapping, and Sapphire joined in quickly and Mrs Lewis was struggling to get out of her chair.

'Oh dear, I'm afraid I feel a bit emotional. I don't want to spoil the party, so I'll go and check the lamb.' Then she waddled out of the drawing-room without a backward glance.

'Is she okay?' Sapphire asked.

'She's fine,' said Lulu cheerfully, 'Mum always cries because she misses Dad. I'm going to have some more champagne,' she said filling up her glass.

'Steady on Lu,' said James, 'you're not used to alcohol, you need to pace yourself.'

'What's this big announcement?' asked Phoebe.

They were all still standing in the middle of the room together. Sapphire wondered why nobody sat down. Perhaps they wanted to create a party atmosphere, instead of a wake. Seeing as there were only four of them, they'd all have to work especially hard to create any kind of atmosphere at all. They couldn't rely on Mrs Lewis for back-up.

'I told Mum all about it yesterday. Are you ready?'

'Oh for Pete's sake, get on with it Lulu,' said Phoebe irritably. James shot her a warning look, but she just stared back at him in defiance.

'I've got a date!' Lulu was beside herself with excitement.

'Is he from the dating site?' asked Sapphire.

'Yes, I've spoken to him twice already. Do you want to see his picture?'

'Love to,' said Sapphire.

'This must be the closest you've ever come to a man, isn't it Lu?' Phoebe sounded bored, but there was a flicker of something in her eyes. Sapphire wondered if she was jealous. Then she realised how ridiculous that idea was. Phoebe had everything; a career, smart car, apartment and she knew how to dress. Doubtless she also had a string of men she could call on whenever she needed some down and dirty time.

'Look—what do you think?' Lulu showed Sapphire the picture of an ordinary looking man, who wasn't smiling at all. He didn't look particularly attractive to her; his eyes were too close together, but Lulu seemed smitten.

'What does he do for a living?' Sapphire asked.

'Something in the city, he said.'

'Well that's helpful,' said Phoebe, 'He could be anything from a politician to a road sweeper. Don't you think it would be a good idea to find out more about him before you meet?'

'No, I'm meeting him after work on Monday.'

James, who had been quiet up to that moment, said, 'I think it would be a good idea if I came with you. Just for the first date.'

'Don't be so utterly ridiculous, James.' Phoebe put her empty wine glass on the hostess trolley. 'You can't baby her forever. Lulu's a grown woman—isn't it time to cut the apron strings? Even Dad wouldn't have been as protective as you are.'

'I beg to differ,' said James stiffly.

'Look guys,' said Lulu loudly, 'no one's coming with me, okay. This is my life and I am going on a date—alone!'

Well said, Louisa Lewis, thought Sapphire, but she wisely stayed silent. It was nothing to do with her anyway. This wasn't her family. Thank goodness.

'I'm going to help Mum with the lamb,' said Phoebe and strode out of the room.

'Aren't you pleased for me?' This was directed at James and Sapphire watched him for the tell-tale signs that he was being economical with the truth.

'Yes, Lulu, I'm pleased, but I can't help being concerned too. You're my little sister and I love you and want you to be happy. But it's a tough world out there and you have to be on your guard.'

'Against what? Nothing is going to happen to me.' Sapphire wanted to cheer Lulu for standing up for herself.. But James was right to be concerned as well. Sapphire found herself on the fence with this one.

'Where is he taking you?' asked James.

'I don't know, he didn't say.'

'Well, before you go, find out and I want you to give me his phone number and the name and address of the restaurant or pub... or whatever...'

'I think that is a good idea, if I may say so,' said

Sapphire, 'All the people I know who do internet dating have a friend that they text periodically during the evening to let them know how things are going.'

'I can't text all night, Sapphire!' said Lulu with a horrified expression.

'Not all the time, of course, but when you go to the ladies, or when he leaves for whatever reason—fire off a quick text.'

'But don't go to the ladies too often or he'll think you've got cystitis.'

'James!' said Lulu and Sapphire together and then they both burst out laughing.

'Just trying to lighten the mood,' he said, but Sapphire could tell he was still worried.

Sapphire had to admit that the lamb was the best she had ever tasted, and she adored roast lamb, especially with a hint of rosemary. Mrs Lewis had done a wonderful job; the meat was succulent, medium rare, and served with blackcurrant jelly, crispy roast potatoes, buttered cabbage, carrots and the richest, most flavourful gravy she had ever had.

'This is gorgeous, Mrs Lewis,' she said.

'Thank you. I make a good roast dinner if I do say so myself.'

'It's one of the best I've ever had.'

'Have some more then,' said Mrs Lewis.

'I will, thank you. Is there any more gravy?'

'Can I have some more?' asked Lulu.

'Yes, but only when you've eaten what's on your plate.'

'Okay,' said Lulu.

Sapphire glanced at James who was watching her reaction. She'd talk to him later, as the dynamics in this family were puzzling to say the least. Lulu acted and was treated like a child, but she was celebrating her twenty-sixth birthday. There were secrets in the Lewis family, and she wanted to know what they were.

For now, though, it was enough to be enjoying this glorious roast dinner and listen to the conversation around the table. Sometimes you picked up a lot about people from small talk and body language. People gave themselves away, especially when they had something to hide.

'How's the job going, Phoebe?' asked James.

'It's fine. In fact, although I didn't want to say anything yet, I might be in line for a partnership next year.'

'Well done!' said James.

'Yes, that's great,' said Sapphire, 'Many congratulations.' Another woman pushing through the glass ceiling. Sapphire approved.

'Mum? Got nothing to say to me?' Phoebe asked.

Sapphire could feel James tense next to her and she wondered if it was all going to kick off. There was a lot of emotion simmering under the surface in this family. She put her head down and kept eating, pretending she wasn't listening.

'Well done, dear.'

'You could say it as if you mean it.' Phoebe deflated as if it wasn't worth the effort.

'I'm glad you're doing well in your job, Phoebe, but it's only what we all expect. And anyway, you've never cared about my feelings before.'

'That's rubbish, Mum, and you know it. I've always wanted your approval, but you and Dad never had much time for me. Not after Lulu was born, anyway.'

'Well you know why. She took up all of our time.'

'Right,' said James, 'If we've all finished, let's get the cake in and we can sing Happy Birthday.' He stood up and left the room, carrying the tureen that had held the vegetables.

Lulu, who had been sitting quietly with her head down, suddenly perked up.

'Happy Birthday to me, Happy Birthday to Me…' she sang quietly to herself.

Sapphire stood up and started to collect the plates. She wondered if someone would stop her, telling her that, as a guest, she didn't need to do that, but no one did. She hurried into the kitchen after James.

'Sorry about that,' said James, putting the tureen into the dishwasher. Sapphire added the plates.

'No need to apologise. You did warn me.'

'Yes, I did, didn't I?' He put his hands on each side of her head and kissed her deeply. She responded, luxuriating in the scent of his skin, the feel of his hands holding her.

'We'll go after Lulu's blown the candles out. I want to be alone with you.'

'Fine by me.' She wanted to be alone with James. It seemed ages since they had made love and she was feeling horny. What she had in mind wasn't like the wild, passionate coupling that occurred the first time. She wanted to lie next to him and take her time. Turn him on slowly so he was desperate for her, then let him take her to new heights…

'I know what you're thinking about,' he said huskily.

'Do you?' she whispered.

'I can see it in your eyes, hear it in your irregular breathing and taste it on your skin.' He kissed her on the side of the neck, then licked her there, causing a surge of need to pass through her.

'Come on,' he said, 'I'll take the cake, you bring the matches and tapers.'

They went back into the dining-room, where the three women were sitting silently and avoiding eye contact, each in their own space. The only one who looked happy was Lulu, whose eyes lit up when she saw the cake.

'Oh, James! Will you take a picture when I blow out the candles?'

'Of course. Sapphire? Would you help me light them please?'

'Yep.' Sapphire lit a match and then the wax taper and proceeded to light the twenty-six candles that huddled together on top of an ordinary looking cake, with white icing and Happy Birthday Lulu in pink icing. She imagined there wouldn't have been much point in having anything else as the candles obscured the top of the cake anyway.

'Okay, are you ready?' asked James as he aimed his mobile at Lulu.

She blew, then blew again, twice, and, eventually, all the candles were out.

'Hooray,' shouted James and Lulu beamed.

'Right. Lulu—we need to leave now, but I'll see you back home, okay?'

'Okay.'

Sapphire had expected Lulu to beg them to stay a bit longer, but now the meal was over, she seemed quite happy for them to go. She realised that she couldn't help thinking of Lulu as a child, and expecting her to act like one, but she was a grown woman. She was puzzling and Sapphire decided to ask James about her on the drive back.

'Yes, I think I'll go too,' said Phoebe, standing up and walking into the hall.

'You okay on your own with Mum?' asked James.

'Of course,' said Lulu.

'We've always been alright together before. You lot go and leave us in peace,' said Mrs Lewis, making shooing motions with her hands. She smiled to show that she didn't really mean it.

It'll be a pleasure, thought Sapphire who couldn't get the measure of the woman at all. She was an enigma, a bit like her younger daughter. Except for her cooking skills. James just laughed and kissed his mother on the cheek.

'Bye then,' shouted Phoebe from the hallway.

'Bye,' replied Lulu and Mrs Lewis in muted tones.

When they got outside, Phoebe was waiting on the driveway. 'Thank God that's over.'

'Amen to that,' said James.

'It was nice meeting you, Phoebe,' said Sapphire.

'Likewise, I like your fashions and the perfume. I'm glad James is working somewhere decent for once.'

James said nothing but headed to the sports car. Phoebe didn't move but watched them both as they climbed into the car and sped off towards the motorway. Sapphire glanced back at the house. Phoebe was reversing her car out of the driveway.

Chapter Eighteen

'Okay, so how bad was it, honestly?' James asked as he turned onto the roundabout that took them to the motorway.

'What? Meeting your family? It was fine. I enjoyed myself. Lulu was sweet over the cake and your mum's a great cook. I loved the lamb. After all, you're not the Addams Family are you?'

James laughed, the most relaxed sound she'd heard from him all day.

'Not quite. Who would I be? Uncle Fester?'

'You'd be Gomez and I would be Morticia.'

James laughed again and Sapphire couldn't wait to get home, she put her hand on his leg and squeezed.

'That means you'd have to become one of the family. I think you'd hate that,' James said.

Sapphire took her hand away and clasped her hands together in her lap.

'Why didn't Lulu come back with us? Isn't she working tomorrow?'

'It's half term and she wants to spend next week with Mum. She'll get the train back on Friday morning.'

'Then she'll have the rest of the day to prettify herself for her big date.'

'I wish she wasn't going on it,' said James with feeling.

'May I ask why? I know Lulu hasn't had much experience with men but she's a pretty girl and... well, she deserves to fall in love if that's what she wants.'

James was silent and Sapphire took the opportunity to study his face. He looked strained; he was frowning, and his hands were tense on the steering wheel.

'Has something happened to Lulu? Has she had a bad experience in the past with a boyfriend?'

'No, nothing like that. Lulu is... well, different. The truth is she's-'

Just then, Sapphire's phone rang. She took it out of her handbag. 'I need to get this,' she said to James, then speaking into the phone she said, 'Hi, Monica, how's things?'

While James drove fast, but safely, down the motorway, Sapphire caught up on all the news with her bestie. She would have to quiz James about his family some other time.

When the call ended, she turned her attention back to James. And all she could think about what how much she wanted him. She put her hand back on the top of his thigh.

'Are you trying to get me to break the speed limit?'

'Who me? Perish the thought.' She squeezed and he put his hand over hers briefly.

'Although for you it would be worth it. It's been too long,' he said quietly.

They had started undressing each other as soon as they were in the house in Primrose Hill. It was unhurried, as if what they were going to do was inevitable, but they had all the time in the world. There was none of the wild desperation they felt at the beginning of their relationship. Sapphire helped him to pull off her dress, she then undid the buttons on his black shirt. They left a trail of clothes from the front door, up the stairs and across the landing. By the time they reached James's bedroom, they were both naked.

James wanted to savour the moment, as if it was all they had, and he needed to make the most of it. Sapphire's skin was soft. He stroked her arms from her shoulders, down to her elbows, then further down to her wrists, stroking lightly so goosebumps stood up on her skin. He held her hands in his and simply gazed at her. Her hair was loose and mussed from being blown about in the car. Her eyes were bright, and the pupils dilated with desire. He let go of one of her hands and traced the features on her now familiar and beautiful face. Perfectly shaped eyebrows, a straight nose, wide generous mouth, small neat chin and long slender neck.

'What are you thinking about? You look deep in thought.'

'I was wondering which one I would be if I could be either a painter or a sculptor. If I could paint you, I would capture the many shades of colour—your skin, eyes, hair, not to mention nail polish. If I could sculpt, I could capture your lines—the beautiful curves, dips, and hollows, and, of course, your voluptuous breasts.'

'Can you do either?'

'No, I'm afraid not. Art has never been my strong point. Can't even sketch.'

'Pity,' said Sapphire shaking her head.

'Yes,' said James as he pulled Sapphire to him. 'But I can do this.' He kissed her hand. 'And this.' He kissed her forehead, then her nose until their mouths met in a deep, passionate kiss. Neither wanted it to end, but eventually Sapphire pulled away.

'Let's get into bed.'

'Good idea.' He pulled back the duvet and Sapphire climbed in. Della was looking after Sparkle for the weekend, so Sapphire was free to spend the night with him. They had the place to themselves. Bliss.

'James, tell me about Lulu. You have hinted that she is different, but in what way?'

Sapphire's question slowed him down for a second but then he climbed into the bed and covered Sapphire's body with his own. His erection was getting harder and this was not the time for a serious conversation.

'I will tell you all about Lulu, but not right at this minute. There's only one person I want to focus on now and that's you.' He kissed her, then rolled over onto his back, taking her with him, so that she lay on top of him. 'Now that feels good.' His erection was pressing into her stomach and she moved upwards and straddled him.

'Condom James?'

'Top drawer of the bedside cabinet. I can't reach from here.'

Sapphire got off the bed, opened the drawer and took out a packet of condoms. He would have loved to have had sex without one, but it was safer if they were protected.

A thought came into his head. Did Lulu know about protection if she met someone and wanted to…? He couldn't continue. The image his thoughts produced were disturbing and inappropriate. He had to keep in his mind that Lulu was a grown woman. He had always known this time would come eventually. He needed to deal with it.

He kissed Sapphire and lay obediently still while she rolled the condom onto his erect penis. The touch of her fingers as she sheathed him forced thoughts of anyone but Sapphire out of his mind.

Then she moved over him and guided him into her slowly and steadily. He watched her face as she did so, marvelling at how quickly her arousal grew. She was moaning softly and moving gently with him inside her.

James reached up and cupped her breasts. She took his hands and held onto them around his wrists as he played with her nipples, running his thumbs around them in small circles, feeling them harden at his touch. He knew what she liked now; how firm or how soft a touch on her breasts, a light brushing stroke on her stomach which always drove her wild, kisses on her neck and inner thighs.

He wondered if he was in danger of becoming too predictable. If he did, would Sapphire grow bored and find someone new? Neither of them had mentioned the time limit on their relationship, but James was constantly aware that this could be the last time he made love to her.

Then all his doubts came to nothing as Sapphire orgasmed. He hadn't realised she was that close. She spasmed and threw her head back as her orgasm ripped through her. He held her hips as best he could and thrust up at the same time as she squeezed harder. She cried out and James was glad that Lulu wasn't in the house or she might have thought someone was being murdered.

She was riding him as hard as she could, and James loved every second. She was chasing another orgasm, thrashing around on top of him and he could feel all his inhibitions drift away as his arousal peaked.

'Yes, yes, yes…' he cried as he came in spectacular fashion.

'Mmm,' moaned Sapphire, slowing coming down from her multiple orgasms.

When they were still, Sapphire carefully got off him and he removed the condom and disposed of it.

When he returned, Sapphire was lying on her back, her arms out to the sides, her breathing slowly returning to normal. He had never known a woman who put so much effort into her sexual fulfillment. He wondered if she was like this with every man she had been with. He didn't really want to dwell on her other lovers. She was with him now, for as long as they were both happy to enjoy sex together.

She opened her arms and he climbed into bed and hugged her.

'That was amazing,' he said.

'It's always amazing with you. Your previous lovers must have taught you well.'

He was about to say that there hadn't been that many, when a picture of Ruth came into his mind. They had enjoyed a satisfactory sex life and it could have been better with time. But Ruth chose to be with Malcolm not him, so that was that. Seeing her again, through the leaves of the palm tree, had brought back memories. He had enjoyed being engaged and planning the wedding, choosing a venue for the honeymoon. He had enjoyed sex with her, too. Nothing compared to the way he felt about Sapphire. The sex they enjoyed was the best he had ever had. And he enjoyed Sapphire's company, loved wining and dining her. Even Sunday lunch at his mother's house was more enjoyable having Sapphire to share it with him.

As he lay in the dark, Sapphire's head on his chest, he wondered if his feelings for Sapphire were changing. Maybe it was time to admit, if only to himself, that he was beginning to fall a little bit in love with Sapphire Bell-Johnson.

Chapter Nineteen

James spent most of his spare time trying to discover the identity of the mystery investor, but by Friday afternoon he had to admit defeat. Fortunately, he knew someone who would be able to do a better job—at a price. A man whose services he had used once before.

When he had suspected that Malcolm wasn't being entirely honest with him, he employed a private investigator to look into his business dealings. Ian Nightingale had come highly recommended and James understood why. He looked more like an accountant than the image James had of a PI. He was middle-aged, short, slightly overweight, sandy haired with no distinguishing features. A nondescript type of man who could blend in with any crowd or pass unnoticed in a pub or restaurant.

But, the man had a brilliant mind, could think on his feet, and get to the core of a problem in record time. He could hack into any website and extract information from the most encrypted account and had no compunction in ignoring confidentiality to obtain the information he needed. Phone tapping came as standard. In short, the man was a genius.

James had sent Angie out on an errand, so had the office to himself. He rang Ian's number and it was answered almost straight away.

'Ian… James Lewis here. How are you?'

'James, nice to hear from you. I'm fine thanks. I take it you have a job for me?'

James smiled. Ian was a man of few words and had little time for small talk. 'I have. Two things really. The man you investigated before has a new company called Dalton Mackenzie. I'm sure it's a front. I want to know what he's up to.'

'Of course, I remember him well. And the second thing?'

'I'm working for a company called Sapphire Enterprises, which includes the House of Sapphire—it's a fashion house.'

'I've heard of it.'

'Good. Well, we have a mystery investor. He's buying shares but we can't find anything on him at all. We need to know who he is. I'll email you the information.'

'No problem. Leave it with me. Usual fees apply. I'll contact you when I have something.'

'Great. Thanks Ian.'

James sat back in his chair, lost in thought. He really didn't want anything to do with Malcolm Steele and hoped the information Ian turned up proved that he had turned over a new leaf and was trading legitimately as an honest citizen. *Hah! Fat chance.*

His thoughts turned to Ruth and her betrayal. He must have been stupid not to have seen what was in front of his eyes. He trusted her, believing that she loved him.

How did the song go? What a fool believes? Something like that.

James turned back to his computer screen and a spreadsheet he had been working on, just as Angie came into the office.

'There's a woman in reception who would like a word, James, shall I bring her up?'

'What woman?'

James felt irritated at the interruption. He was behind with the figures he needed to balance in order to impress the board members. He had yet to find the perfect company for Sapphire Enterprises to invest in, but there were three that looked as if they might be suitable. He needed to convince the members of the board and, more importantly, Sapphire, that the money they would sacrifice would have a good return on investment. So far, though, it looked as if the numbers were falling short. They needed to invest a small fortune in order to recoup the losses the company was making.

'She didn't give her name,' said Angie hovering around him and straightening papers on his desk. It was one of her more annoying habits. She seemed to think that all the papers should be in a neat pile, whereas James had papers fanned out on his desk so he could see the ones he wanted at a glance.

'What does she want?'

'She didn't say.'

James bit back a sarcastic comment and sat back in his chair. 'Does she want to speak to Sapphire?' Wannabe designers, fresh out of college, were always calling without an appointment, on the off chance that the frantically busy designer/owner would drop everything, cancel appointments and go without lunch, just to take a look at designs she wouldn't be seen dead wearing. They were young and believed in their own talent. Some of them might eventually go on to become world famous. If Sapphire had a spare five minutes, she might take pity on them and give their portfolio the once over. But not today; Sapphire had wall-to-wall meetings which were going on into the evening.

'No, James, she asked to speak to you.'

'She asked for me by name?'

'Yes. She said she would wait as long as it took.'

'Well, whoever she is, if she wants a word, she can have this one—no. I'm far too busy to speak to randoms wandering in off the street. Don't bother going down, just phone the receptionist to tell her to make an appointment. And find out what she wants.'

'Yes, James,' said Angie who hurried off to make the call from her own tiny office. Angie was proving to be quite a good PA all things considered, despite her various irritating habits. Giggling being one, flirting, bad time keeping, chewing gum, straightening his papers... Five minutes later she was back.

'She said to tell you her name is Ruth, as if that would make any difference. It wouldn't, would it James?' Angie grinned expecting him to share in the joke, but James was stunned and could only sit and stare at Angie in disbelief.

'James? Are you okay? You've gone a bit pale.'

'Yes, I'm okay.' He got up and strolled over to the water cooler in the corner to get himself a drink and try and get his thoughts together while his back was to the room. 'Listen, maybe I've been hasty. I will see her after all, just briefly. Could you go and collect her please, Angie.'

'Shall I make coffee?' She was staring at him in amazement. He didn't usually make such dramatic U-turns. If he made a decision he stuck to it.

'Not yet, let's see what she wants first. She may not be staying long.'

'Okay.' Angie left the office and James stood, holding his paper cup of water, and wondering what the hell Ruth wanted to see him about and how she had tracked him down. Maybe she *had* seen him hiding behind the potted palm after all.

He swallowed the water and scrunched the paper cup into a tight ball, then threw it angrily into the bin. He needed to be calm and collected when she arrived. She mustn't see how much her turning up like this had rattled him. He loved this woman once, had been prepared to give her everything he possessed, and she betrayed him in the worst possible way. He would be cold and distant, unemotional. Except part of him felt excited at the prospect of seeing her again. He mustn't let that part have the upper hand. He would hear her out, then ask her to leave. What the hell could she possibly want with him after all this time?

He walked towards his desk, taking deep slow breaths as he went.

'James, Ruth is here.' Angie's voice sent his heart racing and he turned slowly to face the two women.

'Thank you Angie. I'll ring if we need anything.' Thankfully his voice didn't betray his emotions. He wanted to go and sit behind his desk, making Ruth stand. He was determined to be the one in control in this meeting, but he just stood there like a dummy and stared at the woman who had broken his heart.

He had expected her to look defiant, gloating possibly. When he studied her face, her eyes held fear and shame.

She looked beaten down, not triumphant. Whatever had happened to her since she trampled all over his feelings and kicked his heart around like a football, she was suffering now.

That thought should have made James feel pleased, vindicated. But it didn't.

'It's good to see you again,' she said quietly.

'It's a pity I can't say the same. I'm very busy, so please just say whatever it is you've come here to say and then go.'

'Yes, of course, I didn't expect you'd see me at all, but I had to try.'

'May I take your coat?' She was wearing a rather heavy red winter coat, despite the warm weather, one hand holding it closed in front of her. Then she nodded and turned away as she slipped it off her shoulders.

James got the second shock of the day. Ruth was pregnant. He was no expert on these matters, but he would guess she was at least six months into her pregnancy.

'I see congratulations are in order,' he said stiffly, glancing briefly at her expanding waistline.

'Thanks,' she said quietly.

He glanced at her hands. She wasn't wearing rings. That in itself, of course, proved nothing, many people didn't bother wearing wedding rings these days. James wondered why some people got married at all, if they had no respect for the traditions. If things had been different and their marriage had gone ahead, he would have worn a ring and he would have wanted Ruth to as well.

Ruth lifted up her hands and splayed her fingers, turning them around so he could inspect them. 'No rings,' she said with a sad little smile. 'We never got that far.'

'What makes you think I'm remotely interested? What you and lover-boy do is no longer any of my concern.'

'I have a lot to apologise for, haven't I?' Ruth was standing a few feet away from him and he had no choice but to look at her face as she spoke. But it was tearing him apart.

'It's a bit late for an apology. Anyway, you got what you wanted. Did he make you a partner in the business? Are you doing well? I have to confess I've lost touch with Lewis Leathers. I haven't bothered checking share prices so I've no idea how you're doing.'

'James...'

'Not that I care. I've moved on. A long way.'

'James...' Her voice was fainter this time and he looked at her closely. She was pale and her eyelids were fluttering in an alarming way.

'Oh God, Ruth, sit down. Are you feeling faint? Let me help you.' He was beside her in seconds and holding her up with his arm around her waist and his other hand holding her hand. He half dragged her to the only comfortable seat in his office; a small two-seater settee with no cushions or arms. He guided her gently so that she was sitting with her head resting back.

She kept her eyes closed but her breathing was deeper.

'May I have some water?'

'Of course.' He got up and grabbed a paper cup, filled it to the top, spilling some on the carpet in his haste. Then he sat next to her while she drank it and watched her face for the colour returning to it. Thankfully it didn't take very long.

'Better?' he asked. Without even thinking of what he was doing, he took her hand and stroked it as he used to do when they were together.

She nodded, then burst into tears.

James jumped up again and grabbed a couple of tissues

out of the box on his desk, then returned to sit next to her, pressing the tissues into her hands.

'Oh, James, I'm so sorry, so very sorry.'

'Hush, just calm yourself now, you've got the baby to think of.' Malcolm's baby. That didn't matter, he just wanted Ruth to stop crying.

Gradually her tears dried, and her head fell naturally onto James's shoulder. They sat like that for a few moments, James experiencing déjà vu and wondering how to extricate himself, when he heard a quiet knock on the door. Before he could answer, the door opened, and Angie walked in.

'Sorry to bother you, but I wondered if you… oh.' She trailed off when she saw them sitting closely together. 'I thought you might like…' She was staring in bewilderment at Ruth's belly and her head on James's shoulder. He dropped Ruth's hand as if it were a hot potato, but realised it was too late. Angie was a known gossip and this little tryst would be all over Sapphire Enterprises by the end of the working day.

'Tea, yes. Thank you Angie, that's a splendid idea. Ruth felt faint and I had to help her to sit down.'

'Right,' said Angie as if she didn't believe a word. 'Tea. Milk and sugar?'

'Yes, bring the lot, please,' said James who just wanted her out of the office. 'And biscuits.'

'Of course.' She smiled and left.

'Are you feeling better now?' asked James.

'Yes, thank you. I'm sorry about that. I have low blood pressure.'

'When's the baby due?'

'In three months' time.'

'Well, I wish you both the best of luck with it all.' He stopped, his throat dry. They had talked about having a family, himself and Ruth; they'd talked into the early hours about their hopes and dreams for the future, and it always included children.

'James,' said Ruth quietly, 'it's not the way you think. Malcolm and I are over. He was screwing around and when I told him about the baby, he ended it. He doesn't want kids you see, and…'

'The bastard! He made you pregnant and then dumped you? The rotten, lousy—'

'James…' Ruth put her hand on his arm, and he stopped talking but he was seething inside. He had a good mind to go around and punch the man's light's out. Only he didn't know where they were living and the woman he was thinking of defending didn't want him anyway. None of it was any of his business.

He stood up as Angie brought the tea in. He took the tray from her and put it on the coffee table in front of the couch.

'Is there anything else you want, James?' Angie asked.

'No, that's all, thanks.'

'Right. Okay, then, I'll go back to my office. I'll be there if you need anything.' Angie was staring at Ruth as if she was trying to memorise her appearance, clothes and shoes.

'Angie?'

'Yes?'

'Just make sure we're not disturbed again would you please?'

'Of course, James, I'll make sure nobody comes anywhere near.' She left, not realising that the subtext to his request was that she herself was to stay away and not disturb them.

James poured tea into the cups and added milk and sugar; two teaspoons for himself and one for Ruth. Then he opened the biscuits and put two in the saucer. He gave Ruth hers and she took it and murmured a thanks.

'Tell me something,' he said after he sat down again. 'How did you find me?'

'Really?' she asked and smiled up at him. 'It wasn't difficult, James, your photo was in all the local papers, and splashed all over social media, carrying Ms Bell-Johnson out of her own fashion show. I imagine you've become quite the celebrity after that little stunt.'

'It wasn't a stunt, she was ill.' At the mention of Sapphire, he felt a twinge of guilt. What would he tell her? Angie was probably on the jungle drums right now, spreading the word of the woman in his office.

'Oh, I'm sure,' said Ruth, 'I didn't mean anything by it. That's how I tracked you down, anyway.'

'Does Malcolm know you're here?'

'Good God, no. He mustn't find out either. I need your help and he mustn't know we are back in contact again.'

'Help with what?' James swallowed the rest of his tea and gave Ruth his full attention. Now that the shock of seeing her again was starting to wane, he wanted to find out exactly what was going on.

'I didn't realise what a dishonest man he really was. Everything he told me was a lie. He said you were the one who was putting the company at risk by insider trading and that you were making money hand over fist and was planning to buy him out. He said he had to get in first and— stupid I know—but I believed him. I would never have got involved with him if I'd known what he was really like.'

'And what's he really like?' James wasn't buying this. Ruth must have known what a devious bastard Malcolm was. They were lovers after all.

'He's corrupt. He's been using company money to buy

shares using aliases, with the intention of becoming a majority shareholder and taking over the companies. That's what he did to you, wasn't it?'

'You know it is, Ruth, you were part of it.' James felt cold. She was just as guilty as the slime ball that James used to call a friend.

'I don't blame you for being angry, but you must believe me, James, I never wanted to hurt you. I'm so sorry for what we did to you.'

He got up and started pacing. 'Hurt doesn't come even close. You nearly destroyed me. Between the two of you I lost everything that meant anything to me, except my mother and sisters and you would have taken them too if you could.'

'No, you're wrong, I never wanted you to lose everything.'

'So why did you have an affair with him? What did he give you that I didn't?'

'I can't explain it... Malcolm was, well... persuasive. He promised me a life that I'd only ever dreamed of. He said we'd have exotic holidays in the Bahamas and go to Las Vegas... Monte Carlo, the glamourous lifestyle. It was intoxicating listening to him and I believed everything he told me. He swept me off my feet and promised me the world...' she trailed off and looked at him helplessly.

'Surely you knew that what he was doing was illegal and if he got caught you could both go to prison?'

'He promised me we wouldn't get caught and that there was no proof of anything, so we were quite safe.'

'And you believed him?' James could hardly keep the incredulity out of his voice. He'd always thought Ruth had more sense.

'I had no reason not to.'

'Apart from the fact that you knew how dishonest he was.'

'Don't be angry, James, please. I know I've been a fool but I'm paying the price now.'

'How?'

'I found out he had other women and I challenged him about it. He said that he had never promised me exclusivity.' Ruth wiped her eyes, but James wondered how much of this was real.

'And had he?'

'Well… maybe not in so many words, but he led me to believe we had a future together.'

'And then you got pregnant? An accident?'

Ruth looked away and James wondered if she had planned it; a ruse to get him to stay with her.

'Yes, of course. I thought he'd be happy about it, once the shock had worn off.'

'I think I've heard enough. I can't believe how stupid you've been to put your faith in a man like that.'

'Talk about the pot calling the kettle black. You went into business with him.' Ruth had lost all pretence of playing the innocent party, her face was hard, and her voice held a hint of sarcasm.

James stood in the middle of the office and stared at Ruth. How could he have ever thought he was in love with this woman? She was avaricious, hard-faced and as devious as Malcolm in her own way.

'I think you'd better leave,' he said, 'I've got rather a lot on in my life at the moment and I would rather like to get back to it. I'm sorry you've found yourself pregnant and alone, but I'm sure you'll survive. You never know, maybe you could persuade Malcolm to take you back.'

'I don't want him back,' she spat the words out. 'I want

to bring him down, expose him for the grubby little philanderer he is. I want to see him rot in hell.'

James was shocked by her vehemence, but not really surprised. The Ruth he fell in love with bore little resemblance to the woman sitting in front of him. Hell hath no fury like a woman scorned.

'And you need my help?'

'Yes,' she looked at him and smiled, 'together we could expose him. I can't do it without you, James, I need you.'

'Give me one good reason why I should help you?'

'Well isn't it obvious? You've just been telling me how we took everything away from you, and I'm offering you the chance to get it back again. All of it.' She was looking at him in a way that was unmistakable; a predatory look. A look that told him everything he needed to know concerning her intentions.

'I'm afraid it isn't obvious, so please enlighten me—what exactly are you offering me?'

'The chance to turn back the clock, to regain control of the business that is rightfully yours—'

'Just to clarify, do you mean Lewis Leathers?'

Ruth laughed and swept her hair back from her face, 'Of course I mean Lewis Leathers, what other company is there?'

There's Dalton Mackenzie for a start. It was obvious to James that Ruth hadn't seen him behind the overgrown palm. If she had, she'd be the one grilling him about his intentions.

'And how do you intend to bring him down and steal his company? Not the same way you did it to me, surely? He's going to be wise to that trick.'

'It's not stealing, James, it's just giving the company back to its rightful owner. Isn't that what you want? Surely you're not happy playing second fiddle to the design queen are you? Don't you want to be back in the driver's seat? In charge again?'

Of course he did, he wanted all those things. He intended to achieve them honestly, with hard work and transparency in all his dealings. The big question hadn't yet been answered.

'What's in it for you, Ruth?'

She smiled then, a slow seductive lifting of the corners of her mouth and her eyebrows, making her expression gentler. Her eyes flashed a message that at one time James would have responded to, but now just left him cold. It was so contrived.

James gave her his best poker face; neutral, relaxed and unsmiling. Never again would he let this woman know what was going on in his mind for he trusted her as much as he trusted Malcolm. Not at all.

'It's like I said before,' she murmured, 'you can have it *all* back if you help me.'

'What about the baby?'

She sat back and gazed at him. 'I didn't think the baby would be a stumbling block for you. You love children, don't you? You always said you did. You could grow to love this one. Malcolm doesn't want anything to do with it, he's made that plain and to be honest, I'm relieved, he's hardly father material.'

'Perhaps you should have thought of that before you let him get you pregnant.'

'James!'

'You must think I'm a mug. I may have been once, because I mistakenly thought I was in love with you. Those days have gone, Ruth. I think you should leave now. You've said your piece and the answer is no. Please go.'

Ruth got up and stood in front of him, her gaze piercing

and defiant. 'I expected this. You were never the spontaneous kind. A man who could see the potential in a deal or opportunity straight away. You need to go home and think about it. No change there then.' She rummaged about in her handbag and produced a business card. 'Take my card and ring me when you've come to your senses. If we work together, we can bring Malcolm down and make sure he stays down. Then he can't hurt anyone else. Isn't that what you want? You could have your company back and you could have me. Think about it.'

Ruth strolled over to the chair where James had put her coat. She didn't put it on but carried it over her arm. She'd only worn it to hide her pregnancy. She'd thought of everything, but she was leaving empty-handed. James had a good mind to throw her card in the bin, but something made him slip it into his pocket.

'We'll speak later,' said Ruth as she opened the door and left.

'Over my dead body,' James murmured, to himself.

Chapter Twenty

'I'm going to work from home for the rest of the afternoon,' James said to Angie as he stood in the doorway of her office.

'Okay, James. See you on Monday then. I hope you have a lovely weekend.'

'Yes. Thanks. You too. Ah…Angie?'

'Yes, James?'

'Have you mentioned my visitor to anyone?'

'Oh no. Discretion is my middle name. Well, it isn't really, it's Barbara.' Angie giggled then said, 'I've never liked that name anyway.' James gave her a strained smile.

'Good… I think we should keep it to ourselves for now. Okay?'

'Oh yes, of course. Only…'

'Yes?'

'Well, I did say something to Della, but that was because she was in reception when I went to fetch the woman. She made a joke about her wearing a big coat and I said she was probably trying to hide something, and…'

'And?'

'Well, Della asked if she was pregnant and I said I'd let her know. So I rang her later and told her that she was. Sorry—did I do the wrong thing?'

James held back a sigh. 'No, don't worry about it. See you on Monday.'

'Bye, James.'

He would have to talk to Sapphire before he left now. If Della knew, Sapphire knew; that was how they operated.

As if he didn't have enough to worry about with Lulu's date that night, he now had to explain why he had his pregnant ex-fiancée in his office. He could take the easy way out and tell her the truth, or he could lie. By the time he reached Sapphire's office, he still hadn't decided which way to go.

Sapphire's next meeting started in twenty minutes, but instead of preparing herself and getting her notes together, she lounged in her chair, staring into space, tapping the desk with her biro.

Della had told her that James had a pregnant woman in his office. Nothing unusual in itself, but Angie had told Della that they had been sitting close together and holding hands. That fact was tearing her apart. Who was she? An old friend? A family member who had come to James for help? A woman called Ruth. The name of his ex-fiancée. Was it the same Ruth?

Sapphire knew she wouldn't be able to concentrate on work unless she had the answers to her questions, and she had important meetings to get through.

She picked up her phone and dialled Angie's number.

'James Lewis's office.'

'James please,' she barked at Angie's cheerful greeting.

'Oh, hi Sapphire! You've just missed him I'm afraid. He's going home to work. That visitor has upset him a bit.'

'Visitor? And which visitor is that, Angie?'

'Oh, I'm not really at liberty to say. James asked me not to tell anyone.'

'Did he indeed.'

Just then, James put his head around the door of Sapphire's office.

'Never mind,' she snapped and slammed the phone down.

'Sapphire… just wanted to tell you that I'm working from home for the rest of the day. I want to be there to talk to Lulu before her date.'

'You're worried about Lulu?'

'Yes, you know I am.'

'Come in a minute, James, would you?'

He came in reluctantly and put his briefcase on the floor.

'What's up?'

'I was hoping you could tell me. Is it the same Ruth?'

James sighed and collapsed on the sofa before answering. 'Yes. It appears she and Malcolm have split up and she needs help.'

'What kind of help?'

'Advice mainly, about her rights. She's pregnant and Malcolm is refusing to pay for the baby.'

'So, what—you're an expert on family law, are you? Know everything there is to know about paternity suits?'

'No, of course not. She came to me because, at one time, we were close, and she doesn't have anyone else to turn to.'

Sapphire didn't believe him. James was an honest man and she had learned that, on the few occasions he told her a white lie, he tugged the collar on his shirt, as if his lies were choking him, and couldn't meet her gaze. He was tugging now and staring at the floor.

'Are you going to help her?'

'I've given her the details of contacts to get in touch with, that's all.'

'Will you see her again?' Sapphire tried to be cool but could hear the pleading tone in her own voice, which meant that James would hear it too.

He looked up. His eyes were gentle and his voice soft, 'No, Sapphire, I won't be seeing her again. I feel nothing for her except pity. She's firmly in the past. I've moved on and I'm very happy in the place I'm in now.'

This time she knew he was telling the truth.

'Good. And for what it's worth, I'm pretty happy you're here too.'

He grinned and she wished she didn't have the wretched meetings. She'd much rather go home with James for a bit of afternoon delight.

'Will I see you tonight?' she asked.

'You can bet on it,' he said standing up and picking up his briefcase.

'See you later', she said as he blew her a kiss. 'And don't worry about Lulu, she'll be fine.'

When James got home, the house was empty. Lulu wasn't back yet. He sent her a quick text asking when she was leaving Mum's and she replied almost straight away and said she'd be leaving in an hour or so.

Although he felt too restless to work, he logged onto his computer to check his emails anyway. Perhaps the process of reading would calm his mind and help him to think more clearly. There was one from Ian Nightingale saying he had discovered something and asking him to ring as a matter of urgency. James phoned him straight away.

'Ian—what have you uncovered?'

'Quite a lot. The same man I investigated before is also behind both your other enquiries.'

Ian never mentioned names when he was on the phone just in case it was being bugged. James felt compelled to do the same.

'Hang on… do you mean the man who had the affair with my fiancée is the mystery investor in the company I'm working for now?'

'Correct. He'd been buying shares in a few companies, all in assumed names, taking them over and selling them off. He then transferred the money to an offshore bank.'

'You're using the past tense—is he not doing this anymore?'

'I need to do some more digging, but he started losing money recently. I'm trying to discover why. I'll get back to you with that.'

'And the other thing—the company I asked you to look into?'

'Bogus and being run by the same man.'

'Thanks Ian.'

James got up and went to the kitchen for a bottle of water. He would have dearly liked to have opened a bottle of wine, or had a snifter of brandy, but he needed to keep a clear head. He was seeing Sapphire later on, but before that had to watch Lulu get ready for her date and impose on her the importance of telling him where they were going and to text him as soon as they arrived. He was still debating whether to follow her—just to make sure she was okay. He wanted Lulu to be happy, second only to being safe.

As he drank the water, he quickly sent Ian his fee, his mind on the information he had just received. If Ruth had seen the photo of him carrying Sapphire out of the fashion show, then so must Malcolm. He picked Sapphire Enterprises because it was where he, James, was working. He certainly didn't pick it because of its profitability. The company was starting to slowly pick up but hadn't reached the level that a man like Steele would consider rich pickings.

Malcolm was still engaged in his dirty dealing, but it wasn't going to happen to Sapphire. He'd stop him somehow.

He felt claustrophobic. Even pacing around the room wasn't bringing him any release. There was only one thing that would.

James ran up the stairs to his bedroom and changed out of his suit into blue jeans and a sweatshirt. He put his trainers on and took his leather jacket from the wardrobe. He wouldn't bother with the leather trousers. Apart from the fact that it was far too hot, he wouldn't be out long as he needed to be back for Lulu. He grabbed his helmet and rang back down the stairs.

Once on the open road, James started to feel more in control. It was a glorious summer day and the sun bathed London in welcome warmth. He wanted to get out of the city, even for a short while, so he headed towards the countryside and relished the feel of the open road with the deep blue sky above and the roar of the bike's engine.

He planned his next move as he drove. He had to stop Steele without Sapphire knowing. He didn't want her to be involved in anything underhand. She had her reputation to think of, and a designer's reputation was the most important thing she had. He couldn't be responsible for the name of Sapphire Enterprises being tarnished in any way. He had been employed to help her company, not hinder it.

Thinking about Ruth's visit made James feel restless and anxious. Normally riding his bike had a calming effect. It was his way of meditating. Emptying his thoughts to everything but the truth. The only truth he was fixating on now was the fact that he needed Ruth's help after all to bring down Malcolm Steele and save Sapphire's company. The last thing he wanted was to need that woman for anything.

Ruth didn't know everything that had gone on when he lost his company, and he doubted very much that Steele would have enlightened her. For James had discovered, via the admirable Ian Nightingale, exactly what Steele had been doing. James knew dates, numbers of contacts, companies, and other things that, if made public, would have meant that Malcolm Steele would have served a considerable amount of time at Her Majesty's pleasure.

Ruth didn't know, for instance, that he and Steele had struck a deal of sorts. He had agreed not to go to the police with his information, in exchange for far more than his company was worth. He knew Steele had the money because he had worked out exactly how much he had made from the insider trading and it ran to millions. Steele had agreed as he had no choice, but he had made James sign a disclaimer agreeing never to share details of the company with anyone.

He needed to get that document back. Doubtless, Steele had made copies, but the original would be sitting in his safe. And the only other person who would have access to the safe was Ruth.

So, he had no choice. He needed Ruth's help. A thought that brought bile to his throat. He didn't want to ever see her again. He had promised Sapphire he wouldn't and now he would need to break his promise. He couldn't tell Sapphire the truth or he would never see *her* again, and that thought was unbearable.

He had been driving on autopilot, not aware of his surroundings or his place on the road. He didn't normally drive in such a fashion, but his mind was like a hamster going round a wheel relentlessly and getting nowhere.

Up ahead was a bridge, too narrow for two cars to pass, but adequate for his bike. Normally, he would have slowed down and gone across slowly and sensibly. Today, his feeling of reckless anger and frustration provoked him to accelerate. He hit the bridge at speed. Everything would have been fine—he still had perfect control of the Harley—if it hadn't been for a boy racer in a bashed-up Ford, who wasn't going to stop for anyone, or slow down for that matter, coming in the opposite direction.

The bike hit the car head-on. James felt himself being flung into the air and tossed like a bag of rubbish, over the bonnet. When he landed on the side of the road, awkwardly, he felt pain in his left leg, the like of which he would never have been able to imagine before. He started screaming. Mercifully, he lost consciousness.

Chapter Twenty-One

Sapphire was just leaving her office, having said goodnight to Della, when her mobile rang. She was surprised to see Lulu's name on the screen. She should be getting ready for her hot date by now. Perhaps she needed her advice about her make-up or was panicking about what to wear. Sapphire smiled as she answered.

'Hi, Lulu, how's it going? Not too nervous I hope?'

'I need your help. Can you take me to the hospital? We need to go straight away. He's not dead but I have to be there.'

'Hey, slow down. Who isn't dead? Lulu you're not making any sense.'

'James has broken his leg. He's in A&E. I rang Mum but she's out and so is Phoebe. Can you please take me to the hospital?'

'Of course, darling, just stay put, I'll come straight away.'

The line went dead, and Sapphire hurried down the stairs, not bothering to wait for the lift. When she got outside, she managed to flag a taxi straight away and sat back in the seat taking deep breaths while she phoned Lulu's number. She was in danger of hyperventilating and her heart was beating far too hard to be healthy.

'Lulu—it's Sapphire.'

'Yes, Sapphire,' said Lulu sounding remarkably calm.

'I'm in a taxi and am only a few minutes away, so tell me what this is all about. Start from the beginning. Did the hospital ring you?'

'Yes, about an hour ago.'

'An hour ago! What have you been doing? Why didn't you ring me straight away?'

'Because I was trying to ring mum and Phoebe. That is what I have to do if there is anything wrong—James first, then mum, then Phoebe. But they weren't there.'

'Well, I'm glad you rang me. You did the right thing. Okay, so what exactly did the hospital say?'

'It was a nurse. She said that James had been in an accident and had broken his leg, but he wasn't dead.'

'What… the nurse just came out and said he wasn't dead?'

'No, I asked her if he was dead and she said no.'

Sapphire was starting to feel lightheaded but this time it had nothing to do with her diabetes. She felt as if she was in a parallel universe and had no idea what was going on. The sooner she got to the hospital the better.

'What kind of accident was it?'

'It's called an RTA which stands for road traffic accident. His bike crashed headlong into a car, and he was thrown over the bonnet and landed on the road.'

'Oh, poor James. Why was he on his bike? Where was he going?'

'I don't know. The nurse didn't tell me that.'

Sapphire wondered if Lulu was in shock. She was speaking slowly and calmly, seemingly repeating things exactly as they had been told to her.

Then Sapphire remembered the hot date.

'Have you told your date that you have to cancel?'

'No.'

'Don't you think you should?'

'I don't know. Will he be angry?'

'Oh, Lulu, sweetheart, it doesn't matter if he is—this is an emergency. Look... don't do anything until I pick you up. You can ring him in the taxi, and I'll talk to him if he gets nasty.'

'Okay.'

'Right, I'm outside your house now. Are you ready?'

'Yes.'

Sapphire told the driver to wait. She got out of the taxi just as the front door opened and Lulu appeared with an overnight bag that looked stuffed to bursting.

'What's that for Lulu?'

'It's for James in case he needs to stay in hospital. The nurse said to bring a few items he might need. I didn't know what he'd need so I've brought as much as I can.'

'Right.' Sapphire eyed the bag suspiciously. She hoped his injuries weren't so severe he needed to stay in a long time, but if he did, Lulu had it covered. 'Let's go then.'

In the taxi, Lulu tried her date's number. 'It's gone to voicemail.'

'Send him a text,' said Sapphire.

'What shall I say?'

'Just say you have to cancel as your brother has been in an accident. You don't need to go into details.'

'Okay.'

Sapphire sighed and closed her eyes for a moment while Lulu texted.

'James never mentioned going anywhere on the bike,' Sapphire said as she mulled things over in her mind, 'he said he wanted to be home for you.'

Lulu said nothing but glanced at her phone periodically, then out of the window.

'Lulu, did you see him at all before he went out on the bike?'

'No, he wasn't there when I got home.'

'I wonder where he was going.' Again, Lulu said nothing, but continued to stare out of the window. She was too calm in Sapphire's opinion, almost as if she had gone into autopilot or had shut down emotionally.

Sapphire, however, was a mess. She felt sick at the thought of James lying in the road hurt. The memory of the accident she had seen previously, even though it was many years ago, still haunted her—the red blood against the green of the paramedic's uniform and the smashed-up bike lying on its side in the road. And James had been alone, with no one but strangers to tend to him, albeit strangers who were qualified medics and would have known exactly what to do to help James. What would she have done if she had witnessed it? She doubted she could have stayed calm. She would have lost it big time.

The taxi pulled up outside the doors of the Accident and Emergency Department and Sapphire pushed some notes into the driver's hand. They hurried into the chaos of the department, hardly registering the noise, the heat and the smell, and headed for the reception desk. Once they had been told where James was, they took off in the direction of the cubicles and eventually found him.

'James! Oh my God, are you okay?' Sapphire couldn't

maintain the calm manner she had told herself to adopt. Seeing him lying on the trolley, covered with a white sheet, his face cut and bruised and blood stains mingling with gravel from the road, she wanted to take him in her arms and hug him.

'Sapphire… Lulu… I'm so sorry…' he reached out his left hand and Sapphire took it.

'I brought your things like the nurse said,' Lulu put the bag on the floor and stood staring at her brother. 'I'm glad you're not dead,' she said calmly.

'Yes, I'm pretty relieved about that too,' he said trying to smile.

'How bad are you?' asked Sapphire stroking James's hair back from his forehead and examining the cuts on his face.

'They've x-rayed me, and the good news is that it's a closed fracture, I think they said a transverse fracture which means the bone is still aligned, so I just need a plaster cast— no surgery thank God.'

'That's a relief,' said Sapphire resisting the urge to kiss him. He looked so fragile lying on the hospital trolley with blood drying on his face and his leg supported by a strange looking contraption that Sapphire tried not to stare at.

'The bad news is that I'll never play rugby again.'

'Oh, that's a shame,' said Sapphire.

'You don't play rugby,' said Lulu.

'No and there's no chance I ever will now.'

Sapphire looked from James to Lulu in bewilderment. James groaned.

'Sorry, that was my idea of a joke. A bad one, obviously. I've been given some heavy-duty pain relief and my brain's frazzled.'

'What about the rest of you?' asked Sapphire, 'Do you have any other injuries?'

'Just cuts and bruises. My ribs ache and my back is killing me. But the x-ray didn't show anything else.'

'What about head injury? You were wearing your helmet I presume?'

'Of course, what do you take me for? On second thoughts, don't answer that. Anyway, my head's solid, nothing can touch it.' He tried to smile, but his eyelids were drooping and Sapphire, who had been holding his hand, brought it to her lips and kissed it.

'You weren't wearing your leather trousers were you?' Lulu was standing slightly away from the trolley and spoke quietly but without any accusation in her voice. She was simply stating a fact.

'No.' James turned his head carefully to look at her. 'I was stupid, wasn't I?'

'Yes,' she replied.

'Why James?!' Sapphire couldn't have been calm if her own life depended on it. She was feeling a mess of emotions and wanted to scream at him. 'You could have died. You have always told me how important it is to be properly attired to protect the body in case of accidents. Wearing leather offers the best chance of protection in case of an accident. You told me that every time we went out.' Sapphire had to make a concerted effort to slow down and stop the flow of words that tumbled out of her mouth.

He was staring at her in dismay and she felt awful suddenly for shouting at him. But she could have lost him and that thought alone was enough to bring her to her knees.

Just then a nurse came into the cubicle. At first Sapphire thought she was going to tell them to keep the noise down, but she spoke only to James.

'Right, Mr Lewis, we're going to put the plaster on your leg now, then you can go.'

'Oh, great—thanks nurse.'

'We'll wait outside, James,' said Sapphire, gesturing to Lulu to come with her.

They sat in the waiting area on uncomfortable plastic chairs. Lulu stared at the floor as if she was wishing herself anywhere else but there.

Sapphire tried to calm her beating heart and took slow and deep breaths in. She had her eyes shut, but the image of James lying on the hospital trolley, the blood stains obscenely red against the white of the sheet, wouldn't leave her mind.

'I need to get out of here,' Lulu said in a quiet trembly voice.

'Do you feel faint?'

She was looking desperately pale, much more than usual. She wore no make-up and her eyes were red-rimmed and darted here and there as people walked past her hurriedly and voices rose and fell in a wave of sound.

'I have to get out. I'm going outside.' Then she got up and started walking with her head down and her shoulders scrunched up as if she was dodging invisible missiles.

She was taking this very badly, thought Sapphire, as she watched her exit the hospital. Maybe she'd be better away from it for a while. Once they got James home, she'd be okay.

Sapphire wasn't used to just sitting—unless she had a glass of chardonnay in her hand and she was watching the waves break on a Caribbean beach, or was outside a cafe, sipping a cappuccino in an Italian city, people watching as smartly dressed locals promenaded up and down at dusk.

Sitting in a hot, noisy accident and emergency department with the smell of blood and urine in her nostrils was something entirely different. No wonder poor little Lulu had to get out. She was just about to get up and look for Lulu, when the curtains of James's cubicle were drawn back, and she got up and hurried over to him.

He was upright, looking a bit dazed with his hair sticking up. He was trembling slightly. He managed a brave smile as she came up to him.

'Hi, gorgeous,' he said.

'I'd like to return the compliment, but you look a sight,' she said feigning distaste, when all she wanted to do was throw her arms around his neck and make him promise never to buy another motor bike.

'Sorry. I am, Sapphire, really sorry for all this. I've been a fool.' He put his head down and she noticed the gravel that was stuck in his hair. She picked it out absentmindedly while thinking of how much this man was beginning to mean to her. Far more than she wanted him to. They had gone far beyond the no-strings-sex stage.

'Right, Mr Lewis, it's time for your departure.' A plump nurse carrying a pair of crutches interrupted Sapphire's musing. 'Here's your transport, so let's have you out of here. The fracture clinic will send you an appointment in about two weeks to see how you're getting on. Any questions?'

Sapphire had lots, but James just smiled weakly and shook his head.

'Right. Grab hold of the crutches and I'll give you a quick lesson in how to use them.'

Sapphire stepped outside the cubicle to phone a taxi while James huffed and puffed as he struggled off the trolley and swayed precariously between the crutches. The nurse stood by, making encouraging noises.

Sapphire ordered a black cab so there would be plenty

of room for James and his crutches. Then she stood, staring into the middle distance and thinking hard. There would have to be a few changes made. Would it be better if he came back to her apartment as it was all on one level and there was a lift from the ground floor? Or would he insist on going home? Maybe, once his mother and Phoebe found out about the accident, they would want him with them so they could look after him. And then there was Lulu. She was such an enigma. She wouldn't want to be separated from James. Maybe it would be better if he managed to get home and Lulu could take care of him.

'Right, he's all yours,' said the nurse who obviously couldn't wait to discharge James so she could deal with the multitude still in the waiting room. Who'd be a nurse these days? Obviously, someone dedicated with lots of stamina.

'Thanks,' said Sapphire trying to sound sarcastic, but desperate to get James out of the hospital and reunited with Lulu. Then they could get home and have a glass of wine— well, she and Lulu could, James was on strong painkillers— then talk through how they were going to manage everything.

Lulu was outside, gazing around and occasionally throwing anxious glances at the entrance to A&E. Sapphire could see her through the glass of the automatic doors even when they were still only halfway through the waiting area. She obviously hadn't wanted to move too far away in case she missed them.

Progress was slow. James was obviously still in considerable pain and was sweating profusely. He occasionally let his foot hit the floor accidentally and yelped which made Sapphire grab hold of him and they stopped until he had got himself together again. It was a tortuous journey but eventually they made it outside just as a black cab pulled up in an ambulance bay. Sapphire didn't care whether it was hers or not, they were taking it.

Eventually they were all settled in the back, which was another mammoth task. Fortunately, the driver got out to help. James looked as if he was about to pass out and Lulu kept throwing him anxious glances and looking away again.

'Lulu,' James said quietly, 'could you try ringing Mum and Phoebe again but tell them I'm fine and not to come over until tomorrow.'

'Okay.' Lulu got her phone out of her pocket and started pressing buttons.

'Did your hot date ever return your text?' asked Sapphire.

'No. I don't want to think about him at the moment,' said Lulu. She was looking at her phone and didn't even look up. Then she became quite animated when the call was answered.

'Mum? It's Lulu.'

With Lulu relaying events to her mother, Sapphire turned her attention back to James. He had given the driver his address as soon as they got into the cab and Sapphire was concerned.

'Are you sure you're going to be able to manage at home? Wouldn't you be better at mine?'

'Probably. In fact I did think about that for a couple of seconds, but I don't want Lu to be alone. And I'm going to have to get used to these things, so I may as well get thrown in at the deep end.'

'Thinking about practicalities for a moment, how are you going to get up the stairs? Or are you going to sleep downstairs? Is there even a bathroom downstairs?'

James grabbed her hand and kissed it the same way she had kissed his hand earlier. 'Stop worrying. The nurse said I need to get used to going up and down stairs as I need to be mobile. It's a balancing act, apparently; getting enough rest and not putting too much pressure on myself and keeping active so I don't seize up. She gave me some advice and I'm going to Google it when I get home and see what tips I can pick up.'

'No you are not, Mister. You're going to get in bed and sleep—you look absolutely shattered.'

'Only if you get in with me.'

'Tempting as that thought is, you need to rest. I'll stay for a while, but I need to go home eventually.'

'Thanks, Sapphire, you've been wonderful, I don't know what poor Lulu would have done without you. I'm really in your debt.'

'Well, I was in your debt at the fashion show, so let's call it quits. Agreed?'

'Agreed,' he said softly and gave her hand a squeeze.

Lulu was watching them solemnly from the other side of the taxi. She had taken the seat facing backwards to let them sit next to each other.

'Okay Lulu?' asked James.

'Mum is angry. She was ranting about how dangerous bikes are. She's going to get Phoebe to bring her tomorrow.'

'Where's Phoebe now?'

'A hen-night.'

'Oh, not her own I take it?' James grinned.

'She didn't say.'

'That was a joke, Lu.'

'Sorry.'

'Are you alright, sweetheart?' James sounded so concerned that Sapphire studied Lulu's face which was drawn and sad.

'Do you remember when Dad died?'

'Of course, darling, I'm hardly likely to forget it.' James turned to Sapphire. 'He had a heart attack on a Sunday. It was lucky that the whole family were there. We all went to A&E with him. He had another attack once there and they couldn't revive him.'

'Oh God, that's awful, I'm so sorry.'

'Is that it, Lu? Did the hospital remind you of that time?'

Lulu nodded her head and stared at the floor of the taxi.

'I'm so sorry, darling, I wouldn't have put you through that again for anything. God, I'm a total dick.'

There was silence in the taxi. Neither of the women contradicted him.

Chapter Twenty-Two

By the time the taxi drew up outside James's house, he was feeling sick. His leg was throbbing, every part of his body hurt, and he was so full of self-hatred that he didn't ever want to look at himself in the mirror again. How could he have been so utterly stupid as to ride his bike recklessly like that? He prided himself on being a careful bike rider, obeying all the rules and guidelines to the letter. Today, he let his emotions get the better of him and look at the consequences.

He had made poor Lulu relive the horror of the night their dad died, made her miss her first real date and heaven knows what Sapphire was missing out on because of him. Then he remembered that they were planning on spending time together tonight. He was going to take her for a meal, then bring her back to his place and wait for Lulu to come home. Then, after listening to Lulu telling them all about her new man, they would retire to his bedroom and make slow, sensual love all night.

Now, he didn't have enough strength to get up the stairs.

Lulu got out first, lugging the huge overnight bag. Then the driver helped Sapphire manoeuvre James out of the taxi. He managed it by moving slowly and inching his way across the seat, so he was almost out of the door. Then he grabbed hold of the sides of the open door and shuffled forwards, hopping slightly. Then, with Sapphire holding the crutches ready, he launched himself out on his good leg and swung his plastered leg after it. Everybody, including James, seemed to be holding their breath until this act of daring was accomplished.

'I'm out!' he croaked. He would have shouted his triumph if he could, but his voice was hoarse with pain. The thought of all the stairs he had yet to negotiate made him want to sit down in the road and cry.

'Thank gawd for that,' muttered the taxi driver and James watched as Sapphire tipped the man handsomely for his help.

'Thanks, mate,' said James as he stood on the pavement, swaying slightly on his crutches. He had never felt so weary in his life, but his ordeal wasn't over yet.

Lulu had unlocked the front door and stood on the top step waiting for them. Sapphire walked by his side as he inched his way down the path. Then the next obstacle course loomed as he pulled himself up the steps and into the house. If only that was the end of it, but he was still on the ground floor and had the equivalent of Mount Everest to climb before he could collapse on his bed.

'Do you want to have a rest before you try the stairs?' asked Sapphire.

'No.' He shook his head. 'If I sit down I'll be asleep. I need to do it now.'

'Right. Let's go then.'

He heaved a sigh. Then told himself to stop being such

a wimp and get on with it. He brought this on himself and everyone else by his irresponsible behaviour. He needed to suck it up and just do it. He looked down at himself. The medics had cut away the leg of his jeans and he wondered how the hell he was going to undress himself. He looked at Sapphire and realised he was going to rely very heavily on her support for the foreseeable future. How long would it be before she was sick of him and walked away?

Eventually, with Lulu ahead of him and Sapphire bringing up the rear, he negotiated the stairs the way the nurse had explained. Let your strong side do most of the work, she had said. Up with the good, down with the bad. Step up with your uninjured leg and hold on to the bannister then pull the injured leg up second. It was agony and by the time James got to the top he couldn't help moaning slightly, but he had made it to his bedroom and now he could sleep.

'Thanks, ladies,' he said as he made his way to his bed, 'but if I don't lie down, I'm going to pass out.'

'You'll need help getting undressed,' said Sapphire, 'Lulu—could you fetch a bowl with some warm water and a flannel please?'

'Of course.' Lulu left the room and shut the door.

'Are you going to give me a bed bath Nurse Sapphire?' Despite his exhaustion, the thought of Sapphire running a wet flannel over his body took his mind to places it shouldn't go. Not in the condition he was in. An injured man with a hard-on wasn't an attractive prospect.

'No, so don't get excited. I'm just going to wash the blood off, then you must sleep. We'll think of how the hell you are going to perform your ablutions tomorrow. One step at a time, James.'

By the time Lulu returned with the washing up bowl, a

flannel and a towel, Sapphire had undressed him, and he was lying under the duvet. He was so tired that he didn't think he could stay awake to enjoy Sapphire's administrations.

'Thanks, Lulu. Now, I'll give him a quick wash, so how about you rustle us both up a light supper. I'll stay for a while, but I do need to get home at some point to feed Sparkle.'

'Okay. Pasta?'

'Perfect.'

When Lulu had gone, Sapphire pulled off the duvet and began to gently wipe the blood away. Despite how careful she was being, every touch hurt; his skin was covered with abrasions and sores and what should have been an enjoyable, sensual experience, turned into an ordeal, and James was glad when she was finished.

'I need some more pain killers,' he said hating how pathetic he sounded.

'Of course,' Sapphire replied, 'I'll get you some water and put everything within easy reach on the bedside cabinet. Don't try to get to the bathroom on your own—shout for me or Lulu okay? Keep your phone with you, so you can text us if you need anything.'

'Sapphire, much as I appreciate your help, I have no intention of imposing on you or Lulu in that way. The nurse said I need to keep mobile, so tomorrow I'll be out of this bed and moving around the house.'

'We'll see. Let's take things one step at a time.'

He watched her as she left the room, then he let go. He wanted to stay awake to take more medication but keeping his eyes open was totally beyond him. And he didn't want to think anymore. He could feel the darkness descend and he gave in to it gratefully.

As Lulu bustled about cooking the pasta and defrosting Bolognese sauce, Sapphire poured a generous glass of Chardonnay for them both. They deserved it after the evening they'd had.

'Any message from your date?' she asked.

Lulu shook her head and concentrated on cooking the meal.

'Maybe you should try him again?'

'No, there wouldn't be any point. I don't want to meet him now anyway.'

'Why, Lulu?'

'Because every time I looked at him I would think of poor James injured and the sight and smell of the hospital.'

'That's not his fault. He might have been looking forward to meeting you.'

'I don't think he was, or he would have phoned to see how I was. Or how James is. I don't think he's interested. He told me he's been on a lot of dates.'

'Well, maybe he wasn't the right one, but you must keep trying.'

Lulu carefully drained the cooked pasta, arranged some on each plate and put the plates on the table. 'Do you want parmesan?'

'Yes please.. This is lovely.' And it was. In fact, it was delicious. Sapphire was hungry.

'When James is better. I'm not going to have time now. We need to look after him. He's our priority.'

'I was thinking about that,' said Sapphire, trying not to speak with her mouth full, but enjoying the food so much she was wondering whether to have seconds. 'For the first few days at least, somebody will have to stay in the house with him in case he needs anything. Once he gets used to the crutches and moving around, he'll be okay alone.'

'Yes,' said Lulu, nibbling at the garlic bread she'd warmed up. She ate daintily and never stuffed her face as Sapphire did.

'What time are your mum and Phoebe coming tomorrow?'

'They'll arrive just in time for lunch, which means we'll have to cook something. I'll do it if you like, I like cooking.'

Sapphire wanted to ask if that was a tradition—arriving in time for lunch—when they visited anyone. Then she decided she couldn't be bothered with the eccentricities of the Lewis family; she was just too tired.

'Do you think your mum will want to help look after him?'

'No, I shouldn't think so. She can't drive so someone will have to collect her. I don't drive either. Phoebe will be too busy at work.'

Which just leaves me, thought Sapphire. 'Do you think I should offer to collect her?'

'No.' Lulu shook her head but didn't elaborate.

'Why Lulu?'

'Because she'll feel pressured into coming when she doesn't want to.'

'So… what? I wait for her to ask me to collect her?'

Lulu shook her head again. 'No, she won't do that.'

'Right.' *Well, that clears that up*, she thought in confusion. She decided to speak to James about it. Perhaps she'd get more sense out of him.

'Well, that was lovely, thank you. Shall I load the dish-washer?' asked Sapphire.

'No, I'll do it, then I'm going upstairs.'

'Okay.' Lulu obviously had enough excitement for one day.

Sapphire went back upstairs to see how James was. He was lying on his back with his mouth open, deeply asleep. The poor man looked shattered. She tiptoed out of the room and left the bedroom door open slightly in case he woke up and needed something. Lulu would be bound to hear him.

Then she went back downstairs to say goodbye to Lulu, but she was nowhere in sight. Willow was curled up in her bed in the kitchen and the sound of the boiler humming gently was the only sound in the house.

Sapphire let herself out and started walking. She'd take the tube. It would give her time to think and unwind, and the fresh air would do her good. She thought about how busy she was at work and wondered if she could get away with swerving the meeting of the Lewis clan the following day. After all, Lulu would be there. But James would want her with him, and she couldn't leave Lulu to fend off all the questions that were bound to follow, on her own. That was a strange thought, considering they were Lulu's family, but she just felt, instinctively, that she should be there for moral support.

Chapter Twenty-Three

When Sapphire arrived at Primrose Hill the following morning at eleven o'clock, she was amazed at the scene of peaceful domesticity she found. Lulu was in the kitchen cooking a chicken casserole and a lemon meringue pie for lunch and James was in the living room, sprawled on the couch with his laptop on a lap-tray, which was balanced on his good leg. He was typing furiously with a frown on his face.

'Hi, you look better.'

James put one hand out to her without looking up from his screen. 'Come and join me—you can give me the benefit of your wisdom with this.'

Sapphire sat next to him and was pleased at the aromas that surrounded James. Unlike the day before when he smelled of blood and sweat, he now smelt sweet and clean; a mixture of citrus cologne, soap and shampoo.

'What are you working on? Did you manage to have a shower this morning?'

'It's my report to the board. I've thought of a few

companies I want to look at, but I need approval for the finances. If we are going to do this properly we need to up the ante with the amount we are prepared to invest. We need to go for the big guns.'

Sapphire started reading the report while James put his arm around her shoulders and kissed her cheek.

'It looks okay to me, but I'd have to check the figures. Will you email it to me?'

'Sure.' James started typing again. 'And the answer to your second question is yes. The creative genius that is my baby sister came up with a way to wrap plastic bags around the cast and secure them with masking tape. I didn't think it'd work but it did.'

'You seem much brighter today. It's good to see.'

'Ah well, that would be the pain killers and the pleasure of seeing you.' He kissed her on the cheek again, 'they're obviously a winning combination.'

'Shall I go before the rest of your family arrive? You don't seem to need me today and I don't want to intrude.' She had so much to do that the temptation to nip into the office for a few hours was irresistible.

James sighed and hugged her to him. 'Don't let appearances fool you. This is all for Mum and Phoebe. We want to present a united front and let them see how well we are coping. If you were with us, then the argument would be rock solid. The truth is Lulu and I are crumbling wrecks inside.'

'I don't believe you. Anyway, why are you so frightened of your mother and sister?'

'Have you met my family?' he said with a smile. 'Lulu and I are a team, we support each other. Mum would think she had to have me home and do nothing but complain about it and Phoebe... well, she'd be tempted to put me in a convalescent home and throw away the key.'

'Don't you and Phoebe get on?'

'On the surface, for the benefit of others we do, but there has always been intense rivalry. Phoebe will lose no chance to see me brought low and a broken leg is a golden opportunity for her.'

'I think you're exaggerating.'

'A bit maybe. Remember the way she parked her car in the driveway so I couldn't get mine in?'

Sapphire remembered. 'Yes, I was going to ask you about that.'

'That's the kind of thing she does. She's continually proving that she's better, richer, more popular than me. If you think Lulu's insecure, it's nothing compared to Phoebe, but she hides it under the veneer of her successful lawyer image.'

'I see,' said Sapphire who didn't really see, but it explained Phoebe's cool reception when they met.

'Does she have a boyfriend?'

'If she has, she wouldn't tell me.'

'That's quite sad.'

'Yes it is, but now you can see why I want you here, can't you?'

'To prove something to your family?' Sapphire didn't really see what he was getting at, but she had no frame of reference for this kind of sibling rivalry.

'To get them to stay away because we don't need them. Lulu has offered to help as much as she can and if you could call in now and again...' He trailed off and looked at her with sad eyes.

'Fine. I'm sure the three of us can manage. I wasn't planning on abandoning you anyway. I'm here for you,

James, in whatever way you need. You know that, don't you?'

'Thanks. That's all I need to hear.' He kissed her gently, his mouth warm and soft against her lips. Then his mouth opened, and their tongues touched, sending messages to her erogenous zones that she hadn't had sex for a while and this was nice—more than nice, in fact. The kiss deepened, and he played with her hair, running his fingers through it, untangling her curls and his other hand came up and cupped her face. He moaned softly and shifted restlessly under the lap-tray.

'Will you stay with me tonight?' he whispered.

'Are you sure you're up for sex?' She knew that he was as aroused as she was. It had been too long since they had been together. A week, in fact, and for them, that was a long time.

'Of course. I'm always up for having sex with you, Sapphire. If I take my painkillers at tea-time, I'll be fine. We could always have an early night.'

'What about Lulu?'

'She won't mind. She'll probably be in her bedroom anyway.'

They kissed again and the promise was there. Sapphire ran her hand under his T-shirt and stroked the smooth skin of his stomach. He was wearing a pair of baggy navy-blue shorts that were probably the only things he could get over the cast. It would be so easy to slip her fingers up the leg and stroke his hardness, but that wouldn't be fair, seeing as there would be no opportunity to take things further. His family wouldn't appreciate James greeting them with a massive hard-on.

Reluctantly, she pulled away. 'I'll go and see if Lulu

needs any help in the kitchen and leave you to work in peace.'

'Tonight… okay?' The poor man looked almost desperate as he hid himself under the lap-tray. She was feeling extremely horny herself.

'Yes, James, tonight.' She blew him a kiss as she walked away.

Mrs Lewis and Phoebe arrived about thirty minutes before the casserole was ready. Just enough time to berate poor James about the danger of riding a motorbike and how stupid he was for not wearing his leather trousers. Lulu had let that slip when she was trying to defend him. Unfortunately, she seemed incapable of being anything but scrupulously honest.

Lulu stayed on her own in the kitchen and insisted she didn't need any help, she preferred to do it herself. She had a system and other people just confused her, she said. The rest of them retired to the living-room and Sapphire poured them all aperitifs; sherry for Mrs Lewis and limoncello for everyone else.

She refused to take any part in the conversation. They were James's family, and he could deal with them. He did in his own indomitable way, by apologising profusely over and over until it started to become meaningless, and by being excessively cheerful about how well the three of them were coping.

Phoebe didn't say much, letting her mother do the dirty work.

'I've lost track of the number of times I've told you to be careful on that bike.'

'Yes, Mum, I know you have, and you're absolutely right to be angry—'

'It's not as if you need it… it's not like when you were a youngster and couldn't afford a car. You've got that sports car.'

'Bikes negotiate London traffic more effectively—'

'Until you crash them,' said Phoebe.

Sapphire noticed the look of triumph that flashed across Phoebe's face, as she spoke. To an outsider, it appeared that she really didn't like her brother, and was enjoying his disgrace. Sapphire would never understand some families and how they were with each other.

'Anyway,' said James with a sigh, 'the police have told me that the bike is a write-off, only good for scrap.'

'I'm sorry,' said Sapphire, 'you didn't tell me that.'

'No, I was going to later… I phoned the police this morning.'

'Well, that's that then and I can't say I'm sorry, James. Not if this is what happens when you ride the thing. You gave me and your sister such a shock, hearing you were in hospital. You should think of other people more.'

'Sorry, Mum,' said James wincing slightly as he pulled himself to his feet. His crutches were next to him on the couch and he fitted them neatly into his armpits and started across the carpet to the door. Sapphire was pleased to see that he didn't sway anymore. In fact he moved quite competently now. He had mastered their use very quickly. When James was determined to do something, he just got on with it. One of the many things she admired about him.

'Where are you going now?' his mother asked crossly.

'I'm going to organise the wine,' he said cheerfully. Sapphire wasn't fooled. Although he was doing his best to be upbeat and let his mother's attitude flow off him, she could hear the bite in his voice and see the tension in his jaw. His self-control in not reacting to her was admirable.

'I'll come too,' said Sapphire. 'I can set the table or something.'

When they got to the kitchen, however, Lulu had everything under control and was serving out. Thank goodness. The sooner they got this meal over with the better.

The chicken casserole was delicious, and the Lewis family was too busy eating to snipe at each other over lunch. James played the charming host to perfection, not letting his mother's anxious nagging and his sister's spite bother him, and Lulu took all the compliments she received in her stride. Even her mother said the chicken was cooked well and that she could taste the lemon in the pie. Mrs Lewis said she was never comfortable with lemon meringue pie unless it was one of her own, as they usually disappointed, but the one Lulu made was very nice. High praise indeed. Lulu didn't seem bothered one way or another. Her relationship with her mother was strange, Sapphire couldn't work it out. And she couldn't remember Lulu and Phoebe exchanging one word to each other since they had arrived.

It wasn't her problem. She intended to escape as soon as she could and spend a few hours in the office before coming back when Mrs Lewis and Phoebe had gone home. Then spend a relaxing evening with James screwing each other senseless. She had never had sex with a man in a plaster cast before.

After lunch, when she had helped load the dishwasher

and James had led the procession back into the living-room, Lulu whispered to Sapphire, 'Do you want to see my bedroom? Leave the rest of them to talk?'

Sapphire, curious about all things to do with Lulu and not wanting to be in the company of her mother and sister, agreed straight away. Lulu beamed and Sapphire realised what a compliment it was to be invited into the woman's sanctuary.

'I hope you don't mind,' said Lulu, when they had climbed the stairs to the top of the house and arrived at the attic conversion where Lulu lived, 'if I ask you to take your shoes off.'

'No, not at all.' Sapphire slipped off her shoes and walked bare foot into Lulu's bedroom.

She stopped in the doorway and stared at the spacious room. It took up half the attic space and was divided neatly into two areas. The first part contained a four-poster double bed which was piled high with teddies, sitting on the most exquisite quilt that Sapphire had ever seen. It looked to be made from ivory satin and gave the impression of an heir-loom of some kind, but Sapphire was sure Lulu had made it. The bed was enclosed in an ivory material tied back with pale blue ties. It gave the room a floaty, dreamy feel—ultra-feminine and graceful. There were bedside tables on either side of the bed and the wall was a dark blue colour. There was also a couch, wide-screen TV and a coffee table.

It was the other side of the room that fascinated Sapphire. It was a crafter's paradise.

'May I see?' she asked Lulu.

'I want to show you,' Lulu replied, 'I've been dying to show you my work from the first day I met you. Come on.'

She led the way and Sapphire stopped and gazed in

fascination at the wall-to-wall shelves packed with materials, pattern books, scissors, cushions, quilts, curtains, and table-cloths. There was a small table with a sewing machine on it and several old tins that had once held chocolate and biscuits but, Sapphire would have bet, now contained buttons, bows, ribbons and other crafting items. The tins were organised according to size and sat neatly in towers at the back of the table. Sapphire knew without looking that each tin would have its own label with the contents accurately annotated.

The shelves in Sapphire's workshop were, to be honest about it, organised chaos, because that was how she worked. She always knew where to find things. These shelves, however, were immaculate. Everything was neat and tidy, labelled meticulously and colour-coded. Talk about micro-managing. This was the epitome of it.

'Are all these designs yours?' Sapphire asked.

'Yes. That space over there is where I photograph everything for my website.'

Sapphire turned to look where Lulu was pointing. A corner of the massive room, where the light from the skylight was strongest, was set up like a photographer's studio. There was a large wooden table that looked as if it had been distressed to look like a country pine table. On it were a few objects that Lulu obviously used as a background when displaying her crafts. There was a vase with dried grasses, a wicker basket with artificial flowers laid in it, a bowl of fruit—all standard stuff to Sapphire's trained eye.

'I didn't know you had a website.'

'Oh yes, I sell my things on it. Do want to see?'

'Yes please.'

They went back to the other side of the workroom

where a desk with a computer was set up against the wall. It reminded Sapphire of the workstation of any office worker, with a framed photograph of Willow on one side of the desktop computer, and a printer on the other side. Again, everything on the desk was in its rightful place. It was tidy to the point of obsession.

And when Lulu showed Sapphire her website, she realised why.

Confessions of an autistic crafter by Louisa May Lewis.

Sapphire turned away from the computer and looked at Lulu as if she was seeing her for the first time. The expression on her face must have given her away because Lulu raised her eyebrows and then shook her head.

'James didn't tell you. I was convinced he would have done.'

'No, Lulu, he didn't tell me.' She should have guessed, she realised.

'Oh.' Lulu looked sad suddenly and Sapphire resisted the urge to hug her. Autistic people didn't like being touched, did they? But then Lulu had hugged her lots of times.

'Tell me about your website.'

She brightened and smiled. 'I have a blog where I talk about what it's like to be autistic. I try to make it funny and entertaining to attract readers. Then I have a separate blog that is just for my crafts. I sell my quilts, cushions and some other small items.'

She stopped and waited. Sapphire's mind was working overtime. She hadn't seen designs as perfect and professional as Lulu's in a long time. The shades she used were wonderful together and she wasn't afraid to use bold sweeps of colour. She had designed a cushion which had a back-

ground of rainbow colours with tiny beads in the shape of
birds flying across.

'Lulu—do you ever take commissions?'

'Not really. I just sell the things I make.'

'I think your work is of an incredibly high standard.
Where did you learn all this?'

'A bit from school. Most of it from the internet, books
and magazines, and by trying things to see if they work,
then adapting them. I've got one design that I love, and I
use it in different ways by combining it with other designs.'

'How much time do you spend up here?'

'As much time as I can. After work, weekends, holidays.
Sometimes I can't sleep and will work all night.'

'And the autism. That must be hard?' She had so many
questions she wanted to ask Lulu about her condition but
didn't know where to start. She realised how ignorant she
was. She had heard snippets about what it is like to live with
autistic children and had always felt sorry for the parents.
But she had never, until now, considered what life must be
like for an autistic adult. She wanted to know but didn't
want to be rude or upset Lulu.

'Yes.' Lulu gestured to the couch and they sat next to
each other. Lulu stared at the wall opposite and Sapphire
tried not to stare at Lulu.

'Do you want to talk about it?'

'I don't mind. Being autistic I mean. It's who I am after
all. Other people can be unkind because they don't understand. My senses are more pronounced, so smells, noises
and very bright lights, can hurt. My head sometimes feels as
if it is going to explode.'

'I can't imagine how frustrating that must be.'

'Yes. I don't like people with loud voices, shouting, or
sudden noises like someone dropping something near me.

The kids at school used to do that on purpose just to watch me jump.'

'Were you bullied, Lulu?'

'Not exactly, but the cool kids used to say I was weird. I am so I didn't blame them.'

'Did you have many friends?'

'Oh yes, I had quite a few.'

'That's good.'

'Yes.' Lulu fell silent and Sapphire did too. She didn't want to seem as if she was interrogating the girl and there would be other occasions to ask her about herself. But, for now, in the companionable silence and peace of Lulu's bedroom cum workshop, Sapphire's mind was working overtime.

Sapphire Enterprises was always looking for ways to expand. James didn't seem to be having much luck with finding companies in other industries for them to invest in, and she had thought about broadening her design portfolio for quite some time. She had never, until now, thought about interior design. Lulu's ideas combining shapes, colours and patterns would translate easily into many items for the stylish homemaker. Not just the ones Lulu had been concentrating on such as cushions and quilts, but throws, tablecloths and matching serviettes and even furniture and wallpaper. There was no restrictions for clever designers. And Lulu was undoubtedly an extremely clever designer.

Then the phone rang. A house phone that linked Lulu's world upstairs to James's downstairs. Her mother and sister were going, and their presence was required to say goodbye.

Sapphire followed Lulu downstairs and stood on the sidelines watching as one half of the Lewis family said a relieved farewell to the other half. When they had gone, she too, left, promising to be back for tea. James was looking ill again and needed to sleep off the stress of his family's visit. Lulu would retreat to her sanctuary.

Sapphire was eager to get to the office to see how feasible it would be for Sapphire Enterprises to move into interior design. She was buzzing with ideas and plans and couldn't remember feeling as excited about anything for a long time.

Chapter Twenty-Four

When James woke up the house was quiet, and he was alone. This meant that Sapphire hadn't returned, and Lulu was upstairs in her space. Lulu needed to be alone frequently throughout the day; he understood this and had accepted it a long time ago. She would sidle up to him and whisper that she didn't want "people" and needed to get away from them. He would let her stay in his bedroom until she had recharged her battery, or got her head together, or whatever it was she needed to do. She had to share a bedroom with Phoebe when she was very small, and she never felt that it was her place.

Now, of course, things were different. Phoebe had never understood her little quirks which were not her fault, but the result of being an HFA— high functioning autistic. Therefore, the two girls, now women, weren't close. But then, Phoebe wasn't close to anyone really. She felt responsible for their mother but, James suspected, she didn't like her very much.

James sighed. Families. They weren't easy for nonautistic people to understand so how Lulu managed he didn't know. But manage she did. She was happy living with him, they were a team and supported each other. And then there was Sapphire...

He smiled as he thought of her. She was his lover, co-CEO—even if she insisted on saying he worked for her—and friend. They still hadn't decided on an end day to their relationship. The one night of sex to get it out of their systems had stretched to several nights, to the point where James never wanted it to end.

His thoughts led to Ruth. In the drama of his accident and the pain and discomfort he had been feeling, he had pushed that little problem out of his mind. But he had to face it soon. He needed her help which meant seeing her again. He would wait until he was more mobile, then meet her on neutral ground. He didn't want her in his home. And, whatever happened, he had to avoid her bumping into Sapphire and Lulu.

He got out of bed, slowly and painstakingly, but he was determined to be mobile and independent as soon as he could. He had slept in his shorts and T-shirt, so just needed to brush his hair to make himself presentable. At least he had managed to shave that morning.

By the time he struggled downstairs, he was in pain and sweating again, so he went to the kitchen and got a drink of water. He closed his eyes and tried to will himself to feel better.

'Hi, how are you feeling now?' Lulu's voice behind him made him smile. He turned around carefully.

'Hi, sweetheart. Getting better by the minute. Shall I help you make something for tea, or shall we get a takeout?'

'The second. Sapphire will be back about six.'

'Good, how about Indian? Or what you prefer pizza?'

'Pizza.'

'Yes, good choice.'

'You need to sit down, James. Come on.'

She walked by his side, carrying his glass of water. When he had settled himself on the couch again and Lulu was sitting in the armchair, curled up, with her feet under her, he broached the subject he had been curious about since earlier that day.

'What were you and Sapphire talking about when Mum and Phoebe were here?'

'I showed her my designs and website. She liked everything.'

'Great, what's not to like?'

'I want to be a famous designer like her.'

'Really? What about the attention? All the people clamouring for a bit of you?'

'I wouldn't have to appear in public, would I?'

'If you became famous you would.' That thought reminded James of the fashion show and the thousands of hits the picture of him carrying Sapphire off the stage had generated. 'Have you taken your blood sugars today?'

'Yes, James, they're within the acceptable range.'

'Good. You'll be able to have a small sweet after the pizza then. Maybe some ice-cream.'

'That's the door,' she said getting up quickly and almost running out to the hallway.

'I didn't hear anything,' James said after her retreating figure. It was quite normal for Lulu to hear things before anyone else. She had the hearing of a bat.

He stayed where he was, even when he heard Sapphire's voice talking excitedly to Lulu. He was so glad they got on well. Lulu needed friends.

'Hi, James, I bought something for you.' Sapphire threw

herself down on the couch next to him and handed him a parcel.

'Thanks. I think. What is it?'

'Open it.'

He opened the packet that had a green cross on the front and discovered a strange plastic object inside. He shook it out and held it up.

'It's a giant condom. You really do have plans for tonight, don't you? But I'm sorry, honey, even I can't fit into that.'

'Don't be so ridiculous,' said Sapphire, grabbing it off him. 'It's a protective sleeve for your cast. Now you can have a shower without poor Lulu wasting all her masking tape on you.'

James grinned at her.

Lulu sauntered into the room with a handful of takeout menus. 'We're having pizza. What kind do you like? I'm having Hawaiian.'

'Why don't we get a selection? I'll ring them,' said James.

'That sounds like an excellent idea,' said Sapphire stretching like a cat.

When the call had been made, Lulu went to the kitchen to organise plates and cutlery. Sapphire had switched the TV on to watch the news and James sat back with a sigh. He had taken his pain killers, so he was feeling kind of floaty and peaceful. He was going to eat pizza then have a night of sex. He was happy, content to be exactly where he was with his two favourite women. Lulu had taught him to live in the now and in this precise moment, he had everything he needed.

Finally, James had Sapphire all to himself, exactly as he wanted her, naked and warm in his bed.

'Thank you,' he whispered to her.

'What for?'

'For everything. For being supportive, for being here with me.' He realised he didn't know how to express it, but he was so grateful to her for being in his life, he just wanted to tell her.

'You'd do the same for me.'

'Yes I would.' There was a lot he would do for this beautiful, sexy woman who lay next to him, one hand propping up her head, the other caressing his chest.

'I want to ask you something and I want you to be honest,' said Sapphire.

'Of course,' he replied.

'Why didn't you tell me that Lulu was autistic?'

'High functioning autistic.'

'Okay, but why?'

'Because it isn't fair to her. How would you feel if, every time I introduced you to someone new, I said, "Meet Sapphire, she's a diabetic." You wouldn't like it, would you?' Sapphire was silent. 'Her autism doesn't define her as a person. She's Lulu first and foremost. The autism is just a feature of who she is.'

'It's a big feature. Okay I get what you're saying and you're right, I don't like people knowing I'm diabetic as it shouldn't make a difference to the way they are with me.'

'When people know Lulu is HFA, they treat her differently.'

'Do you mean, they don't treat her with respect?'

'Sometimes. Other people are just afraid of her.'

'That's awful. Lulu's lovely and talented. She says she's happy being autistic.'

'She doesn't know what it's like not to be.'

They were silent for a while, both lost in their own thoughts.

James was just thinking about sex again, when Sapphire said, 'I want to offer Lulu a job.'

'What kind of a job?'

'As a designer. I've been thinking of how hard it is to find a company we can invest in. Personally, I'd like to invest our profits, such as they are, into expanding Sapphire Enterprises. I'm toying with the idea of moving into interior designs with Lulu working with a team of experienced designers at the beginning. Eventually, once she settles in, she could be promoted to chief designer with younger, lesser experienced designers under her. She can help train them up—a sort of succession planning.'

'I don't think that's a good idea. Not the interior design idea but asking Lulu to head it up.'

'Why?'

'Because she's not experienced enough to do a job like that.'

'I won't throw her in at the deep end, I'll teach her everything she needs to know, and she can work from home a lot. James, Lulu's designs are the best I've seen for a long time. She's got such a good sense of colour and shades, I got quite excited when she showed me. I haven't felt like that after being presented with someone else's work for ages.'

'Have you asked her what she thinks about working for you?'

'No, not yet. I wanted to get your views first.'

'Let me think about it, too, okay? Maybe sound her out first. If she doesn't want to do it, then that's the end of it, right? And I think you should consider keeping Lulu part of a team, without the responsibility of management. She works well at the school because she has people to ask if she gets stuck.'

'Fine. I think she'll be on board with it. It could be the answer to all our problems.'

'Maybe, but there's only one problem I've got at the moment, and that is—what do I do with this?' He took her hand and guided it to his erection. Sapphire, never being one to resist a challenge, did what he had hoped she would and stopped talking. Instead, she shuffled down the bed and took him in her mouth.

Soon the heat from her tongue and her hand gently squeezing his balls pushed all other thoughts from his mind. He closed his eyes and allowed himself to be carried off on waves of ecstasy as Sapphire performed her magic on his aching flesh. It was over too soon, and Sapphire carefully cleaned him up.

'Is that better?' she asked with a mischievous smile.

'Yes, much better, thanks. Now I want to return the compliment so come closer, I might need some help with this.'

'You don't have to seeing as you're a poorly soldier.'

'I do, for both our sakes.'

Sapphire looked lovely in the subdued light. Her hair was loose and flowing, exactly as he liked it, and her eyes were sparkling.

'You are so beautiful.'

'Thanks.'

She cuddled up to him while he was "recovering" which he appreciated. He was starting to feel tired despite his mind being wide awake and eager for round two. His body was letting him down badly.

'Damn plaster cast,' he muttered.

Sapphire sat up and stared down at him. 'Is it itchy?'

'Not yet. That part will come later, so I'm told. It's just an encumbrance I could do without. I want to make love to you all night, but I'm afraid this thing is just going to get in the way.'

'Then we'll have to be creative,' said Sapphire as she reached into the top drawer of the bedside table and extracted a condom. She sheathed him expertly, then looked at him as if she was measuring him up for something. 'Umm, I wonder if you would be more comfortable on your back or your side—what do you think?'

'We could try both. Seeing as I'm already lying on my back, how about you straddle me, and I'll tell you how it feels?'

She did as James suggested, being careful not to add too much weight to his damaged leg.

'How does this feel?'

'Amazing,' he said huskily. He started to move carefully, and Sapphire matched his movements. He reached up and caressed her nipples, rolling them gently until they hardened. She lowered her body down so that he could take one of her nipples into his mouth.

'Oh, that's good,' she whispered. Her eyes were closed and, with her hands on each side of his head, her hair fell over her face and swept the pillow. He reached down and stroked the silky skin of her back, then cupped her breasts as his tongue played with the hard nub of her nipple so it stood erect and proud.

She sat back up again, so she was, once again, riding him and he held on to her hips as she rose and fell.

'You okay?' Her voice was husky as she grew closer to her climax, but James felt tenderness for her that she was thinking of him at that moment. Even though his leg was hurting, he smiled and nodded.

Sapphire was close now and she threw her head back and cried out as she orgasmed. James took longer to follow than normal, which he put down to the painkillers, and he lay still afterwards, as Sapphire disposed of the condom.

Not his best performance by a long shot, but at least they both managed to climax.

Sapphire got back into bed and cuddled up to him, after covering them both with the duvet that had slipped off.

'Sorry,' he said.

'Whatever for?'

'For a mediocre performance.'

She sat up and looked at him but the expression on her face was unreadable. Then she lay back down with her head on his chest.

'What was that look for?'

'I'm just a bit surprised that's all. I thought we'd got past the "just sex" stage— the one where you feel the need to "perform"—to a different kind of understanding. Obviously, I was wrong.'

'What are you saying, Sapphire? Are you saying that you want commitment?'

'I'm not sure what I'm saying except that I think we have a strong connection which goes beyond just sex.'

'You told me once that we couldn't be friends with bene-fits—do you remember?' He would be happy to be her offi-cial partner, both at work and in private, but he needed to be clear that it was what she wanted.

'That was then. I'm very fond of you James. Perhaps I'm saying that we could agree to be exclusive for now.'

'That's fine by me. I haven't wanted another woman since I met you anyway.'

'And I haven't wanted another man.'

'Good. So that's settled then.'

'Good.' She sighed and hugged him closer. It wasn't long before her breathing became deeper as she fell asleep.

James lay staring at the ceiling. Despite his post-coital relaxed state, he found it difficult to fall asleep. They had just admitted they had feelings for each other. Was this something that was going to last? Or would they grow tired of each other eventually? And then he had the problem of Ruth and Malcolm to contend with. He felt helpless being confined to the house, but the doctor had said it could take up to eight weeks before his leg was completely healed. Anything could happen in that time. Malcolm could take over Sapphire Enterprises while he was laid up. He couldn't let that happen. Maybe Sapphire was right, and they should be thinking of expanding the company to include interior design. There was a lot of money to be made from branching out.

Then he thought of Lulu being part of the plan. He had no idea whether it would be the best thing for her or the worst. There was only one person who could answer that and that was Lulu herself.

Chapter Twenty-Five

A week later, James knew he couldn't put it off any longer.

The house was quiet. Sapphire and Lulu were both at work. James could shower now without any problem, his plaster cast protected by the giant condom. He was more mobile, even though he still swallowed pain killers as if they were going out of fashion. He could write a book on how to use crutches and was bored stiff.

He stared at the screen of his mobile phone, took a deep breath, then phoned Ruth. She, irritatingly, didn't sound surprised to hear from him. It was almost as if she was waiting for his call. She agreed to call round to see him when he explained that he couldn't leave the house as he had broken his leg. He would have to risk the chance of Lulu and Sapphire arriving home while Ruth was in the house.

He sat down and tried to read the paper, but couldn't concentrate and, when he realised he had read the same article three times and still had no idea what it was about, he stood up and threw the paper on the floor. He'd pick it up later. He went into the kitchen, opened the fridge door then stood staring into the interior as if the fresh produce, cheeses, milk and wine would help him to decide what to do. He couldn't offer her wine because she was pregnant. Tea or coffee? She didn't deserve either, but he was going to ask her to do him a favour, so he would have to be civil.

When he opened the front door to Ruth, he felt a jolt of something that he could only describe as tenderness. She looked vulnerable and lonely standing on the doorstep, her hands over her stomach as if she was protecting the baby.

'Ruth, thanks for coming.' He shuffled backwards on the crutches to leave her enough space to enter.

'Of course, I came. And I'm sorry about…' She looked him up and down and her gaze rested on his plaster cast. He was wearing another pair of baggy shorts with an old T-shirt and his feet were bare. The ankle of his bad leg had a habit of swelling slightly if he didn't raise the leg for several hours a day. This caused a dilemma as he wanted to be as mobile as possible as quickly as possible, but the more he moved around on the crutches, the more likely it was that his ankle swelled.

'Thanks. My own fault, I wasn't wearing the leather trousers.' Ruth had always hated the motorbike; one of the few things she shared with his mother and Phoebe. In fact, probably the only thing.

'You silly boy! Why ever not?' Ruth smiled coquettishly.

'Do you want to sit down?' He wasn't prepared to have a conversation in the hallway, and he needed to raise his leg.

'Can I just nip to the loo? He lies on my bladder, the little devil.'

'It's a boy then?'

'Yes, I had the scan. We're having a little boy.'

'Would you like something to drink?'

'Have you got any juice? I'm not drinking at the moment and I've gone right off tea and coffee.'

'Fine.' He turned away and moved himself into the kitchen. They had mango juice. In fact they had about ten cartons of mango juice because it was Lulu's favourite and she had a fear of running out of the stuff in the middle of the night. Not that she ever drank it at night, but James had long since given up trying to understand some of Lulu's little quirks. It was easier just to accept them.

James managed to reach for two glasses from the cupboard, then the carton of juice from the fridge, without wobbling, dropping anything, or knocking the juice off the counter. He poured them both a generous amount. Then put the carton back in the fridge. When he turned to wait for Ruth to come back as he couldn't use the crutches and carry the glasses at the same time, he found her behind him, watching everything he did.

'I'll take those shall I?' Ruth said.

'Thanks.' He led the way out of the kitchen to the living-room.

James sat on the couch and rested his leg on the stool that had two cushions on it, bringing it to exactly the right height. Ruth sat next to James, sipping her mango juice.

'When you came to see me in the office, you said we could work together to bring Malcolm down.'

'That's right. And the offer still stands. Together, we could do it, I know we could.'

'There's something you need to do for me first.'

'And that is…?'

'Malcolm made me sign a disclaimer to safeguard himself if I ever decided to expose him.'

'What does it say?'

'The exact wording doesn't matter, but the fact is, I

need to get hold of the original. It'll be in his own private safe, not the business one, but you need to find a way to get it for me. While that is still in existence, my hands are tied. There is nothing I can do against Malcolm.'

'I don't understand, James… what could he possibly have on you to make you sign such a thing? And is it even legally binding?' James had often wondered the same thing himself. Even if it couldn't be used in a court of law, it showed that Malcolm paid James a lot of money to keep quiet. It would do his reputation in the business world nothing but harm. He needed to get it back. But he really didn't want Ruth to know what it said. It was an impossible situation.

'You know Malcolm, full of trickery.'

'What happens once I get the document?'

'I'll let you know later. One step at a time.'

'How do I go about this?'

'You need to get access to anywhere you think Malcolm might have hidden it. I suspect it's in his personal safe in his home. He wouldn't risk it being seen at the office. I'll go and see him at work, to leave the way clear for you to search his house.'

'What are you going to say to him?'

'I'll play it by ear, but if you could send me a text as soon as you've got it, then I'll be in a strong position to negotiate.'

'Malcolm isn't the type to negotiate. He's a taker. I hope you know what you're doing.'

Ruth sounded as she didn't trust him to do the job properly. Well, he didn't trust her either, so they were in the same boat. A leaky one, miles away from shore and safety. In this situation, working together was the only way to beat the dastardly Steele at his own game. They had to trust each other; they had no choice.

James had taken to going to bed early. The painkillers and the effort of trying to keep mobile usually wiped him out by early evening. Sapphire took advantage of this to talk to Lulu about her plans.

They were sitting in the lounge with the TV on, staring at a quiz show that neither of them were particularly interested in. Sapphire had Sparkle on her knee. James had asked her to stay for the duration of his convalescence, to help Lulu in the evenings, and she had agreed so long as her cat could come too.

Lulu was curled up in the armchair and Willow was sitting, sphinx-like, on the arm. She was keeping her eye on Sparkle. If the cats felt any familial loyalty they were keeping it well hidden. They ignored each other most of the time, and if one got too close to the other, they both backed off sharpish.

'The answer's 1984—it's obvious,' said Lulu without taking her eyes away from the screen. 'George Orwell wrote the novel in 1949.'

'I'll take your word for it,' said Sapphire who hadn't even listened to the question.

'Thank you,' said Lulu.

Sapphire sipped her wine and wondered how to approach the subject. Lulu groaned and shook her head in disgust.

'Why do people go on quiz shows when they are basically devoid of any general knowledge?'

'Have you ever thought of going on a quiz show? With your ability to remember facts you'd be good.'

Lulu hugged a cushion to her as if for protection and stared wide-eyed at Sapphire. 'Me? On television? In front of zillions of people?'

'Why not? You could win a lot of money.'

'I don't care about money.'

'You could give it to your favourite charity... or start your own business. Your designs are so good, they'd sell. You could develop your own line in interiors.' Sapphire wondered if she was getting through to her. Lulu was staring hard at the TV, but Sapphire suspected her thoughts were elsewhere. Eventually she turned to Sapphire with a frown.

'No one's ever told me I could do any of that. I don't know who to believe.'

'What did your parents tell you?'

'Mum said I needed a nice, quiet, safe job with little contact with people. Dad said I was his little girl and that he would always look after me. I was fifteen when he died. He never saw me grown up.'

'And James? What does he say?'

'James helped me find the teaching assistant's job. I love the little ones and am happy there. I sell a few of the things I make online. I'm grateful that I can do both those things.'

'What if I told you that there is a way you could sell more of your things, make a name for yourself and make a living as a designer instead of a teaching assistant?'

'You mean, just sell my things online and not go to work in the school?'

'No, Lulu, I mean come to work for me at Sapphire Enterprises. I'm looking to expand, and you gave me the idea that interior design is the way to go. Your ideas are innovative, inspirational and—quite frankly—blew me away with your colour choices, the patterns you manage to create. You have a natural instinct for what goes together. Can you imagine a room, furnished entirely by you? All the soft furnishings; cushions, curtains, rugs, throws, wall hangings—oh, the list is endless…'

Sapphire stopped as she was getting louder, something she tended to do when she was excited, and Lulu was gnawing on the side of her thumbnail which she did when she was on edge.

'I don't know,' she said quietly.

'I tell you what—why don't you think about it? Talk to James. There's no hurry about anything. I would love it if you said yes. It would be the start of something really big for my company and I want you on board.'

'Can I ask you something?'

'Of course, anything you like.'

'If I say no, will you go ahead with your plans anyway?'

Sapphire thought before answering. It was a good question and she intended to be brutally honest. It was how she did business. She didn't want to scare Lulu off the idea.

'Yes, once I make this kind of decision— something that is going to be beneficial for the company and for my future —I rarely change my mind. I have given this a lot of thought, Lulu, and I sincerely believe that this is the way to go. It will only work if I have the top designers in the business. I think you could become one of them. But, if you don't want to do this, I will look for someone else.'

'Thank you for being honest. I think I'll go to bed now. I will think about everything you've said.' Lulu got up and picked Willow up, cuddling the cat to her chest. 'Goodnight.'

'Goodnight Lulu. Sweet dreams.'

When girl and cat had gone, Sapphire continued to

stroke Sparkle. Her purring was the only sound in the room. Thinking about her ideas for her business had opened the floodgates of creativity in her mind. Not only would she expand into interior design, but she would develop a new perfume and call it Lulu. James had told her how hypersensitive Lulu is, her senses turned up to the max. So a strong smell would be three times as strong. And some smells, especially a mix of strong aromas, could make her feel really sick. She would come up with a perfume that was milder—subtle but still evocative—something Lulu could wear without it making her feel ill.

Sapphire felt too wired to sleep, so went to the kitchen and poured herself a large glass of wine. She returned to the living-room and opened her laptop. The cat was curled up in the corner of the couch.

'Okay, Sparkle, let's get to work.'

Chapter Twenty-Six

James dressed carefully in a white shirt with rolled up sleeves and a clean pair of baggy shorts. He wished he could power dress in his best Italian suit and silk shirt with matching tie but, as that was impossible—he would never get his suit trousers over the cast—he tried to look as smart as he could in the circumstances. At least it was summer, and he could wear casual trainers.

Not that Steele would care what he wore, but he hated the feeling of being at a disadvantage in front of his arch nemesis. And to think he used to consider the obnoxious little shit a friend.

He felt a sudden pang for what he was about to do. The money that Steele had paid him for his business had been sitting in a high interest rate account and was a nice little earner. He hadn't touched any of the money and had enjoyed watching his pay-off building up month by month. And now, he was going to give most of it back to Steele in exchange for the shares he had bought in Sapphire Enterprises. Provided the man agreed to sell.

Ruth had texted to say that she had managed to convince Steele to let her back into the house to collect a few possessions she had left behind. He had handed over the spare keys and she was going in the morning while Steele was in a meeting. James would arrive just after the meeting and demand to speak to him. That would, hopefully, give her enough time to find the contract. When she did, she would send him a quick text. Steele would then have nothing to bargain with and James would have the upper hand.

James had no idea what he would do if Ruth failed to find the contract. He would have to wing it.

He phoned a taxi and waited for it to arrive. The house was quiet as Sapphire and Lulu were at work and both the cats were asleep, curled up together in Willow's bed. If only people could heal their rifts as easily as Willow and Sparkle.

When James arrived at Dalton Mackenzie he was feeling less confident of the success of the venture than he had when he thought it through in the safety and comfort of his home. For one thing, he had to get past the receptionist. Luckily, due to his attire and general dishevelled appearance, she didn't recognise him from the first time he had visited. Then he had been a confident, smartly dressed CEO with an appointment and the right to be there. This time, he struggled to get through the main doors on his crutches and had to wait for someone to take pity on him and hold the doors open for him.

When he confessed that he didn't have an appointment, the receptionist told him in no uncertain terms that Mr Steele wouldn't accept unsolicited visitors. James had to get quite aggressive in his manner, telling the girl that he needed to see him as a matter of some urgency and Mr Steele wouldn't be happy that he had been kept waiting.

Fortunately, James was convincing, as he was told to take a seat and she would see what she could do.

Sitting down was too problematic as the chairs were lower than he was used to, and getting back up again was even worse, so James leaned against a wall and tried to look as if he meant business. It wasn't an easy look to achieve when looking like a helpless invalid. He was nervous too and was afraid that he would soon need to use the bathroom. Perhaps he should have waited before confronting Steele, but who knows what mischief the man might make in the time it took James's broken leg to heal.

Finally, the receptionist walked over to James and said in a tight voice, 'Mr Steele has agreed to see you, but he can only spare five minutes, he's a very busy man. Can you find your own way to his office?'

He was tempted to say that he was also a very busy man but thought his appearance might suggest otherwise, so he just asked, as politely as possible, if he could be shown the way as he had difficulty opening doors. The last thing he needed was to fall flat on his face in front of Malcolm; that would be the ultimate humiliation. As it was, Ruth hadn't sent him a text, so he would need to play for time.

The receptionist sighed heavily and said she would show him the way. She made it seem as if deserting her post for his convenience was a big deal, and that might have been true except there was no one else in the reception area, and they didn't meet anyone in the lift either. James would have loved to have found out what Steele's meeting was about and with whom. The receptionist didn't seem in the mood for small talk, so he stayed quiet and thought about what he would say when he saw his ex-partner.

The receptionist looked to be in her thirties and was quite attractive in an obvious kind of way. James wondered if she was one of the women Steele had been unfaithful with. Ruth had hinted that there was more than one. The man was a fool. He could have had a happily married life with Ruth and been looking forward to fatherhood, but he had thrown it all way. For what?

The building that housed Dalton Mackenzie was the most depressing he had ever set foot in. Far from looking cutting edge and prosperous, it looked abandoned and unloved, as if the owner had forgotten he had a business and let it go to seed. Even if Steele was using the place as a front for his shady dealings, he should still make it look as if he was head of a legitimate company.

They stopped outside a closed door and the receptionist knocked once, then opened the door without waiting for a reply. She stepped back and stared at James who stared back at her. He had never experienced such rudeness from a staff member before. If she had been working for him...

James took his time moving slowly on his crutches as he inched his way into the office. Then he stopped in the middle of the room as the door slammed behind him.

Steele sat behind a desk in front of grimy windows with no blinds or curtains. The sun on the glass showed more streaks than a rasher of bacon. In fact, it didn't look as if it had been cleaned in months.

'Well, well, well, look what the wind's blown in. What happened to your leg, mate?' Steele looked James up and down with a grin.

'Good afternoon Steele. I came off my bike and broke my leg. It's a clean break and will heal well, so I'm told.'

'Glad to hear it. Do you want to sit down?' Steele didn't get up to help him but gestured to a chair that was placed at the side of the desk. He watched curiously as James manoeuvred himself onto the chair and let the crutches slide to the floor.

'Drink? There's only water, I'm afraid. I could ask Shirley to make us a coffee, but she's run off her feet peopling the reception desk and would snap my head off if I asked her.'

'Peopling? What kind of expression is that?' James was surprised at how easily he had slipped back into the banter that he and Steele used to enjoy in their youth, before his old friend got greedy and tried to ruin James's life.

'Well you can't say "manning a desk" it's sexist and "womaning a desk" sounds rude, so… "peopling". It's nice and neutral.'

'A bit like the décor in here,' James said, 'in fact in the whole building. I expected something a lot more upmarket. Are times hard for you nowadays?'

Steele's smile slipped and he adopted his poker face, which James had always been able to read. Steele was annoyed but not overly so.

'What do you want, Lewis? Not that I'm not over the moon to see you again after all this time, but—well, a bit surprised, that's all. What are you after?'

Now that he was here and face to face with his ex-old friend, he was no longer nervous. In fact, he was more curious than anything. With all the businesses he had acquired, Steele should be a rich man by now. But he looked on his uppers. The suit he wore was old and shiny, the cuffs of his shirt frayed. He had bags under his eyes, and his hair needed cutting.

'I couldn't help noticing that there was no one in the lobby, no one in the lifts and there was a definite absence of the sound of fingers tapping away on keyboards. Don't you have any staff? And what exactly do you do in this place, anyway?'

'Import and export.'

'Stolen goods?'

Malcolm smiled. 'This is a legitimate business I'll have you know, we have a high turn-over rate.'

'You and Ruth?'

Malcolm narrowed his eyes. 'Yes, me and Ruth.'

James wasn't supposed to know that they had split up and that Ruth was pregnant. He had to pretend ignorance. Shame, he would have loved to ask Steele what the fuck he thought he was doing, getting a woman pregnant, then dumping her like he did.

'Things going well for you then?'

'Yes, mate, they are. I'm pretty sure you didn't struggle all the way here on those crutches to ask after my welfare. What do you want?'

James's mobile phone was deep in the pocket of his shorts. He had turned it to silent but kept the vibrate on so he would know when Ruth texted him. He was tempted to sneak a look in case he had missed her text, but he couldn't risk Steele seeing. There was nothing else for it, he would have to tell him the real reason for his visit.

'Okay. Cards on the table. I want to buy your shares in Sapphire Enterprises. And please don't tell me you don't have any because I know you are using an alias.'

'I wouldn't dream of lying to you, mate. We were close friends once.'

'Good. I'll offer you a competitive price.'

'That's jolly decent of you, old bean, but they're not for sale.'

'What possible interest could you have in a fashion house?'

'I could ask you the same question. But... oh, wait... I don't need to, do I? It's bleedin' obvious really, you would own the majority of shares, and the place, to all intents and purposes, would be yours. Am I right, or am I right?'

'Yes, you're absolutely right. So—how about it? You don't need another company do you? How many have you got now?'

'As you know, I don't keep them. I sell them on at a huge profit. This place is all I have.' Malcolm opened his arms and gazed around.

'Why don't I believe you?'

'Because you always were the mistrustful type. If you'd stayed with me, you too, could have everything I've got. But you threw your dummy out of the pram and left. You chucked it all away, Lewis, never forget that.'

'You were having an affair with my fiancée; how could I have stayed as your business partner after that?'

Steele leaned forward on the desk and grinned. He was obviously enjoying James's discomfort.

'Never mix business and pleasure. You never did understand that, did you?'

'And isn't that what you're doing now—you and Ruth?'

Steele leaned back in his chair and turned his face away from James. 'We've split up, so no, I'm not mixing business and pleasure. Not that she ever gave me much pleasure moaning all the time, demanding this, that and the other. I've never met a more needy woman. You dodged a bullet there, mate, you should thank me.'

What James wanted to do was hurl himself over the

desk and punch the idiot's lights out. Common sense and a plaster cast kept him glued to the chair. While Steele had his head turned away, James pulled his phone slowly out of his pocket, then made a show of coughing so he could put his head down and sneak a look. No texts.

Steele got up and poured a cup of water from the water cooler in the corner of the office. One of the only pieces of useful furniture in the room. He handed it to James.

'Thanks.'

'You're welcome.'

Steele sat down again and stared into space. James was conscious of the vibes he was feeling—from the man behind the desk and the set-up in general. Something was wrong. He would have to tread carefully.

'Do I take it that you and Ruth aren't the perfect couple after all?'

Steele made a snort of disgust and looked down and muttered, 'No comment.'

'What's that supposed to mean? She left me almost at the altar to be with you, the least you can do is tell me it was worth it.'

Steele looked up and glared defiantly at James. 'Like I said—you dodged a bullet.'

'Tell me. After all, we used to be friends. What harm can it do?'

Steel leaned forward but kept his gaze away from James's. That could have meant he was lying but could be because he was embarrassed.

'She's very ambitious, wants the best that life has to offer, but isn't prepared to lift a finger herself to contribute to the dream. Oh no, that was my department. I was working sixteen-hour days just to keep her in the style to which she wanted to become accustomed. I was knackered, on my knees, but still she wanted more.' He stopped and the tension showed in his face.

'Go on,' James said softly.

'Well, something had to give, didn't it? I started messing up, so the business was suffering. We were losing money, but Ruth wanted more—of everything. I started gambling as a way to make money but lost more than I won.' He stopped as if he had said too much, then shook his head.

'So what happened?'

'When she found out that the company was bleeding money she left me. Just walked out. She was pregnant. Did I mention that?' James shook his head. 'Not mine.'

James sat up in surprise, 'Really?'

'Oh yes, she was fooling around with a guy from accounts. That's how she found out about the financial state of the company. She told me it was mine, but I had a vasectomy years ago because I don't want kids. I never have. Lying bitch.'

James was stunned. He didn't know who to believe, the man who used to be his best friend or the woman he nearly married. Right now he didn't believe either of them. They were both after what they could get.

'What happened to my company?'

'I sold it. It's in good hands.'

It should have been in James's own hands. It was his pride and joy. He built it up from scratch and worked around the clock to turn it into the profit-making machine it was today.

He needed to get out. There was a lot to think about and Ruth hadn't texted. Maybe she had no intention of helping him. Perhaps she was just using him to get back at Malcolm.

'Listen,' James said, trying not to let his dislike of the

man he used to call a friend show, 'I'll give you a good price for the shares, more than you'd get elsewhere. Here's my card.' He threw his business card onto the table, but Steele just glanced at it and looked away. 'I'll be in touch as I'm not prepared to give up.'

'Yeah,' said Steele yawning, 'It's been just like old times.'

He struggled to his feet thinking that it was nothing like old times. Then he had trusted Malcolm Steele with half his business; now he wouldn't trust him to feed the cat.

'If it's any consolation,' Steele said, 'I wish I could turn back the clock and we could be in business together again. It's no fun on your own.'

James gave him a thin smile. Like that's ever going to happen. It was obvious now why Steele's businesses had failed; because he didn't understand the work ethic. You had to work like stink at a new business, and expect to make losses for quite a long time before things turned around and the money started coming in. Steele never understood that. He was good at playing the suave businessman, enjoying liquid lunches and entertaining the great and the good, but he knew nothing of burning the midnight oil, anticipating the moves that rival companies made. Business was like a game of chess, you had to think ahead of the game. Something he, James, excelled at.

'I'll be in touch. Let me know when you're ready to sell and I'll make you an offer.'

'Not going to happen mate, but it was nice catching up. Hope the leg heals soon.' Steele grinned but James shrugged and turned on his crutches to leave the office. He hoped Steele would get up and open the door for him, but he didn't. James balanced precariously on his good leg and managed to get the door open.

'Thank you for your time,' James said.

'Cheerio,' Steele said brightly.

James smiled to himself as he moved cautiously towards the lift. He knew the sale was in the bag. Steele was in trouble, as he had suspected, and would sell eventually. All James had to do was be patient.

Chapter Twenty-Seven

Sapphire was enjoying a rare, long lunch break. Her best friend, Monica, had invited her to lunch. Sapphire had been working flat out since early that morning, sustained only by copious amounts of coffee and a few biscuits, and she needed a proper lunch.

Since the fashion show, and motivated by Lulu's example, she had made a concerted effort to check her blood sugars and eat regular meals. But she found it hard, as she worked long, erratic hours and sometimes the need to eat slipped her mind.

Sapphire and Monica had been friends since college. Monica was an artist whose work was being recognised by those in the know the world over. The painting of London at night that hung on Sapphire's office wall had been a present from Monica when she launched House of Sapphire.

'So,' said Monica spearing rocket leaves with her fork. 'What's been going on? Tell me everything.'

They had both ordered the same healthy lunch—salmon, avocado and rocket with a wasabi dressing—and Sapphire felt quite smug as she tucked in.

'I've got a new co-Ceo.'

'Good. That means you can cut down on the hours and have a life.'

'Work is my life. But you're right, he does take a lot of the pressure off.'

'Okay. And are you two... you know?'

'Are we what?' asked Sapphire trying to hide a grin.

'You know what, you can't fool me, girlfriend, we've known each other too long.'

'Okay. Yes, we are. But it's only temporary as neither of us want commitment.'

'What's he like?'

Sapphire frowned and wondered how to answer. *What is James like?* 'He's good at his job, sexy, can be serious but has a good sense of humour—'

'Was he the guy that carried you out of your own fashion show? My goodness, that caused a media stir.'

'It was nothing. I was going into a hypo as I, foolishly, hadn't eaten all day. Hence...' Sapphire gestured at the salad. 'I'm determined to look after my health from now on as I can't risk it happening again. I'm thinking of joining a self-help group to get advice on lifestyle choices for diabetics.'

'Great idea. You're looking well, honey. You know I've been worried about you for a while. Working too hard, no holidays, no fun... but it looks as if this guy, James is good for you.'

'Thanks. I feel well. In fact I feel better than I have for ages.'

Sapphire was determined that she would never again be out of control in public. There won't always be people like James and Lulu around to catch her if she fell. She needed to keep a tight rein on her condition. If Lulu can do it then she can.

'So, tell me why you don't want commitment. Is it because of what Roland did?'

'Partly, I suppose. Monty warned me not to trust men. In business or in private. He was right. Roland took me for a fool and I'll never let that happen again.'

'Okay, so tell me more about this guy. Come on, give, let's have the statistics. How often do you get together?'

'Well… I'm staying at his place to help his sister look after him. He came off his bike—a Harley Davidson—and he needs a bit of help at the moment.'

'So, you've met his sister. What's she like?'

Sapphire hesitated. She remembered what James had said about Lulu not being defined by her autism and decided not to mention it.

'Lulu is an artist too, specialising in interior design. In fact—and this is the exciting thing I wanted to tell you—Sapphire Enterprises is branching out and I'm planning a whole new department for interior design. I'm hoping Lulu is going to be part of that.'

'Wow, that is exciting. Good for you.'

They ate in silence for a while, then Sapphire became aware of Monica watching her closely with a smile on her face.

'What? Why are you staring at me?'

'Because there is something different about you and I'm just worked out what it is.'

'Go on.'

'Usually, when we discuss the men we've had sex with, we mention the size of his dick, and how good he is at using it, the number of orgasms we've had and how often. When I asked you about this one, I've heard about his sister, his sense of humour, you've moved in with him… do you see where I'm going with this?'

Sapphire knew Monica was right. She felt disloyal to James talking about that stuff. She was silent.

Monica summoned the waiter to order two more glasses of wine.

'Oh, not for me thanks, I'll just have a mineral water. Got tons to do this afternoon.'

Monica said, 'You have changed. But you know what? I like it. When are you going to meet his family?'

'Oh, I already have. His mother's an odd woman and his older sister is a lawyer.'

Monica gave her a narrow eyed look. 'Don't tell me you're actually falling in love for this guy?'

'No way. I'm fond of him. I owe him a lot. And we're good together. But love? Never. Not going to happen.' Sapphire thanked the waiter as he put their drinks on the table. 'You're staring at me again.'

'I'm known you a long time, Sapphire. And I love you, you know that, don't you?'

'Of course, and I love you two. You're my best friend.'

'Be careful. Remember Monty's advice. But if he is as good as you make out, then grab him with both hands and never let go.'

Ruth was waiting for James when he got home. She was sitting on the front step reading a paperback. She stood up as the taxi stopped outside the house but made no attempt to help as he struggled out of the back. It was getting easier though to manoeuvre himself around on crutches.

He stopped in front of her. 'How long have you been waiting?'

She put her book into the enormous bag she was carrying and said, 'Not long. Can I come in?'

He shrugged. 'Of course.'

He turned his back on her, shuffled up the steps and unlocked the front door. Then he pushed the door open with one of his crutches and waited until she had walked past him. He caught a whiff of her perfume as did so. He used to love it back in the day when they were together. It wasn't as pleasant as Sparkle by Sapphire.

'How are you?' he asked.

'Fine. You?'

'Fine.'

They wandered into the kitchen and she sat at the table with her hands folded over her stomach and stared at him. Okay, something was up, and he was sure he knew what it was, but he wasn't going to be the one to bring the subject up.

'Would you like a tea, coffee or a cold drink?'

'A cold drink please.'

He opened the fridge door and took out the mango juice, her eyes piercing his back. He collected two glasses from the cupboard and poured two generous helpings. He'd have to put mango juice on the next on-line shopping list, or Lulu would start getting anxious. There had to be ten unopened cartons in the cupboard, and they were down to nine. He put one glass on the table in front of Ruth.

'Did you find the contract?'

'Oh yes, I found it.'

'Can I have it then, please?'

'No James, you can't. I am keeping it and the copies that were with it. What idiot keeps copies of an important document with the original? Apart from that idiot, Malcolm, of course. You're no better are you? You're two of a kind. I don't know why you didn't stay business partners, you're both tarred with the same brush. You're a fool you know. You could have had everything you wanted but knowing how much money Malcolm paid you and realising that our company suffered because of it, makes my blood boil.'

James sipped on his juice during this tirade. He shook his head sadly.

'You never did have a head for business, did you Ruth? The money Steele paid me was a drop in the ocean compared to how much the company could have been worth in the future. And the reason your new company is going broke is because Malcolm is lazy and not prepared to put in the hard yards. I have no idea what you two do in that place, but it obviously has nothing to do with making money.'

'You don't know what you're talking about. Malcolm is a businessman and it would take a better man than you to bring him down.'

'So why did you ask me to help you?'

'Because I thought you were better than this!' She reached into her bag and pulled out the disclaimer. She waved it at him, and he was tempted to make a grab for it, but then she quickly stuffed it back into her bag.

'Did you really think I would walk away from the business I loved with nothing to show for it? What do you take me for, Ruth? I'd already lost you, I wasn't prepared to lose everything.'

'You should have fought him. Behaved like a man. Instead, you did a deal. Blackmailed him into giving you money in exchange for your silence. How noble is that?'

'Noble! What the fuck are you talking about woman? Noble… you're pregnant with the accountant's baby, you blame it on Malcolm and try to get me to play daddy. How noble is that?'

'It's Malcolm's.'

'He told me he's had a vasectomy.'

'He's lying.'

'One of you is lying. The jury is still out as to which one.'

Then she seemed to soften as if she realised she was getting nowhere being belligerent. 'We were lovers once, James, we meant something to each other. Have you forgotten that?'

'If I remember correctly, you were the one who forgot when you cuckolded me with Malcolm.'

'Oh, for God's sake, don't be so pompous! Who says "cuckold" these days?'

'Can I help it if I've got an extensive vocabulary?'

James was getting bored. He knew, if he bided his time, he would get the shares he needed. He really wanted to get his hands on the disclaimer but wasn't prepared to beg. With a sick feeling in the pit of his stomach he realised she was going to keep the disclaimer as a bargaining tool. If she thought for one minute they were going to get back together, she was sadly deluded. He needed to get her out of the house but didn't know how to go about it. She was sitting there, looking as if she belonged and sipping her mango juice thoughtfully.

'What did you and Malcom talk about?' she asked.

'We strolled hand in hand down memory lane reminiscing. What do you think we talked about?'

'There's no need to be nasty. I was asking a civil question.'

James's leg was starting to throb, so he poured a glass of water and swallowed two painkillers. Then he sat at the kitchen table opposite Ruth.

'We talked business. And he told me about you and the accountant.'

'There was nothing between us. We were work colleagues, that's all.'

'Not how Steele tells it.'

'How did he seem?' Ruth, surprisingly, sounded genuinely interested. Maybe she still had feelings for Steele. Maybe she was realising she had made a mistake in coming to James for assistance.

'He seemed exactly the same as he always has. Older, tattier, but still as "Jack the Lad" as ever.'

'He was your business partner once; you must have liked and trusted him then.'

'I was younger when we agreed to go into partnership. More naïve and willing to give people the benefit of the doubt. He had money I needed, and I had skills he needed. It worked—then.'

'What about now, James, what are your plans now?'

His plans were none of her business. 'I'm happy where I am. I like working for Sapphire and can contribute much to the business. It's on the up and I'm happy to be part of that.'

'You're not at a job interview, James. This is me you're talking to.'

Which was precisely why he wasn't prepared to tell her his plans. He didn't trust her an inch.

'What about you, Ruth? What are your plans for the future? Apart from finding an appropriate daddy for the baby.'

'That's unkind.' It was, but he didn't care.

'Sorry, but you're coming across as slightly desperate. I'd just like to know the truth that's all. If it's the accountant's baby, why don't you take up with him? He'll always be able to find work. Good accountants are constantly in demand.'

'It's Malcolm's baby. I don't know what I can do or say to make you believe me, but it's true. Malcolm is lying.'

'Why would he?'

'Because he's a dirty two-timing rat who'll say anything to get out of his responsibilities.'

James knew that to be true. They were both capable of subterfuge to further their own ends. Suddenly he was tired of the whole situation. He wanted the day to be over so he could see Sapphire. He glanced at the clock on the wall and realised it was nearly four o'clock. Lulu would be home at any minute.

Ruth had seen him, and she raised her eyebrows in a question, 'Expecting someone?'

'Lulu will be home anytime. Maybe you should go.'

'How is your sister? Still single?'

'She's dating now and moving into interior design. We're thinking of expanding and taking her on as chief designer.'

Why had he said that? It was none of Ruth's business what they were doing and the least she knew the better. He hated the patronising way she spoke about Lulu and wanted to show Ruth how well she was coping with life.

'My, my, quite the little autistic savant. And this woman that you were seen carrying out of her fashion show? Are you two just work colleagues, or…' Ruth stopped and looked at him speculatively.

'We're work colleagues.'

'Fuck buddies?'

'None of your business.' James spoke more sharply than he intended, and a slow smile spread over Ruth's face.

'I'll take that as a yes then.' Her voice was as smooth as cream, but her eyes were flashing and the muscles around her mouth had tensed.

'Take it any way you like,' he said angrily.

Then the front door closed, and Lulu came into the kitchen.

'Hi James, is Sapphire back yet? Oh…' She froze when she saw Ruth sitting at the kitchen table.

'Hi Lulu, lovely to see you again. How are you? James has been telling me all about your new life. It sounds exciting. More exciting than the teaching assistant job anyway.'

'Yes,' Lulu said, looking to James for clues. But the damage had already been done.

'So—Sapphire lives here too?' Ruth looked from one to the other and James knew there was no point in lying.

'Yes,' said Lulu, 'she's here to help James.'

'Of course she is,' Ruth said brightly. 'They make a lovely couple, don't they Lulu?'

'Yes,' Lulu said still looking towards James to rescue her.

'Ruth was just going, weren't you Ruth?' James said, gathering the glasses together. Lulu came forward and put them in the dishwasher. 'I'll just show her out.'

Lulu was looking worried and so James smiled at her. It wasn't her fault. And if Ruth thought she and Sapphire were an official couple, maybe she'd stop bothering him. Perhaps she'd try and get Steele back.

As he hobbled down the hallway, Ruth walked ahead of

him, her head held high and her enormous handbag on her arm. The bag that contained the disclaimer.

'So—you and the designer are together after all. Why did you lie to me, James?'

'I didn't lie, I told you to mind your own business.'

'But it is my business. So long as I have the documents you want, you and I have unfinished business.'

'That disclaimer is worthless to you. In fact, if anything, it just proves that I am a shrewd businessman who is not prepared to let anyone walk all over me.'

'It proves you're dishonest.'

'No, it proves Malcolm Steele is dishonest. He was the one engaged in insider trading.'

'You blackmailed him—money for silence. It proves you knew what he was doing and didn't say anything.'

'It proves nothing—read it again. There is no mention that I knew what he was doing. It merely says Malcolm has paid me for the company. It's as if I sold it to him. I promised not to disclose anything about the business. That's all.'

'So why were you so desperate to get it back?'

'Because, Ruth, I want a fresh start. I want nothing to link me to Malcolm Steele, or you, or anything else concerning Lewis Leathers. I'm in a different business altogether now.'

'Do you love her?'

'Love whom?'

'You know *whom*,' she said sarcastically.

'No, I don't know what you are talking about. Now, if you don't mind, I think you should leave.'

'You haven't seen the last of me, James. I'll be in touch.'

Then she left, walking carefully down the steps and strolling in that special way only pregnant women use, as if they were aware of every step and that they were carrying precious cargo. James felt a pang that lasted a couple of seconds. That could have been his wife and baby. Did he feel relieved that he had dodged a bullet as Steele suggested, or was there part of him that felt he had missed out?

Then he thought of seeing Sapphire that evening, and the question was easy to answer.

Chapter Twenty-Eight

James didn't have to wait long for Steele to make contact. Two weeks later, on a Monday at about lunchtime, he phoned to ask James to call on him again.

'Why don't we meet somewhere neutral this time? The George and Dragon at about seven?'

'George and Dragon it is.' Then he hung up.

Steele hadn't said why he wanted to meet him but there was only one reason that James could think of and that was to sell his shares. He did a mental happy dance.

He was getting used to mobilising on his crutches and taking taxis everywhere, while looking forward to the time when he didn't have to rely on anyone again. That Monday night, Lulu and Sapphire had gone to a Diabetes Self Help group, so James was free to see Malcolm without having to explain where he was going.

The George and Dragon was packed, and James struggled to get through the crowds to the corner table where Malcolm sat nursing a pint of bitter. Thankfully, he had been kind enough to get one for James.

'Evening,' said James as he collapsed onto the chair and rested his crutches on the floor.

'Good evening to you, mate. How's the leg?'

'Not hurting so much now, I'm weaning myself off the pain killers albeit slowly.'

'Great,' said Steele. James doubted he had been listening to a word he said. He wanted to cut to the chase and ask Steele about the shares, but he was settled now, and it was pleasant to be back in an old-fashioned London pub with its unique smell of beer and onions and the general background noise of people enjoying a night out.

'Cheers,' said James, lifting his pint glass in a mock salute.

'Yeah, cheers,' Steele replied as he did the same.

James drank deeply and licked his lips in appreciation. 'You can't beat a good old-fashioned beer.' Steele didn't reply, and James studied his face. 'Is anything wrong?'

'You may well ask,' Malcolm replied.

'I just did.'

'Okay, then I'll tell you. I've got myself into a bit of debt and need money fast.'

'So, you're willing to sell the shares?' This was almost too easy, thought James.

'The shares? No, mate, I can't sell them, they're all I've got. Like you say, the company is starting to do well, and those shares are going to be worth a lot more in the immediate future. In fact, I was planning to do what you were thinking—buy more and then I'll have a majority.'

'Well, that's not going to happen now, you must realise that.'

'Look, this is just a temporary blip. If I could just borrow enough to pay off my debts, then I'd be able to get back to doing business. The sooner I do what I do best, the sooner I can pay you. You see?'

'It appears that what you do best Steele, is lose money hand over fist. I'm hoping that you're not going to ask me for a loan because the answer is no.'

'Have a heart, we used to be good friends once. Do anything for each other. For old time's sake. How about it?'

James couldn't believe what he was hearing. The cheeky bastard was asking him for a loan. After everything that had happened. Was he, James, really so gullible? Did he have "Mug" tattooed across his forehead?

'I don't believe you're asking me this.'

'I'd do the same for you, mate, you know I would.'

'No, Steele, you wouldn't, and, for the record, I am no longer your *mate*. I stopped being that when you tried to ruin my life. We were doing well and could have been top of the financial tree by now, but you just got greedy. Not content with taking my fiancée you had to steal my business as well. I loved that company. It was mine, my pride and joy, the one thing in my life that I had done well. And you just ....'

James trailed off, feeling emotional suddenly. He thought of his father, of how successful he had been and how James wanted to follow in his footsteps. He wanted something of his own that he could be proud of. That his father would have been proud of him for. Then it was gone. All down to the man who sat opposite him, staring at him as if he had never seen him before. Perhaps he hadn't. They never talked about anything personal or deep, it had only ever been about the company or superficial stuff. Things that didn't matter. They never spoke about their feelings.

'Sorry. I didn't know you felt like that.'

'Well how did you think I felt?'

'I dunno. I just thought it was work, just business, you know. All's fair in love and finance, that kind of thing.'

James took a deep breath in to get himself together. Then he took another long draught of his beer, wiping his mouth on the back of his hand.

'So… let's get down to business then, shall we? I'm willing to buy your shares but it's going to cost you. I'll write the price down to save you any embarrassment.'

James took a piece of paper out of the top pocket of his shirt, and a short stubby pencil. Since he broke his leg, he had taken to wearing clothes with lots of pockets, so he could carry small items he needed around with him. Keys, tissues, his phone, pencil and paper, even safety pins and paperclips but he couldn't remember what he needed them for.

When he had written the amount, he handed the piece of paper to Steele.

'What?! You have got to be joking. I paid more for them than this.'

'Tough. That is the amount I am prepared to pay. No more.'

'Ridiculous. Some friend you are. I could sell my shares online and get more than that.'

'You could, but that would take you longer and I can transfer the money to you now, no questions asked.'

'It's not enough, James, I need more to cover my debts. I really thought you would help me out here.'

'Sorry, this is my final offer.'

'I'm disappointed, I really am. But if that's your final word, then there's nothing more to say. Good evening, James.'

Steele got up and strode out of the pub. James sat back to wait, sipping his beer, and eavesdropping on the conversations around him. He'd give him an hour and then he'd leave. If Steele wasn't back by then he would have severely underestimated his old friend.

James had debated telling Sapphire who the mystery shareholder was and giving her the chance to buy the shares. That would have been the sensible and morally right thing to do. But, if that happened, his chance to play the Knight in Shining Armour, riding to the rescue of the damsel in distress, would be gone. He wanted Sapphire to praise him for his good business sense. He wanted her to look up to him and see him as an equal, not just the man who was helping her obtain her goals.

If Steele didn't come back within the hour, he'd arrange a meeting with Sapphire and Hector and come clean about Malcolm Steele. Then the decision would be out of his hands. If Steele returned before that however, he would go ahead with his plan.

Forty-five minutes later, Malcolm was back. 'Still here? Do you want another?' He gestured at the empty glass.

'Yes I am,' said James, 'and yes, thanks. Scotch. Make it a double.'

Steele tutted, but took the empty glass and fought his way to the bar. James watched him, feeling smug. He hadn't changed that much then.

By the time they left the pub, having sealed the deal with more glasses of whisky, James was feeling quite drunk. He wondered whether he should try to "crutch" home, as he called his style of walking. He felt invincible as if he could fly, but Malcolm, thankfully, wasn't feeling so ecstatic and hailed a taxi, practically shoving James in the back before waving him off.

'Bye Steele!' he shouted as the taxi moved away from the kerb. 'It's been jolly doing business with you.' He laughed at his wit and decided that it had been an exceptionally good evening. All he needed now, was Sapphire, waiting for him in bed, warm and naked, to make it perfect.

Sapphire listened intently as the speaker informed the group about cheese. The title of the talk was "Dairy and Diabetes" and Sapphire had already learned that she should be eating low-fat cheese and reduce her favourites; cheddar, Brie and Edam. She could still eat them, but just had to watch her portion sizes.

Sapphire glanced at Lulu who was also soaking up the speaker's words of wisdom. When Lulu listened to someone she gave them her full attention and Sapphire knew that Lulu would be able to repeat everything the woman said, word for word. It was an enviable skill. One that Sapphire didn't possess, and she would have to study the handouts with tables containing information on the glycaemic index when she got home.

She was glad she had come, had met some interesting people and the feeling that she wasn't alone with her struggle with diabetes was a comfort. She also had a lot of blogs to read. Personal accounts of how people managed their diabetes. Sapphire liked blogs and regularly checked out Lulu's.

But now, she was getting bored and hoped they could go soon.

Sapphire was a bit concerned about the situation with James. It had been three weeks since his accident and he was doing well. He worked from home, collating information, researching companies, and answering emails, but Sapphire looked forward to the time he could return to the office. She had grown used to having him around and relied on him for moral support as well as the practical things.

The mystery investor remained a mystery, despite James's efforts to discover his identity. Ruth hadn't been mentioned again and Sapphire hoped that meant James hadn't seen her again.

Then there was Lulu. Sapphire really wanted her on board with the new interior design range but didn't want to pressurize her for an answer.

The speaker had stopped speaking and everyone was clapping. Sapphire joined in and then the meeting was over.

Chapter Twenty-Nine

The phone rang in Della's office, but Sapphire didn't look up from her computer. She was busy trying to arrange a meeting of all the staff who would be involved in the new interior design section of the business. Sapphire hadn't felt this excited for ages. It would be amazing, especially if Lulu agreed to join them.

Sapphire realised that Della had left her office and was standing in front of her desk waiting for her to look up.

'Della—what is it?'

'There's a woman by the name of Ruth Mitchell in the lobby asking to see you.'

Sapphire thought for a second then shook her head. 'I don't know anyone called Ruth Mitchell. Is she a designer? What does she want?' Maybe word had already spread about her expansion plans and she was asking for a job.

'The receptionist said she's been here before. A heavily pregnant woman who came to see James.'

'That Ruth? Is she asking for him, not me?' James had

assured her that they'd seen the last of that woman. Sapphire had never even met her but disliked her anyway.

'No, she's asking for you. She has some information for you. Important, so she says.'

'What about?' Sapphire was puzzled. She didn't have time for this. What did the woman want?

'About James apparently,' said Della. 'Maybe you should hear her out?'

'I don't like the sound of this, Della. Can you sit in on the meeting as a witness?'

'If that's what you want. Shall I go and fetch her?'

'No, tell her to find her own way. It's not difficult, you just take the lift to the top floor. She's been here before after all. You can meet her at the lift.'

Della left the office and Sapphire finished an email she was typing. She pressed send, then turned her thoughts to Ruth Mitchell. James had said she asked him for advice concerning claiming child maintenance, but why go to James? He's never had a child and, anyway, all the information would be online these days. For the first time, she felt a twinge of doubt about James and Ruth. After all, he had loved the woman once.

Sapphire was standing when Della escorted Ruth Mitchell into the office.

'Coffee?' asked Della. Sapphire looked at her visitor who smiled.

'Could I just have water, please? Coffee makes me need the loo.' She spread her hands over her stomach as if to show that she was pregnant.

Della walked over to the water cooler and filled two cups, then put them on the table next to the couches.

'Thank you, Della,' said Sapphire.

'Yes, thanks,' said Ruth.

'Have a seat.'

As Ruth waddled over to the couch and plopped down on it, then picked up her water and sipped at it, Sapphire took the time to study her. She wasn't what she had expected. She looked too… well, neat was the only word she could think of. Her hair was bobbed and shiny, her make-up simple and she wore varnish, not colour on her nails. There was nothing in her looks or manner that would make anyone look twice at her. And yet this woman had been engaged to James and had left him for another man, breaking his heart in the process. She must have something about her.

'Thank you for agreeing to see me, I realise how busy you must be.' Her voice was well modulated and slightly husky, but quiet as if she didn't want to stand out.

'What's this all about?' Sapphire didn't have time to waste on nonsense. She still didn't trust the woman who looked at her with a wide-eyed innocent look that had to be false. She remained standing to give herself the advantage.

Ruth glanced at Della, who was perched on the edge of Sapphire's desk listening.

'I've asked Della to stay, I hope that's okay with you.' *Tough if it isn't*, thought Sapphire.

Ruth didn't look very pleased but shrugged and smiled at Della.

'So, Ms Mitchell, perhaps you could tell us why you're here.'

'Okay. I realise this isn't going to be easy to hear, so I'll just come out and say it. I don't know what James has told you about the two of us, but… well, the fact of the matter is that I'm carrying his baby.'

Sapphire glanced at Della who raised her eyebrows in amazement.

'James is the father?'

'Yes. It didn't work out with Malcolm, and James and I... well, we never stopped loving each other.'

'I don't believe you. You're lying. It's Malcolm Steele's baby.'

'It can't be his as he had a vasectomy years ago. He doesn't like children.'

'I don't believe you.'

'I'm so sorry, I really am.'

'Why are you telling me this?'

'Well, I've only got six weeks to go before the birth and I want everything to be out in the open. I know James hasn't told you about us yet because you have such strong feelings for him, and he really is fond of you and doesn't want to hurt you—'

'I think you need to leave now, Ms Mitchell. You've said enough.'

Sapphire, who couldn't keep still with all the adrenaline pumping around her system, started pacing.

'I understand how upset you are—'

'I'm not upset, I'm furious. How dare you come here lying to me about the father of your baby. Do you really think I wouldn't have known if James had still been seeing you? I don't know what your game is, but it's not going to work. I don't believe a word of it.'

'I'm sorry you're taking this view. I only came here to clear the air—'

'Please leave now. Della? Could you please escort Ms Mitchell off the premises.' Sapphire turned abruptly so she didn't have to see the woman's self-satisfied smirk.

'Certainly,' said Della.

'You'll be sorry you didn't listen. James isn't the perfect gentleman you seem to think he is. He is just as capable of dishonesty as any of us. I was just trying to stop you from making a fool of yourself. He told me it was just sex between the two of you. I've always been the one he loved.'

Sapphire stared at Monica's painting of London at night, hoping it would ground her and didn't reply. She was shaking with rage and something else that she took a while to identify—panic. For one moment there, she had started to believe it. She felt the pain of loss and betrayal, until common sense won and she realised that it was simply a pack of lies.

'This way, Ms Mitchell,' Della said, trying to encourage their unwelcome visitor to leave. But, as Sapphire turned back to face her, it was obvious she hadn't finished. She had struggled back to her feet and was holding out a document to her.

'Take this and read it. James didn't lose his company. He sold it, for a considerable amount of money. And now that he owns the majority shares in your business, he's a rich man. James was always the brains of the partnership, while Malcolm was the brawn.'

'You're wrong,' Sapphire glared at the woman who stared back at her brazenly with the smirk still on her face. 'I am the majority shareholder and intend to keep it that way.'

'I'm sorry, I really am,' said Ruth looking anything but sorry. 'James has been buying shares, sometimes using aliases. Check with your accountant. James owns this company now.'

Then Sapphire thought of something. 'Has Malcolm

Steele being buying shares in my company under another name?'

'Yes, shares that are now in James's name. They've been planning it for months.'

'Why are you telling me this? What's in it for you?'

'Like I say, now that James and I are together again, I want a fresh start, everything above board. James has promised me a job here once the baby's born.'

'Over my dead body. Della—get her out of here!'

'Of course.' Della had hold of the woman's arm, but she left willingly. She had already done all the damage she could do.

When she heard the door close, Sapphire collapsed into her chair and put her head in her hands. She took deep breaths and closed her eyes for a few minutes. Only then did she look at the document which was scrunched up in her fist. She put it on her desk, smoothed it out and quickly skimmed it. It appeared to be a contract of some kind between Malcolm Steele and James Lewis. Sapphire put her glasses on and read the whole thing carefully. It stated that James had willingly sold his part of the company to Steele. There was a small paragraph at the end of the document signed by James and witnessed by someone else—a someone with an illegible signature—stating that he would not disclose any information about the company or its activities to a third party.

James, far from having lost his company as he had claimed, had sold it to Steele for an incredibly generous amount of money. It wasn't an obscene amount, but it was definitely enough for James to start up again.

Sapphire was shaking. She'd tested her glucose and had eaten a healthy lunch, so it wasn't caused by her diabetes. It was the shock of finding that a man she had grown close to, admired, respected and—even though she was reluctant to use the word— had begun to love, had lied. What else had he lied about? When she had got herself together, she sat up straight and picked up the phone.

———

'I was sure you'd already know about this, of course, as you've been working so closely together for a while now, but…'

'What is it, Hector?' Sapphire's heart was beating fast and her hands had started trembling. She was desperate for her accountant to deny it; to say that everything was as it should be, then she could dismiss Ruth's vitriol as jealousy and desperation.

'You do know, don't you, that you no longer hold the majority shares in Sapphire Enterprises?'

'What? No, I didn't.' *Oh God, it's true.* 'Who does?'

'James Lewis. That mystery investor that he was investigating has sold all his shares to him. He now has a fifty-one percent majority.'

Sapphire was stunned. She'd braced herself for this, but now that it was out in the open, she just felt like crying. She didn't think she could cope with any more shocks but kept her voice calm and even. 'Did we ever find out who the mystery investor was?'

'James obviously knew, but he didn't pass the information on to me.'

'So James is the majority shareholder?'

'Yes, he is. I was sure you'd know about it.'

Hector looked at her with sympathy in his blue eyes. Sapphire didn't want pity, she wanted to yell at someone, scream at them, tell them to do something. Sort it out! But the only person who deserved that kind of treatment was herself. She had taken her eye off the ball. She was an astute businesswoman who never let anyone get the better of her. She was clever and ambitious, kick-ass and smart. So how the hell had she let this happen?

Sensible Sapphire looked at herself over the top of her glasses and tutted. *You know full well. You trusted a man. You let a man take over. Handed over full control of your body, your heart, and your business. And now look what's happened. You silly bitch.*

Sapphire groaned and Hector looked at her in alarm.

'Are you alright, Sapphire? Shall I get you some water?'

'No, I'm fine. Thanks.'

She forced a smile to her face and touched him on the forearm. It was an innocent, reassuring gesture and, fortunately it worked. Hector patted her hand, then closed his laptop.

'Well, if that's everything. I have another meeting to go to. The board members are buzzing about the new plans. Interior design—what a wonderful idea.'

'Yes, I think it's just what we need. A complete change of direction. Thanks Hector.'

'A pleasure, my dear, as always.' Hector stood up and Sapphire did too.

In her heels she was at least two inches taller than he was, but he seemed oblivious of that fact. Or he didn't care. Why couldn't younger men be as kind and honest as Hector? Because younger men, like James, were ambitious and greedy.

When he'd left, Sapphire remained standing in the middle of her office. She could hear the muffled sounds of London traffic, watched birds flying above the buildings through the windows. She loved this company. She loved her lifestyle. She'd worked hard for this. Monty's money had set her up and she wasn't going to let some lying bastard take it.

Then she thought of James. His gentleness and strength, his hands as they caressed her body and his mouth as he kissed her gently… or not so gently. Passionate, sexy, clever, she had believed him to be a man of integrity. He'd lied. About everything.

Chapter Thirty

James and Lulu were both in the kitchen preparing a meal when Sapphire arrived home. No, she could no longer think of it as her home. In an hour or so, she'd be gone, never to return. The adrenaline was still flowing but this time it resulted in cold, hard anger that fueled her determination to tell James what she thought of him before she packed the few things she had here, put Sparkle into her carrier and phoned for a taxi.

'Hi, darling,' said James over his shoulder as he stirred something on the cooker. He was wearing his apron again, but this time was fully clothed. She pushed the thought of never being able to hold that hard masculine body against her and feel his growing arousal, ever again. She would miss the sex, that was for sure. But hey—there were more selfish-bastard fish in the sea.

She didn't reply but smiled at Lulu who was setting the table. 'Hi, Sapphire,' she said sweetly. 'We're having spaghetti carbonara. It's one of James's favourites.'

'Hi Lulu.' She was beginning to realise everything she

was losing. She'd loved being with these two people. She'd started to believe they were a team—one that could live together happily and work together profitably and productively. Hopefully, she could still have that with Lulu.

'Don't I get a kiss?' asked James. He hadn't even turned around, and she knew he expected her to come to him, put her arms around his waist and press her body against him. She would have kissed his neck and maybe risked a quick feel of his growing erection if Lulu hadn't been in the room.

James turned and looked at her for the first time. It must have been written all over her face.

'Sapphire, what's wrong?' He frowned and she inhaled slowly. This wasn't going to be pretty.

'I had a visitor today.' She tried to speak calmly and slowly, but her heart was beating out of her chest and she felt ill.

'Oh? Who?'

Sapphire took the crumpled contract out of her bag and held it out to him. 'She gave me this.'

James put the wooden spoon onto the counter and hobbled slowly towards her. 'Ruth.'

'Correct. She told me some interesting things.'

'You do know, I assume, that she is a liar and a cheat.'

'Takes one to know one.'

'What's that supposed to mean?'

'I think you know.' Her voice was starting to get louder and Lulu, who had taken over the sauce stirring, looked behind her in alarm.

'Are you going to argue?' she asked quietly.

'No, of course not. Are we Sapphire?' said James.

'I'm leaving.' They needed to talk in private. She couldn't tear a strip off him with Lulu listening.

'What? Why? Sapphire…'

She left the kitchen and James followed after her. He caught up to her at the bottom of the stairs as he could now work up quite a speed on those wretched crutches. At least he didn't need help any longer. In fact, he was going back to the office on Monday. Oh God... how was she going to avoid him?

She ran up the stairs and he came after her. Using one crutch and hanging on to the bannister, he could move at an impressive rate. By the time he got to the top he was sweating, and his T-shirt was sticking to him. He was also panting, and his eyes were wild.

'Sapphire! I'll explain about that contract... give me a chance to explain...'

She stood at the door of his bedroom and waited until he reached her. He was breathless and his face was red, but she wasn't going to let herself feel the slightest bit sorry for him.

'In here,' she said curtly, holding the door open for him, 'You can *explain* while I pack.'

'You're not serious? Sapphire, please tell me what's going on?' He collapsed on the bed still panting. Sapphire started emptying drawers and tipping her make-up and toiletries into carrier bags. She could sort it out when she got home. For now, she would listen to his excuses for as long as it took to collect all her things. Then she would never be forced to listen to his lies again.

'That contract—legally it's worthless. That's what Ruth didn't seem to understand. It would never hold up in a court of law. I signed it to keep Steele off my back. He thought he could buy my silence, so I went along with it. And the money, well... I'm a businessman, Sapphire, I wasn't about to walk away with nothing.'

He stopped talking, no doubt expecting her to reply, but

she continued to pack, taking her trouser suits off the hangers and folding them neatly before placing them on the top of the suitcase that was already stuffed to the gills. She had never been good at packing suitcases.

'I don't give a flying fuck about that contract. You double-crossed me. When you said you wanted to be in charge of another business, I never dreamed you meant mine. I thought you were helping me achieve my dreams, but no, you were just looking out for yourself.'

James seemed to slump in relief. 'The shares. That's what this is all about isn't it?'

'Like I said, Ruth told me some very interesting and enlightening things about you.'

'Did she also tell you who the mystery investor was?'

'Of course. She said the two of you had cooked up this little scheme right from the beginning. You targeted me. I suppose you thought that, being a mere woman, I'd be easy prey—'

'Sapphire! Don't be so utterly ridiculous! Of course I didn't *target* you. How can you think that of me? Steele was the one trying to take over your business, so I had to stop him. He's in dire straits financially and I got them at a knock-down price. I did rather well, actually.'

Sapphire turned on him, her rage making her voice so loud she was almost yelling. 'Oh yes, you miserable bastard! You've done very well for yourself, *actually*, haven't you? You own Sapphire Enterprises, you still have the money from your company and the majority shares in mine and you're about to become a father. Congratu-bloody-lations!'

Her words didn't have the desired effect. James stood up with a smile on his face and tears in his eyes. He crutched towards her, then let the crutches fall to the floor and put his arms out for her to embrace him.

'Oh Sapphire, that's wonderful! When did you find out? You're pregnant? That's fantastic. I'm going to be a dad!'

'I'm not the pregnant one you idiot! I'm talking about Ruth.'

He deflated visibly in front of her as if he'd been a balloon that she'd just stuck a pin in. 'I don't understand.'

Sapphire felt a twinge of doubt. Was Ruth lying about the baby? Or was James a better actor than she had given him credit for?

'It's not difficult to understand, even for you. Ruth is carrying your baby and the two of you are an item. Oh, and the best part is that when the baby's born you have promised Ruth a job at Sapphire Enterprises.'

'What in God's name has that bloody woman been telling you, and why do you believe her?' James was starting to lose his cool and veins stood out on his forearms and his jaw clenched tightly. Sapphire took a step back out of his reach.

'She told me that it can't be Malcolm Steele's baby as he has had a vasectomy.'

'Bollocks!' James shouted, 'if you'll excuse the pun.' He shook his head in disbelief. 'Steele is the biggest coward I know; he'd never let anyone holding a scalpel near his crown jewels.'

Sapphire continued her packing, with James shadowing her. He pleaded with her and she nearly gave in, but what would be the point? The facts spoke for themselves. James had lied about losing his business and about buying Steele's shares.

'Please, Sapphire, you can't go like this. Can't we just talk about it?'

'When you found out that Steele was the mystery

investor, why didn't you tell me? Why did you buy the shares yourself?'

'Because I had the money from the sale of my company. Time was of the essence. I was worried he would sell them to someone else or buy more shares and became the majority shareholder, which was what he wanted. I had to move fast—surely you can see that.'

'A few days wouldn't have made any difference, James.'

'It might have.'

'Okay, but why didn't you tell me what you were going to do? I had to find out through Ruth and then Hector that I was no longer in charge of my own company. How do you think that made me feel?'

'It makes no difference to the company, as I don't intend to make any changes. You will, obviously, have to run things by me, but you are answerable to the Board of Directors anyway…'

Sapphire glared at him, took her phone from her handbag, and ordered a taxi.

'I am so disappointed in you, James. I thought that, at last, I'd found a man comfortable enough in his own skin to be honest with me and treat me as an equal. I thought you were someone I could trust enough to go into partnership with. We could have had it all, you and I, but you threw it all away. I'm going now. We have to work together, but let's keep the contact to the absolute minimum, shall we?'

Sapphire wheeled her suitcase out of the bedroom and didn't look back. The last picture of James that she would keep in her mind was of him staring at her in disbelief. He had looked shocked and defeated, which was exactly how she had felt after Ruth's visit.

She went downstairs and picked up Sparkle, giving her a quick cuddle before putting her in her carrier.

She stopped at the kitchen door. Lulu was sitting at the kitchen table biting her nails.

'I'm going back to my apartment, Lulu. Have you decided yet on the designer job?'

Lulu shook her head, her finger still in her mouth.

'Could you make a decision soon do you think? I really need to move fast on this one. There's a lot to organise.'

Lulu took her finger out of her mouth and nodded. The doorbell rang, and she jumped.

'That's my taxi. Bye, Lulu.'

'Sapphire?'

'Yes?' She turned back.

'Are you coming back?'

'No, but I'll stay in touch whatever happens.'

Lulu didn't speak, so Sapphire left with her suitcase and cat carrier. As she climbed into the taxi, she felt drained. Never again would she trust a man. And yet… James had never shown her anything but courtesy and consideration. During sex, he thought of her needs first. At work he deferred to her. Was it really all an act? Was he so deceitful that he could have spent so much time with her, secretly plotting to take over her business and run Sapphire Enterprises himself? And was he really, all this time, leading a double life and going from her bed to Ruth Mitchell's? It didn't seem possible, even for a highly sexed man like James.

The facts spoke for themselves. He had lied. Directly with the disclaimer and by omission with the shares. He wasn't trustworthy. What a fool she was. Never again. Monty had told her never to trust anyone, and he was right. Especially men.

When James eventually dragged himself down the stairs, after spending a considerable time lying on the bed staring at the ceiling, Lulu had eaten her tea and was cleaning the kitchen cupboards, putting everything back in regimental lines, each line equidistant from each other. She did this when she was stressed. Just another thing for James to feel guilty about.

'She's gone,' said Lulu.

'I know,' James replied before collapsing onto a chair and staring into space.

'She says she's not coming back.' Lulu closed the cupboard door and then opened the adjacent cupboard door and started taking out packets of macaroni and rice.

'I know that too.'

'What have you done?'

'I haven't done anything. Well… nothing much. I bought shares from Malcolm Steele, but instead of doing the sensible thing and telling Sapphire first, I went ahead and bought them in my name, so I am now the majority shareholder. Sapphire thinks I was trying to take over, but I wasn't. I was just trying to help.'

'Why didn't you tell her about the shares first?'

James sighed. It was a reasonable question, one that Sapphire had asked. 'Because I wanted to be the one who rescued Sapphire Enterprises from the clutches of Malcolm Steele. I knew I could get him to sell to me for peanuts. I was playing the big man so Sapphire could admire my prowess as an entrepreneur and look up to me as her saviour. I was being a complete dick to be honest, Lulu, and now I've lost everything.'

Lulu had cleaned the inside of the cupboard and arranged the packets and boxes to her satisfaction.

'Not exactly everything. You've still got the shares.'

'They mean nothing now that I haven't got Sapphire. I don't want to take over her business. Oh, I might have thought about it in the beginning, but her love means more to me than shares.'

'Do you love her?' Lulu sat down at the kitchen table and frowned at him.

'Yes.'

'Have you told her?'

'No.'

'Then how is she going to know?'

James smiled. Lulu's cool logic always cut through to the heart of the matter. 'She doesn't know. She never will now. It doesn't matter Lulu. It's over. She has made her feelings perfectly plain.'

'Then you should do the same. Make your feelings perfectly plain.'

With that Lulu got up and left the kitchen. James moved slowly and lethargically into his study. That dash up the stairs had really taken it out of him. He had two weeks to go before his plaster was removed, so he was far from being back to full strength. His muscles had weakened in the weeks he'd been laid up. A few trips to the gym were in order.

James thought of the irony of the situation. Two women, in the space of a few days, had told him he could have had it all. Now he had nothing.

He sat in front of his computer and stared at the screen. He had been working from home for the last few weeks and was still in touch with the goings on at Sapphire Enterprises. He had been looking forward to getting back into the office, but with the rift with Sapphire, he was thinking of staying away for a bit longer.

The doorbell chimed and for one instant, James

wondered if Sapphire had returned to talk things through. He struggled to his feet and crutched out of the study and into the hallway, but then stopped when he heard the voice of the person Lulu was speaking to. Shamelessly eavesdropping, he moved closer so he could hear but not be seen.

'Is James in?'

'Yes.'

'Can I come in then?'

'No.'

'Excuse me? I said I wanted to see James and if he is in. Please step aside and let me pass.'

'James doesn't want to see you. He loves Sapphire, not you.'

'I don't think it is any of your business what James does, now please move aside.'

'No.'

'James!' Ruth's voice shouted which James knew wouldn't be pleasant for Lulu. She hated people shouting.

James watched as he lurked in the hallway, peering around a corner. Lulu was trying to shut the front door and he wondered if he should intervene.

'He doesn't want to see you ever again, so do one.'

'I beg your pardon! What did you just say to me?'

'I told you to do one.'

'I'm pregnant and I need to use the bathroom. You have to let me in.'

'No, I don't.'

'You callous little bitch! Let me in right now.'

James had heard enough and moved slowly and deliberately down the hallway.

'Ah… there you are,' said Ruth, 'and about time. Your sister won't let me come in.'

'Good for her, Neither will I,' said James as he reached

Lulu. The two of them stood next to each other and Ruth looked from one to the other in exasperation.

'Will you just move aside?'

'No.' James and Lulu said together. 'There's nothing here for you, Ruth. Your little scheme to try and split us up hasn't worked, so you need to leave, and please don't come back. There's a pub at the end of the road if you genuinely want the toilet.'

'You're making a big mistake.'

'The only mistake I ever made was asking you out in the first place. Now please go.'

'You're pathetic.' Ruth turned and walked carefully down the steps and down the path to the gate.

James and Lulu watched as she waddled off down the street, then they closed the front door and moved back into the kitchen.

'Cup of tea?' asked Lulu.

'That would be lovely, Lulu, thank you.'

She filled the kettle and switched it on, then took two white mugs down from a pristinely tidy cupboard.

'I've made a decision.'

'What about?'

'I'm going to work for Sapphire. I will probably never get another chance like this ever again. I want to be a designer and I love Sapphire. You don't mind do you, James?'

'Of course not. I'm delighted and, for what it's worth, I think you've made the right decision.'

'What do you mean "for what it's worth"? Your opinion is always worth a lot to me.'

'Thanks for that, but I seem to be making a lot of wrong decisions at the moment.'

'About the shares?'

'Yes, mainly them.'

Lulu put the mugs on the table and sat down. 'Perhaps something that causes so many problems isn't worth having.'

'I've been thinking along the same lines.'

As they sat together, sipping their tea, James knew what he had to do.

Chapter Thirty-One

Sapphire threw herself into work. The phone call she received from Lulu late on Sunday night had cheered her up immensely. Her instinct had been to dash around to Orchard House with a bottle of champagne and celebrate with them. Instead she'd ordered a crate of champagne for the meeting scheduled for Monday afternoon. Lulu was to meet the other designers and they could crack open a bottle then. She intended to introduce Lulu to people gradually so she could get to know her colleagues, one or two at a time.

Sapphire left Lulu alone in her new office, to familiarise herself with it and to put her few belongings in strategic places. She had promised to return in half an hour. Lulu was wide-eyed and nervous, and it was important that she wasn't left alone for too long if she was going to settle in at Sapphire Enterprises and start to feel at home.

James had sent her an email that morning, saying he had decided to stay at home for another couple of weeks, until his plaster was removed. Sapphire was relieved as she had dreaded seeing him again. It was all wrong. He was running the show now, and she would be answerable to him. A situation she hated. This was her company and she would do everything in her power to regain control of it. The designs were hers, the ideas and plans too. The décor was her choice and she wasn't prepared to change anything.

Then a horrible thought struck her. Would James insist she move out of her office so he could use it? And would he take Della off her as well? And if he thought for one moment that Angie would take the place of Della as her new secretary, he had another think coming.

She couldn't settle, so left her office and took the lift to the floor below her where Lulu's new office was situated. She had chosen a spacious room with plenty of light and a pleasant view of the London skyline. She wanted Lulu to be happy with everything at Sapphire Enterprises and never to regret her decision to become one of the team.

When she knocked, and then entered the office, she was pleased to see Lulu sitting at her desk, already busy on the computer. Two framed photographs were on the desk—one of James and one of Willow. A large mixed bunch of flowers was sitting on the top of a small table surrounded by congratulations cards and the large table in the corner was spread with pieces of fabric, cotton, and scissors. Lulu had obviously wanted to get stuck in to work straight away. A good sign.

'How are you settling in?' asked Sapphire.

'Everything's fine, thanks. James has just sent me an email wishing me the best in my new job. He gave me a card as well.' She nodded in the direction of the table.

'Is he coming in today to join the celebrations?'

'No. He wants to give you space. He knows you're angry with him.'

'You understand why I'm angry with him, don't you

Lulu?' It was important suddenly that Lulu didn't think badly of her.

Lulu nodded but then looked down. 'He didn't mean to upset you and he doesn't love Ruth, he loves you.'

'Is that what he told you?'

Lulu nodded again but didn't look up.

'Anyway, we're here to work aren't we? We're going to have the meeting of all the designers you'll be working with in your office as I want them to see your portfolio and the examples you've brought with you. Is that okay?'

'Cool.' Lulu looked up and grinned. 'I'm so happy you're giving me this chance and I promise I won't let you down.'

Sapphire felt a lump in her throat at the look of joy on the girl's face. 'I know you won't.' Whatever happened with James, she was determined that nothing was going to spoil their plans for the interior design side of Sapphire Enterprises.

'So, what happens now?'

'After you've met the team, we need to get as many samples done as possible with as much variety as we can. Then, in a week or so, we are going to have the biggest launch party Sapphire Enterprises has ever seen. We'll invite all the important people who are going to invest in us, including rival designers in the hope we can coax some of them to come and work for us and the media so they can spread the word and we can win some orders. Then we'll hit every retail outlet we can think of with our stunning new range.'

Lulu's eyes were shining, and the grin was firmly on her face. It was a look that reminded Sapphire so much of James that she felt as if she'd been punched in the gut.

'Can we invite family and friends to the party?'

"Of course. Anyone in particular?"

'Yes. Can I show you his picture? I met him on a different dating site. This is one for people who have autism. We've been talking in the chat room and he wants to meet. I'll meet him before the party though, just to check we're compatible. He suggested just a coffee first, which James says is a very sensible idea.'

'Right. That does seem sensible. And I'd love to see his picture.'

Lulu passed her phone across and Sapphire looked at the photo. This young man was completely different to the first man she never got to meet. Which was probably a good thing as the man in the photo looked perfect for Lulu. He had a mop of untidy blonde hair, twinkly blue eyes and a crooked smile.

'He looks lovely. What's his name?'

'Pete. He's an Aspie.'

'What's that?' Sapphire wondered if it was like a goth only more conventional.

'He's got Asperger's.'

'Oh, I see. Well, I think he looks very promising. What are you going to wear?'

Lulu had quietly reverted to her original look in clothes and hair, but Sapphire hadn't given up hope of improving her wardrobe.

'Would you like me to help you choose something?'

'That's very kind of you, Sapphire, but I want him to see me as I really am. And this is me.' She looked down at her simple dress and cardigan with flat shoes and then back at Sapphire. Sapphire had another lump in her throat. Would this young lady forever make her feel emotional? Or was it because her nerves were already frayed by the situation with James?

'Well, whatever you wear, you'll look good and Pete is a lucky guy to be taking you out.'

'We might end up both being lucky.' Lulu smiled sweetly and Sapphire smiled back.

Then there was a sharp rap on the door and Della came in carrying a bottle of champagne and a box of champagne glasses. Following her were four women of varying ages, each carrying food.

'Ah, there they are. Let the party start,' said Sapphire.

Lulu was introduced to the team, who all welcomed her to Sapphire Enterprises and then turned to admire the items she had brought with her.

Sapphire decided to take a back seat and sat in the corner, sipping her champagne and listening to the conversation. They were all enthusiastic for their future plans and were soon immersed in talk of home interiors, shades that were "in" at present and their favourite designers. Pleasingly, Lulu seemed to be in her element. These were her people, and Sapphire felt herself relaxing. It was going to be okay. She had made the right decision in inviting Lulu to join them. And James would be pleased.

Thinking of James was the only negative to the day, but she would have to think about him soon. They still worked together, with James making all the final decisions. She wasn't sure if she could do that. It would be too humiliating when she had been her own boss for so long. But what was the alternative? Losing Sapphire Enterprises and everything she had worked so hard for. Now, at least, she understood how James had felt when he was forced to sell his company to Malcolm Steele.

It was late when Sapphire returned to her own office, but Hector Winthrop was waiting to speak to her.

'Is something wrong, Hector?' she asked.

'Not wrong, no, just a trifle puzzling. Maybe you know what's going on?'

'What is it?' She gestured for Hector to sit down, which he did with a look of relief.

'James Lewis has just signed all his shares over to you.'

'What? Do you mean he wants to sell them to me? What kind of price is he asking?' Maybe this was a way out for all of them. If the price was one she could afford.

'Well, no… not sell. He has just transferred them all to your name. Not just the ones he bought from the mystery investor but the ones he bought in his own name as well. Which, of course, makes you the majority investor at sixty percent or thereabouts. I'll need to double check the figures, and the good news is that the shares are increasing in price as we speak. The news of the new line we are moving into has had a positive effect. Sapphire Enterprises is definitely on the up.'

'I don't understand. He has just gifted all his shares to me. Just like that. Why?'

'I have no idea. I was hoping you could throw some light on it, but you're obviously as much in the dark as I am.'

'Maybe I need to ring him. Could it be a mistake?'

'Oh no, it's no mistake. He emailed me this morning asking me to take care of it. Which, of course, I promptly did.'

'Of course.' Sapphire was gobsmacked. Why would James give her all his shares? He said himself that he was a businessman and wouldn't dream of throwing money away like that. He still had cash from the sale of his own business, but it wouldn't be enough to start a new business of his own. He was losing big-time from this, whereas she was much closer to her dream of being on the Forbes list of richest billionaires. It was a thought that should have had her jumping up and down with excitement and punching the air. All she felt was deflated.

Was this James's way of cutting all ties with her? Was he freeing himself from her, Sapphire Enterprises, and any future they could have had together? Perhaps Ruth was right, and he had decided that his first love was the one he wanted to be with. But according to Lulu, who knew James better than anyone, he didn't love Ruth he loved her.

'I don't know what to think, Hector, if I'm honest. The only person who knows is James. I'll have to talk to him.'

'Yes, I think that's a good idea for your peace of mind. But really, my dear, you should be thanking him. It looks to me as if all your financial problems are behind you.'

Chapter Thirty-Two

James couldn't decide what to wear. He wanted to get it right because it might be the last chance he'd ever have to plead his case with Sapphire. The party would be overflowing with the great and the good of the fashion world, with a special emphasis on home décor, and Sapphire would be playing the hostess for all she was worth, but James was determined to make Sapphire listen to him when he told her he loved her. He would tell her how very sorry he was for everything. He was a clown who didn't deserve her love. He wasn't worthy to as much as clean her shoes. Those lovely red stilettos that she wore the night they first got together…

He needed to get a grip. He hadn't had sex for weeks and thinking of Sapphire and that night was guaranteed to drive him mad if he didn't exercise some self-control. He wanted her now, on the floor, the bed, in the bath, on the kitchen table. He didn't care where they did it as long as they did.

He opened the doors of his wardrobe and stared

vacantly at the suits hanging up in rows. Then suddenly, he knew what he would wear. His dark blue Italian suit with the pale blue shirt and silver silk tie. The outfit he wore to the restaurant that first night. And to think he had only wanted sex with Sapphire then. Now he wanted her for life. He wanted to love her forsaking all others. But what were the chances of her even listening to him, never mind agreeing to spend the rest of her life with him?

True to his word, he had given her space. He hadn't gone into the office at all in the weeks since she left Orchard House. Sapphire hadn't contacted him either, even after he gave back all his shares. There had been no contact between them at all.

Lulu had come home each day, full of happiness and stories of everything that was going on at Sapphire Enterprises. She had found her niche at last.

He got dressed quickly, savouring the feeling of being able to wear trousers again like any other man. He no longer had to think of his leg and the monstrosity that had encased it. He was free! He flexed his knee and waited to feel the twinges and cramps, but he felt nothing. So far, so good.

Then, catching a glance at the clock on his bedside table, he realised he was running late. It wouldn't do to be the last to arrive. This was Lulu's big day—and Sapphire's —and he wanted to support them in any way he could.

The Grand Ballroom of the Grand Rossini Hotel was buzzing. James could hear the noise of merrymaking as soon as he walked through the doors into the lobby. There was a security guard at the entrance to the ballroom, checking everyone's ticket and James was thankful he had remembered to bring his with him. The man was friendly enough, however.

'Enjoy your evening, sir.'

'Thanks, I will.'

He strolled in, searching the crowd for Sapphire or Lulu, but couldn't see either of them. Phoebe and his mother had also been invited but he hadn't been surprised when Lulu told him that they had both declined, pleading prior engagements. He could believe it of Phoebe who had an active social life, but his mother never did anything in the evenings except watch television. It was probably just as well, it wasn't her thing and Lulu had Pete as her plus-one. He had met the young man and liked him instantly.

He accepted a glass of champagne from a waitress and loitered in the corner, watching everyone having fun. They were loud, both in voice and attire, typical of the type of people for whom fashion was the most important thing in their lives. James had grown to love these people in the months he had worked at Sapphire Enterprises. They were outgoing, brazen and outrageous. He thought he looked okay in his Italian suit but amongst this crowd he was a crow in a field of peacocks.

'James, thank goodness you're here. I don't know whether I can stay in this room much longer. It's too noisy and there's too much of everything. I need to get out.'

James turned and Lulu clutched his arm. She was pale and looked as if she was going to pass out or have a meltdown. His heart broke for her. This was a massive occasion for his little sister, and it seemed that she wasn't going to be able to enjoy it after all.

'Okay, Lulu, take deep breaths. Come on, let's get some air.'

She kept hold of his sleeve, and he led her outside. He spoke to the security guard and told him they would be back. The man nodded but seemed unconcerned.

They moved away from the entrance of the hotel where luxury cars were stopping to drop off their passengers before moving away again. Then they turned a corner and found themselves on a quiet street.

'What if I can't do it? I can't be in crowds, James, it's too much.'

He stopped and held Lulu by the arms so she was forced to look at him, something he knew she avoided when she could, but he needed her to listen. 'Lulu, you can do the job in your sleep, you know you can. A party is a different thing, and no one expects you to shine in that environment. Have you told Sapphire how you feel?'

'No, I wanted to see if I could do it, but I've been peri-odically hiding in the toilets then coming out again and trying to mingle until I couldn't stand it any longer. It was fortunate I spotted you.'

'Oh Lulu, honey, you can't spend the night in the loo.'

'I know. I feel so stupid.'

'You're not stupid. Don't ever feel that. Where's Pete?'

'At the bar. He's not entirely comfortable either. He keeps dropping things.'

'Right. Here's what we're going to do. We are going to go back to the hotel, you and Pete can stay at the quieter lounge bar and I will explain things to Sapphire. We'll do it calmly with the minimum of fuss. How does that sound?'

'Thank you, James, I knew you'd save me.'

He grinned. 'Yep, saving damsels in distress is a specialty of mine, didn't you know?'

'Yes, I did know. I hope Sapphire remembers you saved her too.'

'I'm hoping that the party will put Sapphire in a mellow mood, and I can talk to her and ask her forgiveness. Wish me luck.'

'Good luck.'

'Thanks. Right, let's go.'

After he had located Pete who looked as lost and nervous as Lulu had and escorted them to a hidden table behind a pillar where people wouldn't bother them, he went back into the ballroom in search of Sapphire.

It didn't take him long to spot her. She was surrounded by men—admirers, probably —and she was laughing and tossing her hair back over her shoulder. He stayed a good distance away so he could watch her. Every now and then, when the men were guffawing at something one of them had said, Sapphire glanced quickly around her as if she was searching for someone. Had she got her eye on another man already? The lady was a quick worker if so.

Slowly he moved nearer to the group. He needed to talk to Sapphire, but he didn't want to annoy her by interrupting their conversation. He stood far enough away so he wasn't intruding but near enough so she could see him. He didn't notice someone sidling up to him.

'James, good to see you again. It's been an age.'

'Hi, Della, yes, it has been a long time. How are things?'

'Pretty good as it happens. We're on the up, apparently. At least, that's what the board members are saying. When are you coming back to work? Is your leg better?'

'My leg is much better thanks, but as for me coming back…'

'Oh but you must. It was mainly your input and sage advice that resulted in the upturn of our fortunes.'

'Is that the company line now, "upturn of our fortunes"?'

Della put her head back and laughed. 'Yes, it did sound rather like a quote for the media, didn't it? I think I've been spending too much time around corporate types.'

'That's what you get when you work too hard.'

'Who's been working too hard?' Sapphire had come up behind him and now stood at his shoulder.

'Your secretary. You work her far too hard, Sapphire,' said James as he turned slowly to face her.

Their gazes locked. For James, it was if they were alone in the world. The noise of the party blended into the background and he hardly registered it. He stared into her green eyes and never wanted to stop looking. He tried to read the emotion there but, as usual, Sapphire was keeping it all hidden. She had a half-smile on her face as if she couldn't quite make up her mind whether to bother smiling properly. It was her default look in meetings with difficult clients, or when someone was about to tell her something she didn't want to hear.

James couldn't help himself. He broke into a huge grin.

'And what's amusing you?' Sapphire asked.

'Nothing. I'm just ridiculously happy to see you again, that's all.'

'Really? Why? I thought you didn't want anything to do with me or Sapphire Enterprises?'

James was shocked. 'What the hell made you think that? Nothing could be further from the truth. You walked out on me remember? It wasn't the other way around.'

'Keep your voice down, people are starting to look.'

'Let them,' he said belligerently. This wasn't going as he had planned. But then, had anything ever gone the way he planned where Sapphire was concerned?

'James!' she hissed.

'Sorry, I'll be good. I know this is important for you and

I was planning to come here tonight to support you and Lulu, not make a nuisance of myself.'

'Where is Lulu by the way, have you seen her?' Sapphire glanced around the room again and James watched her. He had missed her so much that he couldn't get enough of drinking her in. He longed to touch her but didn't think the lady would appreciate PDA's in front of her peers. Then he remembered how easily she had shrugged off fainting at the fashion show and being carried out in his arms. Maybe he could risk stroking her cheek if he did it surreptitiously.

'James?' She had turned back to look at him and he realised he needed to behave, at least until he discovered if she was willing to forgive him.

'Lulu and Pete are in the lounge bar, hiding from everyone and recovering from the sensory assault that neither was able to cope with for long.' Sapphire frowned as if she had no idea what he was talking about. 'The noise, the colours, the smells, the swirling lights, too many people talking at once.'

Sapphire gasped and put her hand to her mouth, 'Oh my God, I never thought of that. Why didn't she say something?'

'Lulu can be very stubborn at times, it's a family trait, I'm afraid. She wanted to see if she could cope and when she couldn't she had to retreat. At least she knows when to give up and admit defeat.'

'Is that another Lewis trait?'

Sapphire stopped a waiter as he circulated with a tray laden with glasses of champagne and took two. She passed one to James.

'Thanks. No, that's just Lulu. I never give up if I want something badly enough.'

'What never? What about your business? You gave up on that quickly enough.'

'Ouch!' He grimaced. James sipped his champagne and gazed at Sapphire over the glass.

'What about your fiancée?'

'I couldn't forgive her infidelity. I'm a bit old-fashioned like that. I believe in faithfulness in a relationship. I'm a one-woman man.'

'And Ruth is definitely not your woman?'

'Definitely not.'

They were moving closer together slowly, imperceptibly. James was about to raise his hand and tuck a lock of Sapphire's hair behind her ear, when he felt someone's elbow in his back, and he lurched forward into her arms.

'Steady…are you okay?' Sapphire had one hand on his shoulder to steady him and he put his right arm around her waist and pulled her in closer. They were still holding the champagne glasses as there was nowhere to put them down.

'I'm totally okay now. Wonderfully, perfectly okay.' He brushed her lips with his, and she opened up to his kiss. It was the most exquisite kiss he had ever experienced. It was gentle, caressing, hot and sexy, and promised so much more.

'James?' she whispered.

'Yes, Sapphire?'

'Why did you give me all your shares?'

He could have told her it was because they had caused problems between them. He could also have said that he didn't feel he had the right to them, considering how he had acquired them. He knew that there was only one answer that fitted her question.

'Because I love you, Sapphire, more than I have ever loved another human being. I want you to be happy and you will be when you've made the Forbes list. If I can help you achieve that, then I will be happy too.'

'You love me?' Her voice was hesitant, as if she wanted to believe him but couldn't quite bring herself to.

'Yes, with my whole heart.' He ached for her to reciprocate but she didn't.

'But what about your dreams, James? You want your own business again. You told me that. You had the majority shares, but you gave them all away.'

'Yes, but they didn't make me happy because I lost you. But they do make you happy.'

'So, what do *you* want, James?' They were still so close that James was sure Sapphire would be able to detect the obvious thing that he wanted. He grinned.

'I meant in the long-term. I know you want sex, that goes without saying.'

'I want your forgiveness and I want us to be friends again.' He wanted so much more, but that decision now lay in Sapphire's hands. He'd put his cards on the table, told her he loved her. It was down to her now.

Sapphire was still holding on to his arm, but he gently let his arm drop from around her waist and stepped back.

James downed the rest of his champagne. 'If it's alright with you, Sapphire, I think I'll go home now. I'm feeling a bit tired. I only had the plaster off yesterday and I've been on my feet for hours.'

'Okay,' her voice was quiet with a trace of disappointment. 'Thanks for coming.'

'I wouldn't have missed it for the world. Look after Lulu and Pete, won't you?'

'Of course.'

He turned and walked away, depositing his glass on a tray the waiter was holding. He wanted to look back at

Sapphire but resisted the urge. He would find Lulu and Pete and make his farewells.

As he walked out of the Grand Ballroom, he was aware that it could be the last time he ever spoke to Sapphire if she didn't feel the same way about him. He could have made a dick of himself again and she was glad to see the back of him. Or, this could be the beginning of the best years of his life. It was all in Sapphire's hands.

Chapter Thirty-Three

Sapphire was drunk. Totally, gloriously three sheets to the wind. The launch party had been a roaring success. Everyone she spoke to had positive things to say about her new line and she had networked like mad, for most of the night, and—after James had left and she had put Lulu and Pete in a taxi—secured quite a few orders. As most of the guests had been hitting the champagne like the hardened drinkers they were, some of the orders wouldn't be forthcoming, or even remembered, but some, she knew, were genuine.

As she lay on the bed, propped up by six pillows, cuddling Sparkle and sipping iced water she knew the real reason for her euphoria was James. He had said he loved her. More than he had ever loved anyone else. And he hadn't waited for her to say it back. He said it almost as if he was simply stating a fact. Something that just was. How long had he loved her and why hadn't he ever said anything before? And why, now she came to think about it, hadn't he stayed at the party after making such a momentous declaration? He could have sat down for goodness sake. He didn't have to dance or anything.

He wanted her to be happy and rich. If she was happy, he was too. That *was* love, wasn't it? So what did she do now? She could wait for James to contact her, but what if he didn't? He would be waiting for her to contact him wouldn't he?

As she mused, sipping her water and stroking her cat, she realised that she had never been in this situation before. One-night stands were just that. Friends with benefits were men she didn't see that often anyway and there hadn't been any since James. Poor Monty had died. God rest his soul. Several men she had thought were potential relationship candidates had dropped her after a few dates. She had put that down to them being intimidated by her. She did put men off with her attitude and outspokenness. But if they weren't man enough to handle a bit of straight talking... well...then there was Roland and the less said about him the better.

James Lewis was different. She had always felt that he supported her in everything she did. He'd been there at the fashion show. He'd given her Sparkle. He'd given her his shares, leaving himself with nothing.

He really did love her, didn't he?

The thought thrilled and terrified her. Real love. Not just sex, although sex with James was out of this world, but love. He'd seen her looking her worst—when she'd had the hypo—and he loved her anyway.

She reached for her phone to ring him. Then hesitated as she realised that she hadn't sobered up yet and probably wouldn't until she'd had at least five or six hours sleep. She finished her water, then wandered into the kitchen to make herself a large black coffee. Then she'd have more water and sleep. Nothing was going to happen tonight. James was probably already in bed. She sighed. She should be with him. But no, this was too important to stuff up. When she rang him, she would be clear-headed and adult, even though she felt like a kid on her birthday and someone had given her an enormous present and she couldn't wait to unwrap it.

Sapphire woke on Friday morning with a plan in mind. She had promised herself before the party that she would go to work, take advantage of the progress her new venture had made at the launch party and start working on the orders that would swiftly come flooding in. Then she would phone James in the evening and maybe they could meet on the weekend.

The trickle of orders that disappointingly arrived could easily be dealt with by the designers. Perhaps the guests hadn't sobered up enough yet to get into their offices.

Lulu was already hard at work on an order for throws and matching cushions. Sapphire didn't have much to do.

So, she went home and sat cross-legged on her bed, staring at her phone. Why didn't James ring? Because the ball was firmly in her court, he'd made that plain. It was up to her. Isn't this what she had always wanted? Complete control of her life? James had given her that, and she was dithering like a schoolgirl with a crush on an older boy.

She picked up the phone, then texted a message, *"Hi. Fancy a drink?"* It was a matter of seconds, probably only nanoseconds, that she got a reply. *"Great! Thought you'd never ask. Be round in 20 mins."*

Sapphire smiled in delight, then realised the implications of only having twenty minutes to get ready. Oh shit…

She dashed to the bathroom, shrugging her clothes off as she went, then piled her hair on her head loosely and jumped into the shower. She loved to take her time and luxuriate in the hot water, the smell of her favourite shower gel and the sense of relaxation showers always produced. This time she was like a whirling dervish, and the bathroom floor was swimming in water. It was times like this that she would appreciate a wet room. Then she got lost in a daydream of herself and James making love in the middle of a hot and steamy shower room and she nearly forgot the time.

Oh bugger! She quickly dried herself and pulled on knee-length shorts, a vest top and jacket and a pair of sandals. Never had she looked so boring and ordinary, but she didn't even have the time to apply her usual coats of foundation and mascara. A bit of lipstick and a quick brush with the mascara wand and she was almost ready. The only thing she would never leave the house without was a generous squirt of Sparkle by Sapphire.

She was just thinking about the perfume she wanted to design that she intended to call Lulu, when the intercom buzzed, and Victor told her that her visitor had arrived. The amount of disapproval in his voice warned her that it was James. Poor Victor. Unrequited love—or lust—was a bitch.

She practically skipped down the steps. She had too much restless energy fizzing around her veins to wait for the lift. Then she called thanks to Victor as she left her apartment block.

James was standing on the pavement, with a huge grin on his face. Luckily he had dressed down too in jeans and a white T-shirt. He watched her approach and the grin got wider.

'You look gorgeous,' James said.

'I do not. Don't ever make me get ready in only twenty minutes again, okay?'

'Anything you say, Sapphire.'

He stood grinning at her and looking as if he had just won the lottery.

'Why are you so happy? You've lost your business, your fiancée, and the shares in Sapphire Enterprises. You've still got your job of course, unless you're planning on moving on.'

'I'm actively seeking employment opportunities as we speak.'

'Oh, what?'

'I fancy being a barista. I make a mean cup of coffee. Or... I might open a home for stray cats. Another one's been hanging around lately and Lulu insists on feeding it. That's how we got Willow. She was a stray.'

'Or...' said Sapphire walking up to him and standing as close as she could without them touching, 'you could put on one of those dark but sexy suits and return to where you belong; running Sapphire Enterprises with me.'

'Do you still want me to be your co-CEO?'

'Oh, James, I've missed you so much. Of course I do.'

'Thank you. You don't know how much that means to me.'

'But we need to talk about a partnership. Fifty-fifty. I'll tell Hector to split my shares, so we have half each.'

'No, you don't need to do that, really—'

Sapphire stopped him by putting her finger across his lips, then replacing it with a kiss.

'Yes, James, I do.'

One of the many things she loved about James was his ability to sense when she wouldn't take no for an answer.

'Okay. Thanks.' The grin was back.

'Right, let's go and have a drink. Did you bring the car?'

'No.' There was a hint of mischief in his face now.

'So… shall I get a taxi?'

'No.' James's grin was in danger of splitting his face in two.

'Okay, I give in. What's going on?'

He stepped back and gestured at a motorbike that she hadn't noticed, surprisingly, considering its size. She had been so focused on James that she'd missed the huge, black, shiny beast that sat waiting for the attention it was due. It was even bigger than the blue beast.

'Please tell me that thing isn't yours.'

'No can do. That beautiful machine is completely mine. She's bigger, faster, sleeker…'

'And more bloody dangerous. Oh, James, how could you? Your mother will go spare.'

'When did you start caring what my mother thinks?'

'Ever since… well… you know, if you and I are going to…' He was grinning again, the bastard. He seemed to delight in her discomfort.

'If we're going to do what, Sapphire?' He moved closer to her and took her in his arms as if she was his property and he had every right to do so. Sapphire loved it.

'If you and I,' she said primly, while trying to control the rush of heat that moved through her in a lustful wave, making her knees buckle, 'are going to be an item of some description, then I imagine I'll be seeing more of your mother. Possibly…' She ran out of steam, then forgot what she was going to say as he kissed her deeply, holding her to him and tangling his fingers in her hair.

When he broke the kiss she found she was clinging on to his shoulders as if he was the only thing holding her up. James was still grinning.

'If you and I are going to be an item of *any* description, then I demand exclusivity. That is my only demand by the way. In everything else, I am yours to command.'

The thought of commanding James to do her bidding was making her wet and needy. If they didn't get to a private place soon so she could feel him inside her again, she was going to scream.

'I agree to that. Now, shall we go?'

James moved to the bike and took out the leathers and helmets that Sapphire knew he would have brought with him. She believed that he had learned his lesson and safety would now be paramount.

'I got these in your size so Lulu can have hers back.'

She pulled on the trousers, enjoying the feel of the leather against her skin. The jacket was smart and fitted perfectly. Shame that she didn't have the heavy boots that James wore, but maybe it was time to invest in a pair if she could find some that were attractive enough. As she dressed, her mind started whirring. Leather wasn't the easiest fabric to work with, but it never dated. It's one of those things, like blue jeans, that would always be in demand. Why shouldn't the leather gear that bikers wear be practical *and* fashionable. What about a range of affordable, sexy leather clothes that the average bike rider could afford and look good in? It could change the image of bikers forever. They weren't all Hell's Angels after all. And James knew all about the leather industry.

'Okay, now I'm getting worried. You've had that look on your face for too long now.'

Sapphire realised that James had been watching her while he put his leathers on.

'What look?'

'That "I've got an idea" look. That little frown that appears just there.' James stroked her face between her eyebrows. 'What are you thinking about?'

It was her turn to grin. 'Our next big thing, James. Come on, let's go and I'll explain when we get to the pub.'

'Will the Hare and Hounds do?'

'The one with the woodland nearby? The woodland with that lovely secluded spot where we made love?'

'That's the one.'

'I think it will do very nicely.'

'Lunch and then a gentle stroll in the woods?'

'Sounds perfect.'

'Let's go then.'

They didn't say much as James skillfully negotiated the London traffic. Once they were on the country roads, James picked up speed and Sapphire felt the tension slowly leaving her. It was going to be all right. James was a good, safe, bike rider. He was coming back to work with her, and they were going to take Sapphire Enterprises to a whole new level. As far as being on Forbes's list was concerned, she really didn't care about that anymore. She counted her riches in a different currency now. She had family, friends, a loyal workforce and a man she adored. There was only one more thing to do.

'James,' she shouted, 'I love you too.'

He didn't take his eyes off the road, but she could tell he was grinning. 'I love you, Sapphire Bell-Johnson.'

'And I love you, James Lewis.'

'Tell me again,' he shouted.

This time they both shouted at the same time, Sapphire's voice slightly louder than James's.

'I love you!'

They laughed for the sheer joy of it and the blue of the sky overhead and the thought of all the days ahead of them, working, living, and loving together.

vinci-books.com/touchmeagain

Life doesn't always give you what you want but it can often give you what you need.

When Colleen visits her sister in London, she finds illness and squalor—not glamour. Meanwhile, Adam plans a tame stag night for his friend. But a strange man, a damp flat, and a cardboard box ignite a chain of events no one saw coming.

Turn the page for a free preview…

Touch Me Again: Chapter One

Colleen O'Shea stood on the pavement gazing up at the block of flats. Next to her was her suitcase on wheels that she had pulled along beside her for what felt like miles from the tube station. London wasn't a complete mystery to her; she'd visited plenty of times, with her mother and sometimes on her own. But she'd never been to this part of London before. She loved the centre with the Houses of Parliament, Big Ben, Buckingham Palace and the art galleries and museums. Especially the art galleries. She was on a mailing list and was notified of interesting exhibitions that were to take place and occasionally she found the money for a trip.

She glanced down at the piece of paper in her hand containing Nora's address then back up to the building. It was the right place. But it wasn't as she'd imagined. Nora had given her the impression that she was living the high life with friends, parties, and men. Just one mad social whirl is how Colleen had pictured it. She'd imagined her living in a smart, bijou apartment with a balcony, and a lovely view of one of London's many parks. But this building was dirty, dark, and cold looking. The small patch of grass at the front was littered with dog dirt, broken bottles and even a super-market trolley with no wheels lying abandoned on its side.

A man came out of the front door, letting it swing shut behind him. He stood on the patch of grass, swaying slightly, and trying to make a roll-up cigarette. He had a tin, presumably for the tobacco and dropped it twice on the grass. He cursed each time and on the third time he dropped it, he tried to kick it, swearing loudly. He missed and landed on his backside then noticed Colleen watching him.

'Don't just stand there you bitch, help me up.'

Colleen was frozen to the spot. She watched him strug-gling to get to his feet, then, swallowing her fear, went to help him. He was a big man, heavy and drunk as a lord. He stank of beer, sweat and nicotine, and his clothes were grimy with dirt. Colleen took hold of his arm and tried to pull him up, but he was too heavy for her. Somehow the man ended up on his hands and knees and Colleen backed off.

'Leave him, love, he's not worth your efforts.' A younger man stood in the doorway of the flats, holding the door open. 'Are you coming in or what?'

Colleen retrieved her suitcase and moved towards the front door.

'Thanks,' she said as he held the door open for her.

'You're welcome,' he said and hurried off down the street.

Nora's flat was number five, which meant it was on the next level. There appeared to be four flats to each storey, making twelve in all. There was a lift which had tape across it and a sign declaring it to be out of order. The sign was written on a piece of paper in blue biro and was so faded Colleen could hardly read it. The lift had obviously been out of action for a while.

Colleen started towards the stairs, dragging her case with her. There was a strong smell of urine, and the stairs were filthy. Colleen tried not to breathe in too deeply as she hurried to get to Nora's flat. At least it'd be clean and tidy. Nora had always been a stickler for cleaning her room. She had kept it spotless. Until she reached the age of fifteen when she suddenly lost interest in everything.

Colleen knocked on the door of number five. There was no answer, so she knocked again. It had never occurred to her that Nora wouldn't be home. Friday evening at teatime. Everyone was at home then. Nora would be back from work and looking forward to the weekend. Colleen intended to join her in whatever activities her sister engaged in on a Friday evening. She knew she'd be welcome; Nora would be delighted to see her, she was sure.

Colleen pushed the door carefully and it swung open. That was bad, not locking her door. She'd heard about London and the crimes that went on. Manchester was bad enough, but London would surely be worse. Nora should be more careful.

'Hello,' she called. No answer. 'Nora?' she called again, louder this time. Still no answer. Oh to heck with it. Something was very wrong, and she needed to help her sister. It was a good job she'd come.

Colleen went into the flat and was hit by the stench.

Weed. Dope. Cannabis. Whatever you called it, it was bad news. Nora had started smoking it while she was still at school but when their mother had found out, had promised faithfully that she wouldn't touch the evil stuff again. Well, so much for promises.

The flat was cold. Although it was May, there was a nip in the air and, despite the heavy smoke-laden atmosphere, the cold and damp were obvious.

A man lounged in an armchair, a spliff in his hand, his head back and his eyes closed. He wasn't quite as dirty as chummy outside with his roll-ups but wasn't far off. Colleen stood in the middle of the room, not daring to move, but the man looked as if he was asleep, or unconscious. The spliff had burnt down, the hot ash dangerously close to his fingers. Should she wake him up and tell him? And, more importantly, where was Nora?

Colleen looked around the room for signs of her sister. Maybe she'd wandered into the wrong flat. Perhaps she lived at number seven or three. Then she heard the sounds of someone retching, then groaning. Was that Nora? Whoever it was needed help.

'Nora? Are you okay?'

Colleen left her suitcase and moved towards the bathroom. Nora was lying on the floor with her head in the toilet. She was almost unrecognisable from the pretty young girl who had left the family home in Manchester to make her fortune in London. She had told them that, without her father, there was nothing for her in Manchester anymore and she was moving on.

This comment had stabbed their mother in the heart, and it took all Colleen's powers of persuasion to convince Mum that she didn't mean it, she was grieving and didn't know what she was saying. Eventually, her mother accepted that Nora needed to go, and she hadn't tried to stop her, although she wept buckets the night Nora left.

Colleen knelt down on the floor and took Nora's hand. It was cold and clammy. She wanted to envelop her in a hug and take her back home, but Nora was struggling to stand up and she wasn't looking pleased.

'What the fuck are you doing here?'

'I've come to visit. I've not seen you for ages and just wanted to see for myself how you're doing.'

'Well, as you can see, I'm living the dream.' Nora was pale and she avoided eye contact.

Then Nora pushed past her, and Colleen had no choice but to follow her back to the living room. With one last glance at the bathroom—no bath or pedestal mats, no shower curtain, and the bath looked like it was used for everything but washing—Colleen followed her sister.

The man was awake now and had lit a new spliff.

'Hello, darlin',' he said.

'Hello,' said Colleen trying to avoid looking at him.

Nora collapsed onto the sofa and accepted the spliff from the man.

'Manners,' said the man. 'Perhaps your guest would like a drag.'

'Oh shut up, Maggot.' Nora took a deep drag and offered it to Colleen.

'No thank you. You know I don't take drugs.' Colleen was horrified and heartbroken at the same time. This was her baby sister, the girl she loved more than anyone, and she was living in a slum and doing drugs. She needed to help her but felt completely out of her depth.

'Please yourself,' said Nora and continued to smoke defiantly.

'Let me make you a nice cup of tea,' Colleen said cheerfully, 'I'd kill for one, not had anything for hours.' She'd had a stale sandwich and a can of orange on the train but had been hoping for a nice meal sometime that evening.

Nora and Maggot burst out laughing.

'Tea? Is that still your answer for every problem in life? You poor sad old woman. You'll be living with cats soon and taking up knitting.' Nora was staring at her with contempt in her eyes. This wasn't the baby sister she knew and loved. Colleen wanted her back and vowed to help her in any way she could. Nora needed to stop the drugs and start looking after herself. And it would be their secret, not a word would they breathe to Mum. It would break her heart.

'Nothing wrong with cats or knitting. And yes, tea can help in any situation. That's why, when people have had a shock, they give them sweet tea.'

'I'm a coffee man myself,' said Maggot.

'Oh shut up, Maggot,' said Nora. 'Anyway, we haven't got either.'

Colleen went into the kitchen which was littered with drug paraphernalia. A tin on its side spilt its contents onto the kitchen table. Needles, spoons with a black sticky substance caked on, dimps. Ash littered the table and the floor.

Colleen braced herself as she slowly opened the fridge door. Half a bottle of milk looked as if it had turned to cheese. No food, but strange packets pushed to the back. She shut the fridge door and looked in the cupboards. Mice droppings and dirt.

'Right. I'll just nip out and get you some supplies. I noticed a supermarket on the corner. Shall I buy something for our tea as well?'

'Fish and chips, darlin', with salt and vinegar.' Maggot grinned at her with a mouth full of broken, brown teeth.

Nora said nothing, so Colleen left the flat and hurried down the stairs to the outside and fresh air. She breathed deeply and suppressed the sob that rose to her throat at the thought of the way Nora was living. Her poor baby sister.

She took her time strolling to the supermarket, dreading going back to that flat with the putrid air and the filth. Even as a child, she'd hated getting her hands dirty or sticky. Where was she going to sleep? She hadn't even seen the bedrooms but if they were anything like the rest of the place, she couldn't stay there overnight, she just couldn't.

After buying milk, tea, coffee, bread, butter, and jam, she went to the chippy and bought fish and chips three times with plenty of salt and vinegar.

Her footsteps dragged as she approached the block of flats. Never had she been so reluctant to enter a building as this one. But the fish and chips would get cold if she didn't hurry up and her stomach was rumbling and if she didn't eat soon, she'd get the shakes from low sugar. She took a deep breath and pushed the front door which, despite it being a security door, wasn't locked.

After she handed out the fish and chips, she perched on the edge of a chair, dreading to think what the stains on the upholstery were. The food was hot and delicious, but she was the only one who finished the lot. Maggot ate about half and left the rest on the floor in its polystyrene tray. Nora said she'd have hers later. She looked unwell and, before Colleen had finished eating, she was in the bathroom again throwing up.

'You need to eat something, Nora, that's why you're being sick, because you've got no food in your stomach.' Colleen knelt down next to her sister and stroked her hair.

'I've got a stomach bug, that's all.'

'Then you should be in bed. Shall I ring a doctor?'

'Yes to the first, no to the second.' Nora tried to get to her feet, but she was weak, so Colleen helped her up. She put her arm around her, shocked at how thin she was.

'Come on, let's get you into bed.'

Nora let her lead her to the bedroom and help her onto the bed. There was only one bedroom in the flat and it contained a double bed, a wardrobe and little else. The duvet was filthy, and the room smelt rotten.

'You need to drink some water, you'll be dehydrated after all that vomiting.'

'Fine.' Nora sounded lethargic as if she didn't care anymore.

Colleen went back to the kitchen and found a glass. She washed it as best she could despite the fact there was no washing up liquid, ran the tap until the water turned cold, then filled the glass and took it back to Nora. Maggot seemed to have succumbed to sleep again; he was slumped in the armchair snoring heavily.

'Here you are. Drink this and you'll start to feel better.' Nora took the glass and drank.

'Now. Listen to me. You need help to get yourself out of this situation. I'm here to help you, Nora. I hate to see you like this. You're a bright girl and can do so much better for yourself.'

'How do you know I don't live like this from choice? I might enjoy it.'

'I don't believe that for a minute. You're clever. You could have the world at your feet if you went to college and learned a skill…'

'So, if that kind of life is so wonderful, why don't you go

to college?' Nora was watching her, and Colleen felt she deserved the truth.

'I'm not as clever as you are. A secretary is all I'll ever be and I'm content with that. But you take after Dad. He was clever and he wouldn't have wanted to see you in this mess.'

Colleen was dismayed as tears fell from Nora's eyes and traced a path down her cheeks.

'Oh my darling girl, I'm so sorry, I've upset you. I didn't come here to do that, I want to help you. You know I love you, don't you?'

Nora nodded and wiped her face on the pillowcase. 'There is something you can do if you really want to help me.'

'Oh? What?'

'I've got a job tonight, but I'm too sick to go. Could you go in my place? We can share the money.'

'I didn't know you worked. Well done, you. Tell me all about it.' Colleen imagined she was a waitress or worked behind the bar in one of the swanky wine bars or nightclubs.

'I work for an agency. They text me when they have a job for me. I never know when and they don't give me much notice. Anyway, this is a good one. A stag night at the Spice Club.'

'Okay. What do you have to do?'

Nora looked embarrassed but defiant at the same time.

'Don't judge me. It's hard getting work when you're not qualified. At least you've got secretarial qualifications. I've got nothing.'

'Well, that's more reason to consider going to college. Learn something that'll earn you a wage.'

'Whatever.' Nora lay down and put her arm over her eyes. 'Do you want to do this job for me or not?'

'Yes. Sorry. Of course I do. Tell me.'

'I'm a stripper. They want me to burst out of a box shaped like a present and then strip.'

'A stripper! You have got to be joking. I can't do that. It's degrading. Why are you doing this, Nora? I don't understand you.'

'No, that's the problem, isn't it? You don't understand. Anything.'

Nora turned her back on Colleen and pulled the duvet over her head. Colleen put her head in her hands and shut her eyes. This day was going from bad to worse. Her sister was taking all kinds of drugs and keeping herself alive by taking her clothes off in front of men. And now she was asking her to do the same. Well, not the drugs, of course. But if she really wanted to help her, maybe she needed to stop being so judgemental and do as she asked.

Colleen sighed, a sound that came up from her boots. She was tired and heartsore. Mum had asked her to ring her and let her know how Nora was. But how could she tell her the truth?

Nora was still. Had she fallen asleep?

'Nora? Listen to me. I'll help you all I can and first thing tomorrow I'll go out and find a job. But please don't ask me to strip, I can't do that, okay?'

Nora turned over slowly. 'Can't or won't?'

'Both.' The thought of taking her clothes off in front of strange men made her shudder.

'Okay. If you won't do it, I'll have to do it myself. I'm not throwing away the chance to earn two grand.'

'How much? Did I hear right? They're paying you two thousand pounds? Who are these people?'

'They're rich knobheads that's who they are. They pay well to ogle women.'

'I can't believe it. It's incredible.'

'No, Colleen, it's London. Now, if you aren't going to help me, can you leave me alone to get some sleep so I can get through tonight?'

'I can't let you go, you're not well enough.' Nora lay still with her back to her. 'Nora, talk to me, please. Tell me why it's so important to do this job.'

'I owe people a lot of money. Bad people.'

'What people? How much do you owe?'

'I owe five thousand pounds. And if I don't pay, they'll…'

'What? How did you get yourself in so much debt? What have you been doing? And what will these people do?'

Then the penny dropped. Drugs. Oh God, this was far worse than she'd realised. She owed drug dealers five thousand pounds.

'They're coming back for their money. You shouldn't be here, or you'll be a target. You need to go, Colleen. Trust me, you don't want to mess with these people.'

'But if you owe them five and the stripping job is only paying two.' *Only*, what was she saying? What kind of world had she become involved with? 'What about the other three thousand?'

'If I can give them two, it'll get them off my case for a while, but they'll come back. They always come back. And every day they add more and more interest. I'm trapped but as long as I work, they let me be.'

'Oh my darling girl, what are we going to do?'

'*You're* going to do nothing, it's not your problem. I'm going to work as much as I can and pay it off gradually. What else can I do?'

'Meanwhile, the interest is making the debt impossible

to pay off. They've got you for life, Nora. We have to do something.'

Colleen knew she couldn't let Nora go out feeling so ill. She was worried sick about her but the thought of drug dealers turning up and frightening her baby sister made her sick to her stomach. She wasn't leaving London until Nora was off the drugs and clean again. That money would just keep them sweet for a short while. And then what?

'Okay, I'll do it.'

Touch Me Again: Chapter Two

Adam arrived at the Spice Club before any of the others. As best man, it had fallen to him to organise Jeremy's stag night. Adam had known Jeremy since their university days, and he considered him one of his closest friends. In fact, the closest, as most of his other "friends" were work colleagues and CEO competitors from rival companies in the city.

Adam was determined that Jeremy would enjoy himself tonight as he had waited a long time for his fiancée, Lady Theodora Blakely, to agree to marry him. She had kept him dangling for days when he proposed and even after she had agreed to wed him, he had to wait an inordinately long period of time before she agreed to make the announcement official.

'She likes to do things properly,' Jeremy had said to him with a smile.

'We know who wears the trousers in that relationship,' said his friends.

Everyone in their social circle despaired of Jeremy and

Theo ever tying the knot and most of them had lost interest in the couple, with the exception of Jeremy's parents who were desperate for an announcement so they could boast to everyone who would listen, of the wonderful match their son had made.

Jeremy had a lot of friends and even more acquaintances, being one of the richest, most eligible bachelors in the country, who was also unusually generous with his money. Consequently, Adam was ruthless in choosing only people he knew to be genuine friends of Jeremy to invite to the stag night. The gold diggers and hangers-on would be denied entrance.

Jeremy Baxter was considered to be an odd fish by people who didn't know him as well as Adam did. He came across as a bit of a hooray henry and could be a bumbling oaf on occasions, tactless and outspoken, with a loud, braying laugh and a penchant for dirty jokes. Adam had quickly seen through his outer persona to his quirky sense of humour, sharp business brain and almost infallible talent for picking winning horses. In fact, Jeremy had won more money on the races than anyone Adam had ever known.

Adam hated stag nights. They were all the same; a group of men who were old enough to know better, getting drunk and boasting of how many women they'd shagged while trying to get off with every waitress, bartender and female customer who was unfortunate enough to stray into their orbit. They got louder and more obnoxious as the night went on. And the nights usually went on a long time after the club had closed, well into the early hours. He flatly refused to go to any stag night that was taking place in

Amsterdam, or weekends in Scotland for the shooting, hunting and other upper-class obscenities.

This stag night would be different. Adam had spoken to the manager and told him that there would be no strippers and no raucous or unseemly behaviour. It would be a civilised occasion of friends having a few drinks to celebrate Jeremy and Theodora's nuptials.

The manager had grinned and nodded. 'If you say so,' he said.

Adam was checking over the venue when the manager came into the bar.

'Just the man I wanted to speak to.'

'Really? Okay. What is it?' Had he missed something important?

'You know what you were saying the other day about there being no strippers?'

'Yes.'

'Well, who ordered that then?' He pointed to a large cardboard box in the corner, wrapped up in shiny paper and tied with a blue bow.

Adam hadn't noticed it before. Someone must have delivered it when his back was turned.

'Well, it wasn't me. What's in it?'

'Nothing at the moment, but there'll be a stripper in it later, waiting for her cue to burst out of the box and do a strip in front of your friend.' The man was grinning, no doubt at the thought of a woman taking her clothes off. Lecherous old sod.

'I'm sorry I have no idea who ordered it. I certainly didn't.' Damn, it must have been one of Jeremy's moronic friends having a laugh. 'Can we get rid of it?'

'We could. But the stripper will be showing up any time

now. She has to hide in the box before any of your guests arrive.'

'Couldn't we just apologise and say there's been a mistake?'

'She'll want paying. Are you prepared to pay her? What if she makes a scene?'

Adam was flummoxed. The man was right, of course, he couldn't expect the girl to go away empty-handed but his strict instructions from Theo had been no strippers or someone would be in trouble. He wasn't sure if she meant himself or Jeremy. Maybe both. Theo took no prisoners if her demands weren't met exactly as per her instructions.

'It's not very big,' Adam said staring at the box. 'And it sticks out like a sore thumb wrapped in that shiny paper.' He felt sorry for anyone who had to spend time crouched in such a small box.

'It'll be covered until the moment the stripper bursts out of it. I'll put the cover on when she turns up if she ever does. She's late.'

Adam sighed. 'I guess we'd better let the show go on.' Jeremy and his mates would love it. They seemed to enjoy tacky entertainment. So much for his idea of a civilised stag night. Perhaps there really was no such thing.

'What's this?' Colleen stared in dismay at the pile of red ribbon the manager of the Spice Club had shoved in her hands.

'It's your outfit apparently. That's what the man from the agency told me anyway.'

'It's just a handful of ribbon. What the heck am I supposed to do with it?'

'Why are you asking me? You're the stripper, you should know how these things work. And don't shoot the messenger. If you're not happy, take it up with the agency, it's nothing to do with me.'

The manager was smirking in an unpleasant way. She hoped he wouldn't be watching when she stripped. He gave her the creeps.

Colleen had no idea what she was letting herself in for. Nora had been non-committal telling her it was a straightforward job. Wait for the cover to come off the box, which was her cue to jump out of it, then do a quick strip and go. No physical contact of any kind was required. It sounded straightforward the way her sister told it. But now, standing in front of this big, smirking man who looked as if he despised her, but would watch the show anyway, she was having serious reservations.

Two thousand pounds she was being paid. Just to jump out of a box and wiggle around a bit. There had to be more to it than that. Was it too late to back out? Then she thought of Nora being threatened by drug dealers. She had no choice.

'Well, are you just going to stand there or are you going to put your *costume* on?'

The man's voice dripped sarcasm and Colleen marched off in the direction of the Ladies. She took her clothes off and put them in the plastic carrier bag that she had brought the groceries home in. It was the only bag she could find as there were none in Nora's flat and she didn't want to lug her suitcase all the way there and back.

She started to wrap the ribbon around herself, trying desperately to cover her breasts and pubes. Fortunately, there was a lot of ribbon and she managed to cover up most of her private places, tying a massive bow at the front that looked ridiculous but did offer her a modicum of protection.

After covering herself as best she could, she scrutinised herself in the mirror to see if she'd missed any important bits. Good God in heaven this was ridiculous! What was she doing? She tiptoed out of the Ladies.

Finding it hard to walk naturally as she'd had to put some ribbon between her legs to cover her pubes properly, she shuffled back into the lounge area where the action would take place. The manager was leaning on the bar with his back to her talking to a customer. Luckily, there was no one else in the place.

The customer stopped in mid-sentence, his mouth hanging open and his eyes on stalks. The manager turned around to see what he was staring at and did the same.

'What's the matter? Have you never seen a woman wrapped in ribbon before?' Colleen wasn't usually so outspoken, but the adrenaline was flowing, and she just wanted to get this pantomime over with so she could get dressed and collect her money. Which reminded her. 'When do I get paid?' she asked the manager.

'Take it up with the agency. You better get in the box, the guests will be arriving soon.'

'Right.' Colleen still hung onto her plastic bag. She wasn't prepared to let it out of her sight as it held all her worldly goods at that moment. The most important ones being her clothes and phone.

The manager took the lid off the box and stood back, watching Colleen struggle to climb inside. Not a gentleman then, but maybe that was a blessing, she didn't want any man near her while she was dressed in nothing but ribbon. His gaze moved over her like strobe lighting which caused her to hurry so she almost fell inside the box. There wasn't enough room to stand up, so she crouched, trying to cover herself from his penetrating eyeballs as best she could.

'You better make yourself comfortable, you could be in there for a while,' said the manager.

'Okay.' How the heck she was supposed to get comfortable in a box while trussed up like a festive turkey she didn't know.

'The holes are in the front. You'll know when the cover's taken off as you'll be able to see through them. Do you understand?'

'Yes, of course. I'm not stupid.' Although her present situation might prove otherwise.

'Right. Wait for the cover to come off, then jump out.'

'Yes, thank you, it's perfectly clear.'

The man was starting to get on her nerves. Did he treat all women as if they were imbeciles or just the strippers?

It went dark as the cover was put on over the lid. Colleen didn't think she suffered from claustrophobia but had never been stuck in a box before. How long would she have to stay there? The manager had said a while. How long was that? A few minutes or a few hours? Oh God, no, not hours. She'd have to get out before then. What if she wanted the loo? She took a deep breath and breathed out slowly. Think of the money. Just concentrate on two thousand pounds. Don't think about anything else.

Not only could she not see through the holes in the box, but she couldn't hear anything. Were they still there? They hadn't just gone away and left her like this had they? As some kind of joke?

Colleen willed herself to calm down and concentrate. She listened intently and then breathed a sigh of relief when she heard voices. Men's loud voices, sounding as if they were out for a night of fun. The stag party. There was one man in particular who had a loud voice and an even louder laugh. She wondered if he was the stag. Would he expect her to remove the ribbon? Well, he could think again, it was staying put.

At one point she thought she heard someone doing something to the box. There was the sound of rustling nearby, but it must have been her imagination as it stayed dark, so the cover must still be on. She had been hoping that it was her cue to leap out and strip. She might just remove a tiny bit of the ribbon as a tease, but no way was she going to do a full strip. She just wanted to get it over with now, she was growing more anxious by the minute.

Colleen crouched in the hot, stuffy atmosphere of the box. Her long legs were starting to grow numb, but she couldn't turn around or stand up to ease the discomfort. How much longer would she have to be in here listening to the sounds of men getting drunk? Their voices were growing louder and there was more laughter.

Maybe she should just burst out now and get it over with. Colleen pushed at the lid to see how easily it moved. It didn't. She pushed again, harder. It was completely immobile. The cover must be heavy. So, she was totally reliant on someone to get her out of her prison. What if they forgot she was in there and the party just continued into the early hours? No, that wouldn't happen, she was just scaring herself witless and needed to calm down.

She did her deep, slow breathing again, but started to feel dizzy so stopped. There was no air in the box. She felt around the lid, trying to find the holes that the manager had told her about, but couldn't find them.

Music started up, sounding a lot like "The Stripper" which was presumably her cue to jump out of the box.

Then she felt and heard something as if the cover had

been dragged off. She looked frantically for the holes to see
if it was time for her to exit but couldn't see them anywhere,
the box was completely sealed.

Grab your copy...
vinci-books.com/touchmeagain